I0543792

THE SWINDLER
A NOVEL

THE SWINDLER
A NOVEL

O.B. Counter

SWIFTSURE BOOKS · SEATTLE

The Swindler is a work of fiction. Names, characters, places, and incidents are the product of the author's imagination or are used fictitiously. Any resemblance to actual events, locales or persons, living or dead, is entirely coincidental.

2012 Swiftsure Books First Edition

Copyright © 2012 by Kevin Stamper

All rights reserved.

Published in the United States by Swiftsure Books, an imprint of Swiftsure Press Publishing Group, a division of Swiftsure Films LLC.

Counter, O.B.
The swindler: a novel / O.B. Counter
1st ed.

ISBN-13: 978-0615506104
Library of Congress Control Number: 2012935032

Printed in the United States of America

SWIFTSURE BOOKS
Seattle, Washington
www.swiftsurepress.com

For the kiddies, who must never read it

THE SWINDLER

1

Daniel Zakian hurried across the reception area, his effete loafers barely touching the floor. Moonlight streamed through the windows and lit the way, though he could have found it blindfolded. He skirted the extravagant display of glass art and glanced over his shoulder to confirm he was alone, then pushed open one of the massive mahogany doors.

When the second corridor appeared he turned down it, stumbling forward into the darkness. He slowed his pace and trailed a hand along the wall until he found the edge of another door. This one was plain wood and cheap varnish, unremarkable in every way, except for the oversized banker's lock that bolted it shut. He scraped his key across the metal, searching for the keyhole, and slid it in.

The door closed behind him and he switched on the lights, flinching in the sudden glare. The room was a windowless box, not much bigger than his wife's main closet. A high-end printer sat on rollers near the door and a tangle of cords snaked across the thin carpet. A long folding table was pushed against one wall, its white plastic top strewn with broken pencils and empty Diet Coke cans. In the center of the floor, squatting like a pagan god, was the ancient IBM AS/400 computer.

He glanced around the hidden room with its bare walls and soup-kitchen furniture. What a contrast to the gleaming trading room just two floors down, where young hotshots executed orders at lightning speed, phones in each hand, their hungry eyes reflected in a phalanx of flat-screen monitors. The real money, though, was made right here.

He normally wouldn't come on a Thursday. He visited the room twelve times each year, always the first Saturday of the month. He would update the old IBM from his spreadsheets, plug in the trades, and then wait for Beth to arrive. She printed the statements and wheeled them to the mailroom, the wealth on her wobbly cart swelling month-by-month for over a decade, the accounts somehow immune to the tempests that otherwise roiled the markets. Zakian Global was now the highest-rated hedge fund in the country, and by a fair margin. Not bad for an oddball outfit in Seattle. Should he use the word? Genius? Others certainly had.

There were whispers he made his relentless returns by "front-running" – executing private trades in advance of his regular customers downstairs – but that was penny-ante stuff, not worth the bother. The SEC had been out to investigate more than once and never found anything to complain about.

It was considered a privilege to have your money in Zakian Global. Well-heeled investors pestered him to let their friends in too, and after putting on a little show of head-scratching and a few sighs, he always took the cash. A smug lot, all of them, convinced they were part of some super-caste because they could write a check. He liked to put a bit of their money in the other projects as well: the real estate and aircraft deals, biotech programs and Internet startups. It gave them something to talk about at cocktail parties. Nothing beats good word-of-mouth.

Wouldn't it be something if it were all real? If those trades had actually been executed, just like the old computer said?

He dragged a battered folding chair to the table and set down his laptop, then accessed the Reuters feed. Things had gone badly in Asia again, and the London market was a looming disaster. New York would open much lower. He was going to get a lot of calls. How many would ask for their money back today?

Despite his best efforts to pour oil on the water, the redemption rate was spiraling out of control. He needed a big infusion of cash to ride this thing out. Africa would be the key. The panic began to well up again and he made a conscious effort to slow his heartbeat. The important thing was to set everything in motion. It was a complicated plan; it would take some time to unfold. He may have waited too long already.

It was clear from the start he couldn't do this alone. He needed help from someone who trusted him. Someone he could control. A person smart enough to get it done, but not *too* smart. Desperate for money? That would be a plus.

He took out his phone and scrolled down to Jake's number.

2

Jake Morrow shifted his weight on the plastic stool, his leg aching from the nightlong vigil outside his house. If they didn't come soon, they wouldn't come at all. The eastern sky was already beginning to pale, a barely perceptible easing of the black. He could almost see the earth's rotation as it turned to meet the sun, his life spinning away faster every day.

Shadows flickered along the fence. He crouched deeper into the foliage. The shadows moved again and three forms emerged: slightly-built young men in baggy pants and hoodies. They edged closer and Jake raised his camera.

The phone in his pocket burst to life with a high-pitched cackling. Shit.

The boy in front lifted his head like a deer at the snap of a twig. A split-second later all three turned in unison and darted down the fenceline. Jake heaved himself off the stool and jabbed at the camera, the flash shattering the night for an instant. He shouted, willing the boys to look back, but they were professionals, and kept their faces down, shrouded by the hoods. The last one held a can of spray paint at his side, and laid down a long black tag on the freshly-painted fence, recording his lope like an EKG.

The three artists were around the corner when the chicken cackled again. He fumbled in his pocket for the phone and checked the message: "U NEED 2 GO 2 LIBERIA 911." That would be Daniel. Jake felt the familiar pang in his gut, and pictured steaming acid squirting onto soft pink stomach tissue.

BETH SMITH'S EYES homed onto him as he approached the inner sanctum. Waspish, with wire-hard hair and the look of a woman disappointed by her children, she arched her back and squinted hard. Even Daniel's best friend since the third grade couldn't get past her without a damn good reason.

"Where have you been?" she said, like he'd stumbled home at four in the morning without his shoes. "Mr. Zakian's in the conference room with Mr. Pease. They're really going at it too."

Jimmie "Snap" Pease was well on his way to squandering, with some panache, a staggering inheritance. "What's Snap up to?" Jake asked, curious about the oversized Texan's next financial pratfall.

"Wouldn't know. Just a worker bee."

Jake rolled his eyes in a show of solidarity and headed for the conference room. He was almost free of her gravitational pull when she singsonged "I know something you don't know."

Another squirt of acid. She said the same thing at last year's Christmas party right before Daniel dropped the bomb: Jake's small firm was being replaced as General Counsel after a 12-year run. The flow of work from Daniel's companies started to decline almost immediately, and the personal rebuff still smarted.

The conference room was empty. Two glasses of softening ice cubes sat side-by-side at the far end of the long table and a pleasant hint of Diplomaticos lingered in the air. Jake opened the side door to the office and poked his head in.

Daniel Zakian sat splayed behind his desk in a pose a body-language expert might mistakenly describe as submissive. He was well over six feet, quite tall for a man of Armenian descent, but behind the enormous desk he looked like a little boy. There was something slightly amiss about his proportions, his torso overly long and his head a bit too small for the rest of him. Face flushed, he mumbled into his headset and waved Jake into the room.

Snap Pease sat across from Daniel on a small antique chair, looking like an elephant squatting on a footstool, his body dripping over the tiny seat and making it almost disappear beneath his mass, the chair possibly in real danger. "Howdy pardner!" he boomed, rising and enfolding Jake in a bear-hug.

Jake took the nearest seat and gazed out the window at the high-priced view of Seattle that seemed to stretch all the way to Canada. He was 40 now, and technically a lawyer, though he hadn't seen the inside of a law library or courthouse in over a decade. He specialized in repossessing aircraft, but the meaty projects from Daniel dried up months ago. He was going soft, blurring around the edges, and the latest batch of summer interns looked even younger than last year's, bouncing around the office, making him feel two-dimensional. He was augering into another financial bind too, and his wife seemed suspiciously content lately.

Snap put a pre-Columbian clay lizard back on the desk and nudged him. "How much you weigh?"

It wasn't the first time for this routine. "190," he lied, then quickly recanted, remembering Snap was a world-class cattle breeder who could tell at a glance and to the pound how much rump, chuck, brisket, and stewing meat a steer would produce. "Maybe 200," he said, his weight continuing its steady upward trajectory. He pictured his body laying down luminescent strips of yellowed fat, like soggy lasagna.

"About six feet?"

"Yep."

"Still sedentary?"

"Afraid so."

Daniel ended his call and swiveled to face the two men, the big smile not quite masking his irritation.

"Jake's burning 120 calories an hour right now," Snap said. "Two calories a minute. The boy needs some nourishment." A few years back Snap swelled to almost 300 pounds before an intimation of his own mortality, caused by a one-time experience with impotence, drove him to a spareribs and Dr. Pepper crash diet. When the dust settled he was at 340 and no longer able to squeeze into his mid-life roadster. He refused to try again, and now experienced weight-loss in a more roundabout fashion, poring over diet books and devouring before-and-after stories in women's magazines. "The boy's wasting away—"

"Everything's arranged," Daniel said, staring Snap down.

"That's real good. Sure?"

"Positive."

"Great. Wonderful. Finally." Snap's face softened with relief, like another kidney stone had made it out. "Guess I ought to vamoose then. The plane's waiting." He slid a thin envelope across the desk to Daniel, then turned and squeezed Jake's shoulder. "Good luck pardner. I'll just slip out that way." He nodded toward the back door, as if Jake might be interested in the exact routing of his departure.

After he was gone, Daniel slouched into his seat. "You've got to grab the red-eye to New York tonight. There's two million at Hanford Bank that needs to be in Liberia tomorrow."

Jake examined Daniel's face. He had gone to West Africa for him many times, often on short notice, but never hauling cash. Despite the maxed-out credit cards clogging his wallet, getting roped into some squirrely payoff nonsense would be bad baseball.

"The whole thing is totally legitimate," Daniel volunteered. "You've got to cowboy up here, Jake. It's important."

"It's a holiday weekend."

"So what? You never do anything on weekends."

"But other people do, so they're less likely to bother me. Plus I need to paint the fence again."

Daniel smiled. "This is right up your alley. No real work. Just sitting on airplanes mostly. It'll be like a vacation."

"I don't want to traipse all the way to Liberia just to deliver a package."

Daniel appeared to mull this over as he shuffled through a stack of mail, most of it going unopened into his wastebasket. He extracted a letter from a large padded envelope, read it quickly, then shook out a thin box. "Here, it's a gift from that leasing company in Taiwan. A pen."

"I've got a pen."

"Not like this you don't. They retail for over twelve hundred bucks. The waiting list is longer than the Seattle Tennis Club's." He jabbed the pen at Jake like he was poking at a dead bird with a stick. "Take it."

Jake didn't want the damn thing – he liked his two-dollar Razor Points – but it was going to be easier to take than not. "Get a courier," he said, pocketing the gift.

Daniel pushed aside the stack of mail. "It's more than a delivery. I need someone I can really trust on this one."

"Get a bonded courier."

"Hell, a courier would unlock the handcuffs and give the case to the first black face that asked to see his cholera card. I need someone with steel elbows attached to that thing."

"I'm handcuffing myself to a briefcase? You're kidding."

"Only if you want to. Lot of cash, though. Don't want to leave it standing next to some third-world urinal."

"What's it for?"

"The 747 renewal. I'm close to salvaging the deal at the same rate."

Another amazing rabbit out of Daniel's hat. Government-owned Liberia Airways had been leasing a 747 from him for almost five years. With the current glut of aircraft on the market, a renewal at even half the old rate would have been a coup. "The whole thing kind of blew up in my face this morning. The deal's off unless they get the cash. It's a signing bonus. Hard currency for fuel. Has to stay clear of the Central Bank though, or I'll be greasing palms from the Head of State to the guy who brings in the tea."

Jake walked to the window. The story was plausible, but it didn't make the trip any less dangerous. Daniel was no pushover down there though. He nurtured a web of relationships with bearer bonds and stacks of convertible currency; and Abu Bello, his strutting, belligerent, Mercedes-driving representative, was ex-Nigerian intelligence and connected throughout the region.

"I was going to deliver the money myself but something's come up." He pointed to a svelte suitcarrier sitting by the door as hard evidence. "Help me get this done and I'll make it up to you. Promise."

"They're in the middle of a civil war."

"It's more civil unrest than civil war."

"Oh, well then."

"I kind of need you on this one," Daniel said, resorting to the magic words. "A car will get you at JFK, Maddie has the cash, and Bello will meet you at the other end. Try not to lose the money. It's only two million, but without it the 747 deal craters and I'm screwed. Beth has your tickets."

Maddie, at least, was a slender ray of light. Jake shook his head and headed for the door, waving to Daniel without looking back.

Beth slapped a thick envelope into his hand, beaming. "Thanks," he said, mustering a grin to match hers, really wanting to look like he'd hit paydirt with this Liberia trip. "I'll call from New York to see if Daniel's got any last minute instructions." Maybe the trip would be cancelled.

Beth turned back to her magazine. "I'm taking a spa day tomorrow. You can check in with one of my girls though."

Jake glanced at his watch as the elevator descended. He had all day to kill. His passport and a packed bag were sitting in his office closet, ready for a last-minute trip. He could shower at the health club and change into comfortable clothes later, then head over to Dino's for a good steak and a few beers. He needed to pamper himself while he could. Other than getting a glimpse of Maddie in New York, he was looking at a nasty five-day ordeal.

It would be two consecutive red-eyes just to get to Liberia, 18 hours on planes in all, no real chance for sleep between flights. He would need to work his way through Monrovia's airport carrying two million in cash (like swimming in a shark tank with a tenderloin Speedo) and hand the money over to a glowering Bello. Then it would be off to a shabby hotel room – sagging mattress, intermittent electricity, rattling air conditioner pushing out anemic streams of mildewed air – assuming no problem with the reservation. In the three humidity-soaked days before his flight back out he'd have to dodge amoebic dysentery, armed street-toughs, and transdermal parasites dripping from the tree leaves.

But hey, it might beat going home.

3

"What's wrong with *this* place?" bellyached Snap, a rivulet of melted butter creeping down his chin, "we haven't hardly finished building it." Just back from his trip to Seattle, he was still a little grouchy from the bumpy ride in the tiny jet.

It was early evening and 102 degrees, hot for September, but the newly installed industrial-grade air-conditioner had the room chilled down like a meat locker. He and Lucille sat close around one corner of a huge banquet-sized table, the overdone dining room put together by a decorator he needed to fly in regularly from West Palm Beach, no Texas homosexual up to the task, apparently. It could have passed for a lavish New York penthouse except for the view out the oversized picture window: endless red-tan land interrupted by the sheds and outbuildings of a typical Texas cow-and-calf operation and a handful of dusty pecan trees.

"I'm not suggesting we leave the ranch; just that we get a place in town," Lucille said.

"We have a place in town."

"Something nice. The Hayburns are building a *gorgeous* house up on Cambridge Avenue. Over 10,000 square feet and a pool for swimming and another one for the kids."

"We don't have kids."

"Of course we have kids; and you have to think about the grandbabies."

"We don't have any of those either," griped Snap, wondering if she were holding something back. The three girls were at college back East, tied much closer to their mother now than to him, but none of them yet married as far as he knew.

"It's got a wine cellar, and a room just for watching movies in, and phones in all the bathrooms. They have almost two acres."

"We've got 40,000 acres."

"I'm talking about being in the city."

"What about the Dallas house?" He reached for another corn-on-the-cob from the platter and rolled it in what was left of a stick of butter, now collapsed to yellow mush. The plan to discuss some belt-tightening with Lucille was seriously off course.

"That's Dallas, I'm talking about a house here, like the Hayburns'."

"The kids are never here anymore, not even for vacations." He tried to calculate how many gardeners it would take to keep two acres at least as nice as the Hayburns'.

"Still. It would be nice."

Sop sop sop went the slab of white bread in the bowl of barbecue sauce. He didn't want a new house; he was seriously worried about losing the ones he already had, especially the one they were sitting in right now. His granddaddies had ranched vast swatches of land near Odessa, first becoming wealthy cattle barons, then watching the oil money flow in. They pitched in and bought the Lubbock place for his daddy as a wedding present. He grew up in the big country house on this very spot, recently bulldozed to make way for Lucille's new palace, a lure to get her out of Dallas and onto the parched ranch, which sported some of the best turkey, whitetail and hog hunting in the state. He raised his prize bulls here too, and the miniature cattle, breeding smaller and smaller versions with less and less marketable flesh, having over the decades built up a large enough store of admiration and respect from his ranching peers to withstand even that endeavor.

Eons of unbroken evolutionary success finally hit a bad patch, squeezing down the line: he was the only child of two only-children, same as Lucille. The inheritances all funneled to him, the gene pool's hope for immortality riding on his beefy shoulders, the Pease name set to die out regardless.

When his parents passed, he cashed out of the oil business and returned to the ranch. The girls liked the idea of coming from a big Texas spread; it had a certain cachet back at school. In truth, the children cared little about the place – they were more in the vein of moderately-spoiled city kids than ranchers' daughters.

"Will you meet me in New York?" Lucille said, ringing for Chela to clear the plates.

"A little soon for Christmas shopping."

"It's the same as always. I like to beat the rush and just worry about the odds-and-ends when I go back in November."

"I'm traveling next week, but maybe I could meet you on my way back."

"That would be wonderful, Pumpkin! Did you have a good time with Daniel in Seattle?"

Snap sighed. Only a portion of his current predicament could fairly be laid at Daniel's feet. He certainly wasn't responsible for the Dallas "see-throughs," empty office buildings with views clean through them. Daniel didn't have anything to do with the Classic Weather Channel either; or the all-smoking airline; or his getting into potatoes in such a big way, right before the FDA came out and said a french fry was deadlier than a cigarette.

On the other hand, he most definitely did have a pile of money tied up in Daniel's hedge fund and other projects, and some kind of payback was long overdue. All the airplane deals were hurting: Liberia, Sudan, Uzbekistan, Nauru, every last one of them. The artificial sphincter R&D partnership was producing nothing but huge tax write-offs and bad jokes down at the coffee shop; and that unfortunate canard of a golf course community in Oregon was still sitting half-built, Daniel making a bad situation worse by telling the tree-huggers their much-loved forest was no more sacred than the mold on an orange, just taller. A lot of money had been pissed away on the photo-voltaic cell program too; and the Kona waterfront duplexes, at nine million a pop, were selling to the Japanese like chitlins to a white man.

He placed too much faith in Daniel, relied on him too much, a man who couldn't whistle or spit. These days it seemed he needed to beat Daniel over the head with a stick just to get his damn attention.

Africa really needed to pan out. It was the one that gobbled up the real money. He checked it out good too, before putting up the cash, wanting to be sure the decision to go in big wasn't swayed by emotion. A money pit so far, but the potential payoff was enormous and Daniel was certainly adamant that everything was on track.

"Did you hear about Jeb Davis filing for bankruptcy?" Lucille said, startling him out of his thoughts, making it sound like Jeb was peddling kiddie porn. "Audrey and Bea say the Davises owe just *everybody* money. It's a disgrace, them living so nicely and all, and there being nothing behind it. I feel so sorry for his wife."

Snap hadn't seen Jeb for years, but watched the drilling rig equipment slowly stack up on his back lot. He felt a sudden camaraderie with the man. It was time to quit stalling. He needed to tell Lucille the cat was on the roof – they would be ruined if the loans were called right then, before there was anything to pay them with. "Things are a little tight for us too, Biscuit," he managed to squeak out.

"Oh you always make things work out, Snap. You are truly the smartest man in Texas. I must make my friends sick the way I brag on you, but it's true, you have more ideas in your little finger than any two of their husbands have in their whole darn bodies."

"Well, it doesn't hurt to be a little careful with spending the money."

"Of course it doesn't, but what difference would one little house make in the whole scheme of things?"

She was right: he was in such a huge fix that any kind of belt-tightening would be like shooing a gnat off a mule's hundred-pound pack. What a mistake to personally guarantee those big loans. What a mistake.

"Were you playing with the dollhouse before dinner?" Lucille asked. "I believe you've spent more time with that thing than all three girls put together."

It was probably true. He built it for Ellie's sixth birthday, an exact replica of their big Victorian in Dallas, sitting up nights gluing a thousand little cedar shakes onto the roof. He improved it over the years; it was wired and wallpapered now, filled with the most expensive furniture in the world, pound-for-pound. It had been handed down to Janie and then Lu-Anne, and if he added it all up and paid himself a decent wage, it cost more than most homes in Lubbock went for.

He continued to upgrade it, even after the baby headed east to join her sisters. His huge hands looked out of place as they refinished thin strips of crown molding, or repaired the delicate furnishings. Lately, Lucille looked for him there first, sometimes finding him just sitting on the bed staring at the little house, its miniature sconces giving a warm glow to the tiny wainscoted rooms.

In the beginning he was everything to them, their little faces bursting with happiness each time they saw him, all three running through the house and jumping into his arms when they heard the front door swing open. He used to sit and watch them: they couldn't just walk anywhere, they skipped and hopped and bounced. Now their love had moved on, they didn't need him anymore, someday soon that love would be shining on their own little babies. He was just the check-writer, the guy put on the phone for a few minutes when they called to talk to their mother. It made his chest ache to think about the old days. In the evening they would crawl onto his lap without thinking about it, to color or read or just sit, like climbing Everest for the littlest, preferring him to a chair or a couch. They would end up falling asleep there like a pile of puppies, and he would carry them off and tuck them into their little canopied beds. That pure love had waned and he knew they didn't remember how important he had been to them, how as little girls they had needed him so much.

After Lucille left the room to work on the Texas peach fried pie with home-made ice cream, not trusting it to Chela, he gazed out the window at the darkening expanse of ranchland. He was left with no choice. There could be no second-guessing his decision at this point. It was extreme, like dropping the atomic bomb, but he needed to salvage things for Lucille and the girls. They were counting on him. He wouldn't let them down, even if it meant other people got hurt.

He tried to identify a new sensation. Was this what a person felt right before beginning to cry?

No, it was a familiar feeling after all, like he was about to throw up.

4

A hand slipped under the netting and moved toward the man's shoulder. "What?" Finis said, before it got there, his eyes suddenly wide open. He had been dreaming of Fiona again, her diamond earrings the size of apples, her ear lobes stretching to her waist.

"The animals are loose," came the anxious voice from the blackness.

He groped for the electric lantern and switched it on, then swung his legs over the edge of the cot. Francie was pressed against the tent's sidewall, as far from him as she could get.

"The monkeys?"

She hesitated, the bearer of bad news. "Yes."

He picked up his frayed bathrobe and put it on, moving at half-speed, and shuffled to the wooden porch. The quarter-moon was so different from back home – it always made him think he was seeing the beginning of an eclipse. He glanced around the darkened compound, thankful for the pre-dawn cool. In a few hours the sun would begin to bake them like a sheet of cookies.

"And the rabbits? Are the rabbits loose too?"

"Not all of them."

"How many?"

"Half. Three-quarters."

"The new ones?"

"No. Those are locked in."

He could see the outline of a dark form sleeping under the karité tree. The men and boys with their automatic weapons and ragtag uniforms were everywhere now, scattered in the shadows, leaning against the perimeter fence or sitting on their heels. Like with strange dogs, it was best to avoid the eyes.

"What about the cats?"

"Everything is loose."

"The cats are loose?"

"Cats, and the rats too."

"How many?"

"I don't know. A lot. I came straight here." She was crying.

There was no way this was an accident. Ever since last month's debacle the lab animals were well secured. And even the cleverest of those pampered monkeys, with their amazing dexterity and little tricks, even the cleverest couldn't undo a padlock without a key. It was sabotage again. Plain and simple.

Then the question he had to ask.

"What about the women?"

5

Jake passed a fifty-dollar bill to the barista and scanned the airport hall for a likely seat. He sifted the change in his closed fist, then flicked two pennies and a nickel into the tip jar with a satisfyingly large clatter. There was one empty table in the area. A well-dressed woman in his periphery picked up her pace a bit, and vectored toward the prize. He beat her by half a step and slapped down his cup. She murmured something – *asshole?* – as she moved away. There was a surge of remorse. He used to be a nice guy. Ah well, it was a victory of sorts.

He nursed his Frappuccino and rearranged an abandoned *Seattle Times*. He was dawdling in the obituaries, calculating the percentage of the dead people who were younger than he was, when a wild-eyed Daniel plowed through the crowd toward him.

"We finished early. I thought I'd see you off. Let's get some coffee." The Starbucks kiosk had just closed, its metal screen pulled halfway to the floor. Daniel ducked under it and talked the barista into a triple Americano, not looking like he needed it.

They settled into conjoined plastic seats away from the havoc of the gate area but close enough to pick up the boarding announcements. "What's up for the weekend?" Jake said, not meaning it to sound like a complaint.

"I've got a meeting Saturday morning. I'm hoping to get up to the boat before noon."

Jake considered asking about Glenda, but Daniel included her in his life only when a spouse was absolutely mandatory. "Don't forget to pump the bilge," he said instead. "Nobody's been on board for a while."

Passengers were beginning to droop, their all-night ordeal barely begun. Ostracized smokers sat in a glass box in the corner of the hall, trying hard to make themselves invisible. An elephantine woman left the vending machine area with a slight man trailing in her wake, his jeans slung well below where his waist should have been, even his facial hair looking anorexic. "When you get right down to it," Daniel said, "the human race is not all that attractive." He stretched out his arms to encompass the milling crowd, the people making his point for him.

"They must think we're gods," Jake said, mocking him.

Daniel nodded. "Did you know the average American gained over ten pounds in the last ten years? That's a pound a year. You're holding up your end, by the way." Daniel was only 9% body fat himself and looked like a professional cyclist. He worked out religiously, monitored each bit of food he ate as though it were a prescription drug, and took full credit for never being sick.

"If I ever bring the 747 back from Liberia I'll need to change out the seats to accommodate our fat American asses. We're 50 pounds overweight, on average. Picture me with one-pound packs of hamburger hanging all over my body, 50 of them. That's what it's like, the extra fat."

Jake dutifully envisioned the meat dangling from Daniel's lean frame on little plastic hooks: 25 packs on the front, 25 on the back.

"If you've got 400 people on a 747, that's ten tons of extra lard. You could put another 80 people on board if you got rid of it. Costs more than a billion a year in fuel to haul that blubber. The output of a nice little oil field. Forget about drilling offshore – just push back from the third helping of candied yams, for godsakes."

Daniel's obsession with other people's weight had been growing for months and was now beyond the merely eccentric. "You've been hanging around Snap too much," Jake muttered, and in truth Daniel *had* been spending a lot of time with his diet-obsessed investor – unusual in that Daniel didn't have many male friends. On more than one occasion Jake was forgotten while Daniel and Snap talked excitedly about downbreeding housecats, or the effect of insulin levels on metabolic rates, their heads close together like new lovers, just happy to be in each other's company, enthralled by any conversation at all.

"Snap can be tiresome," Daniel said. "I asked him this afternoon if you could breed a miniature cow to a regular cow and he said there's got to be a bull in there somewhere. He knew exactly what I meant too." Daniel began to slide into one of his sulks, and Jake thought back to a summer thirty years before.

It was the year Daniel's mother ran away, and old Mr. Zakian took to bringing Daniel with him to Jake's house on Tuesdays to help with the work. In private, Jake's father referred to the stooped and gnarled handyman as "One-Man-One-Day," because that was the full description of services listed on the handwritten bill presented every Tuesday evening at five o'clock, to be settled immediately and in cash.

Tuesdays quickly turned into play days for Jake and Daniel, and the boys ruled the wooded ravines that sloped down to Puget Sound from the big house on the bluff. By the middle of the summer Daniel was an unofficial member of the Morrow clan and spent most of his time at the house. Before bed they would head for the paneled library and sit by the fire. Jake's mother would tell them stories while she knitted, Daniel cross-legged at her feet, as close to her as he could get.

"That Maddie's a piece-of-work," Daniel said out of no-where, barging into Jake's thoughts. "Looks like a prim and proper little banker, you know? In her little tailored suits? Now, that's false advertising."

Jake bristled. It felt completely wrong for Daniel to sit there and disrespect her.

"She's got that purple-and-white urn in her office. You know about the ashes?"

"I guess they're her father's." Jake had never been to Maddie's office, but the urn was legendary.

"No. It's one of her lovers from Paris. The guy commit-ted suicide in the middle of banging her, right on top, with a shotgun. I guess he wanted to leave his wife but Maddie wouldn't have it."

"I heard it was her father in the urn," Jake said again, the shotgun story seeming very improbable. "She likes having him around to motivate her."

Daniel was getting jittery, the shots of espresso hitting his system. "It's her ex-lover."

"It's the father. Trust me. I spend a lot of time with her when I'm in New York."

"She's been one of my Private Bankers forever, over five years."

"We kind of have a personal relationship," Jake said, wishing it were true. "Did she tell you about her ex-husband stealing her laptop?" Daniel might not have heard that one.

"I think so. She tells me a lot of things though."

Jake was clearly getting the upper hand. "Well, it's her fa-ther's ashes. I know that for a fact."

"Whatever. I'm not going to argue with you about a stu-pid vase."

Both men sat in silence until a sequence of boarding an-nouncements emptied the gate area. Jake stood up to go. "I guess I'll see you Tuesday."

"We work out sometimes when I'm in New York," Daniel said, and it took a moment to realize he was still talking about Maddie.

Jake was already feeling separation anxiety, like he was shipping out to boot camp and needed to marry someone. He didn't want an argument with Daniel hanging over his head too. "When I get back, why don't we go down to Arroyo Ranch?" he said, not knowing what other bone to throw. For years Daniel had begged him to go to the celebrity-drenched Santa Fe health spa to get his growing physical disarray under control, Jake always demurring.

Daniel stared at Jake, too long, a bleakness in his eyes, and then he was on his feet. "I've got to go," he mumbled, and headed for the escalators at a half-run.

Jake watched in disbelief until he was out of sight. Who is that guy anymore? He downed the rest of his drink and set off for the gate, his head suddenly hurting. His friendship with Daniel had been on a downward spiral for years, no denying it. What happened to the old Daniel? Maybe without all the master-servant stuff they could be regular friends again. He should drop the Zakian companies as clients; clear the business static out of their relationship.

By the time he eased into his capacious first-class seat, extended the footrest, and asked for a glass of preflight champagne, his thinking had clarified: substantial paychecks in these troubled times deserved some respect. Maybe a good heart-to-heart with Daniel after the trip, maybe that would be enough to get things back to the way they used to be.

6

Jake dragged through the JFK terminal, looking for his name on one of the signs held up by a forest of drowsy-eyed drivers. When he reached the edgy men touting illegal cars, he knew he had been stood up.

He joined the curbside taxi queue and stared out at the gridlock. A Port Authority policewoman frantically blew on her whistle, the blasts getting shriller and closer together. She was making things worse, the panic rising in her eyes as cars and buses congealed in front of her. Officially in charge, she had control of nothing, and Jake immediately recognized her as a kindred spirit.

The taxi driver chatted amiably all the way to the hotel with little reciprocation from the back seat. After a minor skirmish at the front desk when his dayroom wasn't ready, Jake arrived at the 8th floor cubbyhole with a view of the park, turned on the television and flopped onto the bed. The pre-landing coffee and his mistrust of the hotel alarm clock made it difficult to doze: he didn't want to be late for the meeting with Maddie.

Voices from the television mixed with his half-sleep visions of her: the dark brown hair and knowing smile, the hint of mischief in her almost-black eyes. She was five days older than he was, but looked years younger. It was hard to pinpoint exactly what she possessed – a special grace, some kind of sexual charisma — but she definitely cast a powerful spell. What man wouldn't want her?

They met years earlier at a dinner at La Choux, a chance for the bank's top brass to chat up Daniel outside the office, with wives included to foster the illusion of family and friends breaking bread together. Jake showed up early at the private room, looking for a drink. He helped himself from the small bar in the corner, then wandered around the tables. The names of the guests were inked on little paper tents with a calligraphic flourish that made them hard to decipher. The seating plan promised an excruciating evening, so he rearranged a few of the cards, putting himself between Maddie and a man he knew moonlighted as a professional Scrabble player.

Later, after the fawning bankers bid Daniel good night, Jake found himself next to her as they retrieved their coats. "Did you have a good time?" he said.

"Better than you, I think. You're not very good at this mingling and cocktail party chatter."

"It's like bowling. You don't *want* to be too good at it."

"Well you took it like a man."

"Look," he said, emboldened by his fair share of the communal wine bottles, "if my wife and your husband ever, you know, pass away, would you like to get a coffee or something?"

"I don't have a husband. How about a drink right now and get it out of the way?"

At closing time they were still sitting at La Choux's bar. "Let's get something to eat," she said, as the barman picked up their glasses.

"Sounds good." He wasn't hungry, but didn't want the evening to end.

"How about room service?" she asked.

At first it went over his alcohol-dampened head and then he was flustered. Notwithstanding those castle-in-the-sky condoms in his briefcase, expiring and being replaced every few years, he fully intended to remain faithful to his wedding vows, a point of personal honor, until one of them gathered the courage to call it quits.

Maddie smiled sadly at his obvious discomfort, and they ended up at an all-night diner, talking until five in the morning.

He learned she lived with a man who held some type of scouting position with the Baltimore Ravens, explaining it in a way that made him seem...not of great consequence? They spent most of the night plotting an escape to the tropics. Shedding old lives was intoxicating, and they passionately negotiated their differences. Rum or gin? Motorbikes or fringe-topped Jeeps? Barbados or Martinique? Banana daiquiris or strawberry? He wanted to buy a boat and take tourists out fishing; she wanted to make whimsical straw goods and sell them on the beach. They were in agreement though, on palm trees and white-sand; shelves of books and very few appliances; reggae and roofless beach bars with only a few stools; fresh fruit and grilled fish and just one change of clothing. They dared each other to do it, to leave everything behind like an old skin.

"Well, I'm going to the beach," he declared, opening the taxi door for her.

"Look me up when you get there," she said, and it became their ritual, something he told her every time he left town, always garnering the same response, each challenging the other.

Although they never recovered the easy intimacy of that wee-hours diner, each time they exchanged those parting words it reminded him of his best night ever in New York. He still analyzed it like a favorite movie, knowing all the lines. She invited herself to his room, and he acted like an idiot, though, in truth, he wouldn't have traded that night of conversation for anything.

Maddie seemed important, not a soulmate exactly, more like a perfect sunset or a planet passing especially close to earth, something that shouldn't be missed. Each time he came to New York he thought about asking her out, but the moment seemed to have passed. Maybe she pegged him as a Daniel Zakian flunky. Time went by and his strategy for getting close to her came to rely more and more on city-wide electrical outages and propitious elevator timing. But who knows? Lately his libido seemed to be ebbing – that probably meant opportunities would start coming his way.

IT WAS TIME to get the money. He showered and dressed, struggling with his collar button. He would ask Maddie if she wanted to have dinner with him on his way back through. Why the hell not? It would be something to look forward to while he stewed in Africa.

7

Maddie told the receptionist she would be out in a minute to collect Mr. Morrow, then toggled off the intercom. It was hard to believe it had come to this: sitting in a windowless box on the Private Banking floor, in a city she loved so little, working at a job that felt as foreign as camel cheese.

It was six years since she stepped off the plane from Paris and failed to make her connecting flight to Tulsa. She couldn't even remember what the spat was about, just the look of disbelief on Harold's spongy face as she walked away from the boarding gate. It wasn't about the fight anyway. It was a panic attack. One as big as Oklahoma.

She stumbled onto the unproduced playwright the same day, with his seedy walk-up and enormous ego. How did that ever seem like a good idea? A shame you couldn't unfuck someone. By the time she snapped out of it the divorce was final and the children entirely lost, Harold showing a vindictive streak she hadn't noticed before.

Totally without resources, and a man's whim away from being a street person, she applied for the entry-level position at Hanford Bank. Her proficiency in French and Spanish should have been enough to secure the job, but she needed to spend the night with the woman from Human Resources to close the deal, flirting during the interview not nearly sufficient, the woman a real pro.

Once on the payroll, she threw herself into the business of making money like an evangelical, always hoping to get moved to the wire-transfer department, where opportunities must surely abound.

It was so hard to be poor, and then discover you had been incredibly rich from the day you were born, and then be poor again, this time for real.

The buzz of the intercom interrupted her a second time. "Mr. Morrow is still here," came the tinny voice through the cheap speaker.

"Yes, I am perfectly aware of that. Tell him I will be just a moment more." She didn't want to see Jake, but it couldn't be put off any longer.

She knew right away, from that first night at the café, that he didn't understand women at all, didn't realize they resembled men very little, the fact they spoke the same language just an illusion, like color-blind people with different ideas of red. She smiled – he was so embarrassed when she invited herself to his hotel room.

THAT WAS THE smile Jake saw beneath the sparkling dark eyes as she came down the corridor toward him, her hair swinging above the starched collar of her pure-white blouse. The clothes, the walk, she was clearly in play: this was not the look of a woman who had exited the market. They shook hands; it felt warm and personal, and he followed her down the hall to her tiny office. She should have a much bigger job at the bank. She was more capable than her bosses, he was sure of it. He sat down across from her. "Nice view."

"Funny."

"What's in the urn?"

Maddie turned in her chair and looked at the vase. "Father's ashes," she said distractedly.

Jake beamed and wished Daniel were a fly on the wall.

Maddie unlocked a steel cabinet. She pulled out a polished aluminum briefcase and set it on the desk. It was thicker than a standard case, with two latches bracketing a three-digit combination. She unlocked the side latches with a small key on a plastic chain, spun the tumblers to the combination, opened the case and turned it toward him.

"*Voila*. Two million in $10,000 packets. Forty pounds of pure Americana."

He hesitated. What exactly *was* the etiquette when handed a few million in cash by a woman you really liked? He didn't want to stoop to counting it, like a diner meticulously examining the check instead of just tossing a credit card on the tray. Not that there couldn't be a mistake, but how big, after all, could the mistake possibly be?

On the other hand, he was in a position of trust and responsibility – just one bill from each packet would amount to twenty grand – and he had plenty of time. He methodically removed the money from the case and piled it on the desk in twenty stacks of ten packets each, like chips at a blackjack table. The paper band on each packet said "100 - $100's" and that looked about right. He picked one up and fanned through it, then repeated the process with the top packet from each stack. When he was done, he began to repack the case. It was clear halfway through the process it wasn't all going to fit, so he removed the money and started over. He glanced up. Maddie seemed amused.

When the briefcase was finally closed and locked, he picked it up and tested the weight. "So I guess this is a size $2,000,000 AluminAir. Pretty heavy. Let's do thousands next time. You're a bank; you can still get those, can't you?"

"Only on eBay. Be thankful it's not gold."

"You smuggle gold *out* of West Africa, not in."

"Well then be thankful it's not Naira. They're worth so little now the bagmen need dump trucks to close a decent-sized deal in Abuja."

Was she intimating he was a bagman on his way to make a payoff? Or just educating him on bagman logistical problems in sub-Saharan Africa? It was hard to tell.

She pushed a paper across the desk. "If you'll just sign this we'll get you on your way and not take up any more of your valuable time."

Even his feeble effort to count the money was clearly too much. He signed the receipt and pushed it back.

She handed him the little key. "This is for the two side latches."

"What about the combination?"

She pointed to the file cabinet behind him. "There's a box for you in the top drawer. Can you grab it?"

He twisted around in the cramped space and opened the drawer. When he turned back he had a small cardboard box in his hand, heavy for its size. "You shouldn't have."

Maddie seemed flustered, a look he hadn't seen before. "It's not a present. You don't need to wait for the cake. Go ahead and open it."

He held up a gleaming pair of chrome handcuffs. "Nice. Sure you have time?"

"Daniel said you'd want them."

"Think I'll pass." Things were definitely not going as hoped. "What's the combination?" he asked again.

"You know, Jake, I'm not really authorized to give that out. You need to get it from Daniel."

"Come on. I've got to have it. What if they make me open up at the airport?"

"You'll be put on the plane the back way. I've already done the paperwork for taking the money out. And surely Daniel has the African side all arranged."

"I'll get the combination from him."

"Wonderful." She put the receipt in a folder and stood up.

The meeting was clearly over. Their relationship had plummeted to a new low. He moved toward the door, then turned and made full eye-contact. Last chance. "I'm going to the beach," he said.

"Good-bye, Jake." She kissed him on the cheek for the first time ever, opened the door and pointed down the hallway. "The lobby is thataway."

8

Jake's taxi nosed into a too-small spot not far from the Liberia Airways sign. He had budgeted time for a leisurely meeting with Maddie, maybe coffee afterwards or even a drink, so he was very early.

A stream of people spilled out of the propped-open double doors and stretched down the sidewalk for fifty yards. Mounds of suitcases, trunks, cardboard boxes and large black garbage bags littered the walkway. He moved along the motionless line of people toward the doors. A woman squatted on the sidewalk at a small paraffin stove. He realized he hadn't eaten all day.

He elbowed through a group of passengers clotting near the entryway and went into the small ticketing hall. Shared by a handful of low-frequency foreign carriers, today it belonged to Liberia Airways. The hall was packed. There were no discernible lines, the people eventually just washing up in front of one of three besieged agents at the check-in counter. A handful of other employees milled around behind the counter with no obvious purpose, ignoring the yells from the crowd, their neon green uniforms lighting them up like laser targets.

Jake scanned the impossible flood of people and baggage. Passengers normally began showing up as early as the night before, knowing that nothing as flimsy as a paper ticket would guarantee them a seat.

He elbowed his way to the side of the room, cutting across the grain and bouldering through mounds of luggage. The other passengers took his jostling with grace, long conditioned to the assertion of privilege by arrogant politicians and tribal heehaws. The plane everyone wanted to get on was Daniel's 747, and it was Jake's current purpose in life to make sure it kept coming to New York for another five years.

He reached the side wall and began to work his way to the front, making quicker progress along the edge. Minutes later he was at the counter next to a passenger with a dozen enormous suitcases. A day-trader, the man would be heading home after a few hours in America, his bags stuffed with batteries and scarves and cheap radios, everything checked as luggage, the cost of the round-trip ticket and a modest bribe easily recoverable from the street vendors who would be hawking his stuff on the streets of Monrovia in the morning.

"Excuse me," Jake said, leaning across the counter toward the agent.

Well-inoculated against passengers, the woman ignored him.

He leaned closer, putting his head close to hers. "Excuse me. Alhaji Haruna. Is Alhaji Haruna around?" She looked up and he handed her his card. "He's expecting me."

The woman stared at the card for some time as though it might do something, then wandered off without a word.

Jake avoided looking at the trader and instead watched an agent down the counter struggle to attach an old-style baggage tag to a large red suitcase. He was trying to tie the elastic loop to the handle with a granny knot, like it was a piece of string, his fumbling fingers seemingly shot full of Novocain.

Jake squeezed through the opening in the counter and sidled up to the frazzled agent, set the AluminAir on the floor between his legs where he could feel it, took the baggage tag from the man and showed him how to quickly slip it under the handle and through the elastic loop. He was tagging luggage for his third passenger when Haruna arrived, grinning like a maniac.

"Mr. Jake! My good friend! It is so good to see you! How are you? Where are your bags?"

"Hi, Alhaji." Jake picked up the AluminAir and pointed to the suitcarrier sitting by the counter, his leather briefcase hidden behind it.

"Come, come. I've got it." Haruna grabbed the suitcarrier. "Are you checking anything?"

He normally wouldn't let go of his bags on an Africa trip, but this time he needed to tend to the cash, so he let Haruna tag the suitcarrier and put it on the belt.

"Let's get you settled in the lounge," Haruna said, leading Jake out the back door.

Alhaji "Fadi" Haruna was the Station Engineer, second-in-command in New York. The driving force in his life was avoiding a transfer back to Monrovia. He had hung onto his plum assignment for almost eight years, an unprecedented span, by catering to the bigwigs who regularly passed through the station.

Liberia's first-class lounge was furnished with the same tired chairs as the main terminal. A television murmured in the corner next to a stack of worn magazines. An unapproachable woman presided over a folding table covered with soda bottles and plates of cookies, possibly a flight attendant doing double duty.

"I'll be next to you on the flight," Haruna said, as Jake staked out a couple of seats for himself. "My youngest brother is a father for the first time and I'm going home for the naming ceremony."

"Boy or girl?"

"We find out at the ceremony. The mother and baby don't leave the birth house until then. You should come with me. There will be goat cooked with rice and all the tea you can drink."

"If it's a boy they should name him after his esteemed uncle in America."

Haruna laughed. "I will be right back with your boarding pass."

Minutes later a boy returned and handed the boarding pass to Jake, telling him with averted eyes that Mr. Haruna would come later to personally escort him to the plane, after the other first-class passengers were called.

The first muffled boarding announcement came much later. Jake knew the drill: there would be too many people; duplicate seat assignments bought under-the-table; shouting and mayhem in the aisles; ten pounds of potatoes showing up for a nine-pound sack. It would be hours before the last coach passenger was seated. To alleviate his festering anxiety about the AluminAir, he waited until no one was looking and slipped on the handcuffs. It was surprising: they made him feel small.

He pulled out his cell phone and called Daniel's backline. There was always the chance Daniel had canceled the trip and neglected to tell him. It wouldn't be the first time.

"Zakian," said Daniel, after one ring, sounding harried.

"It's me. Just checking in. Is the 747 renewal still a go?"

"What do you mean?"

"Is everything still a go? Money still needed?"

"Still a go. Any problems?"

"No problems. I made the pickup from Maddie. I'm waiting to board."

"Great. Have a nice flight."

"I need the combination to the case. Maddie wouldn't give it to me." She would surely get a serious tongue-lashing for that gaffe.

"Oh for heaven's sake. I'm not sure what it is myself but Bello has it at the other end. Hang on, Beth can get it for us."

Jake heard Daniel shout: "Beth! Get in here a second okay?" There was a moment of silence, the phone muffled, then clear again. "Jake, there's a call I've *got* to take. Can I get right back to you?"

"Sure. I'm on my cell. We're getting ready to board."

"I'll make it quick."

After the coach section was fully loaded, an agent came and fetched the first-class passengers and paraded them off in the direction of the boarding gate. Jake stayed behind, alone in the lounge with the bored attendant. Haruna finally appeared carrying a locked metal case with a red seal and an FAA repair tag. "It's an HSI," he said. "One of yours. We got it back from Seattle this morning. It needs to be switched out right away. I'm hand-delivering it since I'm going down anyway."

The 747 had a lot of built-in redundancy and Jake tried to remember if it could be legally operated with a malfunctioning HSI. Daniel's company provided all of the rotable spare parts for the aircraft, repairing them as needed. It was a hugely profitable sideline, and gave Daniel a stranglehold over the airline's operations. Give away the printer, he always said, make it on the toner.

They strode down the hall past a woman with an infant being escorted by three immigration officers. "She came in on our flight a few weeks ago," said Haruna. "The little boy was born on the floor of the forward galley. Missed by about 15 minutes. Unusual headwinds."

Jake had seen it before: the carefully timed trip to the U.S. on a tourist visa, swollen belly hidden under billowing yards of traditional cloth. The baby missed being an American citizen by less time than it took to grill a hamburger, mother and son whisked away to detention before getting a taste of the free air.

Haruna stopped at an unmarked door and slid his ID card through the reader. Jake was well-accustomed to being escorted through airport back halls, a pseudo-employee, avoiding the security frisks and screening machines. He followed Haruna down the stairs and through a maze of hallways to the airline's Operations Office. The room was deserted, the Liberians swarming the ramp for the twice-weekly ritual that justified their existence in New York, the process seemingly more complicated than a NASA launch.

The ground-level room looked out at the nose gear of the 747. The plane was in the green and gold livery of Liberia Airways, a huge bongo antelope on its tail. A half-dozen odd-shaped vehicles nuzzled up to it like mutant puppies.

Haruna led Jake outside and up the jetway's exterior stairs. The first-class cabin was mostly empty, the rest of the elite passengers still clearing security. Jake's window seat was on the left side of the plane, and Haruna carefully placed the HSI in the bin above it. "Don't let anyone walk off with this," he said, before rushing away.

Jake set the AluminAir on the seat beside him and covered the handcuffs with a blanket. A dour flight attendant poured him warm orange juice from a large can with no label. His seat was right above the forward cargo door. He watched the luggage move up the conveyer belt and disappear beneath him, the airline apparently short of containers. His suitcarrier joined the procession. One less thing to worry about.

He knew a little too much about the airline to be 100% comfortable flying on it. He was in Monrovia the day Daniel first handed the plane over, in the middle of a rain storm that threatened to wash the world away. The airline's maintenance team showed up in tattered clothes, each man carrying a single tool. He glanced at the overhead bin where the HSI was snuggled. At least the spare parts were being professionally repaired.

He took out his cell phone and started to punch in Daniel's number. The phone beeped and the screen went blank. He tried again with the same result. He meant to charge the batteries at the hotel. Daniel had probably been trying to reach him for a while.

The first-class cabin filled up. The captain, a squat man who managed to strut and waddle at the same time, made his way through the section in full uniform, glad-handing the important passengers, his four stripes shining like spun gold.

"Mr. Jake! Welcome aboard, my good friend."

Jake didn't recognize him.

"We have this slight delay because of a problem with a broken bulkhead handle. Have you heard my news?"

"No, I don't believe so. Good news I hope."

The gleaming white smile that spread across the man's dark face indicated it was. "This is my last flight for this worthless government outfit. I have my own airline."

"Congratulations." Jake remembered him now. He was cornered by the man a year or two earlier about acquiring aircraft. It was hard to keep them separate, these Liberian captains, every last one of them in some stage of airline development.

"Our first plane is a 727. We will be flying cargo from Kampala and Luanda up to Leipzig."

Jake nodded appreciatively. The ancient freighter would burn more fuel on each trip than the plane was worth.

"Mr. Jake, we must talk. There are some fantastic opportunities. I will come see you after the workload settles down up there." He nodded toward the winding staircase that led to the upper deck and cockpit.

"Great," Jake said with little enthusiasm behind the smile, and the captain moved off to his next potential investor.

Haruna reappeared. "The handle is fixed. It won't be long now. We are just waiting for the paperwork. I am sure Captain Agom will make up some of the delay in flight. I will be back after I sign for the fuel."

Jake could see the handle duct-taped to the bulkhead. He tried the phone again. It was completely dead, no longer able to produce even the desolate beep. He glanced out the window at a half-dozen large carts overflowing with luggage. They still needed to be hand-loaded into the belly. The conveyer belt seemed to be set at an unnaturally slow speed. The ramp rats put on a bag and watched it roll all the way to the top before putting on the next one. Getting one of these flights off was like giving birth to a ten-pound breach baby.

Jake eyed the lined-up baggage carts again and did a quick extrapolation. This would take at least an hour.

Haruna was nowhere to be seen. Jake got up and made his way to the boarding door, the AluminAir still handcuffed to his wrist. He retraced his path down the jetway stairs to the deserted Operations Room and dialed Daniel's backline. Busy. He hung up and tried Beth's number. He didn't recognize the voice at the other end.

"Is Beth there? It's Jake Morrow."

"She's out of the office today. Would you like her voicemail?"

He was confused. Daniel was just talking to her. "Is Daniel available?"

"Mr. Zakian is on the phone. Would you like his voicemail?"

"Would you tell him it's Jake, please?"

"I can't disturb him."

"Just pass him a note that it's Jake. I only need five seconds."

"I'll tell him you called as soon as he's off the line. Is there a number he can reach you?"

"It's an emergency."

"Is there a number? Or would you like his voicemail?"

"I'll leave a message. Tell him there's been a mudslide and his house is slipping down the bluff. See if he wants me to save the dog."

"I'll pass that along."

He hung up. Damn. He couldn't even get through to Daniel. He was turning into a nobody.

The first thing he noticed was the yellow light flashing on the other side of the window. Then he heard the muffled sound of the warning bell as the jetway nestled back into the terminal, contracting like an accordion. A tug pushed the aircraft toward the center of the alleyway and the string of luggage carts came into view, sitting forlornly on the tarmac, still overflowing with bags, no room for them on board. Two men uncoupled the 747 from the tug, freeing the plane to lumber down the taxiway. Jake glanced at the silver AluminAir handcuffed to his wrist.

Daniel was not going to be a happy camper.

9

The abrasive ringing of a phone worked its way into Jake's consciousness. He walked out of the Operations Room and headed for the center of the terminal. The 747 renewal was hanging in the balance: he had felt Daniel's anxiety and knew it was real. Still, it was hard to imagine a few days' delay actually killing the deal. It was Africa, after all, and time flowed differently there. If you did things on schedule, it only confused them.

It was pointless to reroute himself to Liberia without a passport. The last flight to Seattle was in 40 minutes, but the terminal was on the other side of the airport. No time for the shuttle bus. He ran across the median to the taxi stand and climbed into the first car. The driver turned in his seat, his tall papakha brushing against the roof, its mass of gray sheepskin seeming like overkill on the mild September evening.

"Friendship Airlines terminal," Jake said, breathing hard from the 50-yard jog.

"LaGuardia or Newark?"

"No. Here. JFK."

"Aw, come on, I've been in line for hours," wailed the man, the Russian accent now obvious.

"I'll give you a midtown fare."

"Asshole," the man muttered, just loud enough to be heard but still deniable. He jammed the gear shift into drive and scowled in the mirror. "You oughta, you know, get your shit together."

"You ought to, you know, lose the hat and move to Boise," countered Jake, already weary of New York.

The car accelerated, pushing Jake back into his seat, the transmission clunking loudly into higher gear. The trip back to Seattle would be on his own nickel, the walk-up fare expensive, so he would go coach. He was nervous about the viability of his credit cards, then remembered his wallet was in his briefcase, on the plane. Getting to Seattle was going to be a challenge.

Before dealing with the airline though, he would need to break the news of his temporary financial embarrassment to the bunched-up man in the front seat.

The AluminAir was next to him on the backseat, cradled in his arm like a little silver girlfriend. He was a man of means – two million in cash – he just needed to get to it. He fished in his pocket for the key, found the rough edges of the keyholes in the dark with his finger, and unlocked both side latches. All that stood in his way was the combination lock.

Passwords and PINs aren't much good if you can't remember them, Daniel always says.

Sweeps of amber light periodically illuminated the backseat of the taxi as it passed the poles lining the airport drive. When the next pocket of light arrived, Jake spun the tumblers to 9 - 4 - 4: the combination for the padlock on Daniel's boat. The numbers dated back a half-dozen years to when Daniel got the Porsche. He tried the center latch and it popped open.

It was dark again. Jake balanced the AluminAir on his lap, opened the lid and grabbed one of the packets. It took just the tiniest fraction of a second for his fingertips to signal his brain that something was amiss, the texture not quite right. A millisecond later the confirming data arrived: the packets were too thin. Jake fumbled through them like a blind man. One dropped to the floor and he recovered it on the first stab, almost upsetting the briefcase. He sat back to wait for the glare of the halogen lights that washed the Friendship terminal, then looked down again.

He was handcuffed to a briefcase full of pink telephone message pads.

How odd, he thought, as the driver, sighing and exuding impatience from every pore, waited in the front seat for his fare and tip.

10

Raucous laughter filled the cockpit as the Liberian 747 knifed through the darkness. Zach Bayomi glanced over his shoulder from the right seat. Perhaps Captain Agom was less intoxicated than he appeared.

The Captain stood in the center of the flight deck, hunched over a glass of Scotch from the first-class cabinet. Fadi Haruna was with him, very close, leaning forward. Two other men sat in the back with pinched grins, the plane on autopilot.

Haruna wiped the tears from his eyes. "I must go back to my seat, boys. Really. I need to find my friend Mr. Jake. The American. I haven't seen him since we boarded."

"Come come, *Alhaji*," Captain Agom said, stressing the honorific, "one more drink."

Haruna waved him off. "No, I must talk to the American and then sleep."

The Captain grabbed Haruna's forearm and squinted at him with malaria-yellowed eyes: "You will have time to sleep when you are with your wife."

Haruna held onto his smile and eased toward the door. "I will go back to my seat so *you* can get some sleep, Captain. Don't forget your old friends when you are a big airline tycoon."

The door clicked shut and the four remaining men turned forward. A heartbeat later the first thud came, very loud, shaking the plane. A second thud followed almost immediately, this one muffled, then a staccato banging, like a wooden spoon being slapped hard against a pan bottom.

"What the hell was that?" Captain Agom barked. The nose pitched downward, slamming him to his knees and into the back of the seat.

Zach was pressed hard against his harness. He stared at the glowing panel in front of him. In the vertigo of the moonless night he knew only what the instruments told him: they were pointed at the ocean and going way too fast. He fixed his mask in place and checked the flow of oxygen. Cabin pressure was gone and the aircraft was shaking badly. Something was very wrong. He looked to his left: "Sir?"

Captain Agom was still on his knees. He gripped the armrest and stared blankly out the windscreen.

"Sir! Please," Zach said.

"Get it back."

"Yes, sir." Zach braced his feet and tugged hard on the stick.

"You are taking us down, asshole. Pull up!"

"Sir, I try—"

"What shit are you doing? Go up!"

"It is very heavy, sir."

"Can you both try?" blurted Zach's 19-year old nephew, fresh from flight school in America and a guest in the jumpseat, too green to know the protocol.

An alarm blared. "Why is that sound?" the Captain snapped, struggling into his seat.

"It's the overspeed warning, sir," said Zach.

"I know what it is, jackass. Why is it sounding?"

"We are going too fast," the nephew said.

"And the hydraulics are gone, sir," Zach said quickly, battling the yoke and hoping to deflect attention from the boy. "We have almost no pressure."

"The hydraulics are fuck off?"

"Yes sir. We are dropping rapidly. Have you got the stick?" *The man was just sitting there doing nothing!*

Captain Agom stared straight ahead. When he spoke his voice was flat and distant. "We must make an emergency descent."

"The airplane is doing that for us," the nephew said.

Zach withered him with a quick backward glance, then concentrated on their predicament. He had the sensation they were free-falling out of the sky and looked out the window for something besides the instruments to tell him what was happening. There were stars above him, praise god.

"12,000 feet, Uncle," came the boy's voice from the back.

"Up up up," droned the Captain.

"We're crashing!" weighed in the Flight Engineer, loud enough for the upper-deck passengers to hear. "You must declare an emergency, Captain! You must declare an emergency!"

"Okay. Okay. I declare a fucking emergency. Who do you think is going to help us?"

"8,000 feet, Uncle."

"Help me back with this, sir," Zach said softly. "Please." The plane felt like it might be starting to grab.

"6,000 feet, Uncle."

"What is happening to us?" whined the Captain. He seemed to be getting smaller, the air let out of him.

The dive began to flatten. "I think I may have it," said Zach. "I think we're flying."

The vibration stopped. Captain Agom grabbed the stick and pulled back hard.

"Wait, sir. Easy."

"Now we go up."

"Not yet, sir. We have a control problem. Let's solve the problem first."

Captain Agom squinted across the throttles at his uppity First Officer.

"The engines. We've lost Number 2," Zach said. And some power on Number 1."

Captain Agom slumped in his seat. "What a thing to happen on my last flight. What a thing. Can you believe it?"

FIFTEEN MINUTES LATER the Flight Engineer took a last look at the daunting display of lights and toggles, then slipped out of his harness and stood up. He was charged with understanding all of the aircraft's complex systems, but even the coffeemaker baffled him, the job dropped in his lap by tribal politics. He flew sideways and never corrected anyone who saw his uniform and assumed he was a pilot.

"Should I check the cabin sir?" he said to Zach, not caring what the answer was and screw that imbecile Captain. Screw this airline too. He wouldn't be setting foot in a cockpit again, today or ever. Like tacking in the middle of the ocean to avoid the wind, he planned to move to a new seat on the plane.

He started down the circular stairs to the main deck, panic subsiding with each step. Things were definitely better but this was no time to relax. The best seats for a crash were in the back. Just in case, he would order whoever was in the last emergency row to get out. Though forbidden, he would inflate his life vest early: it would be less to think about later.

He descended into pandemonium. Passengers were pushing and fighting in the aisles, clawing their way to the rear. It was already packed back there, people flattened against the bulkhead. A woman struggled to get an emergency door open. A smoky haze resisted the wind in the cabin, and debris swirled in the air and littered the seats and deck with paper, dinner trays, life vests, clothing.

And the noise! The roar was unbelievable and the pressure hammered his ears. The engines seemed to be inside the cabin. Haruna was next to him screaming into the PA. It sounded like he wanted people to put out their cookstoves, but who could tell? The passengers wore shrieks on their faces but he couldn't hear them. He might be in some kind of shock.

People stared past him to the front of the plane, looking like mice in a snake's cage at feeding time. He turned to see.

A dozen first-class seats had vanished: ripped from their tracks and gone. And that hole, framed by ragged twists of metal and plastic, that gaping ceiling-high hole in the fuselage, it had to be over 30 feet long.

He headed back to the cockpit. If he was going to die it wouldn't be down here with these people.

11

The cabin lights were dimmed on Jake's flight to Seattle. Individual reading lamps beamed down on the few remaining passengers with books or computers open. The drone of the engines was punctuated by the rhythmic hissing of the cabin-pressure regulators and the soft chatter of the flight attendants in the rear galley.

It had been a goat-rope from the moment he opened the AluminAir. The cabbie was apoplectic, more upset, really, than the situation warranted. A one-sided negotiation allowed Jake to escape into the terminal without the authorities being summoned. He agreed to pay the $3.80 on the meter plus a $200 tip, the obligation secured with his $3,500 Bertolucci. The driver would return the watch upon receipt of the money and a prepaid Fed Ex airbill, the deal clinched by the inscription on the back – "To My Darling Husband" and "Five Years" – the words good enough to convince the man that Jake would want it back.

He ran to the counter and cut to the head of the line, unable to keep himself from checking his empty wrist for the time. As a male traveling alone with no luggage, wanting a one-way ticket, he would closely match the airline's profile of a terrorist. The disheveled look, red face and heavy panting were not specifically covered by the profile, but hard to ignore. Not helpful either were the handcuffs and lack of ID, but in the end it was the need for some form of payment that defeated him, and he asked if his friend Smokey Lutz was on duty.

"Geez, Jake. You're going to get me in trouble," Smokey said, once they were sequestered at the far end of the counter. "I can't sneak you on. You'll mess up the weight-and-balance. And there's security issues."

"You can get me around security. Just lend me the money or get me a pass."

"We're ready to push back. I can't get you a pass that fast."

"How about the jumpseat?"

Smokey pecked at the nearest keyboard. "It's open but you need to be a pilot."

Jake shrugged.

"Oh hell. All right." He entered Jake's name into the computer. "The captain's got ultimate authority on whether you ride. What airline do you supposedly fly for?"

Smokey escorted him to the gate and down the jetway. A huffy flight attendant closed the door behind him. He flashed the jumpseat pass and was admitted to the flight deck, where the captain gave it a cursory look. "I'll just go to the back, skipper, if that's okay," Jake said. "There's some seats open." Everyone seemed relieved.

He walked down the aisle and looked for a spot, feeling like a leper. When he took a middle seat near the back the people on both sides appeared angry, their sovereignty over the empty space cruelly usurped at the last moment.

Well into the flight now, he nursed a Diet Coke and resolutely used his elbows to maintain possession of his half of the armrests. The fact is, that briefcase was full of money in Maddie's office. He counted and repacked it with his own hands. What kind of alchemy turned those hundred-dollar bills into message pads?

The hips of the large woman on the aisle bulged warmly against him, and the cowboy at the window snored softly in his ear. He hadn't let down his guard; it was hard to figure how he could have lost the money. Something was escaping him – it was right at the edge of his mind, but he couldn't quite dredge it up. He always felt slow-witted on airplanes, like he'd dropped 20 or 30 IQ points. It was probably the recycled air.

Two hundred miles west of Bismarck, in a half-slumber, the simple truth finally surfaced: this wasn't your basic snatch-and-run. Whoever took the AluminAir replaced it with an identical briefcase, weighted the same, with the same key and combination. It was pre-planned. An inside job. It must be Maddie.

She refused to give him the combination. He wouldn't be expected to discover the phone pads until he got to Liberia. (They would think he was smuggling office supplies!) There was plenty of time for her to make it to some hospitable island before he could raise the alarm. Maybe she finally got her "screw you" money, but she hurt Daniel badly in the process, probably worse than she knew. Or was she working for a competitor, paid to sabotage the 747 deal? Either way, it was a bad idea to exaggerate his relationship with her during the argument with Daniel at the airport.

He tried to muster a little indignation, but, well, it *was* a gutsy move, to just walk off with the cash like that. She beat him to the beach – was probably already snug in some little bungalow. Good for her, really. Then a thought: what if she weren't alone? What if some man was with her? It seemed like the spot belonged to him, even though it was just a stupid fantasy.

His body seemed ready for sleep. There was nothing more to be done until he talked to Daniel – he might want to handle everything privately.

Fadi Haruna would be somewhere over the middle of the Atlantic now, halfway through his eleven-hour flight, worried sick about the repercussions from Jake missing the plane. He would contact Daniel and Fadi's boss first thing in the morning and let them both know it was 100% his own damn fault he missed the flight – no part of it was on Fadi at all.

He descended through the hazy tiredness into half-sleep and now Fadi was gone and Maddie was back, smiling, and then he was above her, cradled on her thighs, her warm breath on his face, loving him.

12

"The left side is gone," the Flight Engineer announced as he retook his seat.

"Say again?" Zach said.

"The left side of the plane."

Zach looked back at him. "What do you mean it's gone?"

"It's missing. You can see right out. Seats are gone. The cabin's a mess. Everyone's fighting. I think we had a bomb."

"You can see out?" the Captain said, confused.

"We must have lost passengers," Zach said.

"And there's smoke in the cabin."

Zach shot the man another look. This was worst of all. The airplane's thin skin would burn like tissue paper if the 220 knot wind streaming past the windshield, working like a giant bellows, got hold of any flame. "Where is the fire?" he said, trying to control his voice.

"I didn't see flames. Just the smoke. Haruna's trying to take care of it. It's from cookstoves, I think."

Haruna. There's a good one. Zach completed the shutdown of the Number 2 engine and decided to watch Number 1 for a while longer before doing anything drastic. They were barely holding altitude as it was. He looked across to the left seat: "Captain." He wished the man would focus. "Captain! There is a big hole in the fuselage. A huge one. Passengers are missing. We have lost engine Number 2 and most of our hydraulics and we are getting reduced power off Number 1. It is almost four hundred miles to Cape Verde, triple that to Dakar. We are at 5,000 feet and having trouble holding it and the passengers are panicking and there is smoke in the cabin."

Captain Agom nodded slowly, like a marionette. "This is what worries me," he murmured. "This is what worries me."

FADI HARUNA STOOD on a seat near the front of the coach section and surveyed the cabin. The people were crammed into the back corner like marbles in a tipped-up box. Things were definitely calmer, an equilibrium reached between panic and exhaustion; fear offset by resignation. Passengers were beginning to sit down, shaky and spent from massive discharges of adrenalin, the good seats at the back commandeered by displaced first-class travelers, their status maintained even under these unusual circumstances. Some prayed. Nobody wanted to be anywhere near that incomprehensible hole in the side of the plane.

They completed a wide turn and seemed to be flying straight and level. Captain Agom should tell them what was happening, say that everything would be okay. The man was an ass, but there were worse things to be.

The PA system was hopeless anyway, with all the noise in the cabin. Another spate of fights erupted in the starboard aisle. Could the people crammed in the corner affect the balance of such a large aircraft? Tip it like a boat? It was an easy question, one he should know the answer to. He had never been on a boat, never in his whole life, not even a little one. That is something he should do: go out on a boat sometime.

One passenger at a time. He would move through the cabin and calm them, restore order, one passenger at a time. Find the girls. Get them back on the job.

ZACH WAS A natural-born pilot, ex-fighter wing, surprise Air Force boxing champion, adoring new husband of the most beautiful and exasperating girl in all of West Africa. He could pull this off. There was plenty of fuel for Cape Verde, even with the engines guzzling it this low. They would get to the islands in little more than an hour. The plane seemed to be flying acceptably despite the massive damage. God bless the man who was in charge of building the 747, it was truly a wondrous plane.

The explosive decompression that first ripped the cabin apart would have blasted pieces of the fuselage out like shrapnel, shredding metal, severing hydraulic lines, damaging the engines, expanding the carnage. Most critical now was the horizontal stabilizer: it seemed to be compromised. The airstream would be working against it like a pressure washer. Every input from the flight deck would increase the chance of total failure.

It was time to walk on eggs.

"Give it more power," the Captain said. "We need to go up."

Zach's instinct was to put as much distance between the plane and the earth as possible, but going up was not feasible. "We cannot climb, sir. We are almost at takeoff power and have trouble holding 5,000."

"You are burning too much fuel," Captain Agom said. "I want to go up. Burn less."

"We have plenty of gas, sir, for Cape Verde."

"I know we have enough, jackass. But fuel costs money, did you know that? You are right now just burning money. This is why you will never run an airline."

"Hold the altitude sir," Zach said sharply as the Captain advanced the throttles and pulled back on the stick. "We're getting the vibration again."

Captain Agom slammed the nose back down as though they had stalled, increasing the speed and driving the aircraft lower.

"We are going too fast now. With the speed down, sir, I think we will be okay."

The Captain pushed forward on the yoke. "What speed do we have?"

"Just leave it alone, sir."

"Huh?"

"Just leave it the way it is."

"Fast, very fast," the nephew said. "4,000 feet."

"We will drop the nose," the Captain said, in a tug-of-war with Zach for control of the stick. When the increased pressure finally stripped the damaged fitting from the stabilizer, the plane snapped downward as though it had been tripped. A two-tone klaxon began to blare, sounding like a meltdown at a nuclear power plant, but otherwise imparting no wisdom whatsoever.

"I've lost it," Zach said, as the plane plummeted.

THE SCREAMS OF the passengers rose above the roaring wind in the cabin, hysteria increasing exponentially. I wonder what happened to Jake, mused Haruna, thinking it odd to be pressed against the ceiling liner.

A MECHANICAL VOICE bleated "sink rate sink rate sink rate" with inappropriate calm. If I just had some quiet, thought Zach, if I just had some quiet I could figure this out.

"What are you doing to us?" moaned Captain Agom.

Another mechanical voice bellowed out its suggestion: "whoop! whoop! pull up…pull up…"

"Help me hold it, Captain," Zach said. "Help me hold it."

"No problem, no problem," murmured Captain Agom.

The sounds from the cabin drifted into the cockpit like faint wisps of wailing from hell. "Pull, pull," said Zach to himself through clenched teeth.

"Piece of cake," the Captain said.

"What's happening!?" shrieked the Flight Engineer, a new smell in the cockpit.

"Altimeters," said the Captain.

The plane broke through the last of the low overcast. The Atlantic came up at them, the eastern sky now bright enough to illuminate the whitecaps. The waves were quite small. The eyes in the cockpit quickly calibrated the distance – they were almost to the ocean, upside down, riding a rollercoaster at astonishing speed.

"Here we go," the nephew said.

"No smoking sign," barked the Captain.

"Terrain terrain pull up pull up," blared the disapproving mechanical voice, seeming to really mean it this time.

"Sorry," Zach said, hanging from his harness and stretching to reach the pedals which were now too far away, talking only to his nephew.

"I love you, Uncle," the nephew yelled back, his voice almost drowned out by the Flight Engineer's screams.

"Seatbelt sign," said the Captain, and the plane, pointed nearly straight down and moving at over 400 knots, was obliterated by the face of the sea.

13

The river was still rising; it must be raining somewhere upstream. He heard the rains were coming here too. That should cool things down a bit.

Finis stepped off the tent's wooden porch and hiked up the path. A desolate cry rose from the huts and he sped up, the frayed bathrobe flapping against his skinny legs. He tried but it was hopeless: he could no more get used to the sobs than to fingernails scraping across a blackboard. His reaction was worse each time, like the peanut allergy. Everything else he took in stride, every privation a badge of honor, but he could really do without all the moaning from the maternity complex.

Most of the men just used the dusty ground behind the tents, but he liked the trek to the latrine, it took him past the Main Laboratory, low and dark, crouched in the dirt like an Idaho potato shed. He felt himself pushed toward it now, as if a powerful wind were at his back, but fought the pressure and came to a stop. He stared at the outline of the structure against the night sky and listened for a while to the hum of the generator and the buzz of the cicadas.

Inside the windowless building it would be brighter than an operating room, and just as sterile, the temperature controlled to within a fraction of a degree, the humidity never varying. In a compound where nothing worked, where communications had been mostly down for months and the vaunted air-conditioning system reduced to a cannibalized pile of sand-clogged machinery in the dump, this building was special, the privileged recipient of all their resources, a spoiled princess amid impoverished peasants.

He considered going in for a quick look but his bladder said no, and he continued along the path. Maybe he would stop on the way back, but only for a minute or two.

They were getting close to putting the pieces together. The Deputy Director would be here in a few days. After years of dreary work in unspeakable conditions, the excitement was palpable. So different from even a week ago when everything seemed ready to fall apart. There were no announcements, just a flurry of helicopters, quickened steps, fervent conversations. The big day must be near, even if no one had the courtesy to tell him officially.

He finished at the latrine and headed back toward the tent, fighting temptation. He passed the Main Laboratory, then suddenly reversed direction, picking up speed as he neared the building's big double doors. He hesitated in the vestibule: it would be best just to go to the observation area.

He let himself into the dimly lit space, not much larger than a closet, and looked out at the pristine all-white room, smaller than the building's exterior seemed to promise. Laboratory benches stretched in tiers to the far wall, and exotic equipment spilled along the countertops and filled the free spaces. Dozens of masked and gowned workers stood in pairs behind the benches, their identical blue latex gloves wielding slender pipettes that seemed to dance like batons to some hidden beat. He rubbed a finger along the filthy window to confirm what he already knew: the dirt was on his side and not theirs.

These kids, his kids, were laboring around-the-clock, taking turns at the expensive equipment, never letting it rest. They were going to save the world, that much he knew. He settled in to watch them work and the rush of pride came so hard he had to brace himself against the windowsill to keep from being knocked to his knees.

"HE'S BACK," HISSED the young man through his green mask, bending over the bench, careful not to make eye contact with the shadowy figure lurking behind the window.

"Surprise, surprise," drawled the pasty-faced woman toiling beside him. "God help us, could somebody slip some Quazepam in his water bottle? Please?"

14

It was just after midnight when the plane pulled into the gate at SeaTac. Passengers scrambled for the aisles, as though only a few would be allowed off.

"Excuse me," the cowboy said in a way that made it clear he didn't care whether he was excused or not. He squeezed past Jake's knees, then stood hunched beneath the overheads, adding one more log to the jam and forcing Jake to lean away to avoid pressing up against his backside.

When the disembarkation finally commenced it was orderly, everyone knowing the right-of-way rules. The passengers traipsed down the concourse toward the main terminal, relentless in their march, an army of zombies moving through a fluorescent world. The airport was in hibernation for the night, all of its shops closed and gated. Silent men with bent heads slowly weaved back and forth, hanging onto their floor polishers. A skeleton-crew of pear-shaped security personnel stopped leaning against the pillars long enough to unhook the rope barriers and let them pass.

Jake crossed a skybridge to the parking garage and inserted his ticket in the payment slot. The screen flashed its message in green and black: he had been gone exactly 21 hours and 54 minutes. When prompted to insert a credit card he cancelled the transaction instead, feeling like a deadbeat even to a machine.

He went straight to the car, despite not consciously remembering where he left it. He stared at his empty hand, the one that normally held the small black briefcase with the car keys tucked inside, then lugged the AluminAir back to the terminal and grabbed a taxi.

The cab headed north on the freeway. Fifteen minutes later they passed through the downtown high-rises and exited onto Mercer Street. He hadn't eaten all day and there would be nothing at home, just bran and broccoli, sprouted-grain bread and cauliflower, skim milk and yogurt, which may or may not have gone bad, but how could you tell? A McDonalds in the shadow of the Space Needle offered the last chance for something that tasted good.

He leaned forward. "Turn here. I need some food." The startled driver hit the brakes hard and swerved into the entryway. Jake rolled down the window and yelled his order into the lit-up menu sign: two cheeseburgers, fries and a large chocolate shake.

"Will that be everything?" inquired a faint metallic voice from someplace near the sign.

"Do you want anything?" Jake asked the driver; and then in case that wasn't clear: "My treat," and then in case that didn't translate well: "It's on me."

The turbaned man shook his head and the car pulled forward to the pick-up window. An acned boy in a paper hat held up the milkshake and a small sack, grease spots already seeping through the side. "$7.58," the boy said.

Happily, it took more and more to get him embarrassed. He could ask the driver to pay for the food and then reimburse him at home, or they could just get out of there. "No, no. No thank you," he said to the befuddled clerk. Then to the driver: "Go, we don't want this food."

"Don't want food?"

"No. No money." He knew before it was out of his mouth it was the wrong thing to say, and noticed for the first time the veins bulging in the man's neck. Was he a Sikh? And were they non-violent? He seemed to recall they were not.

"No money?"

"No money for food. No money right now. Plenty of money at home though."

The driver seemed to ponder his options.

"Go," Jake said. "Please just go." The taxi moved down the empty street toward the waterfront, then headed north along the bay. He rolled down the window, stuck his head out, and shook it in the cool air. He had been mostly awake for over 48 hours, and now, ten minutes from home, his body wanted to shut down. He slapped his face hard to stay awake.

The driver watched him in the mirror and gently increased the pressure on the accelerator.

They looped up the Pier 91 viaduct and headed for Magnolia. The taxi followed the contour of the bluff and wound along a boulevard lit by ancient incandescent lamps on wrought-iron poles. Downtown Seattle glittered behind them. When they approached Andrus Street he told the driver to turn right and head up the hill. This trip, this monumental disaster of a trip, was almost over. In the morning he would dedicate himself to making sure his missed flight didn't cost Daniel the 747 deal. Whatever it took. He'd jump on another plane for Liberia if necessary.

It was a rare sensation – wanting to get home – but tonight the house pulled at him like a magnet, the attraction strengthening the closer he got. It would feel good to collapse into bed amid familiar surroundings. Or better yet, on the comfortable couch in the den.

The house came into view, no lights showing, welcoming even in its darkness. "Right there," he said, pointing to it, and the driver slowed at the corner, executed an almost full U-turn and headed for the driveway. Jake looked around the backseat for his things, then remembered all he had was the AluminAir. They came to a stop and he glanced up. His sleep-deprived stupor was replaced by the instant clarity of a wild animal suddenly at full alert.

At first he thought an armored car was sitting in his driveway. But it was Daniel's Hummer, its metallic-gray paint gleaming in the moonlight.

15

He was no coward but he *was* tired, and the last place in the world he wanted to be was inside his own house. It was just too complicated. He leaned forward. "I need to go someplace else. Downtown"

"This is where you say to take you. I take you."

"Nobody's here. No key."

"There," the driver said, pointing to a reflected glow from the second floor. "You are to pay me to take you here. You must pay me now and leave."

"Just take me to my office and I'll pay you there," Jake said, stuck in a cab with an angry man in an unusual hat for the second time in less than eight hours.

The driver sighed and backed out of the driveway, muttering in a language Jake didn't understand. The two men were silent as the taxi moved through the deserted streets, triggering green lights at every intersection. Was he sent to Liberia so Daniel could be with his wife, like King David and Bethsabee? Could that possibly be what was happening here?

"Please, could I borrow your phone for a second?" Jake asked. He just couldn't leave this alone. "I'll pay for the call."

"I take you where you say. Phone is business only."

"Just give me the damn thing," Jake said softly. He took it and dialed Daniel's number, and was routed straight to voicemail. He pictured Daniel's phone, turned off, dark and silent, sitting on the wicker nightstand in *his* bedroom, beside *his* bed.

He left a message, his voice as normal as he could make it. He was at the office. Daniel could call him there. If he didn't hear from him, he would meet Daniel at the boat at noon.

He passed the phone back to the driver as they rolled to a stop in front of the building. Jake got out with the AluminAir and left the back door open as a signal he fully intended to return with the fare. The driver immediately joined him on the sidewalk. They went in the night entrance together and headed for the security desk, where rows of monitors displayed a changing montage of the building's public spaces. Jake's elevator card was on its way to Africa, so he needed to be swiped on. The security guard was nowhere to be seen.

The cabbie's displeasure was pressing hard on him. Hell with it. He headed for the stairs. The 46 flights were once part of a faintly-remembered exercise regimen.

Somewhere between the fifth and sixth floors, bent over, lungs screaming and heart hammering, the truth became inescapable: the stairs were a big mistake. He already had a lot invested in them though, and if he retreated to the lobby and waited for the guard, it would be paying for the same real estate twice. He tried to visualize the pain as pleasure, just like in the dentist's chair. A dozen floors later he reached a sort of double equilibrium: his body knew precisely how fast it could climb without going anaerobic; and his progress toward the office was exactly offset by his escalating regret.

They exited the stairwell on the 46th floor, which was shaped like a warped octagon to accommodate more corner offices in the lawyer-dominated building. Jake punched his code into the keypad. The two men passed through the reception area and zigzagged down the corridors to his office.

He pulled a large envelope out of a drawer and poured its contents on the desk: spare keys, a handful of twenty-dollar bills, and two credit cards in his wife's name (no reason to pass those on, it would just be gasoline on the fire.) He picked up the twenties, paid the driver especially well, then escorted him to the elevator lobby. Back inside, he liberated a beer from a partner's mini-refrigerator and carried it back to his office.

He checked the AluminAir to make sure the pink message pads hadn't turned into something else, then stood at the window, the city sleeping at his feet.

When did he stop loving her? He wished he had the photo from his wallet, the one of her at the top of Mount Si.

They were only kids, barely 20, when they got married. On the way back from the rehearsal dinner she insisted he pull into the alleyway behind her parents' house. They fumbled in the back of his brush-painted, iridescent-blue panel truck. It was the first time for her. He was surprised and delighted by the early gift, never exactly sure why it was offered, liking the idea she couldn't wait any longer for him, later thinking she didn't want to be an unworldly bride. They never once spoke about it.

The next day they made promises to each other in front of their friends and families. She looked beautiful in her grandmother's gown; he ridiculous in a rust-orange tux.

It seemed like a different lifetime when they laughed, flirted, and looked forward to seeing each other at the end of the day. They were no longer bound by love, or even obligation: it was identity, inertia and her aging parents that kept them together now.

They planned on having a large family, just like his. Both expected the children to be beautiful: nature knew how to do it – pheromones calling out to the perfect set of genes. The miscarriage was a blessing really, her body doing its job, but she was traumatized, her desire to give birth completely smothered. She lobbied hard for a vasectomy. When he refused she told him he was selfish and stepped up her vigilance over the birth control.

He pressured her. The discussions were heartfelt. He didn't understand her withholding this thing he wanted more than anything. Everywhere he looked women were having babies, and he resented her for her weakness.

The night her grandmother died he was in Africa, halfway through a trip and unable to come home (though, in truth, he barely tried). She found comfort with a Boeing engineer from her hiking group, confessing only after the man, ready to leave for a new position in Wichita, sought Jake out and apologized, his sad eyes and hung head not quite masking the hint of triumph in his voice.

The pain was unbearable, and he acted badly. There may have been others. A drunken co-worker at her office picnic propositioned her right in front of him, not knowing he was her husband, and although she turned him down, it was done without any outrage whatsoever, almost tenderly, as if she were apologizing for declining the offer and might just as easily have accepted it. He suspected the fireman from down the street (after she got news of Uncle Fred's passing); and the semi-famous human potential coach at the growth seminar right after her childhood friend died; and the jumping instructor at the horse trials, when her second-most-favorite mare needed to be put down near the log oxer after a fall. He became obsessed with the well-being of anyone close to her, twice taking the cat to the emergency room in the middle of the night.

Over time his jealousy diminished, each suspected infidelity a smaller dagger to his heart, until he no longer cared at all, the few remaining pangs having more to do with nostalgia and competitiveness than with loving her. As she sank further into sadness he realized he didn't have it in him to pull her out. He began to hope she would find a lover who would make her happy, someone in it for the long haul. It would be a relief.

But not Daniel. That would be something else altogether.

The beer, clutched in his fist like it might try to escape, had reached body temperature.

After his night at the New York diner, when he and Maddie plotted their escape to the tropics, he ordered a $299 Delaware corporation: *Barbados Partners, Inc.* He rented a post office box and opened a bank account, depositing money from time-to-time. The money didn't earn interest; there was no need to file tax returns. The entire arrangement was impervious to all but the most determined asset investigation.

Having the cash sitting in a rainy-day fund was a comfort to him, an emergency parachute. When he was discouraged about his life he would put money in. When things were better he might take some out – to fund a vacation for them, or a new sound system. The ebb and flow of the marriage was pretty much reflected in the monthly bank statements.

He peeled the label off the bottle and stared out at the dark city. The balance in his personal slush fund was currently at an all-time high, over $86,000, drawable by corporate check or debit card.

16

Daniel Zakian was experiencing a bad night when the phone rang again. He recognized the federal agent's caller ID. "What?" he said irritably.

"He may not have been on the plane. The cargo manager thinks he got off at the last minute."

Daniel took a moment to process the information.

"We don't know if he had the briefcase with him. The guy just can't recall. First he said yes, then no. It's like he wants us to tell him the right answer and then he'll say it."

"The briefcase doesn't matter." Jake wouldn't let it out of his sight, not for a second, handcuffs or not. "How sure is the guy it was Jake?"

"Seems pretty sure. He knew who Jake was."

"Where is he now?"

"The cargo manager?"

"Jake."

"No idea."

"Is anyone looking for him?"

"Not that I know of."

"Find him. Put on a full-court press." He needed to talk to Jake, and fast. He scanned through the list of missed calls again. Still nothing from Jake's phone. Surprising he hadn't checked in. "It's tremendously important we find him. Do you need help with anyone? Local police? Airlines?"

"I don't think so."

"Well use everyone. This isn't the time to under-react. Call me if you run into any roadblocks."

"Will do."

Daniel snapped the phone shut. So Jake wasn't on the plane after all. God love you, buddy. How do you do that? How do you get to be a golden boy that shit can't stick to?

It was the closest he had come to crying since the day they put his father in the ground.

17

Jake grabbed the spare passcard from his credenza and hurried out the firm's back door to the elevator lobby. When the car arrived, he swiped the card through the reader and pressed 72.

He got off on Daniel's floor and used the glow from the city to illuminate the familiar path to the office. The door was locked. He picked up a metal letter-opener from Beth's desk and went through the conference room to Daniel's side door. It was locked too, but the door to the private washroom next to it wasn't. He went in and turned on the light, passed the Italian-marble shower and the toilet stall with its unexpected view of Lake Union, and tried the door at the other end. It opened directly into Daniel's office, but was secured from the other side. He began to work on the lock with the letter-opener, badly gouging the wood. It sprang open. He was in.

There was nothing on the desk but a tidy stack of documents and a benignly glowing computer monitor, the screensaver merging one flattering image of Daniel into another every ten seconds. Jake turned on the green banker's lamp and sat in Daniel's chair at the edge of a small island of light.

He opened the bottom left drawer and scrabbled through the contents: an assortment of Daniel's business cards with different company names; extra passport photos; a box of pens; ancient Dictaphone tapes; cough drops; a little device for telling the time in different parts of the world; a box of keys

(Daniel never threw any away); cardboard tubes with lead re-fills for long-gone automatic pencils; a cup filled with foreign coins.

The uncovered tin box filled with old desk calendars was at the back, right where it was supposed to be. Rubber bands binding the calendars had deteriorated with age, spilling loose days into the tin. He slipped his hand under the box and pulled out a thin passport wallet. In its zippered right-hand compartment were three sheets of yellow legal paper, no staple, folded over three times.

Daniel had tutored him many times on exactly how to find the sheets, what to look for. He felt he had seen them before, when in fact he hadn't. It was years since they last spoke about them. Daniel was in a different office then, with a different desk. His long-standing instructions were clear and unequivocal though: upon news of his death, Jake was to proceed immediately to the office and retrieve and destroy the papers, before they fell into the wrong hands. Daniel wasn't dead of course, but under the circumstances it seemed like a good idea to finally get a look at what sat concealed for decades in his bottom left-hand drawer.

Jake gently unfolded the sheets and laid them in a row on the desktop. They were well-creased, almost falling apart, like they had been folded and unfolded countless times. He smoothed them out until they lay flat. He was violating a trust, but couldn't stop himself.

There it was, right in front of him: the complete, unabridged list of every woman Daniel had ever slept with, and he very much needed to know if his wife's name was on it.

18

The security guard stepped into the middle of the floor and pulled up his pants, not worried about someone coming in at this hour. He looked around the gleaming restroom: doors on the stalls that came all the way to the floor; little walls between the urinals for privacy; thick quilted toilet paper on the rolls, white not brown, and it didn't bead water either. It was a damn smart move to get out of the shipyard, where the stalls had no doors at all and could be seen from the lunchroom.

He made his way back to his desk and scanned the monitors, manually cycling through the camera positions. He checked the main elevator log. No new activity. He settled back in his chair. All was well.

Halfway through his sandwich he rolled the chair back down to one of the computer screens. He had missed it the first time, concentrating on the main elevators: a second-stage elevator went from 46 to 72 while he was in the shitter, to the headquarters of *Zakian Global*. Odd. He didn't think there *was* anyone on 46.

Most likely it was nothing. You couldn't get to 72 without a passcard. No harm in checking though, right after lunch.

JAKE NEVER DOUBTED the list would be there. Daniel kept a record of every mile he had run in his life, every movie seen and book read, every pound dropped. He had a thick binder entitled "My Best" that listed his favorite sunset, best steak, finest vacation, funniest joke – it was updated regularly as new experiences pushed out the old. He took unabashed pleasure in his accomplishments and narrow celebrity, reflected on them every day, catalogued them, and literally hung them on his wall: professionally-mounted newspaper and magazine clippings permeated the offices. At the urinals, right there at eye-level, you could learn that Daniel Zakian keynoted the 44th Annual Finance Symposium; took another delivery from Boeing; was appreciated by the Boys & Girls Club. Like Nixon and his tapes, he needed the souvenirs.

Jake examined the three pages. The magnitude of it! The entries were numbered, one to a line. Each contained a date and a name. They were in chronological order, going back over 20 years. All were in Daniel's slightly feminine hand. The first half of the list was written in the same ink, the names perhaps copied from an earlier list. The rest of the entries were more varied, some written hurriedly, others meticulously inscribed.

He started at the top of the first page and worked his way down, recognizing fewer of the women than expected. There was an occasional description instead of a name ("girl with bike on ferry"). As he went down the list, the dates got closer together. If you graphed it out, the increased success probably correlated pretty well to Daniel's mounting net worth.

Phil Irwin's daughter was there and Jake rechecked the date, trying to figure if she could possibly have been 18 then. There was a Mrs. Peter Bell. A dozen other names were in the same form: that's how he was identifying the married women. Daniel might have some enemies Jake didn't know about.

It was hard to keep from skipping ahead. On the third page he slowed down. If 'Mrs. Jake Morrow' was there, he would get to it soon enough.

The last name, number 131, was Lizzie Stewart, a local equestrienne who Jake knew slightly, the entry dated less than a week earlier. He let out his breath. Daniel would be religious about keeping the list current, immediately updating it after each conquest, a gunslinger notching his pistol. Unless last night was the first time (or his wife given a pseudonym) Daniel might be in the clear.

He rechecked the last page to make certain he hadn't missed it. Maddie, who at that moment was surely watching the sun climb into a blue-white tropical sky somewhere, was not on the list either. Good for her, he thought, for the second time in as many days. Daniel surely would have tried.

The extent of the list, perhaps not unusual for a rock star or professional athlete, was nevertheless impressive. Daniel wasn't a typical ladies' man: he was abrasive, and not particularly attractive either; with a big beak and ears; sunken, nearly cadaverous cheeks; and short pubic-like hair that carpeted the back half of his head. He would be relentless though, attacking each opportunity with purpose, just like everything else in his life.

Jake's list, had he kept one, would have been inexplicably short for a person who showered every day and drove a fairly nice car. Even if he expanded the parameters to include women who *might* have slept with him if he tried, it still took a great deal of optimism to get himself out of single digits.

He carefully refolded the list and was ready to put it back when he spotted the letter on the desk: a two-sentence notice from Daniel's aviation underwriter. The hull value of the Liberian 747 was being revised downwards, from $90 million to $50 million, because of the dramatically depreciated aircraft market. The change would be effective in 30 days.

Daniel would have been plenty upset about that. He wanted his planes in Africa to be as heavily insured as possible, especially since the airlines paid the premiums.

Beneath the letter was the inch-thick renewal agreement for the 747 lease. He thumbed through it, his professional curiosity piqued, looking for the insurance section. The agreement fell open to the signature page, right before the exhibits. There was a gold seal on the page, as wide as a doughnut, with the imprint of the Ministry of Finance of the Government of Liberia, complete with red, white and blue ribbons. Next to the seal in broad blue ink was the elaborate autograph of the Chairman of the Finance Committee of the airline's Board of Directors; and directly below it the swooping, almost illegible signature of Daniel N. Zakian, President, Chairman and CEO of *Zakian Capital & Aircraft Services*.

At the bottom of the page a notary at the American embassy in London swore she witnessed the two men sign. Ten days ago. Well before Daniel sat in this same chair and begged him to get to Liberia at warp speed to save the deal.

19

Jake took a swig of Pellegrino from Daniel's bar, and examined the photo array that filled the wall behind the desk. There were pictures of mountain summits, finish lines and racing sailboats. Each featured a smiling Daniel, clad in new and expensive-looking gear. The cleanly framed photos almost appeared staged, as though Daniel were sticking his head through the hole in a plywood cowboy at the county fair. Jake half expected to see a picture of him on a flying trapeze, or walking on the moon.

One photo drew his attention. Discolored by age, mounted in a cheap wooden frame and partially hidden behind a candle lamp, it looked out of place with the others, like a ginghamed rural cousin at a big city wedding. Three adolescent boys stood together on a pebbly beach, small sailboats and a canoe dragged up behind them. They were tired and sunburnt and grinning at the camera. A young Daniel, slightly in front of the others, was illuminated by the soft orange glow of the setting summer sun. The other two boys were a step back, shadowed and made smaller by the camera's perspective. Jake, Finis and Daniel. They spent that whole summer at the Utsalady cabin, none of them realizing it was a high-water mark, that nothing again would ever touch it.

He turned his attention to the computer screen. A search of Daniel's recently opened documents didn't turn up anything that pertained to the 747. A file named "cancel insurance" sounded promising, but was just an angry letter from Daniel canceling his policy on the *Nadalia*, effective immediately. The obstinate carrier refused to reduce the premium, despite Daniel's assurances the boat never left the dock anymore.

Just snooping now, Jake opened a document named *"agenda9-7."* It was a blank page. Peculiar, since it took up 87 KB.

He swiveled in Daniel's chair and gazed again at the photo of the three boys at Utsalady Bay. Finis, always the smartest kid in the class, taught them how to make invisible ink, mixing cornstarch with water and heating it, the secret words later appearing in bright purple after a light sponging with an iodine solution. Years later, Finis pestered them with blank e-mail attachments, frustrated no one could figure out his cyber-version of the ink.

Jake turned back to the computer and highlighted the entire document, then clicked on the toolbar for font color. It was set to white, so he changed it to black, and the screen instantly filled with text.

It was a seven-page agenda for an "All Hands Meeting" set for September 7th. He considered reading it, but was having a sinking spell, the last few days catching up with him. He shouldn't be going through Daniel's private stuff anyway – it was dishonorable.

He got up to leave. He would confront Daniel about the already-executed 747 lease after the weekend, man-to-man. The good news? There could be no explanation, no apology, that would get him back on a plane for Africa with another briefcase full of money.

Fool me twice, shame on me, Daniel always said.

He tossed the Pellegrino bottle into the wastebasket, then bent over and stared at the half-full plastic liner. This could be important. If Daniel was in the office after the janitors left, and didn't make a new entry on his list of conquests, well, that would be a good thing. How late did they service this floor on Friday nights?

There were hundreds of paper scraps in the bottom of the liner. He had warned Daniel many times to get a shredder, one of the good ones that cut both ways.

The room suddenly brightened. Someone had turned on the floor's main bank of fluorescents and they were shining through the glass panels into the office.

He reached down and jerked the computer plug out of the strip at his feet. The screen went blank. He slipped the list of women into his pocket, moved across the office and through the washroom and poked his head into the conference room. A security guard was coming his way. He backtracked through the lavatory to Daniel's office and grabbed the liner bag from the wastebasket before heading for the escape-hatch door, the one Snap used two days earlier.

20

It was good to be back on his own floor. Jake crossed the reception area to the lunchroom and started a pot of coffee. It would take a few minutes, so he headed to his office and flopped in the chair.

He hadn't noticed it before: the files and papers that normally spilled across his desk were missing. He spun the chair around. There they were: haphazardly intermixed in precarious stacks on top of the credenza. He spun back. His never-tidy desktop was bare except for an overlapping cascade of multicolored files neatly arranged down the left side.

Someone got into his office and appropriated his desk. He checked the wastebasket: a pile of orange peels sat at the bottom. Okay, even worse. They left their garbage behind.

Whoever did it was trespassing on sacred ground. They might as well have used his toothbrush. And rearranging the papers, that was really over the line. He felt a flash of anger. Everything was organized, even if it didn't look like it.

He grabbed the top file from the desktop. The coding on the tab would identify the attorney responsible for the work. He recognized the client number immediately, it was Daniel's, but not the description: it sounded like a hotel refurbishment project. He certainly recognized the attorney responsible for the file though: the code was "10" – *his* number.

He checked the tab on each folder. They were all Daniel's projects and all "10s." His files were his babies and here were a couple dozen children he never knew he had. He thumbed through the last file: it was thin like the rest and contained information on a bank account.

Coffee suddenly seemed important. He grabbed his mug and headed back to the lunchroom. The coffee wasn't finished, but he pulled the pot out anyway and filled his cup while a stream of brown liquid hissed and bubbled onto the hotplate. He popped the cup in the microwave for a tune-up, liking it really hot.

He was halfway back to his office when the ceiling lights came on. Startled, he splashed coffee onto the carpet. Thank god, again, for the oatmeal weave.

Someone was here with him, most likely the security guard. No worries about the incursion onto Daniel's floor: he certainly had the right to go up and check on his client, at any hour. As for the jimmied bathroom lock, well, he wouldn't know anything about that.

He turned the corner to his office and set his steaming cup on the low glass table just inside the door, relieved to get it out of his hands. If it weren't the guard, it would be a junior attorney; someone with a looming deadline and a spouse with weekend plans. He would go give whoever it was a pat on the back. That would be appreciated, coming from him, and it wouldn't hurt for people to hear the managing partner was working damn early on a Saturday morning.

The firm's back door offered a shortcut past the elevators to the main reception area. He stepped into the corridor, then stopped. There were two men in his lobby.

One was younger, mid-twenties, with an especially bad haircut and buck teeth noticeable even at a distance. He was pacing back and forth. The other man sat behind the receptionist's desk with his feet up on the woodwork, talking on the phone, his bare calves exposed above saggy socks and wingtips big as clown shoes. He extracted a message slip from an attorney's cubbyhole with his free hand, idly perused it, then methodically returned it and took another.

Strange men lounging unaccompanied on his turf, inside the locked doors, at four in the morning? It was bizarre.

He shoved the door open and started into the hallway, but stopped short. He had a plaque in his office with Custer's words at the Little Big Horn: "Come on boys, we've got them now!" This might be a little like that.

He edged back inside and watched through the slightly ajar door. The pacing man jangled keys in his suit pants. The other man pressed the phone to his ear with his thumb – the fingers were all missing from the knuckles out.

It was abundantly clear what needed to be done. And not because of any logical deductions concerning Daniel's recent edginess, the missing $2,000,000, a Hummer in his driveway, critical aircraft renewals already well-renewed, or strange files on his desk. No, these men in cheap suits were transmitting pure menace. Some dangerous shit was going on and Daniel had gotten him right in the middle of it.

He needed to get out of there.

21

Jake gently closed the door to the hallway. He hurried back to his office and stuffed the strange files into a spare litigation case, then brushed in the keys, money and credit cards. He grabbed Daniel's wastebasket liner on the way out.

He peeked out the back door. The reception area was now deserted. He dropped the case and trash bag, wheeled around and ran back to the office. Voices approached from down the hall. He pulled open a file drawer and pawed through it, fingers fumbling, looking for the red file with "*RONNY KNOLL*" on the tab, finally locating it in the "R"s instead of the "K"s. He snatched the file and rushed out, knocking a pansy-orchid off its three-foot stand.

The voices were very close. He slipped into the elevator lobby, expecting the door to burst open behind him. Surely they would have heard the stupid plant hit the floor! He pressed the *Down* button and waited. Could the "ping" that signaled the elevator's arrival be heard in his office? He worked there for ten years and couldn't say.

He squeezed sideways into the car as the doors began to open and hammered the *Close Door* button. They shut with excruciating slowness. Leaning against the rear wall, flooded with relief, he forced himself to breathe, then couldn't stop, his head thrown back, sucking in the air. He was doing okay.

He moved to the front of the car, ready to bolt when it opened, his nose almost touching the crack between the doors.

THE TWO MEN arrived at the office and peered in, then entered single-file. "Think this is it?" the younger one asked.

"Oh, pretty sure, Buck," said his partner, examining a wall plastered with Jake Morrow diplomas. What did he do to deserve this moron? He held his good hand against the grey seat of the desk chair, not sure if he was feeling residual body heat or some natural warmth from the expensive leather.

"Messy guy," Buck said, staring at the swath of dark brown potting soil that marred the carpet. He stuck his pinkie into the coffee mug, and jerked it back out. "Yoww!" he howled.

His partner stared at him a moment, then bumped past and charged down the corridor toward the reception area.

THE ELEVATOR DOORS began to open. Jake noted the vase of silk flowers sitting on a purple acrylic table. It was exactly like the one on his floor. Another company with the identical furnishings? And there was his firm's name in foot-tall silver letters.

He was back on 46. The elevator had somehow returned.

"Come on, asshole step on it," hollered a man from very close.

"Coming," said another voice, this one further away.

Jake eased to the side of the car. He hadn't pushed the button to go down! Relieved to be safely on the elevator, he neglected to tell it where to go. He had just been sitting there, stoned at a four-way stop, waiting for the flashing red light to turn green.

Footsteps hurried toward the elevator and clothing rustled a few feet away. He punched the button for the lobby so hard it didn't come back out. A disembodied hand with just a thumb appeared between the elevator doors as they began to close. Jake's arm came up in an arc and intercepted it, the uppercut slamming the hand back. The doors closed and the elevator began to descend.

He clutched the briefcase and trash bag, loving the empty feeling in his stomach as the car dropped. He got off in the parking garage, then hurried up the spiral ramp to the street. Only the security cameras watched as he stormed up the steep hill toward the darkness.

22

Jake emerged from the shadows beneath the elevated freeway. It was better to keep moving than stand exposed, hoping for a random taxi at this hour. He clasped the trash bag to his rumpled suit and rushed off Madison to the side streets, worried about the two men. A string of rats from a sagging dumpster scurried across his path. Crumbling apartment buildings loomed above him, their windows barred-up as though something inside might be worth stealing.

The eastern sky was beginning to lighten when he arrived at the dilapidated garage on Cherry Street. He walked around the old truck to make sure none of the tires were flat. The firm had taken the pickup in lieu of legal fees, and for a decade it hauled files to storage and furniture to new apartments for the partners' kids. It started on the fourth try.

He drove through downtown and over the Magnolia Bridge, heading for home. From a block to the south he could just make out his driveway. The Hummer was gone. He should go in and talk to her; that's what a grown-up would do.

He passed the house without looking directly at it. Thirty yards beyond the drive an unembellished sedan sat parked by the curb, pointed in his direction. A man in the front seat squinted at a newspaper in the subdued glow from the streetlight. It was odd – a stranger reading a paper in a car before the sun was even up – not that he hadn't done exactly the same thing himself on many occasions.

Daniel said he would be at the *Nadalia* by noon. It made sense to head for the marina and wait for him to show up. Aurora Avenue was nearly empty, with only the hookers and homeless still on its sidewalks. He drove past a string of cheap motels, transmission shops and taverns. The place would be packed with life in a few hours.

He turned east and met up with the freeway. Daniel lied to him. More than once. The truck sped north, doing more than 90, burning more oil than gas. Jake throttled back. The cruise control didn't work. He turned on the radio. The speakers were bad, the bass shredding the air. He started to make a to-do list for himself, like he always did on the way to work, but couldn't concentrate. The sun peeked over the Cascades. The decrepit pickup enveloped the cars behind him in a dense fog of blue smoke.

He thought about the first time he met Ronny Knoll.

23

When Ronny Knoll walked into Jake's office for the perfunctory final interview with the managing partner before being offered the job, he announced before they finished shaking hands that he was freshly diagnosed with AIDS.

Ronny turned out to be the firm's finest word-processor ever, a real Hall-of-Famer. Funny and conscientious, he played his keyboard like a concert pianist. He could knock out 180 words per minute with accuracy, and won Seattle's coveted Best Processor title at Rosita's Mexican Restaurant as a rookie. Jake picked up the tab, on the company card, for the large contingent from the office that showed up to cheer him on.

Ronny took the work at least as seriously as the lawyers did. He never missed a deadline, even when it meant spending all night at his workstation. He read and understood what he typed, was interested in the projects, and Jake came to enjoy the after-hour visits to his office with questions about bartering Mexican oil for crop-dusters, or flying Boeing jets offshore to transfer title.

Ronny was on an extreme drug regimen from the start, but it didn't take, and less than a year after the diagnosis it was clear he was in for a rough ride. Not a public person, he seldom volunteered information about his troubles or his life, which after a while amounted to pretty much the same thing. He never hid things though, especially from Jake, who seemed to have a special status with him. Jake helped him muscle through some legal problems that arose from the illness, once threatening to move the firm's medical insurance to a new provider if Ronny wasn't allowed to have his daily infusions at home instead of at the hospital.

Ronny's paychecks were his only means of support and he budgeted carefully to make it through each month. As the medical emergencies came closer together and his attendance at work turned sporadic, Ronny used the comp time built up in countless late-night work sessions to keep his check whole. When that was gone he turned to his sick-leave, and when that was gone he took all of his accrued vacation. When nothing was left, Jake wrangled an agreement out of the partners to advance Ronny some future sick-leave and vacation time so he could continue to receive a full paycheck. In the end Ronny had taken all of his vacations and sick leave for the next 12 years, a sympathetic bookkeeper conspiring with Jake to not exactly *hide* the extent of the growing accrual, just give it an extremely low profile.

Ronny grew up in Rexburg, Idaho, where high school jocks could letter in rodeo and the biggest thing in town was the small Mormon college. His patent homosexuality was not well-accepted there, least of all by his minimal family, his father long gone, maybe dead, his mother and sister always embarrassed.

Ronny hadn't seen the two women in over ten years when they finally made the trip to Seattle right before he moved to the hospice. They planned on five days but stayed only a night, keeping Ronny awake as they bickered in the living room over the allocation of his modest belongings. Unable to relate to his eclectic group of faithful friends – who ministered to him around-the-clock – they stepped on the plane the next morning, the mother panicked at the thought of catching something.

Jake considered Ronny a friend, but it was an office-hours friendship. He never saw him outside of work, and never set foot in his apartment. Jake made just a single trip to the hospice where Ronny spent almost three months at the end, going there to talk him out of the excursion to Mexico, not knowing why he hadn't visited more often, ashamed of himself even before Ronny died.

When all medical measures were exhausted, Ronny's partner took the news hard. He eventually fixated on a Doctor of Enviropathy who had discovered that the human intestinal fluke and metal toxins were responsible for AIDS, a fact being suppressed by the medical establishment. He begged Ronny to go to Mexico to take the cure, it was now-or-never, Ronny's body well into its final breakdown.

Jake was dead-set against the trip, and told Ronny it was a false hope. Ronny said he had no hope whatsoever, and was going only for his partner's sake. Jake ended up checking Ronny out of the hospice and taking him downtown to get his first-ever passport and a suitcase and a new robe and slippers. Instead of just winding down in peace, Ronny ended up packing off to the airport, his sister enlisted as a traveling companion, delighted to be leaving Idaho in January for a free trip to Mexico.

Barely able to stumble off the airplane, Ronny headed for the Aspiration Clinic in Tijuana where the basic fee for two weeks of black-walnut and nutmeg enemas was $15,500 (including lodging and meals) plus blood tests ($95 each); diagnostic imaging ($750); dental x-rays ($344); tooth extractions ($188 each); and partial dentures ($775); plus tax. Ronny's partner covered everything with funds borrowed from his elderly mother.

After the AIDS parasites were wiped out by the twice-a-day cleansing of Ronny's intestines and his pre-dawn wormwood infusions, it was time to flush the metal toxins from his body. They removed all of his silver fillings and a gold crown, extracted two teeth with root canals (so as not to compromise the immune system), and badly burned his groin while administering treatments with a "Jolter" device that killed the AIDS virus by broadcasting radio waves through his body at frequencies designed to negate the signals broadcast by the virus itself.

They discharged him, exhausted by the torture, carrying over $4,500 worth of books and videotapes, 30 individually-tailored dietary supplements and a Complete Herbal Parasite Program, plus a portable Jolter (that also produced colloidal silver) and a strongly worded letter of advice emphasizing the importance of sending all immediate family members and household pets to the clinic for immediate treatment so as to avoid a relapse.

The airline refused to board him; he was obviously too sick to travel, so his sister headed home alone, done with Mexico, leaving Ronny by himself at the airport. It was fairly clear he died the next day, but much harder to pinpoint exactly where, there being a number of competing stories offered in splintered English by various Mexican officials.

When Jake called Ronny's mother to discuss sending the body to Idaho for interment she said no, and asked whether the firm offered any death benefits. He arranged for the burial in Mexico, most of the expenses paid by the firm, and picked up the small difference himself. Ronny's friends organized a well-attended memorial service in Seattle, but nobody from Rexburg was able to make it.

There was no will to be probated and Ronny's personal effects were distributed to his friends in accordance with an informal letter he had prepared and left with Jake for safekeeping. Ronny's federal burial benefit was never applied for, the pittance not worth the effort to claim it.

JAKE GOT OFF the freeway early so he could drive through the Stillaguamish delta country. The backroads skirted the steadily growing river as it wound through lush dairyland, flat as a countertop. He passed tiny Silvana, where as teenagers they would drink beer in the cemetery to prepare for summer dances at the Viking Hall, passing around a bottle of men's cologne like a joint, splashing it on as if its aphrodisiacal benefits could not be overdone.

Before turning off his memories of Ronny, missing him for the first time in a long while, he reviewed some important facts:

1. Ronny was dead.

2. He exited the world with a Mexican death certificate and minimal paperwork.

3. He had no family worth mentioning.

4. He had a mischievous sense of humor.

5. His social security number, driver's license and passport (valid for another seven years) were sitting in a red file on the backseat of the truck.

At the end of one of their late-night chats at the office, Ronny once said he wished he had Jake's life instead of his own. Jake glanced back at Ronny's file. If it ever became necessary to borrow his identity, he was sure Ronny would get an enormous post-mortem kick out of it.

24

Jake cruised into Stanwood's old Swedish downtown looking for breakfast. A parking spot opened up right in front of the Hearthstone. His crew-cab Ford stuck out a foot further than the rest of the pickups, but otherwise fit right in.

He was lucky to get a table-for-one along the back wall of the busy restaurant. The Duck Hunter's Pork Special was enticing (three eggs, bacon, sausage and ham, hash browns and biscuits) and sported a healthy-heart sticker too, the biscuits no doubt made with a light hand on the shortening and half-and-half. He settled for an egg-white omelette and wheat toast, dry. It was time to start making some changes.

The restaurant's mismatched furniture looked like it had been collected from neighboring farm-kitchens. People chattered between tables. A counter full of farmers and hunters stoked up for another day of husbanding or shooting a variety of creatures.

Jake read the free local paper while he waited for his meal: the town's new cost-efficient self-extradition program was a disappointment so far (the third prisoner in a row failing to show up from California); and the Island County Sheriff's office was investigating the theft of an expensive flashlight from a deputy's patrol car.

He scrutinized the other diners. Everyone seemed to have a real life. He alone lacked substance: a homunculus just watching from the cheap seats. Maybe he should walk out like

Maddie, disappear without a trace, leave everything behind, no explanation to anyone, let the chips fall where they may. Start with a clean slate. Take ballroom dancing lessons.

He ate his breakfast without tasting it. He could renew Ronny's driver's license in Mount Vernon. Did they still hand you the new one right on the spot? The license would be a magic cloak: if he slipped it into his wallet, Jake Morrow would instantly disappear. Costco was right there too. It would be good for another quick piece of picture ID. He loved the place anyway: high ceilings, wide aisles, big carts, jumbo containers of pickles and cookie dough – it made him feel like a kid.

If he moved to a town like this how long would it take to fit in? Five years? Ten? One generation? Two? Three? It would be quicker if he were poor – regular people became locals almost instantly – and that might not be much of a problem. The $86,000 in the slush fund was a pretty meager stake for a new life. Maddie was in a much healthier position.

He asked for a little more coffee and the check. He would miss his brothers and sisters if he did it, and their kids, and they would worry about him. Nothing ever comes without a price though. He had no illusions about that.

The bank wasn't open yet so he gassed up the truck. A greasy-haired woman at the next pump stared at him while she filled her primer-splotched Impala. He stared back and she turned away, shaking her head.

The bank doors opened and he went inside, leaving the truck running in the parking lot, an improbable getaway vehicle. He emerged 20 minutes later with $30,000 in cash and some blank counter checks. It was a scramble getting even that much. The manager handed over the cash begrudgingly, like a librarian who didn't want any books out, and asked him to call a day or two in advance the next time.

If you want to maneuver, Daniel always says, there's nothing like cash in your pants.

Instead of heading back to the freeway, he turned west and drove onto Camano Island. The sun was full in the sky behind him, the day cloudless and cold. Frost covered the ground and the maples and madronas were already starting to turn. Later in the afternoon it would be shirtsleeve-warm. It was always sunnier up here, in the rainshadow of the Olympic Mountains, drier by half than Seattle just 50 miles to the south.

He'd made the decision to detour to Finis's Utsalady cabin during breakfast. He loved the old place and would rather kill time there than at the marina. He could look through the mystery files from the office, rest a bit, take a shower and still get to Oak Harbor before noon.

He drove past the glassblower's studio, the truck running rough, and headed down the familiar lane toward the water. He turned into the gravel driveway and got out to open the wooden gate, breathing in the saltwater smells. After the truck was snug in the shadow of the small cabin, he walked back to the gate.

The last few days had been unusual, no doubt about it. After years of monotony, things were coming at him pretty hard now, gathered together and trying to roll him like a rogue wave. A talk with Daniel and a little rest should set everything straight. He closed the gate and latched it, happy to be inside the stockade, safe from whatever dangers might be out there.

25

"Shut the door," barked the woman from the front of the room, nodding to the fingerless man by the back wall. She was about to repeat the command, figuring he didn't hear her over the soft chatter, when he roused himself and moved lethargically to the door, his insouciance so obvious it had to be deliberate.

Evelyn Schwab was a swarthy, big-pored, menopausal woman. The turtleneck sweater and jeans hid her stocky body well, except for the lower abdomen, which was pushing hard against the denim. She projected her unpracticed smile across the room, but it was coming up short, more like a discolored grimace, the teeth not aging well despite the meticulous attention heaped on them. Jewish herself, she needed to work hard to keep her anti-Semitic feelings in check. She also had little regard for blacks and the rich, and an intense dislike of good-looking people, who seemed to get an unfair ride and took full credit for it, as though they somehow deserved the winning lottery tickets dropped in their laps.

"Grab a seat and listen up." The room was bare except for crooked rows of gray folding chairs and a whiteboard on the wall behind her. Metal scraped against linoleum as the crowd settled in, spots in the back at a premium. She searched the phlegmatic faces for a spark of enthusiasm, or curiosity even. Mostly middle-aged men, they looked like a bunch of miners on their way down the shaft for another day under the earth, half dead already.

They didn't like being rousted early on a Saturday morning. Well, she didn't share the sentiment, not since this was beginning to turn into a pretty big deal. One of the old warhorses had called her in the middle of the night and told her to look for Jake Morrow at his downtown office, definitely not the normal chain-of-command for that sort of thing. She sent Dickhead and Beavertooth, and they missed him of course, little surprise there, but nevertheless staked her claim to the case, planted the flag. So when the whole thing escalated, the guy connected to a plane crash, she was already the case detective, in at the beginning, and she fully intended to ride this puppy right out of her basement cubicle and all the way to the 7th floor.

It was good to be in front of the troops again. The meeting room felt like her war room from the glory days, a miniature one admittedly, but still a war room, and if you squinted you could even imagine these humps as her old task force. People fought to be invited to the early morning briefings then, wanted to be a part of the hunt for the Portage Bay Killer. She ran the case for 11 years, until the FBI came along and screwed everything up. Great while it lasted though, the victims piling up every year, the full resources of the Department at her fingertips. The weekly press conferences were well-attended, at least in the beginning, and she was a local celebrity and a regular on national television.

She didn't appreciate it at the time, having all that clout, people licking her up and down like a hound dog. It faded as the investigation dragged on, to be sure, interest waning even as the death count mounted, the resources slowly taken back, then everything crashing down in one dizzying moment, the Feds not flinching as they tossed her in the dumper. No doubt about it, career resuscitation was badly needed.

"We're looking for Jake Morrow, he's a Seattle lawyer." The murmuring in the room tapered into silence. She wrote the name on the whiteboard. "He arrived on a flight from New York just after midnight pretending to be a pilot. We think he may have been in his downtown office about four this morning." She looked pointedly at the man by the door and his buck-toothed co-idiot. "But we can't be positive."

"SHIT," WHISPERED BUCK to his partner once Schwab looked away, "all this for being a fake pilot? He must've crashed the plane."

"Must have, moron."

Buck took that as an insult, despite the ambiguity of the remark, because of the tone in which it was delivered, and decided to keep his thoughts to himself for a while.

SCHWAB STARTED A stack of flyers around the room. "The top photo was taken less than a year ago for the attorney directory. The rest are computer renditions." The photo had been altered to show a black-haired Morrow and a blond one; one with a beard, one a mustache; glasses; a crewcut; hippie-long hair; even one in a Hawaiian shirt, as though he might have slipped into it to avoid detection. "Our job is to locate and secure him."

"What's the charge?" asked the man by the door, not waiting for her to call for questions.

"Just get him corralled. Let me worry about the charges."

"Hold him without a charge? How do we do that?"

She had asked the exact same question. She decided to give the same answer: "Use your imagination."

She stared into a roomful of disbelieving faces. Even *these* guys were going to need more than that. "He's a person-of-interest in a plane crash that killed 420 people."

Buck gave his partner a look of triumph.

"Just grab him and contact me immediately. You won't have to sit on him for long."

The warhorse had told her the entire Department was behind her, but she was the point of the spear. She was supposed to nab him, then summon the big dogs. The whole thing was low profile, the public not to be aroused. That meant it would be a race to the podium once he was caught, a battle to get in front of the cameras and take the credit. They would expect her to stand in the back row with the rest of the stooges.

Well, she knew how to play that game.

"He's not to be harmed, and I'm there for the bust, got that? You find him, secure him, wait for me to arrive. And there's a metal briefcase. You need to secure that too. Questions?"

"Are the Feds involved?" asked the man by the door.

It was probably a deliberate dig. That ass had never been intimidated by her, even before she hit the skids. "*I'm* involved. That's all you need to know. Everything goes through me."

She was so sick of smelling like a loser. If she pulled this off the Department would have a hard time continuing to pretend she didn't exist. And this Morrow character was a rich lawyer, so that was a bonus.

The meeting went on for another 45 minutes. The most promising leads were parceled out to the ablest officers. Finally there were just two men left in the room with her.

"You've got Oak Harbor," she said to Buck and the man-with-no-fingers, "there's a boat at the marina that needs watching."

26

The well-worn key on the ledge above the cabin door was the same one they reached up and grabbed 20 years earlier. Jake let himself in and lit the pellet stove, the cabin cold, then took a careful look around.

The kitchen was the same, its walls smothered in mucous-colored paint from the Boeing surplus store, slapped on during the summer they earned their keep by doing the cabin inside-and-out. The stuffed chairs in the main room were the same too, looking dusty but no more worn, and the same books were on the shelves: Vonnegut; Hesse; Hemingway; summer reading in a cabin that never knew a TV. The elaborate crystal set that Finis built was on an end table looking ossified; and next to it the crab cooker, an antique now; and in the corner the cheap wood rod that Jake used to catch a 19-pound salmon on 10-pound test before Skagit Bay was declared off-limits to all but the Indians. The whole place had the eerie feel of a private museum, their buoyant younger days frozen in time.

He went back to the truck and retrieved the black briefcase and Daniel's trash bag. The chill was already off the small cabin by the time he returned.

He pulled out the files and arranged them in alphabetical order on the Formica table. There were 22 in all, mostly aircraft deals by the sound of them, with a handful of real estate projects thrown in, a movie syndication, a research and development program, and some ventures with generic handles that could be just about anything.

He picked up the first file: *Alpha Beta Aviation Partners, LLP.* The slim folder contained a corporate resolution granting Daniel N. Zakian and/or Jake C. Morrow unlimited authority to open and manage a bank account for the partnership. There were pages of boilerplate in a tiny font; information about online banking; PINs, access codes and passwords; and a copy of the signature card. His signature was scrawled on the card, one line below Daniel's, dated three months earlier.

He had never seen the card before. He would have remembered signing it. He looked closer: someone used his signature stamp, the one kept in his desk for routine documents.

He grabbed the second file: *Altitude Equipment Leasing Partners IV, LLP.* The contents were almost identical to the first. His name was stamped on the signature card. Same bank too: Industrial Credit Bank of Japan, a financial giant with some money invested in Daniel's hedge fund.

The other 20 folders were more of the same.

He searched through the cabin for a sheet of paper and settled for a take-out pizza menu. Passing through each file again, he summarized the contents in columns on the back of the menu: names, account numbers, user IDs, passwords and wire-transfer codes. Less than an hour later he closed the last folder, his list complete, and went outside.

The tide was halfway out with about 40 feet of shell and pebble beach showing. Tiny needles of steam rose beyond the northern horizon, marking the location of the Anacortes oil refineries. A bank of fog to the northeast blanketed the prosperous farms on the damp Skagit River delta.

Daniel had given him 22 new projects, and made him a signatory on the bank accounts. It was a good sign, this tangible evidence of trust and confidence. It was a long time since Daniel treated him like an equal instead of a lackey. The files were a welcome-home reward, waiting for him to get back from Africa.

Daniel would have noticed his angst and financial distress. That was his special gift, of course, reading people's hearts, knowing what they needed. And it was just like Daniel to make him hang out there for a while, sweating and fretting, before swooping in with the grand gesture.

There was still an hour to kill. He went inside and made a pot of ten-year-old coffee, watching the bubbling liquid splash against the glass knob of the coffeepot lid. Daniel's garbage bag was calling out to him. He poured the contents on the table and culled through the trash for the torn scraps. Daniel wasn't in the habit of ripping paper into tiny bits.

He piled the scraps in a little heap, then refilled the bag with the rest of the high-class junk mail: solicitations for platinum cards; a renewal for Horsebreeder Magazine; invitations to a benefit wine-tasting and Seattle U.'s gala charity auction; an empty box for a handheld GPS (the expensive device no doubt destined to join the other unused gadgets on the Nadalia); postcards announcing oriental rug extravaganzas and art show openings; a brochure for a luxury waterfront home.

He cupped his hands and herded the scraps to the far end of the table where the light was better. Spread out, they appeared to be the remnants of a half-sheet of 8½ x 11 graph paper, the kind Daniel kept on his credenza in a silver tray and used for taking notes. The scraps weren't exactly confetti, but they were small.

The tinier the pieces, the bigger the secret: there were at least 500 of them.

Most of the fragments were blank; the rest marked with blue ink. He set aside the ones with ink, then turned over the blank pieces looking for bits of blue on the other side. The unmarked bits went into the pellet stove. The inked ones lay in front of him like pieces to a jigsaw puzzle.

His nose was almost on the tabletop as he matched up the serrated edges and ink markings. He came up with ten separate groups of scraps. He pieced each group together with cellophane tape from the kitchen junk drawer and lined them up, ten blue-inked islands:

57   53   46   14   3   01   arr 9/7   M   Z   Kona

They meant nothing.

He shifted the pieces around the table like walnut shells in a riverboat game, waiting for something to click. Still nothing.

He tried to call Daniel, but the old phone was dead, probably disconnected by Finis in an economy move. He was already hungry again, the egg-white omelette a mistake. The unheated pantry was filled with empty jelly jars and fondue pots, flower vases and fishing gear. The only thing resembling food was a half-case of beer on the floor. He grabbed two bottles and popped them in the freezer.

A tattered can of *SpaghettiOs* was tucked away on the top shelf in the kitchen. It had no expiration date, so he shook it into a saucepan. There was a loaf of white bread in the freezer. He tossed a couple slices under the broiler.

The radio in the main room was so old it was probably worth money. He settled for a Canadian gospel station, then snatched the toast out of the oven with only seconds to spare, dosed it with a heavy coating of garlic salt and took a bite. It tasted pretty good, even with the freezer burn. He opened one of the beers and grabbed the bubbling pan of *SpaghettiOs* and sat down with it. The ten little chunks of stuck-together scraps were at the other end of the table. He ate out of the pan. Maybe the change in perspective would generate some inspiration.

His mind checked into the radio report somewhere in the middle. He didn't know how much he missed, but did hear, as clear and cold as the air outside the cabin windows, that the investigation was only in its infancy, a terrorist attack was not ruled out, and Boeing and the NTSB were both dispatching teams to Liberia to help determine why the 747 went down.

Liberia Airways had only one 747. They were talking about *his* plane.

He spun the tuner. None of the other stations had anything about the crash. He grabbed the truck keys and headed for the door. There would be a phone in town.

The truck wouldn't start. Maybe he didn't properly finesse the gas pedal. He kept trying until the engine no longer turned over, then went back inside.

There was still nothing on the radio. How many were on board? It was a full load. With the coach passengers crammed into seats with only 29" pitch, maybe less, and the first class section taking up a big part of the plane, it should be around 400 dead, plus the crew, maybe a few more.

Normally he was able to ignore remote disasters but this was staggering. What did their faces look like? It was already hard to recall the faces. The day-trader at the counter; the deported woman and her almost-American infant; that fat-assed Captain What's-His-Name; Haruna, his friend. They were all connected by their journey, then he stepped away.

A broken bulkhead handle. Incompetent Liberians. The loaded baggage carts outside his window. Forgetting to charge the cell phone. The snotty secretary who wouldn't put him through to Daniel. Everything conspired to save his life: if even one element were different he would be dead now, just like them.

He got the second beer from the freezer and realized he had barely touched the first. He washed the pan and straightened the books. He grabbed a plastic sandwich bag, scooped the ten scraps into it, and jammed it in his pocket.

Would the flight records show he was on board? With a free pass, he might not be in the reservations system. He should be listed on the manifest though; it was used for the weight-and-balance. But with Liberia Airways, who knew? He would find out soon enough: if he were officially dead his name would be splashed all over the Internet.

Should he let his loved ones know he was okay? And if so, who would that be exactly?

Maddie would think she was home free. She had a signed receipt. No reason to assume the money was anywhere other than the bottom of the ocean. Her euphoria would be short-lived though, when he showed up alive.

It was definitely unusual to walk off a plane at the last minute and then have it crash. There would be questions about that. Who knew he missed the flight? His buddy at Friendship Airlines. Two cab drivers saw him – he made a big impression – but they had no idea who he was.

So he had surprise on his side. Was there any reason he needed it?

Daniel would figure his two million was gone forever. He would collect $90 million in insurance on the plane though. That would make him happy, a big windfall really, although of course too bad for the people. The replacement aircraft for the Liberians would eat up only half the insurance proceeds, so in Daniel's case a shit-hole place like Liberia and an international air disaster would add up to another golden plume in his well-feathered cap.

He fought the urge to curl up in the warm cabin and go to sleep. It was more important than ever to get to Daniel. The two strange men in his office and the guy parked outside his house probably weren't connected to the crash. It was just too quick, the government wasn't that competent. But something was definitely going on.

He made a list of what he needed:

    1. Daniel
    2. Phone

3. Internet
4. TV news channels
5. Hot water and towels

Everything was available on the *Nadalia*, lying placidly at her berth in the Oak Harbor marina.

27

Evelyn Schwab hung up the phone. Oak Harbor looked like the place to be. Especially with the imbecile twins holding down the fort there.

She thumbed through the latest batch of messages. The picture was getting clearer. They found his car at the airport and identified the taxi that picked him up. The driver was being tracked down. They should have a statement within the hour. Morrow hadn't used any credit cards since he got off the Liberian flight, no ATM withdrawals either, and no calls on his cell phone. He obviously wanted people to think he went down with the plane.

Funny he would come back to Seattle though.

She stood up and smoothed her jacket. She could call for the helicopter, but the paperwork would eat up more time than the drive. It would need to be approved upstairs too, and that might tip them off. No, better to just take the car, she could use the lights if necessary and get to Oak Harbor in under two hours. She picked up the phone to call the garage, then set it back down. There was no reason to make any unnecessary waves. She would go grab the car herself.

This was going to be bigger than the Portage Bay Killer.

No reason to arrange for extra back-up either. Morrow would be a pussy. Pretty sure of that. Soft. Probably curl up in a ball and cry. Better to handle him herself than risk a SWAT team. Those guys were animals. Impossible to control in front of the press.

She should have been more aggressive with the Portage Bay case. Broken the rules. She wouldn't make the same mistake again.

Morrow wasn't to be harmed, she had made that perfectly clear, but if *she* had to drop him she would, and the fewer people around the better. Twice before she needed to shoot-to-kill, and twice before was quickly exonerated. This would be no different: the guy took out a plane full of people. She'd come out of it a hero, whether the Department liked it or not. She'd be bigger than all of them, even the mayor.

She reached into her bottom drawer and removed the pipsqueak revolver, sealed in its plastic bag, and carefully slid it into the pocket of her tweed jacket. Just on the off-chance Mr. Morrow needed to have one in his hand.

28

Jake tried the truck again. Whatever mechanical defect had been bedeviling it was now compounded by an utterly dead battery. He looked down the gravel side-yard to the eight-foot Livingston. The boxy little boat was upside-down and needed a good pressure-washing, its hull blanketed in green moss. Two oversized plastic wheels stuck up from the transom on aluminum stems, like baby-blue crab eyes. He flipped the boat over, uncovering a collection of frayed and faded lines and signs of small-animal habitation.

A five-knot westerly was just beginning to ruffle the water. Oak Harbor was less than eight miles away, a straight shot down Saratoga Passage. He could do it in an hour in the little boat.

A shark's got to keep moving or it'll die, Daniel always says.

Jake went to the bookshelf and grabbed the tide-tables from behind the stuffed owl. He turned to 'September' and ran his finger along the first row. The numbers made no sense, at odds with what he could see right out the window. He checked the cover: the tables were 11 years old.

He went to the window and scanned the near-shore rocks that randomly poked out of the water in front of the cabin, each named for a girl they wanted to have sex with. He spotted the top of Mary Grace just breaking the surface and recalled she represented a four-foot tide. The water was moving slowly from right-to-left, carrying pieces of debris floated off the beaches. It would be the back-end of the ebb. He went out to the bulkhead. The damp upslope of the beach supported his guess. If he got on the water right away the current should be with him the whole way.

The tiny padlock on the shed door looked like it belonged on a little girl's diary, but still managed to keep him out. He finally popped it off with a screwdriver from the kitchen and carried the small outboard to the boat. A battered gas can with flaking paint and a half-inch of something sloshing in the bottom was next. He poured out the contents, cut a section from the garden hose, and snaked the tube into the truck's gas tank. He sucked on the end, tentatively at first, then overcompensated and got a stinging mouthful of fuel. When the can was almost full he added oil, then gargled with warm beer.

The 22 folders went into a plastic garbage bag, followed by the Ronny Knoll file and the cash from the bank. After it was double-bagged and sealed with duct tape, he placed the packet inside a crab-pot, and secured the pot in the bow.

The only life vest in the shed was too-small and covered with mold (it may once have been yellow.) He put it on over his black-pinstripe suit jacket and tossed the oars into the boat. Everything seemed to be in order. He picked up the bow and pushed the boat across the slick grass like a wheelbarrow. Down the crumbling concrete ramp it went, pulling him along as it picked up speed, before banging off the half-foot ledge at the bottom and coming to a sudden stop on the beach.

He pushed it across the rough ground, grinding over mussel and barnacle-clad rocks uncovered by the withdrawing tide. When he got to the water his fingers were white. The boat was heavier than he remembered. It went into the water bow-first, until only the two big wheels remained on dry land. They wouldn't fold up: the cotter pins were corroded. He jerked as hard as he could. The first pin popped loose, cutting his hand.

The second pin came out a little easier, still accompanied by a string of bad language.

When the wheels were retracted and the pins reset to hold them straight above the transom, he pushed the boat into the water and hopped in the stern, almost losing his right shoe to a sucking patch of mud. Out 30 yards, clear of Linda, Sharon and Jeanette, he tipped the motor down. After a dozen jerks on the start cord, the little motor gasped and sputtered to life.

A WOMAN ON the beach in a yellow and gray spray-suit watched Jake as she rigged a small catamaran. Her blonde hair whipped around her face in the growing breeze. When Jake hurtled down the ramp behind the Livingston she smiled. Her eyes followed him as he grunted and cursed his way across the mud in his dress shoes and tiny life vest. Her smile broadened when he got the wheels retracted and tumbled into the boat; and when the little outboard finally started amid all the profanity, she laughed out loud.

HE PUTTED ALONG in the little dinghy. Like a penguin, he was clumsy on land but easy on the water, a natural grace acquired as a toddler, innate, polished by decades of messing around in boats. It was good to be out in the little Livingston, even under these strange circumstances.

The breeze, barely blowing when he decided to take the boat to Oak Harbor, was now producing a noticeable chop. When he came out from behind Utsalady Point he stepped into still more wind, right on the nose, and small whitecaps began to spank the dinghy, which was riding low in the stern. The waves came at right angles, and the little boat pounded into them. He began to take on water and eased off the throttle to temper the flow. The trip had barely begun. He should have brought something to bail with. It may have been unwise to go by sea.

He was berating the pint-sized outboard, all smoke and noise and no power, when it sputtered and died on him, its grating sound now sorely missed, replaced by the hard slap of waves against the hull.

It was funny how the brain worked. Sitting there, dead-in-the-water in the middle of a building storm, the first thing that came to mind was the face of the woman at the gas station, staring quizzically as he pumped unleaded into the tank of the diesel truck.

29

The boat bounced on the chop. Jake wasn't sure why he took off the engine cover. He certainly wasn't going to fix the little motor. He turned to grab the oars and there it was: a small catamaran with a rainbow sail tacking toward him. It was the kind of sailboat usually seen here on hot summer weekends, when powerful thermals sucked the air down the Straits. It came up on his weather side and expertly turned into the wind. The little boat's forward progress stopped almost instantly, and it drifted back toward him, sails flogging. A young woman in a yellow-and-gray spray-suit was at the tiller, with the mainsheet in her gloved hand.

"Ahoy, Jake. What's up?"

Who was this? She knew his name.

"Are you putting out the crab pot? Because the season's over and I don't know about that bait." The woman nodded toward the duct-taped garbage bag, which looked like a huge slab of black and gray bacon. "I'm Carly. Carly Spring. Tommy's little sister. We lived five houses down from Finis. I still do."

The catamaran bumped the side of the dinghy and they both reached out to hold the boats together. He remembered Tommy Spring well, a mean-spirited bully he dodged each summer for a decade. Tommy had been big for his age, coarse and stocky, with a five o'clock shadow in the eighth grade, which is when he stopped growing, stuck forever at 5'7." Surely a wife-beater by now, the little prick.

"Are you adopted?" Jake asked, immediately regretting it, hoping she didn't hear him, but finding it hard to believe this beautiful woman, smooth skin glistening with salt spray, came from the same gene pool as Tommy Spring. "How *is* Tommy?"

"He's still a jerk. Works at the Stanwood glass shop on weekdays; breaks into the customers' homes on nights and weekends."

He remembered her now. She was about ten years younger than he was, a little girl back then, always hanging around the beach with her fishing pole, hoping someone would take her out.

"Do you need help? I can tow you back."

"No. I'm fine." The Livingston bobbed helplessly, taking water from all sides. He wasn't at all afraid, but not exactly sure of his next move either, going forward pretty much out of the question but retreating to the cabin a big step in the wrong direction.

"It's building. The Flattery report says it'll be 20 knots real soon, maybe more." She was excited – clearly out here for the coming wind. "Where are you going?"

"Oak Harbor."

"Perfect. We can drop Finis's boat back at the cabin and I'll give you a lift."

"Thanks but that's okay." Another wavelet hit the boat hard on the beam, adding more water to the growing pool in the bottom. He patted the motor. "I want to see if I can get this thing going." He would wait until she was out of sight before resorting to the oars.

She scanned the clouds that whipped across the sky. The winds aloft were a precursor of what was to come. "I'll take you." It wasn't really a suggestion anymore.

"I don't want to put you out."

"No problem. It'll be a screaming reach home."

Another wave hit the gunwale, dousing Jake and sending cold water down his back.

"Hop on. With you out of the boat it'll ride a lot higher."

He hoped he wasn't being insulted. "I need to grab my bait."

She lashed the duct-taped garbage bag to the netting while he refastened the engine cover, tilted up the motor and stowed the oars. He scrambled across the trampoline and got settled. She eased the mainsheet and they plowed back toward the beach with the dinghy in tow.

WITH THE LIVINGSTON safely on Finis's lawn, they headed back out on the catamaran, speeding through the white-crested waves toward the other side of Saratoga Passage, making a lot of leeway. Hiked all the way out, they were barely able to keep the sailboat at a reasonable angle. When they were under the Whidbey Island bluffs they tacked.

"Do you want it?" she shouted, as they quickly picked up speed again.

He shook his head. He felt stiff and inflexible in the sopping-wet wool suit. The clothes bound his movement; the grubby little life jacket constricted his chest. He was happy to sit and enjoy the ride and didn't want to dispel any image Carly might have of him as the lithe and supple sailor of long ago.

"Come on. You'll hate yourself if you miss this."

He relented, switched places, took the tiller and sheet, slipped his toes under the foot-line. He brought in the sail a bit and pointed the bow closer to the wind. The boat heeled, and they were off again. He looked at her beaming face and knew it matched his. They sliced through the water, going faster than a speedboat, zigzagging to the west.

He cut inside the first red buoy, knowing they drew no water at all, and sailed a perfect line for the dogleg to the harbor. When the wind abated they switched places again.

The boat swept toward the marina, Carly at the helm, both of them making imperceptible adjustments to compensate for the quieting waters and lessening pressure on the sail, each knowing exactly what the other would do, like Olympic dance partners who had been skating together forever.

She ran them down the long channel to the marina and came up to port in the alleyway behind the first row of moored boats. Jake pointed to the *Nadalia*'s stern. He was cold and wet and there was urgent business waiting, but he didn't want the ride to end.

30

Bursting like an over-stuffed sausage from the suit he had bought too early in life, Buck moved gingerly down the long gangway from the shore to the dock. He clutched the railing and concentrated on staying upright, his shoes slipping on the corrugated metal surface. What idiot would design a ramp with that kind of angle? If it weren't for the grating he'd be flat on his ass.

He didn't notice the little sailboat making its way toward the marina.

An elderly man struggled to push an overburdened hand-cart up the narrow incline. There was no room to squeeze by. Buck scowled and held his ground. The frail man braced his load, then sighed and retreated, the pushcart trying to roll him on the way down. Buck pressed until the man was at the bottom of the ramp, then hurried past to resume his stake-out of the rich prick's fancy sailboat.

The wide main dock started at the bottom of the ramp and headed due west into the harbor, spawning six finger piers that branched off to the left and ran parallel to the shore. All of the docks were floating, hooked by metal harnesses to wooden pilings driven deep into the mud, the whole contraption rising and falling with the tides, 300 large boats moving up and down in unison.

Buck tucked himself behind a narrow lean-to at the far end of the main dock, where the water was the deepest. He had stood there for hours already, before taking the bathroom break, and now was really cold, his body's cushion of warmth long since evaporated.

They checked out the boat when they first arrived. Nobody was on board and it was padlocked shut. He couldn't actually see the *Nadalia* from where he stood, with three-dozen or so intervening yachts blocking his view, but he was as close as he could get and still stay out of the wind. The finger pier was a dead end anyway, so anyone heading for the boat would have to go right past him.

He wanted to be back on shore in the harbormaster's office. It was perched over the marina like an airport control tower and had a perfect view of the main dock. You could even see the top of the guy's mast if you knew where to look. The harbormaster pointed it out to them. It was warm in there too, with chairs to sit on.

HUDDLED AT THE bottom of the stairs leading to the harbormaster's office, his back to the wind, Buck's partner pinned a paper coffee cup against his chest with his gloved hand and tried to light the cigarette. The cup began to slip so he pressed harder. The plastic lid popped off and coffee splashed over his jacket. Damn! He really missed those fingers. He looked at his glove, the stiff leather jutting out, filled only with air. It was almost two years now since he lost them, showing off for the little nurse on her five-acre ranchette, taking the lead-line like he knew what he was doing and wrapping it around his hand. Halfway to the loafing shed the fingers were pulled out at the palm like drumsticks from a turkey – a surgeon couldn't have done it any neater. Who would have imagined a horse rearing with that kind of sudden force?

"Pompous ass," he said with vengeance to the timbers beneath the stairway, resenting the harbormaster's request that he go outside to smoke.

He was lucky the Department hadn't forced him out yet — thank god for the Guild's blind allegiance — but it was going to be hard to hang onto this job for much longer, let alone stay in the field. He finally got the cigarette going. He was putting the lighter back in his pocket when a loud report shattered the silence. Startled, he dropped the cigarette in a puddle at his feet and looked in the direction of the noise. A large puff of white smoke was quickly dissipating behind the bronze signal cannon on the yacht club lawn. Retired Navy assholes. He stooped to recover his soggy butt. What a bunch of fucking children.

DANIEL'S BOAT WAS moored headfirst in the slip, the bow pointed toward the prevailing westerlies, her stern sticking a few feet into the alleyway like an old Cadillac in a slightly too-small garage. Jake tossed the duct-taped packet of files up to the afterdeck, then held onto the *Nadalia's* stern rail with one hand and swung himself over the lifeline. He wanted to do it gracefully, for Carly's benefit, but he was wet and stiff and couldn't pull it off.

He helped turn the catamaran and was ready to push it off when a boom reverberated through the marina. Noon. Daniel was going to be late as usual. He wondered if they still woke up the boats on summer mornings with a Dixieland band.

"Thanks," he said, suddenly awkward. He wished she would stay for a bit; they barely talked during the exhilarating ride in.

"My pleasure. Sure you don't want a lift back?"

"I need to be here a while."

"Okay then." She held on to the *Nadalia's* stern for a moment longer, then gently shoved off. The wind pushed her to the middle of the alleyway. She pulled in slightly on the mainsheet and pointed the bow down the row of yachts toward the channel. The catamaran scooted away like it was powered by a silent motor.

Jake watched until she disappeared around the end of the dock, then went to the hatch cover and fumbled with the combination lock, trying to dial in 9-4-4 with numb fingers. When the lock popped open, he slid back the cover and went down the ladder. He turned on the house batteries and the main bank of lights, then moved aft and flicked on the diesel heater. He was soaked and chilled. A hot drink was the top priority. After that he could strip down and hang his clothes in the cabin to dry. He clambered back on deck. There was a coffee machine near the harbormaster's office.

He froze a few steps down the finger pier. A bulky man stood behind the fire-hose cabinet on the main dock, staring intently across the harbor. He was one of the late-night visitors at the office. *These guys are looking for Daniel too!* Jake followed the man's gaze across the water to Carly, who was short-tacking up the channel toward the harbor entrance.

Jake crept backwards to the *Nadalia,* trying to stay as motionless as possible. His feet barely touched the treadles as he slipped down the companionway ladder. He grabbed the keychain and climbed back on deck and started the engine. It coughed to life, running rough, and thick blue smoke filled the air before being whisked away to the east on the breeze.

BUCK WATCHED THE small sailboat zigzag up the channel against the gusting wind. He was trying to determine if the person at the helm was a man or a woman, not wanting to let any fantasies loose until he was 100% certain. When the sound of the diesel engine finally sank into his consciousness he snapped to attention, the catamaran and its androgynous skipper momentarily forgotten. It was hard to tell exactly where the sound was coming from – it echoed off the boats and the water – but it was definitely close, maybe right down the finger pier. He listened a few moments more, like a predator tuned to a rustle in the grass. He took a last sip of cold coffee and tossed the cup into the water, then started down the dock for a closer look.

The engine noise was definitely coming from somewhere near the rich guy's boat, getting louder as he moved closer. Hard to figure, since nobody had gone past him. He slowed a bit, brushed back his jacket and feathered the pistol holstered at his waist. Reassured, he carried on, bent over, head cocked, his right ear thrust forward.

JAKE JUMPED TO the dock again, flipped the *Nadalia*'s thick yellow power cord onto the foredeck, and released the bow line. Glancing under the overhang of the adjacent boat, he spotted the bottom half of a man walking in his direction, coming at him with purpose, the soles of his wide shoes slapping at the dock. Jake scrambled aft and untied the stern line then pulled himself on board. Crouching at the stanchion, he heard the close-by static of the man's radio. There was no way he was getting the *Nadalia* out of here without first dealing with this guy. Panic rose like acid in his throat and then a sudden blur of color flashed in front of him.

"Hey! Hey!" shouted Carly, her voice carrying on the wind.

She's come back. Please, not now.

She was out of sight again, yelling to the other man. Jake snapped out of his paralysis, quickly slacked and untied the spring lines, and tossed them softly onto the dock with a flick of his wrist.

The diesel engine warmed and smoothed out. He moved aft to the wheel. The boat was untethered, the wind already pressing her bow toward the dock. He shifted into reverse and backed smartly out of the slip.

BUCK HEARD THE girl shout and turned. The little sailboat barreled straight at him. He thought it would smash into the dock at his feet, but at the last moment it whipped around, sails flapping, and came to a standstill. The girl, a really nice-looking one, smiled at him over her shoulder.

The little boat bumped gently against the pier. "Can you give me a hand? Grab this?" she asked, tossing a thin coil at his feet.

He got on his knees and grabbed the line before it slipped into the water.

"Have you seen another boat like mine around here? With white sails? I'm meeting a friend. We're going to Coupeville."

"No, I haven't seen anyone." The static made it hard to think. He reached to his belt and turned the radio all the way down.

"Are you new around here? From the base?"

Somewhere deep down he knew he had a job to do, but she was smiling at him and the sound of the motor was quieter and further off and not near the rich guy's boat after all. He turned his full attention to the pretty girl. She seemed to want to talk to him, just like he so often imagined it happening. The catamaran drifted a little to the north. He turned to keep facing her. With his back to the channel, he was not in a position to see the *Nadalia* reach the harbor entrance and motor around the point.

"Well," the girl said, her tone changing fairly abruptly, "I guess my friend's not going to show. Bummer. I'll just have to go by myself. Nice meeting you."

He watched her gather up the lines. She was clearly preparing to leave and he had no way of contacting her. He needed something good to say and needed it right now, something to make her laugh, like in the movies.

"What's your name?" he said.

"Just something people call you." She was working quickly to get the boat turned.

The ball was cleanly back in his court. "What's your phone number?"

"A sequence of digits for communicating with other people." She was talking over her shoulder as she pushed away from the dock.

He was trying to come up with something else, his mouth hanging open, when the catamaran sailed off toward the channel, quickly gathering speed. This was very disappointing, and after such a promising start. He decided to head back up to the restroom for a few minutes of private time.

THE MAN-WITH-NO-FINGERS SUCKED hard on his third cigarette, wanting to get ahead of the curve before going back inside. He idly observed the ripples created by the *Nadalia*'s wake as they lapped against the rip-rap below him. He was getting fatter and slower by the day, his once formidable powers of observation seriously blunted by years of baked goods and apathy, the process accelerated by the painkillers that were at first a necessity and now a pleasant ritual.

There wasn't any activity around the marina all morning, most of the boats still in their slips. Something was very wrong with that, it being such a beautiful Saturday and all. If he had one of those boats, any one, he would be out on it all the time. Fishing, drinking, partying, just driving around. It would be better than getting his fingers back, a real panty-dropper for sure.

How long had it been since he became invisible to women?

He brought himself back to reality. What's the point of dreaming those vice-cop dreams? He flicked his butt under the steps. He should go down to the dock and check on the putz, get it over with, so he could retreat to the harbormaster's office and not worry about leaving for a while.

Halfway down the steep ramp he noticed the blue-hulled sailboat at the end of the channel. He couldn't make out the person at the wheel, but the old alarm was ringing in his head. Shit. He grabbed the radio from his belt and tried to raise numbnuts, but there was no response. He couldn't see him either – he wasn't where he was supposed to be. Yelling didn't do any good; the wind just hurled the words back in his face. He turned and ran back up the ramp.

By the time he barged into the harbormaster's office he was red-faced and wheezing, his lip muscles stiff from the cold. "Wuz bubbas hat!" he yelled, jabbing his finger at the picture window. He worked hard to suck in some air, looking like a fish at the bottom of a boat. The harbormaster reached for the phone to summon the medics.

The detective tried again, this time expelling the words like a piece of dislodged meat: "Whose boat is that?!"

The sailboat's bare mast moved south behind the sandy spit at the far end of the harbor, its hull hidden, but its quadruple-spreader rig clearly recognizable. The harbormaster walked to the map of the marina where each boat was represented by a magnetic namecard. He found F dock and ran his finger down to slip 39. "The *Nadalia*," he drawled. "The one we were talking about earlier. Mr. Zakian's boat."

BUCK WAS THINKING of her thighs, pink and warm, soft and slightly spread, how they met at the top. He didn't hear the door open, but there was no missing the thundering bellow of the man who had run down the steps from the harbormaster's office and sprinted out to the end of the dock, then returned and climbed the steep metal gangway to shore, and now stood at the entrance to the men's room.

"Are you in there you fucking moron?!"

THE CURRENT PUSHED against the buoys, tipping them slightly, showing the beginning of the flood, the barnacles on the pilings waiting for the water to come back and cover them. Jake steered around Strawberry Point, leaving Utsalady Bay dead astern in the distance. He glanced back every few minutes to see Carly's far-off rainbow sail as she reached back and forth across the strait, cavorting in the wind. She was out on the trapeze now, finally getting her ride.

He motored along in the bright sunshine, hugging the Whidbey Island side, avoiding the broad expanse of Skagit Bay, its sparkling surface only the illusion of safety, a thin veneer of water above the mud flats, the silty runoff from the rivers waiting to grab his keel. He headed north on a converging course with the fog bank that slowly crept across the water from the east.

Halfway to the lead-in to the Swinomish Slough he noticed the catamaran coming up behind him, still a long way off. He didn't slow down. She would be enjoying herself. It wasn't long before Daniel's big sailboat, no match for the planing cat, was overtaken by the radiant girl with wind-pinched cheeks.

31

The local deputy stood a deferential step back from the chart-covered table. The two detectives pressed close, hands in pockets, eyes aimed downward. Evelyn Schwab, recently-arrived in the yacht club's multipurpose room, was the only one doing any talking.

"He's been gone less than an hour. The hull speed for a 50-footer – the fastest it can plow through the water – isn't much more than seven knots. That's jogging pace." She placed one end of the spreaders on the chart and drew a circle around the marina. "So it's like he's on foot. And in the open. Running away from us." She tapped the spreaders on the small circle. "This is the furthest he can be right now." She adjusted the spreaders and drew a larger circle. "This is the two-hour envelope. Here's three. Even the three-hour circle is manageable. Most of it's land or tide flats." She remembered her audience. "Shallow water where a big sailboat can't go."

The two men stared at the chart and nodded like bobble-head dolls. They had called her in her car to report the *Nadalia's* escape from the marina. She hung up on them when they got to the part about how it wasn't their fault.

"We should be able to find him pretty easily, but it's important to do it right away. The area inside the ring is growing logarithmically." She looked up at the two men and made a circle with her hands then quickly expanded it. "Whoosh! Real fast."

She turned back to the chart. "He's got to go north or south, up or down Saratoga Passage. It's probably south so that's where the helicopter is heading. We'll have him before he gets to the bottom of Whidbey Island." She slowed down. "Your job is to make sure he doesn't get away to the *north*. It's pretty much a dead end, but there are two possible ways out. One is here, Deception Pass." She rapped the spreaders on a sliver of water that separated Whidbey Island from Fidalgo. "It's unlikely he'd head there, but we'll cover it just in case." She glanced at her watch. It would be almost maximum flood by the time the *Nadalia* could get to the narrow race. The tide would be coming in at a fearsome rate, the swirling waters beneath the bridge extremely treacherous for a slow-moving sailboat with a deep fin keel. She pointed to the gloved man. "You'll cover the Deception Pass bridge. The deputy will drive you up and keep you company."

The two men hurried out of the room. Schwab turned to Buck. "The other way out is the Swinomish Slough." She used her finger to trace the narrow waterway on the chart. "It's an eight-mile canal that connects Saratoga Passage to Padilla Bay. Take the car. Can you drive an automatic? Take the car and set up here, on the highway bridge over the north end of the slough. You need to hustle, even with the flood tide slowing him down."

"What if I see him?"

"Report in, then stop him."

"How?"

"Just do it."

Buck nodded vigorously and left the room.

Schwab sat down and examined the chart. It reminded her of lazy days on the water during the slack years of the Portage Bay investigation, after they pretty much ran out of ideas. Before the bubble burst. The FBI just came out one day and announced they had the killer, got him with some new DNA magic, picked him up an hour before the press conference. There were no platitudes about inter-agency cooperation or the contributions of her task force. In fact, the little shits went out of their way to point out she twice had him in custody for questioning, and twice let him go.

The Department put the best face on it they could – perseverance, no quit in her, monster brought to justice, blah blah blah – spinning her as a relentless bloodhound. There were feelers about doing a book, and even talk of a run for Congress. But people generally know bullshit when they hear it, that's the thing. When the initial euphoria over the arrest wore off, the hero-talk turned to whisperings of incompetence and squandered resources. And of 16 women hacked to death since they let him go the second time.

She was abandoned, buried in the basement, which was okay, she got used to having nothing to do, but her power base was gone. She was a liability now, a joke. They would get rid of her when they could.

It was time to be smart. A 50-foot sailboat with a distinctive 80-foot rig wouldn't be hard to find. A car could be stashed in a shed or rolled down a ravine, but a boat like that had to be in the open, with some water under its keel. Then again, if anyone could let the boat slip away it would be her little band of retards. So enough with the Lone Ranger stuff. If they didn't have the *Nadalia* in an hour she would raise a huge goddamn posse: local police and the Coast Guard, maybe even the Navy. Better to orchestrate the whole thing and share the glory than lose Morrow altogether. They would check every marina, every foot of shoreline, circle all the islands, watch the Straits until they found the yacht. They would have him within hours.

Everything would go through her. She alone would know all the pieces. She could still be at the podium.

32

Carly was on deck with Jake, her little boat tied to the stern. Threading through the buoys that marked the channel, they ran smack into the fog. Jake throttled back and the little catamaran overran its tow-line and gently bumped them. They passed Goat Island 15 minutes later, unseen but hulking right beside them, and rounded into the slough.

Carly said she had a close friend at Shelter Bay, so they dropped the catamaran there and left a note. There were tricycles in the driveway and a wooden swingset on the lawn. Jake was relieved to see them, not sure exactly why.

They nosed back into the channel and moved in slow-motion past the little town of LaConner, trying to run up the down-escalator, the current pushing hard against them. A smattering of determined tourists, invisible in the fog, chattered on restaurant decks perched over the water on stilts.

The canal pointed true north, straight as a needle. The *Nadalia* moved through the heart of the Swinomish reservation and past miles of hidden tulip fields. He tried to keep their speed up, despite the fog. When they hit a thin spot, he caught a glimpse of Carly at the bow. She was clutching the forestay with one hand and leaning forward, trying to push her eyes a little further into the grey. After more than an hour they picked up the first muffled sounds of traffic from the soaring highway bridge at the northern end. They were almost to Padilla Bay.

THE WAITRESS COULDN'T take her eyes off him. Buck shoveled in the second piece of peanut butter pie like he was in a contest. He wasn't enjoying the food, he was provisioning. He might be on that bridge a long time. He stood up and signaled for the check, still draining his coffee cup. He was thinking of everything.

The drive from the restaurant to the bridge took less than two minutes. He pulled the car across the shoulder and well onto the grass, worried about getting hit in the poor visibility. He unracked the shotgun and tramped onto the long span, enveloped in the rumble and vibration of the traffic. Stopping by chance at exactly the right spot, smack over the center of the slough, he peered to the south and let out a thundering belch as the tip of the *Nadalia's* mast swept unseen beneath his feet.

JAKE NAVIGATED BETWEEN the mud flats, keeping to the narrow dredged channel. He left the bright lights and gas flares of the huge oil refinery to port, no amount of cottony fog and halogen able to dispel its sense of foreboding. Visibility improved by the time they reached March Point, and they caught scattered glimpses of Anacortes, its neat Victorian houses stacked along the hillside. Ten minutes later they were past the anchored tankers that waited to offload crude at mile-long piers.

Carly left her bow watch and rejoined Jake on the afterdeck. The sun threatened to break through as they sliced across the eastern end of Guemes Channel, back at full speed. Together for hours, they had barely spoken. A deadhead suddenly loomed at the bow and he swerved to avoid the sodden log.

"Where are we headed?" she asked.

"Right there." He pointed to low-lying Guemes Island, a pear-shaped dollop of land four miles long from stem to base, its beaches strung with blue-collar weekend cabins. "There's a place I know a few miles up the shore." His instinct was to dive underground, get concealed.

They motored alongside the high bluff. For thousands of years it had been dropping pieces of itself into the water like a calving glacier. There were no signs of human habitation at the top, the houses all built back from the edge to delay their inevitable fall to the sea.

The cove came up faster than expected – distances were getting shorter as he aged. He pulled the throttle all the way back and wheeled toward shore, checking the depthsounder. A tiny comma-like indentation appeared in the side of the bluff. He brought the *Nadalia* to a complete stop just short of the entrance, then backed and filled, using the north wind to push down the bow. He rotated the boat until the stern was pointed directly at the opening, then maneuvered her into the snug haven, as easily as backing a car into a garage.

There was no need to drop anchor, the space so close they could almost touch the sides. The bluff lifted the wind over them, leaving the water placid. They tied up to starboard, then slacked the lines and pulled over to the other side and repeated the process. They were suspended in the middle of a little cocoon. Unless someone got within 30 yards, the boat would be invisible from the water side.

"We're home," Jake said.

"How did you find this place?"

"I was messing around in a Whaler. Saw the background shifting when I moved along the shore."

"It's like a secret room."

"I stop here sometimes if the weather's bad." He pointed through the foliage toward a small patch of sky above them. "I climbed up once. I think it was a first ascent."

Out-of-control blackberry bushes covered the sides of the cliff like thick coils of barbed-wire. Trees crowned the top of the bluff, providing an almost seamless canopy. It would be hard to spot them from the air.

"What's up there?"

"Farmland. The closest house is a half-mile away. Maybe more."

They put the deck in order and coiled the lines, like they had crewed together for years. It was almost six o'clock by the time they went below. Carly rummaged through the galley and found a box of hot chocolate packets.

Jake felt a little hypothermic. His expensive suit, soaked on the catamaran ride, was still damp. He scrounged through Daniel's cabin for dry clothes. There was a tiny spoon, hand mirror, and a one-edged razor blade in a little drawer in the forepeak. When did Daniel stop telling him things? He closed the drawer.

He returned to the galley and accepted a steaming cup from Carly. "There's some clothes in there, but I don't think anything's going to fit."

"I'll manage. I might take a shower."

When he heard the water running in the head, he stripped out of his soggy clothes and hung them up to dry. He put on one of Daniel's shirts and wrapped a light blanket around his waist (Daniel's pants wouldn't make it past his thighs). It was slim pickings in the galley: soup, condiments and Girl Scout cookies. He emptied two cans of soup into a saucepan and put it on the stove.

The sound of a helicopter was coming from the east, and getting closer. He went to the radio and scanned the channels. There was no unusual traffic. The Navy and Coast Guard would have their own frequencies anyway.

Carly came into the galley drying her hair. Daniel's clothes never looked so good: jeans with the cuffs rolled up over a pair of heavy woolen socks; a yacht club sweatshirt hanging halfway to her knees, cinched with a narrow braided belt tied in a knot.

"Would you like some soup?" he said. "It's a hybrid. Chicken noodle and cream of mushroom."

SHE WATCHED HIM stir the soup on the propane stovetop. He wore a much-too-small shirt, stretched tight across his chest, his midriff exposed. In lieu of pants, he had a yellow polyester blanket wrapped around his waist like a sarong. The leather slippers were several sizes too small, crushed in the heel, looking like clogs. She took it all in for a moment before speaking.

"This isn't your boat."

33

"Why were you going through Daniel's wastebasket?" Carly said. She stood over his shoulder and munched on a Girl Scout cookie while he rearranged the scraps. She had gone top-side after dinner, saying she wanted to check the lines and watch the night drop. By the time she rejoined him below he had been at it for almost an hour, trying to make sense of the blue-inked notations on the ten little pieces of paper.

"Daniel doesn't normally tear up his notes. So there could be something important on the scraps." It came out sounding pretty tacky, rooting around in your friend's trash, so he quickly added: "I thought he might be in trouble."

During dinner she asked what he did when he wasn't stealing boats, and the whole story spilled out: the phony trip to Africa and plane crash, $2,000,000 gone missing, strange men in his office, even the part about Daniel's car in the driveway. When he turned the tables on her she told him she was a carpenter, and he reached over and took her hand, not meaning to be forward. "You don't feel like a carpenter," he said. It was very intimate, like a French kiss, holding her hand. "Well you don't look like a pirate," she replied, not taking it back right away.

He sat up and stretched his neck. A bit of September sun had made it through and left his pasty face with a slight glow. He went sailing in a little catamaran in a nice breeze and ate food because he was hungry. He took the *Nadalia* out for the first time in a long time. Now he was moored in his secret cove with a remarkable woman who for some reason wanted to help him. Despite all the troubles, he couldn't recall a finer day.

They both concentrated on the scraps:

M   Z   57   53   46   14   3   01   arr 9/7   Kona

He pointed to the 'Kona' piece. "This one's easy. It's Daniel's favorite place in Hawaii." There was a picture of a 360-pound marlin from Kona on Daniel's wall – a teenage girl, he always pointed out. "He goes over all the time. He's got a big real-estate development there." Jake hadn't heard much about the luxury duplexes on the beach for some time, but there were rumors of equipment-eating volcanic rock and money gushing away like lava from Kilauea. Daniel never talked much about the screw-ups.

Jake moved the 'arr 9/7' scrap to the front. "This one, I'm guessing, means he'll be arriving in Kona in six days." He decided not to tell her about the agenda he found while snooping on Daniel's computer. "I figure the scraps with letters on them are someone's initials, MZ or ZM."

"What about the numbers?"

Jake moved the six remaining scraps into a line and rearranged them like Scrabble tiles.

"I think they're a phone number. It's the right number of digits."

Carly moved up next to him and squeezed in for a closer look. He liked her pressed against him, even though it was probably no more personal than sharing a crowded bus.

"I've been trying to figure out the right order. The number of combinations seemed enormous at first, increasing exponentially with each scrap, but there actually aren't that many possibilities."

"Where are the rest of the pieces? If you put the blank pieces together like a jigsaw puzzle you'd get the right order for the numbers."

"I tossed everything that didn't have blue ink on it." He had already mentally banged his head against the wall for that one. He moved the '14' scrap to the front of the row. "This one? It's the only number that starts with '1', so it goes first, for long-distance. That means the area code starts with a '4'. There are only seven possibilities that start with a '4' followed by numbers from the scraps." He pointed to a list he made:

401

~~430~~

434

435

~~446~~

~~453~~

~~457~~

Pride crept into his voice: "Of these seven numbers, only four are actual area codes." He held up the slim Anacortes phone book, opened to a double-paged listing.

Carly glanced quickly at the phone book then turned back to the scraps.

"401 is Rhode Island. 430 is northeast Texas, around Tyler. 434 is eastern Virginia. 435 is the rural area outside of Salt Lake City. I thought it would be Texas because Daniel's got a partner named Snap Pease on the Kona project. He's from Texas and might be mixed up in this." He lined up three of the scraps. "But if the area code is 430, like this, then the first digit of the phone number would start with a '1', and that's not possible. So Texas doesn't work."

He shuffled the scraps into a new sequence. "So it has to be Rhode Island, Utah or Virginia. For the actual seven-digit phone number, there are surprisingly few choices." He moved the sheet full of numbers closer to Carly.

She glanced at the page. The three remaining area codes in the left column spread into 20 prefixes in the middle, then expanded into twice that many four-digit numbers down the right-hand side, the whole thing resembling a peacock's feathers at full fan.

"Bottom line, there are only 42 possible phone numbers. But just like the area codes, most of those prefixes in the middle column don't actually exist, so that narrows down the list a lot, maybe a real lot, like 90%." He was getting a little wound up.

Carly closed her eyes and concentrated.

"So it's not 42 possible phone numbers in three locations, it's more like four or six numbers, probably all in the same place. Once I get online it'll take just a few minutes to check which prefixes are real. Then I can use a reverse directory to see which number has someone with the initials 'MZ' or 'ZM' attached to it."

She furrowed her brow and continued to stare hard at the scraps, like she was trying to ignite them with her gaze.

He summed up with a flourish, a lawyer bringing a brilliant closing argument to an end: "So the scraps represent a person, someone from Virginia, Utah or Rhode Island who's meeting Daniel in Hawaii on the 7th; a person with the initials 'MZ' or 'ZM' and one of these 42 phone numbers."

Carly reached over and divided the numbered scraps into two rows of three numbers each. She grabbed the "Z" and turned it on its side and it became an "N." She moved it to the end of the top row. She flipped the "M" upside down. It was transformed into a "W." She put it at the end of the second row of numbers.

"Or," she said, straightening up, "it's a place."

34

It was obvious now. The numbers were degrees, minutes and seconds of latitude and longitude. The empty GPS box in Daniel's wastebasket should have tipped him off.

The cabin was dark except for the red glow of the goose-neck light over the chart table. He leaned back in the gimbaled seat. Carly was asleep in the quarterberth. Along with everything else, he needed to get her out of here and back home.

He looked at the six numbers again: three of them would mark a horizontal line around the earth; the other three a vertical one. At the intersection of the two lines would be a tall, wiry Armenian with a lot of explaining to do.

The GPS was a treasure map. It would take him right to the spot, give or take ten feet. Two people with the same coordinates could find each other in the middle of a desert or forest, even at night. But first he needed to put the numbers in the right sequence. He pulled an oversized atlas from the shelf above the chart table and opened it to a double-paged Mercator projection of the world.

The "N" scrap meant the latitude was somewhere in the northern hemisphere. So the southern hemisphere could be eliminated, like halving an orange. The "W" meant the longitude was somewhere in the western half of the world. He was down to a quarter orange.

He highlighted the area on the map. All of North America and the crown of South America were inside the yellow lines;

plus a thin slice of Europe; the bulge of western Africa; and all the water in between. He drew six lines of latitude across the page, one for each scrap, then repeated the process north to south. The lines intersected at 36 spots. The one closest to the Kona coast was in Suriname, more than 5,000 miles southeast of Hawaii.

So much for the easy solution.

He was going to have to lose some of the hay if he wanted to find the needle. He put an "X" through the six spots that had the same number in both directions: they couldn't be both latitude and longitude.

Next to go were 18 spots at sea. The GPS could pinpoint a location in the middle of the ocean, but what would Daniel be doing there? Arms deal? Drug deal? It didn't matter: if this was about artificial islands, deep-water sunken wrecks, a submarine rendezvous, something out of a spy novel, it would be impossible to get to it anyway.

That left 12: Labrador; Liverpool; Derbyshire; La Rochelle; two in Scotland; four in the northeastern jungles of South America; two in Mali. Let it be La Rochelle. Or Liverpool even.

Daniel always bragged about his projects, vacations, clients, celebrity encounters. There must be something that linked him to one of the 12 locations. He spent a lot of business and vacation time in France, and was fluent in the language. He took an adventure cruise up the Amazon once, not far from a couple of the spots. Scotland was a regular destination too, golfing at St. Andrews, buying aircraft in Prestwick, arranging for engine overhauls at Scottish Airmotive. As for West Africa, Daniel got his start there, in Senegal, buying used 727s from the government and flying them home at 5,000 feet to keep the rivets from popping out of their corroded skins. He had been all over the continent ever since.

Jake wasn't coming up with anything to narrow the list. The warmth from the heater enveloped him and his body began to sag. He was five years old again and very tired, his dad in the chair beside the bed teaching him how to count sheep, and then he was asleep.

THE SOUND OF Carly in the galley woke him. He felt a moment of terror in the darkness, like he'd been buried alive, before remembering he was on Daniel's boat.

Carly brought him a cup of coffee and sat down on the edge of the quarterberth. "Sorry. I tried to be quiet."

"I wanted to be up."

"Any luck with the numbers?"

"I've got 12 possibilities." He handed her the atlas. "I was just staring at the map after a while."

"Maybe the answer will pop up now that you've slept. That's what happens to me with crossword puzzles."

He stood up and examined Daniel's overhead chart tubes, neatly marked and organized geographically, like alphabetized spice bottles. Daniel always says, when you're stuck, change perspective.

Carly had the atlas open to the index. "Did you know there are two Konas in here? Kona, Hawaii and Kona, Mali."

Jake took the atlas back and got the coordinates from the index, then flipped to the map of Mali. There in the rough square created by his eye, like a tiny tick trying to hide, represented by the smallest dot for the smallest population, was the little town of Kona on the banks of the Niger River. He grabbed the straightedge and laid it horizontally across the map, passing it through the little dot, checking the side of the page for the latitude: 14 North. He spun it 90 degrees and placed it over the dot again and looked at the top of the page for the longitude, already knowing what it would be: 3 West.

All he needed now was an Internet connection and an airport.

35

"Constant bearing, decreasing range," came Jake's voice from the blackness near the mast. A green light moved toward them from the south. They were on a collision course with something.

Carly spun the wheel and pushed the throttle all the way forward. The *Nadalia* was invisible in the moonless night: she had shinnied up the backstay and removed the radar reflector before they left the cove, and the running lights were off.

The green light slowed, stopped, then began to drift aft through the stays. A red light appeared beside it. They were dead ahead of whatever it was. When only the red light remained, she pointed the bow back toward the dark shape of tree-clad Orcas Island and took a deep breath.

After they were well clear of the shipping lanes, Jake made his way to the bow. Normally tethered to the boat at night, or at least wearing a life vest, he was unencumbered this time. It was nice to have someone with him. He lifted the 60-pound plow anchor from the hatch and secured it on the foredeck, careful not to ding the teak. He flaked out the metal chain and nylon rode and tied on the spare lines and halyards, bowline-to-bowline, then secured the end to the base of the mast.

They were near the northern tip of Blakely Island, Carly working the boat through a patch of bull kelp. He went aft and wrestled the rubber dinghy out of the lazerette, inserted the floorboards and pumped the bellows until the pedal wouldn't go down any more. He dug back into the lazerette and pulled out a one-cylinder Yamaha outboard and mounted it on the dinghy's wooden transom.

They would have to hurry to beat the sun and curious shoreside-eyes. He collected the life ring and man-overboard pole and stowed them belowdecks. Nothing else seemed to have the *Nadalia*'s name on it. He went through the cabin and closed all the seacocks, except the engine intake and outlet, and disconnected the hoses, then packed two blankets, Carly's clothes, and the files and money in a large waterproof duffel. The EPIRB – an orange metal box the size of a paperback – sat in a bracket near the hatch. It would go off automatically if immersed in seawater, sending a unique distress signal to pinpoint their location for rescuers. He threw it into the duffel.

He carried two mugs of steaming coffee on deck. Carly was past the eastern tip of Shaw Island and steering for Pole Pass, where Indians long ago strung nets to catch the birds, the gap so narrow you could almost touch the sides.

Up before dawn, gunkholing around the islands. This was a life he could have actually had. Needed to settle for a smaller boat is all. Now things weren't so simple. He stood on the deck with the wind in his face, surrounded by water. It was a funny place to feel it, this claustrophobia.

CARLY WATCHED JAKE coil the lines. Back at the cove she asked him what the plan was.

"Wait for the zebra to show up at the watering hole. Surprise Daniel on his own turf. Get the whole story. All of it. Then figure out how to make things right."

"I'm in," she said.

"No, you're out. You shouldn't get any deeper in this. You'll end up an accessory."

"An accessory to what?"

"Who knows? Somebody put an airplane full of people down."

"Maybe those guys at the marina weren't cops."

"That could be even worse."

"You shouldn't be alone. I want to help."

It was a long time since she last allowed the picture into her mind: 12 years old and alone and standing in the open field, the headlights of the pickup bouncing across the pasture toward her.

"Why?" he asked.

"Karma," she said, and looked away.

HE WATCHED HER steer the boat up the east side of San Juan Island. The green glow from the deck-mounted instruments provided the only light.

"Finis hardly comes up to the cabin anymore," she said.

"I heard he's got a job overseas."

"My mom never got her lawnmower back from that time he went around putting 'free' signs on everybody's stuff."

"I think he was offended by the clutter." On a long-ago Fourth of July weekend Finis went out at night and posted hand-made signs on everything that wasn't tied down. Dinghies, boat trailers, picnic tables, lawn furniture, gnomes, anything left out got placarded. There was a dramatic reshuffling of property the following day.

"It started some feuds that are still going on," Carly said.

"Have you always lived there? At Utsalady?"

"I left when I got married. Right after high-school. We moved to Seattle. Didn't last long."

"How come?"

"Different interests."

"What were yours?"

"I wanted some babies and an orchard. I wanted to build the perfect house. I wanted to fly-fish for salmon on the Sound."

"What happened?" He was prying, but it was hard to stop.

"The city dragged him down."

"He didn't like it?"

"He loved it. Made new friends, tried new things. We hardly saw each other. He sort of had an addictive personality anyway and Seattle gave him a chance to branch out. One night all his buddies were at the apartment and I was in the bedroom trying to sleep. He came in and told me he had a really good hand, a queen-high flush, but had run out of cash."

"He wanted money?"

"No. He wanted to bring the guy with the full house back."

"Do you still fish?"

"It wasn't for sex. Not exactly. But kind of. Cocaine was involved."

"I didn't even know you could get saltwater salmon on a fly."

"He kept saying the pot's almost $500, the pot's almost $500, like he wouldn't be asking if it were less. I slipped out the back door. Didn't take anything. It was all tainted for me, like with mold. My mom was still alive then so I moved back home and got a do-it-yourself divorce."

Jake took the wheel from her and steered the *Nadalia* around the northern end of San Juan Island. An hour later they were a mile off the American shore, running down Haro Strait, the lights of Victoria visible to the southwest, the current helping them along.

Carly went below to check the GPS. "We're there," she said, just loud enough to be heard over the motor.

He put the boat in neutral and let it drift to a stop. The depthsounder wasn't providing any help, the steady green dashes only confirming they were in more than 300 feet of water.

He turned off the engine. The quiet felt good. Carly moved to the foredeck and let the anchor loose. She watched the flaked line run through the hawspipe.

"Long way down," she said, when he joined her at the bow.

"170 fathoms."

"How much line did you cobble together?"

"About 1300 feet."

"That's not going to hold."

"Doesn't have to. Not for long."

When all the line was out they moved aft and unhooked the lifelines. The dinghy slid over the cutaway transom and Carly snugged it up to the *Nadalia*'s stern. She stepped in and he passed her the duffel bag, oars, and a bucket for bailing. The cold ocean water was already softening the dinghy. He reconnected the foot bellows and topped it off. Carly started the little outboard.

"All set?"

She held the dinghy close. "All set." The thin painter was looped around a stanchion, ready for a quick release.

It was Daniel's look at the airport that settled it. There had been something really wrong with those eyes.

Be hot or cold, Daniel always says. If you're lukewarm, I'll spit you out of my mouth.

Jake went below. He started in the stern and worked his way forward, opening each seacock in turn, until all seven were gushing like firehoses, the cold dark waters of Haro Strait spewing into the warm-wooded interior of Daniel's favorite possession.

36

Jake waited until the water overflowed the bilge and spread across the floorboards before going back on deck. The *Nadalia* wallowed in the windless swell. She was settling faster than expected. When the water began to climb the companionway ladder, he stepped into the inflatable.

Carly slipped the painter free and steered for Canada. The *Nadalia*, sated, sat up on her haunches, pointed her bow toward the summit of Mt. Deception, nodded slightly as if saying goodbye, then slipped backwards beneath the surface, going down in the deepest water around, close to the steeply sloping American shore.

They motored in silence for a while. "There'll be insurance," Carly finally said.

Jake stared ahead. He felt nauseous.

She tried again: "It will be a bad insurance company, one that cheats its customers and needs to be punished. One that has annoying ads on TV all the time."

It was the smart thing to do, to scuttle her. The *Nadalia* was the getaway car, no longer useful, an albatross around his neck. He couldn't just let her float away. If he did, they would find her in a few hours, wandering across the traffic lanes. They could calculate the drift, track her back, check saved radar data. They would know before teatime he was in Victoria.

He hoped he hadn't been influenced by the Hummer in the driveway.

DANIEL BOUGHT THE boat a dozen years earlier as a Christmas present for himself, before he could really afford it. He didn't know anything about sailboats and relied on Jake to make the right choice, but it needed to be top-of-the-line. They spent months poring over brochures and specs, like kids with toy catalogs before Christmas, and settled on the 50-foot custom Heron from Finland.

The boat was almost finished when they had the big argument. Jake wanted her christened with a woman's name, with seven letters and a double consonant for good luck, preferably "Loretta," for his maternal grandmother. (He could tell his mob of siblings and cousins, always squabbling over who needed to spend more time with the rapidly dementing real Loretta, that he had been with her all day, or taken her to Vancouver for the weekend.)

Daniel was adamant from the start she would be the *Nadalia*. "It's not your boat, is it?" he finally sneered, and the discussion was abruptly over. Jake vowed right then never to set foot on the damn thing, a promise that needed breaking the second he saw her motor into Shilshole Marina after the long delivery voyage from Finland, bedraggled but beautiful, like a winsome girl in torn blue jeans. They stood on the end of the dock together and watched, Daniel giddy with joy. "I'm going to use her to help others," he told Jake, the grin stretching his face out of alignment.

The sailboat brought the three friends together again, at least for a while. Jake was the talent – he had gone to the Junior Nationals and raced to Hawaii more than once – and liked to handle the foredeck. Finis navigated and Daniel was always at the helm, unless it got rough or they were flying a spinnaker.

THE CURRENT, ALMOST at maximum ebb when they abandoned ship, ate up a couple of the miles to Victoria, pushing them south like a river, flattening the hypotenuse. The sky was lightening when Carly steered into the bay. She headed for the southern end, the masts rising there like a grove of burned-over Aspens, and scrambled out and tied the painter to the floating dock. Jake tossed out the blankets and duffel. It was a common enough sight, a couple arriving in a dinghy at dawn, had anyone been watching.

Jake looked back as they headed down the planking toward shore. Daniel's inflatable was already lost among a half-dozen others and some miniature Boston Whalers, all of them nose-in, suckling at the dock. The little fleet would change every day, Daniel's fungible grey dinghy sitting there anonymously for months. Eventually someone would probably steal it.

They found a good spot for the blankets in the narrow park above the beach, laid one on the ground, and covered up. Carly dozed but Jake couldn't sleep. When the shops across the street began to stir, he slipped away.

He was back an hour later. Carly was wrapped in a blanket, watching the kite aficionados struggle to get their elaborate creations into the light morning breeze.

"The town's full because of the holiday. I was able to get a cancellation near the Inner Harbor. Check-in is at three."

"Great."

"They just had one room; and it only has one bed." He didn't want her to be surprised.

"Still great."

"I need to run some errands; knock a few items off my list."

"I can help. Let's split things up."

Chilled and hungry, the first thing they needed was food. A nearby café served up eggs and thick-cut American-style bacon, baked tomatoes and mushrooms, scalding hot coffee and fresh-squeezed orange juice. It was all so perfect he wished he kept a "best things" journal like Daniel: he would enter it as his finest breakfast ever.

Carly lagged behind him, still working on her second order of everything. A man and a little boy sat together in a large booth across the room, the boy pressed up close against his dad, resting one hand on the man's forearm while he spooned in cereal with the other. The boy's arm went up and down every time his father took a bite. A wave of envy swept over Jake. He didn't know if he wanted to be the man or the boy.

He finished the list and passed it across the table to Carly. She set down her fork and scanned it. "Ooh. A scavenger hunt."

They took a cab to the Inner Harbor, left the blankets with a sleeping man on a marina bench, and put the duffel in a locker near the moored boats in front of the Empress Hotel. Carly set out for Government Street with her list and $3,000 in American hundreds. Jake headed for a salon.

He showed the stylist the passport photo: Ronny Knoll pale and emaciated, wearing a maroon sweatshirt, with black-framed glasses and spiked blond hair. "Just like this," he said. "Exact same cut and color."

"That is so sweet," replied the man, visibly touched.

When the transformation was complete, Jake continued down the street to an enclosed mall, unable to keep his eyes off the caricature reflected in every store window: a bloated Ronny Knoll, exaggerated like a midway sketch.

He purchased shoes and a wallet, and new clothes that he wore out of the shop. There was a perfect pair of thick-framed glasses in an optician's window, so he bought them and waited while they put in plain lenses. He stopped at a drugstore and had his picture taken – he would need visa photos.

Down the street from the museum a small deli offered a couple of computers for hire. He signed up for three hours and brought up the Industrial Credit Bank of Japan's website. Customers jostled him as they serviced their coffee drinks at the station over his shoulder. He took out the old pizza menu with the account information on it, and logged on to *Alpha Beta Aviation Partners IV* as "User 2."

The screen showed a money-market account with a balance of $1,986,237.36. Jake wrote the number on his list. He logged off and moved his finger to the next company: *Altitude Equipment Leasing Partnership*. He logged back on. There was exactly $850,000 in the account. He wrote it down.

After he worked his way through the entire list he reviewed the data: the 22 accounts had balances between $500,000 (*Bum Flights LLP*) and almost $9,000,000 (*Kona Hui Lokahi LLP*). Jake added up the column by hand – it was like fingering gold coins in a counting room. The total available was just over $88 million.

Less than an hour had gone by. He waited until there was no line, then went to the counter and ordered a double-tall non-fat latté, extra hot. He settled back into his seat and accessed the bank's website again. The *Alpha Beta* account still showed a balance of $1,986,237.36. This time he selected "Transfer Funds." The screen asked for another password. He consulted the list and entered it. A new page appeared and asked where the money was going: he filled in the boxes with information for his slush-fund account, taking his time. When he got to the amount he entered "$1,986,000" and hit the "Submit" button. The screen flashed TRANSACTION COMPLETE, and showed a new account balance of $237.36. He was a little dizzy. DO YOU WANT ANOTHER TRANSACTION? Well yes, yes he believed he did.

He logged on to the next account. Methodically moving down the list, immersed like a surgeon in his work, he was oblivious to the passage of time. When he reached *Keystone Aircraft Fund* (a million and change) he was in a rhythm, expecting the "Transfer Funds" page to pop up like the next song on an over-listened to CD. Instead he got:

ACCESS DENIED
USER 2 ALREADY LOGGED IN

Someone else had accessed the account. As him.

The next name on the list was *Pathfinder Aircraft Partners*. He entered the User ID and password. An instant later he was in. He transferred $2,200,000, then logged on to *Pan-Asian Gold & Diamond Corporation*.

Access denied! User 2 already logged in. He and some pretender were both working through the accounts! And the other User 2 appeared to maybe have the faster connection.

He ran his finger down the list. The remaining account with the largest balance was *Shared Executive Jets*: $6,600,000. He logged on, two fingers jabbing at the keyboard. The computer seemed to run slower as his brain sped up. There it was. Transfer funds. Score! Down the list to the next biggest: *Ramrod Aircraft Investors*. Access denied. The other User 2 was skipping through the accounts to the big money too. Jake leapfrogged to *T.A.R.T.A. Corp*. Another big win.

He continued until all the accounts were hit, then went back to the ones he couldn't access. This time he was able to successfully log on, but the accounts were empty. He tallied the score: he bagged 16 out of 22, including the five largest, for a total of just over $82 million. The other User 2 got the remaining six accounts, a little over $6 million. Any way you looked at it, a landslide victory. It was an expensive mistake, though, to get the haircut first.

He researched his travel options to Mali and sent e-mails to an attorney and a banker in Luxembourg who he knew from prior dealings. The adrenalin was starting to wear off. He went to a travel agency and picked up his tickets, paying cash, then headed for the hotel. Was Daniel the other User 2? Would he think Jake emptied the accounts? Probably not. Hard to do that from the bottom of the ocean.

Carly was already checked in, so he picked up a second key and headed for the room, looking forward to seeing her. A cluster of shopping bags sat on the queen-sized bed, but she was gone.

THE ORNATE TEA Lobby of the Empress Hotel was filled with tourists. Carly looked out over the harbor: the town seemed more European than it really was. She shouldn't have come to high tea by herself – it was so romantic – she should have saved it. She poured another cup of the hotel's special blend and examined the finger sandwiches and bite-sized pastries stacked up in front of her on a four-tier tray. Maybe one more smoked salmon and cream cheese, but that's it.

She had started out at the bookstore, always a good place to gauge her mood: the happier she was the more books she wanted. She walked out with a shopping bag full, including the one she went in to get – a travel book on West Africa with a chapter on Mali.

A musty shop on a downtown side street coughed up a large map of Mali in French. She could have stayed there all day too. She sat on a bench by the old Customs Building and used the numbers from Daniel's wastebasket to calculate all the possible combinations of minutes and seconds of latitude and longitude. She penciled the likeliest spots onto the map with little crosshairs.

She bought Jake a watch, and a smallish soft-sided leather suitcarrier. She got clothes for them both, including white polo shirts, a maroon sweatshirt, blue blazer and striped silk tie for him. After a quick cab ride to the hotel to drop the packages, she headed to a grocery for emergency travel food (crackers, cookies, candy bars, nuts); a razor and blades; toothbrush and toothpaste; shaving cream; sunglasses; Tums (giant size); hair-brush; and soap and shampoo (hotels in Mali, Jake said, are not to be counted on). She liked buying the personal things. Then it was off to a chandlery on Yates for a hand-held GPS, the best they had, and a quick walk back to the Empress for tea.

A positive and productive day, if you didn't count sinking the million dollar yacht.

JAKE LOOKED ACROSS the straits to the Olympic Mountains. It was only Sunday. Maddie would be on the beach with Daniel's money. Nobody at the bank would even know she was gone yet. He picked up the phone and dialed her private line. What would her last voice-mail greeting be – she changed it every day – something funny or maybe a "screw you"? She was a smart woman; she would probably play it straight.

He absently listened to the rings. What was the point in leaving a message anyway? She wasn't going to get it and this was no time to be cute. The line connected. At first he thought it was the recorded voice that kept saying hello. By the time he realized his mistake, she had already hung up.

37

Maddie put the phone back in its cradle and turned to the two men. She knew that look: they were thinking about fornication. "Sorry, must be a wrong number."

"Why was Mr. Morrow given the two million?" asked the lumpier detective, picking up the thread again.

"It was on instructions from one of our Private Banking clients." She spun the folder around and pushed it across the desk so he could see the fax, and pointed to the signature at the bottom. "Daniel Zakian. From Seattle."

"When exactly did he get the money?"

"Early Friday afternoon." She flipped the receipt down over the fax, making sure he examined it carefully before she resumed. "He was catching a flight to Africa that evening."

"What was the cash for?"

"Some transaction over there. I'm not privy to the details."

"Anything unusual about him? That you noticed?"

Maddie took her time before answering. "He looked like a little boy on his way to the dentist."

Both men stared at her.

"Nervous. Apprehensive."

"Any idea why?"

She ignored the question. "He's a Seattle lawyer. He works for Mr. Zakian."

"Anything else you can tell us?"

She took a deep breath. Jake would have been terrified on that plane. "He was a good guy."

The lumpy man glanced at his partner. They were out of questions. "Well, thank you for meeting with us, on a Sunday evening and all." Both men got to their feet.

"No problem at all. I know it's important. I'll walk you to the elevator."

She didn't want to come into the office tonight, and especially didn't want to talk about Jake, but it was good to show them the receipt early on. Hammer it in that he picked up the money.

They were halfway to the lobby when her phone began ringing again.

BACK IN HER office, Maddie sat in the visitor's chair so she could look at the purple-and-white urn.

It wasn't easy growing up in Uddersfield, her father's salary stretched thin every month, her dear, plain mother dressed in faded clothes from the vintage apparel shop. She was 15 when Mum's breast cancer was finally confirmed. The National Health Service managed the disease, and there were no trips to leading experts in Switzerland or the United States to interrupt the quick and painful journey from diagnosis to cemetery.

While Maddie made the obligatory mourning trip to London to visit the relatives, all of her mother's personal effects were sent to The Relief Society, including the silver locket she always wore, the one with the sepia photo from her 16th birthday at the Gardens. Mum promised her the locket right before she died, saying she could have it when she turned 16 herself. That way she would always be close to Maddie's heart.

Time for a fresh start, her father intoned when asked about the locket. Time to move on. Let the dead bury the dead.

On that same post-funeral trip to London she finally learned the truth about her family's stupefying wealth: her father was an heir to the Hutton-Foster textile fortune. She was stunned, always assuming the economic disparity among the cousins was a natural course of events, not a deliberate deceit perpetuated by a pitiful man.

After her father had been shunted aside by the family business, he moved to Uddersfield and took a position as a mining engineer, the job perilously close to being blue-collar. He spent all of his free time at a partitioned-off end of the dining-room table, perfecting his coal-log delivery system (get the moisture out; cut down the abrasion; move the stuff like bank documents through a pneumatic tube; kick off a bituminous golden age.)

His rejection of money seemed not at all high-minded, just a monstrous snub of his extended family – a child refusing to eat supper even though it was something he liked. After he made his famous toast at the Easter gathering, calling the group a pack of jackals and whores before stomping into the rainy night, he had no choice but to keep to his new-found principles, no matter how much they hurt. He kept the money in low-yield savings accounts, with no effort to maximize the return, and there was no dipping into the pot to splurge on a vacation, or ease the financial emergencies that regularly assaulted the family.

He barely noticed Mum's passing. A housekeeper was brought in a few hours a week for the ironing and heavy cleaning, but most of the burden of running the household and tending to her dispirited younger brother fell on Maddie.

Living in a city where every conceivable lower-class vice was readily available (her brother opting for home-made, mind-frying, incredibly addictive drugs) she chose a combination of alcohol and sex. On her 16th birthday, when she was supposed to be receiving her mother's locket, she was getting something else altogether, for the first time, surprising the boy in the car, letting him go where he pleased, pretending she didn't see him slip her panties into his jacket before returning to the dance. She followed a few minutes later, face flushed, feeling his dampness on her thighs beneath the short skirt. His friends smirked and the girls sneered at her, everyone a few years older. It made her weak in the knees to realize they all knew exactly what she had been doing.

She became very popular. Her father, shielded by the stack of books and papers in the dining-room, seemed barely to notice her increased absences or her brother's permanent stupor behind his locked bedroom door. A week shy of her 18th birthday she escaped to Paris and enrolled at Cité Université, a student of French language and culture, education being the only thing that could open the family purse strings. Two years later, her brother removed by one overdose too many, a mercy really, she gave up the university (where four years of relaxed and stipended study could surely have been stretched into seven or eight) and took a job at a small Catalan restaurant near the Lourmel Metro stop. She could see her father in it, trading the comfortable life of a student in order to wait tables, and hated that he was a part of her. She wished she could wash his half away but still be herself.

She worked her way up until she managed the restaurant, running it in a responsible manner notwithstanding her fairly dissolute off-hours lifestyle. Most of the people she slept with during the Paris years became her good friends, and it was a wide circle, numbing amounts of alcohol accounting for some of the more unusual couplings. She felt like Gertrude Stein sometimes, holding court in her flat for a group of regulars and wide-eyed newcomers, the agenda strictly carnal rather than literary or artistic, though writers, artists and philosophers definitely in the mix.

After eight years of fairly serious depravity she decided it was time to raise a family. She analyzed all of her acquaintances, looking for someone with a suitable combination of genes and family values. She settled on Harold, a humorless American telecommunications executive on temporary assignment in Paris, who had partaken of her, but only infrequently, and never in the company of others.

Her last visit to Uddersfield was a memorable one: first the wedding to Harold with the humiliating rows of empty folding tables at the pot-luck reception in the Miner's Hall, her dead mother's memory not strong enough to overcome people's distaste for her father; then the heart attack and the long nights at his bedside listening to his frantic mewling about the coal-log papers.

She bought the ornate purple-and-white vase in the Uddersfield thrift shop the day before the memorial service, on her way back to the house from meeting with the solicitor. The entire estate had been left to the Mining Engineering Society to build and endow a worldwide string of museums and interpretive centers for extractive mineral operations, as well as to support the development of coal-log and other transportation technologies, and to provide cash prizes and scholarships in connection therewith, everything to prominently display her father's name. The full extent of her personal inheritance consisted of a handwritten Castro-like diatribe about his relatives (with particular attention to the two older brothers) and detailed instructions on how to retrieve and deliver the coal-log papers to the Mining Engineering Society.

Right after her father was laid to rest in a swale on the dark side of Uddersfield's Miners Cemetery, she returned to Paris and organized Harold's move into the Vasco de Gama flat. He knew she wasn't a virgin, of course, but perhaps didn't fully understand the scope of her prior accessibility until physically on the premises, the stream of would-be suitors at the

door hard to ignore. She was committed to honoring her marriage vows though, and sent everyone away.

She treated Harold badly from the start, she realized that,
like a household employee, and made him sleep down the hall,
the carpet between the two bedrooms barely worn at all.

She quit drinking on the wet day in April she learned she
was pregnant, except for the bottle of absurdly expensive
champagne she consumed each year on the anniversary of her
father's death. Not classically maternal, she bottle-fed both
children and raised them until the youngest was old enough to
attend preschool five days a week, then turned them over to
Harold for further handling, feeling her part of the deal was
pretty much done, wanting to enjoy the children as a person
rather than as their maid or cook. When Harold, never able to
pick up the language and tired of struggling with the fragment-
ed Parisian lifestyle, initiated a transfer back to the main office
against her wishes, showing backbone for the first time, threatening to obtain full custody of the children if necessary (which
the French courts surely would have granted) she packed up
the household, figuring it would be a fairer fight in Oklahoma.

What caused her to run away at the airport? Some sort of
panic. Temporary insanity. Oklahomaphobia. It was a mistake.
She was never supposed to lose the children. In truth though,
it was hard to imagine how things could have worked out well
in Tulsa.

SHE WALKED TO the shelf and picked up the urn. Jake
asked about it on Friday, didn't he? It always surprised her how
heavy it was, the compressed ashes of almost two thousand
pages of original mining research on 20-weight bonded paper,
hand-drawn charts and graphs, footnotes, appendices and bib-
liography. The back-up diskettes were long gone, unceremoni-
ously dumped in the trash bin behind Uddersfield's only Mo-
roccan restaurant.

She set the urn down. It was clear from that first night that Jake wanted her, maybe even loved her. She shouldn't have pushed him off, made it such a game. She always thought there would be a time for him, and now he was irretrievably gone.

38

Jake woke a little after four in the morning. The window was open – it was cold in the room, but warm beneath the down comforter.

It had been a good night. Carly made it back to the room before five and they laughed at his new look until their chests ached, then opened the packages like birthday presents. After taking turns in the tiny shower they dressed for dinner, happy to be in fresh clothes. The inn on Belleville Street was walkable, and they arrived hungry.

The conversation never lagged, their heads bent together over the table all night. They barely noticed the condescending waiters, who could never afford to eat there themselves. Smiling, animated, easy with each other, it looked like they had been intimate for a long time. When he said something about it being their first date, she immediately objected, and no one in the restaurant would have believed it either.

"What about breakfast?" she said.

"That wasn't a date."

"A man. A woman. Food. What's not a date about it?"

He smiled. "What difference does it make?"

"I would never sleep with you the first time we went out."

He was almost certain she was joking.

The first silence came as they sipped their coffee and waited for the check. "I owe you a lot," he finally said.

"No you don't. We might be even. What time do you leave?"

"Early. You'll probably be asleep."

"Wake me. Please. I want to say goodbye."

They were quiet again for a while. "I might end up living on a beach in Africa, selling carved masks," he said.

"I don't want to leave Utsalady Bay. I tried it already. It was a big mistake."

"I know."

"My family's there. It's where I belong."

"That's the kind of thinking that allows Cleveland to exist."

"I love what I do, my friends, the guys I work with. When I have children I want my kids to have what I had."

"I like Utsalady too."

Framed by the white lights of the Parliament building, they held hands while they waited for a cab. By the time they arrived at the hotel the spell was broken. They should have had a bit more wine, or brought a bottle back with them.

Carly came out of the bathroom wearing the extra-large "Charles & Camilla" tee-shirt she bought for him. She was already under the covers when he finished changing. They said good night and then the excellent meal and wine and two days of exertion caught up with them and pulled them into an exhausted sleep. Each hugged a side of the large bed, resisting the sagging mattress that wanted to gather them together in the middle.

Now almost morning, she was curled up next to him, her head by his pillow, facing away. He breathed in the smell of her skin and hair. The closeness and warmth might have caused the dream. And was it all a dream, or had they touched? The ephemeral images were lost forever but the hardness was very real.

Her shirt had tangled and pulled up in the night. He reached out and covered her. She sighed. Maybe she was having a dream of her own.

She said his name. He moved closer and put his hand on the soft curve of her belly and held her against him, then kissed her lightly on the neck.

They moved gently, rhythmically, almost imperceptibly. He pressed and suddenly everything was different. They were connected now; nothing could ever change that, not in an eternity.

She eased onto her back, her breathing exactly matching his. She helped him get as close as possible, and neither spoke a word. He was able to make it good for her.

After she was asleep, he slipped out of bed and closed the window. He took a shower and shaved, holding the towel around his waist.

He zipped up his new leather bag and sat on the edge of the bed. Maybe he didn't have to leave. They could go back to the café for breakfast, this time as lovers, and order the same thing.

THE CITY WAS beginning to stir as the taxi maneuvered through the heart of downtown. He stared at the shopgirls on their way to work without realizing he was doing it. To be swept up by these feelings at his age: it was a miracle. How else could he describe it? He needed to figure out a way to be with her.

He sat back in his seat. It felt good to be heading off to battle – in the game again. For the first time in a long while he felt right, strong, like a man.

There is no substitute, Daniel always says, for getting laid.

39

The last thing into the duffel bag was the little orange EPIRB. Carly handled it gingerly, like unstable dynamite, worried she might set it off by accident. She went to the front desk and paid for the room with cash. The man asked if she enjoyed her stay, leering.

There was no way around it, she slept with a married man, something she swore never to do, a resolution she figured was as easy to keep as not eating snails. She didn't feel at all good about it, but didn't exactly want to take it back either.

She couldn't even use alcohol as an excuse. It was like going to a restaurant for a salad and the next thing you know you're full and a bunch of empty plates are on the table and a Boston cream pie is on the bill.

The 20-mile taxi ride to the Sydney ferry dock seemed over before it began. She stuffed her Canadian coins into the back of the seat: they weren't worth messing with at home and she wanted the driver to have the money, but didn't want to over-tip. The white-and-green ferry loomed over the landing, coming in fast, as she walked to the foot-passenger terminal. At the last moment the bow props churned the water into a boil and the boat gently kissed the pilings.

The ferry filled up with Americans heading back after the holiday. It felt like home the minute she stepped aboard, Canada still a foreign country. A Volkswagen Beetle with two kayaks perched on the roof was the last car squeezed on. Its occupants noisily celebrated their good fortune while dozens of other vehicles sat forlornly at the landing, resigned to finding another way home. She wanted to tell them the boat you miss might be the one that sinks.

She bought a cup of soup at the mid-deck snack bar and carried it out to the narrow promenade that circled the boat, then took the stairs to an uninhabited portion of the upper deck. She tucked herself out of the wind beside a rack of bright-orange lifeboat canisters that looked like cheery depth charges.

Vancouver Island receded into the distance. An airplane climbed over her, heading east. Maybe he was on it. She wanted to be beside him. She wanted to protect him from whatever was trying to hurt him.

The pickup bumped across the pasture toward her, its headlights gyrating through the darkness. It had passed them on the deserted road at least three times, going slower each time, before they decided to split up. All three were 12, young enough to be scared like children and old enough to know what they were afraid of. She was halfway to the lit-up farmhouse when the pickup accelerated and cut her off, then circled back across the field, isolating her like a young gazelle, Tina and Sara long out of sight. At first she didn't run, not wanting them to know she was scared, and then she did. She sprinted back toward the road and they cut her off again. She stopped, not able to run anymore, gasping, her side aching. She could see the silhouettes of the men in the front seat as the truck growled toward her in low gear across the uneven ground. She didn't notice the other set of lights at first, at the edge of the field, coming fast in her direction. The pickup stopped too, its occupants now invisible behind the glare of their headlights, waiting for the new arrival. And then the bright blue panel truck shot between them and the door opened and the driver was telling her they would take her home and she sobbed and said she wanted to go to grandma's and the two city boys from down the beach reached over to help her in, and Tina and Sara pulled her to the back.

THE FERRY MADE a quick stop at Friday Harbor and then they were off again for Anacortes where her friend would be waiting. Most of the passengers had tired of the scenery and gone inside to read or eat in the cafeteria. The boat plowed through Thatcher Pass and started its run across the open water.

She checked to make sure she was alone, then walked to the railing, ready to slip the EPIRB over the side. It would bob to the surface and transmit the *Nadalia*'s unique signal to aircraft and satellites, giving them an exact location. Jake wanted to mislead the searchers and was adamant about where to drop it – showing her the exact spot on the chart.

She hesitated. It might not be a good idea.

If they tracked the signal back to the middle of the ferry route and didn't find the *Nadalia* or any sign of her, it wouldn't take long to figure out where the EPIRB came from. It seemed better to just hang on to it, let the *Nadalia* stay mysteriously missing without a trace. Maybe they would think Jake made it out the Strait and was on his way to the Marquesas. She planned to talk to him about it before he left, but, well, things had gone in a different direction.

She was still mulling over the options when the ferry turned toward shore. It was too late now to deploy it. She was sure she'd done the right thing.

40

Jake reset his new watch to 9:20 in the morning, local time, as the plane touched down at Findel Airport. It had been 18 hours and four flights – two long, two short – from Victoria to Luxembourg. It would be just after midnight at Utsalady Bay: Carly would be safe in her bed.

He deplaned in the middle of the pack and drifted back as more aggressive travelers scurried past. He was in no hurry: this would be the first real test of Ronny Knoll's passport. When his turn came at the booth, he slouched, sucked in his cheeks and tried to look shorter and sicker. He barely came to a full stop before he was admitted to the European Community with a peremptory wave, a handful of darker-complected passengers still clogging the other lines.

Clumps of travelers waited for the baggage carousel to come to life. He skirted them and headed for the "Nothing to Declare" exit. A dozen uniformed customs agents lounged behind a long line of metal examining tables, chatting among themselves. One gave him a desultory glance as he walked by, before turning back to the conversation. He wondered what they did in the gaps between planes.

A damp-pawed vice-president met him in the elegant lobby of Klöden Bank's unmarked two-story building off Boulevard Royal. After a minute or two of verbal salaaming, the man led him up a winding staircase to an office the size of a ballroom, the ornate desk and furnishings trying in vain to fill it.

They sat at opposite ends of the coffee table. The banker passed over a manila envelope. "This was delivered this morning by Mr. LaCouer's office," he said, then turned his attention to the leafy courtyard beyond the double French doors.

Jake examined the Certificate of Good Standing and Apostille for the new company, then handed the papers back. "They are for you, I believe."

"Ah, thank you," the banker said, and signaled to a woman hovering near the door. Junior staff members swept into the room like a bevy of waiters and arranged an assortment of papers on the table. Little red arrows flagged the spots where a signature was needed.

He had to consciously remind himself to sign as Ronny Knoll, his hand not yet accustomed to the new name. After he executed the last of the documents, the banker escorted him down the hall to a windowless room the size of a walk-in closet, with a small desk and a secure Internet connection. It took just minutes to transfer the $82 million to the new account.

An elaborate table for two was set in a room adjoining the office, but Jake declined the invitation to lunch. The banker seemed to take his regrets in stride, as though they were fully expected.

The train to Paris took three hours. Jake went straight from Gare l'Est to the Malian embassy and applied for his visa, citing "see Timbuktu" as the reason for the trip. He walked out right before the embassy closed, a freshly stamped tourist visa in his passport, the staff surprisingly efficient, no private expediting fees requested or paid.

He ignored Paris, took a taxi to Orly instead and grabbed a sandwich there, then boarded Air Maroc's evening flight to Bamako, with a stop in Rabat. He was squeezed into the far back: first-class had been fully booked for weeks.

It would be almost noon in Seattle now. She would be with her work friends, pounding nails on somebody's house, looking forward to her lunch break.

Every cell in his body ached for her.

41

They descended for some time and still nothing marred the blackness below; it might as well have been the ocean. By the time the blue glow of Bamako's fluorescent lights appeared beneath them the plane was quite close to the ground. It swept over the sleeping city and banged onto the runway, bounced, and banged again. Two for the logbook. He was happy to be back on earth.

It was well past midnight when the first-class passengers finished disembarking, and the people in back were released. Jake moved down the concourse as fast as he could without breaking into a run. The heavy suitcarrier slapped against his leg and threw off his stride. He felt the familiar heat of Africa, still cradled in the glass and steel building long after the sun had gone. The air-conditioning was either turned off for the night or in need of repair.

A man in uniform asked to see his yellow fever card. He didn't have one, almost positive the disease had been eradicated and the inoculation no longer required. The man tapped his finger on a sample taped to the side of the glass booth. Jake substituted a fifty-dollar bill and passed through to the next station.

He pushed Ronny's passport across the immigration desk. It would have been nice to have his own: it bulged with multiple-entry visas and arrival stamps for West African countries and branded him as a person who knew the ropes and couldn't easily be jerked around. A seated man gave the passport a cursory look while a woman stood behind him and pinned Jake with her gaze.

"How long of time rest you here?" asked the man.

"One week."

"For why?"

"Holiday."

"Welcome to Mali," he said, returning the passport.

Jake pushed it back across the counter. "Could you stamp it please?" An unstamped passport would cause trouble down the road and cost him money every time he needed to produce it.

"This is not necessary."

"Please, so my friends can see I've been to Mali."

The man stamped the passport hard, as though he wanted to hurt it, then pushed it back to Jake without looking at him.

He lugged the suitcarrier through the Arrivals Hall, steering clear of the luggage belt. He once saw a local policeman come out on it, his throat slit from ear-to-ear, a theft in progress in the baggage room.

Next stop was Customs, where an impeccably groomed official confiscated his travel alarm clock (the FM radio prohibited for military reasons) and the *Us Weekly* (the unwholesome pictures not fit for Mali) and slipped them into his briefcase.

The final station was Currency Control. He braced for trouble: this is where the senior guys tended to migrate, where real damage could be done.

"How much money have you?" the officer said, inspecting the passport.

It was a fine line: too little and they thought you couldn't support your stay; too much and they wanted to share. "One thousand U.S." He was carrying 20 times that much, but didn't want to excite the man.

"Show me if you please."

Jake opened his travel wallet and took out a pile of bills, a mugger's wad. He fanned out two-dozen fifties, like a blackjack dealer showing a new deck.

The man picked up the bills and started to count them. "How long is your stay?"

"Less than a week."

"One thousand is not much for a week."

"I have credit cards," he lied.

"Credit cards are not used in Mali." The man counted through the bills a second time.

Jake was considering offering one of the fifties (the possible downside being a burst of indignation and a much larger gift to calm things down) when the man neatly palmed half the stack and waved him through.

In the country for less than thirty minutes, he was appreciably poorer, the process of extracting money from visitors seemingly institutionalized. If I wanted this, he thought, I could have gone to Venice.

He headed for the exit, pushed open the door, and was suddenly outside in the cool air, a boisterous semicircle of black faces pressing in on him like paparazzi.

A LARGE MAN in a flowing robe and pointed black shoes sat at a high table directly across from the double doors. Mirrored sunglasses shielded his eyes from the dim airport lighting. A collection of cups and saucers were stacked on the table and a pile of newspapers lay at his feet. He had been there all day, carefully scrutinizing the passengers who arrived on each of the dozen or so international flights.

This was the last one. He picked out the whites as they trickled through the door. They were always in the front, first-class passengers given priority all the way through. When the stream of passengers turned black, the man's attention flagged. He looked at his watch. Kedfenou with rice and plantains at the *Café des Deux Continents* sounded very good, and then maybe a woman.

He was on his feet and ready to leave when another white man came through the door. He sat back down and checked the faxed image for the hundredth time. It was not a clear match. The man in the fax had longer hair, darker with not so much grease, and he wasn't wearing glasses. Still, it was close enough that the fellow couldn't be ignored. He got up and peeled off a half-dozen colorful bills and dropped them on the table, keeping his eyes on the white as the airport crowd tried to engulf him.

JAKE BATTLED HIS way to the curb and climbed into the back of the closest taxi, ignoring the bleating of a dozen other drivers and the shouts of their sidewalk pimps. A man jumped in the front seat and began haggling with the driver and another clambered in next to Jake and held the door shut against the people outside, their faces pressed against the windows like maniacal rock fans.

"Hotel Marais, Avenue Al Quds," Jake said.

The taxi maneuvered through the vehicles that jammed the road outside the terminal. Jake looked back at the diminishing pack of men and boys who chased the car. He barely noticed the black Renault that pulled out behind them.

The taxi pulled up to the Hotel Marais, a plain three-story block with only a smattering of trees to soften its bleak lines. The driver demanded more than triple the fare posted at the airport. Both members of Jake's new entourage seemed to side with the driver who, as near as Jake could make out, was insisting the posted fare did not apply to a party of three. He ended up paying much more than he should have, but everyone seemed unhappy, so he probably did okay.

The clerk at the reception desk couldn't find any record of the reservation but eventually produced a room key anyway, and scrawled the address of a car rental company on a scrap of paper.

Jake carried his bag to the almost deserted hotel bar, which was lit up like a Laundromat. Last year's junior soccer match with Cameroon was on the television in the corner.

He ordered three jumbo beers, planning to store them in his room until he was ready (they couldn't get much warmer there). The barman opened all three before Jake could stop him. It was difficult juggling the bottles and his bag on the way upstairs. He set two of the bottles down in the hallway and when he went back for them a few minutes later, they were gone.

The large room had a partial view of the Niger River and a whiff of insecticide. He sipped the remaining beer and finished off a box of cookies Carly got him in Victoria. It was impossible to sleep, his circadian rhythms knocked seriously out of whack by all the time zones. He called down and ordered an American action film he had never heard of, hoping it wasn't dubbed in French. The screen remained blank. He pictured someone in the basement scrabbling through overflowing bins of tapes that needed rewinding. When the set finally flickered and the FBI warning appeared an hour later, he was already dead asleep.

42

The insistent beeping of the alarm dredged Jake from his stupor. He shut it off and checked the time. Daniel would be in Kona in 48 hours. He needed to get there first.

He ignored the elevator and took the stairs down to the breakfast room. Not hungry, he would eat prophylactically, in case food got harder to come by later. An unadorned buffet of bread, goat butter, honey, rice soaked in fish oil, some kind of meat in a leaf sauce, sweetened millet gruel, and Ovaltine sat forlornly on a side table. He settled for a cup of coffee. Daniel would have disapproved, a full breakfast included in the price of the room.

He checked out of the hotel a few minutes after eight and walked past a black Renault filled with silent men in sunglasses. He got into the first taxi and the driver pulled away from the portico and worked the car through jumbled streets. Jake was totally disoriented by the time they stopped at a cinder-block building with no signage and a gas pump in front. Dozens of cars in various stages of disassembly littered the curbs.

"*Société de location de voitures?*" Jake asked, showing the paper with the address again.

"*Oui, oui,*" the driver said, tapping his fingers on the steering wheel.

Inside, a roomful of employees pretended Jake wasn't there. He cornered a man at the far end of the counter, cutting off his escape route. The man listened politely to the bad

French, then walked out the door without a word, returning minutes later with a fellow from the *Charcuterie* across the street.

"Can I assist?" the new arrival asked in English.

Jake pulled out his map. "I would like to hire a car and driver to go to Kona. I need them for a couple of days."

The man examined the map and bobbed his head. The employees were gathered behind him like a grease-stained choir. He turned to them and began to speak. The ensuing discussion was enthusiastic, everyone chipping in, including the other customers and a boy who strolled in from the street hawking toothbrushes and expired antibiotics. The man leaned into the group and listened hard, nodding judiciously from time-to-time and asking questions. Suddenly he stepped back and raised both hands over his head. The babble stopped. He turned to Jake, a hearty smile plastered across his face. "You should take a bus. Much cheaper. Very good buses."

"I need a car."

The interpreter's smile momentarily faded before quickly reappearing. "The driver has been taken ill and a replacement is right now being summoned. The roads are currently dangerous and not safe for driving, and the car is being painted. You should come back tomorrow when all modalities will be organized and the car and the driver fully positioned for hiring."

THE TAXI IDLED in front of the bank while Jake changed dollars into CFA, the local currency pegged to the Euro. They took the Pont des Martyrs over the swollen Niger River to the Gare Routiere, an open square that served as Bamako's bus depot. The streets around the square were lined with buses, minivans and stake trucks in various stages of loading and unloading. Street vendors had commandeered the shadiest spots, and travelers with bundles clustered near the curbs.

"Mopti," Jake said for the second time as the driver began another lap around the square. The town was almost 400 miles away and they were burning daylight. Once he got there he could worry about the last 80 miles to Kona.

The driver cut across the flow of cars and motorbikes and headed for a spot between a bus and an open-sided baché. "Mopti," he announced, as the car came to a stop.

A personal travel consultant with a passable command of English immediately attached himself to Jake. After a brief discussion, he headed off to talk to a man with a straw hat and clipboard.

Three desultory college-aged Americans with Peace Corps patches on their packs sat on the dusty ground near Jake, looking like they were waiting for a prison bus. He watched them try to communicate with a street vendor selling eucalyptus candies, their French worse than his own. What expertise could these kids possibly have, and how were they ever going to impart it to anyone?

The travel consultant was back, wearing a big frown. "The next two buses for Mopti are fully booked. You are to come back at three o'clock."

"That's no good."

The man stared hard at Jake for a few moments, as if trying to assess his level of trustworthiness, then led him down the street to a spot behind the buses. He pointed to a Peugeot hatchback sitting by the curb, like it was the special stuff in the back room, reserved for only the most favored customers. "Very dear."

"No problem," Jake said, unable to spot any empty seats, and the man walked off to find the driver.

The street vendors descended on him. He acquired packets of cheese, crackers, nuts and dried mango. He was negotiating with a boy for a plastic bag of water, like a goldfish would come in, when his travel consultant returned with the driver.

"Good luck," he said, after Jake gave both men some CFA. "You leave at eleven. Always they are on time."

"How long does it take to get to Mopti?"

"Don't worry. Very fast. He is a fast one."

The driver ambled over to the car and motioned for an elderly woman to get out. Jake took her place in the back row. The driver removed a small bale of clothing from the roof, and a goat in a burlap bag, just its head showing, and replaced them with Jake's suitcase, then headed to a massive baobab tree and plopped down in the shade.

Jake sweltered in the hot car, squeezed between two enormous women like a piece of bread in a fleshy toaster. His watch showed 114 degrees, and that seemed about right. He meditated, imagining Carly hand-watering a blue-green lawn as a cool evening breeze swept off the bay. He drank from his bag of water, getting the hang of it, the water as hot as a cup of tea and tasting of plastic. The driver finally returned, used a potholder to open the door, and pulled away from the curb at exactly 11 o'clock.

The narrow road to Mopti ran almost due east. Bicycles, donkey carts and pedestrians flirted dangerously along its edges, too close to the parade of cars, mopeds, and diesel-belching trucks that roared past. As they moved east the flowering bushes and mango trees of Bamako gave way to flat dry summerlands, then changed to naked brown earth punctuated with eerie trees. The houses became smaller and more rustic, evolving into mud huts with rain-softened edges.

Jake was pressed to the right as the car swerved to avoid an overturned truck. He looked out the rear window at the watermelons that littered the road. A black Renault plowed through them without slowing, splattering their red insides across the pavement.

The driver became less patient as the trip dragged on, blindly pulling out from behind the lumbering trucks with their impossible loads, suicide-passing them on the undulating roadway in a kind of Russian roulette. It seemed only a matter of time before a vehicle would appear out of one of the dips and snuff them out in a fiery crash. The swaying car, bursts of adrenalin and reek of dried carp from a basket under the seat made Jake forget about his hunger.

It clouded over and began to rain, cooling things off but creating new problems, the roads slick with oil and water and the driver frugal with the wipers, using them for only a few cycles at a time when the windshield became an opaque sheet of water and dead insects.

The flat African bush rolled by, the monotony broken by an occasional village of thatch-roofed huts or a splash through water that spilled from normally dry streambeds and inundated the road.

Huge raindrops pounded the Peugeot as it pulled into Ségou a little after two in the afternoon. They were only a third of the way to Mopti. The passengers waited in the car until a uniformed man arrived. Jake joined the others in passing forward the entry fee for the city, about a dollar and a half. Another man in a different uniform came to the window and spoke to the driver. The car was already in an uproar before the driver turned in his seat to pass on the news. Jake didn't understand what was said, but everyone climbed out of the car, so he got out too. The driver began to untie the bundles from the roof.

The road to Mopti, it seems, was closed due to flooding.

43

He was on his third taxi driver. With Ségou full of stranded travelers, it had taken a fistful of CFA to get close to a promised room. A military checkpoint held them up for a few moments until one of the dispirited soldiers, sitting on an overturned paint can under a rain-sagged tarp, looked up and waved them through. Moments later Jake stood in front of a sorry two-story building and considered the hand-painted sign over the door:

SEGOU HILTON
Your Heaven Away from Heaven

He paid for the room. The man behind the counter handed him a lightbulb and a half-roll of toilet paper and pointed to the stairwell. The odds that anyone from the Hilton chain had ever heard of this place were very long.

You can't tell whether you're paying 40 a night or 400 if you're asleep, Daniel always says.

He found No. 21 and changed into dry clothes, distributing the wet ones around the room on pegs and corners. The 300 flooded miles to Kona were a worry. Of course, Daniel might not even show up. He flopped onto one of the narrow beds. This whole expedition could be a ridiculous waste of effort, another classic Jake Morrow boner.

He ate the rest of the street food from Bamako and headed downstairs for more. A man in the bar asked if he wanted a seat by the pool. Jake followed him to a table on the covered terrace next to a large hole in the ground. He scanned the menu for the item least likely to make him sick and ordered a *sandwich jambon* and two Cokes, planning to ingest the drinks medicinally, like an IV sucrose drip.

Two drooping laborers, working in slow motion, shoveled sand onto a wooden plank. They carried it like a litter to a hand-turned cement mixer and dumped it next to a haphazard mountain of bricks.

Jake sipped his drink. Could he have invented the wheelbarrow? What could he come up with, knowing what he knew now, if he went back in time? Could he discover electricity? Grow a penicillin mold? Figure out what to do with it? He could describe things, like airplanes and cars and DNA, but could he *make* anything? Paper from a tree? A shirt from a sheep? A wagon wheel? With college and law school under his belt, could he lay out Stonehenge? Skin an elk? Start a fire? And what the hell could he grow?

He finished the first Coke. It was sobering to realize he wouldn't cut it as a cave man. He might subscribe to *Scientific American* when he got home. And those poor, overmatched Peace Corps volunteers. Left on their own, they'd starve in a month.

The skies cleared and he wandered out to the street. Ségou was a pleasant enough place, cleaner and quieter than Bamako, the dust damped by the rains. He asked directions to the market but couldn't understand the lengthy reply. He headed where the fingers pointed and hoped something would develop. Ten minutes later he was in the middle of a large open area surrounded by empty stalls: it was the main market, but the wrong day. He continued down a deserted, tree-lined street, past tan huts with brightly painted doors and goat pens. The buzz of activity picked up as he neared the river. He was joined by a swarm of children begging for *cadeaux*.

A line of women passed him, each carrying a blue wash-tub and balancing a large basket of clothes on her head. He walked along the riverbank past an assortment of small boats being emptied. A man washed a herd of goats in the weedy water. A little beyond, a half-dozen cattle stood with just their heads above the surface, half-bovine, half-crocodile, watching him pass.

Everyone in town seemed to be gathered near a hulking riverboat tied up at the quay. Jake weaved through the crowd. Starchy market ladies presided over portable tables stacked with onions, eggplant, lemons and cantaloupe. Others offered fish hooks, American cigarettes, used hypodermic needles and expired batteries. Cases of beer baked in the sun (how long before they started exploding?)

Long tables were piled high with "dead white man's clothes" from America. A woman moneychanger slept behind stacks of colorful currency for use downstream and across the desert. A blind man sold empty soda bottles and plastic pea-nut-butter jars with lids.

Daniel had his own dumpster at the house, a good-sized one too, like for a restaurant. He was proud of it and filled it week-after-week with his high-end garbage.

Jake bought a plate of flaky white fish, the plainest-looking rice he could find, and a cup of ginger juice. He took his meal to a tree-shaded spot and sat beside two wrinkled men playing checkers with bottle caps. He watched the riverboat. A line of shirtless men hand-over-handed sacks of millet up a makeshift gangplank like a human conveyor belt. The boat had to be half a century old, and wasn't aging well. Its name was painted on the side: *Tombouctou.* Could this rusting hulk, its bow pointed in the wrong direction, possibly be a way to Kona?

A steady stream of people moved in and out of a small building near the wharf. The sun-bleached sign identified it as

Compagnie Malienne de Navigation Bateau. Jake finished his meal and got in line.

"Which way is the boat heading?" he said in English to a pleasant-looking woman behind the counter.

"Down the river."

"Does it stop at Kona?"

"Of course. All the towns."

"When will it depart?"

"That is not certain."

"Today?"

"Not today. The engine is needing repairs. No one is knowing how long it will be. You should come back in December when the weather is cooler."

"But the boat is being loaded."

"Perhaps tomorrow."

A man stepped in and took over. "You are for Kona?"

"Yes. How long does the trip take?"

"One day. Two days. No problems."

It wasn't clear if it was no problem to do the trip in one or two days, or if it was one or two days if there were no problems.

"Do you have space for one person in your best accommodations?"

"The Deluxe cabin is for two with its own toilet and bath, the air is conditioned, the meals are included." He continued, like a waiter describing all the specials, even though Jake already knew what he wanted: "The 1st Class is four berths to the cabin; the 2nd class is 11 berths to the cabin; the 3rd Class is you sleep on the upper deck and may enjoy the wonderful cool river breezes; the 4th Class is you may find anywhere else on the boat you please."

"I'm one person for Kona. In Deluxe."

The man rubbed his bald head then turned up his palms. "No credit cards. Only money." He seemed hopeful this might resolve the matter.

Jake pulled out his wad of CFA. An animated discussion began in French between the man and the woman he displaced. He cut her off with a dismissive flick of the wrist and turned back to Jake.

"95,000 CFA, if you please."

Jake counted out the bills. The man cut a ticket from a printed sheet with a scissors, crossed out the name on it, and hand-lettered Jake's name in its place.

"You can board an hour before we depart."

"When will that be?"

"Tomorrow. God willing."

"When is the absolute earliest we could leave?"

"You will be listening for the bell."

"I don't want to miss the boat."

"*Vous avez de la chance,*" he said, handing Jake the ticket and moving away.

That probably meant he was lucky to get a spot on the sold-out boat, but it might mean he was taking his chances on the old tub. Jake looked at the handwritten ticket as he stepped into the street, wondering if it would work. The man may have done something special for him, taken care of him, asking nothing in return, but he couldn't be sure.

It was getting dark. He retraced his steps to the hotel and headed upstairs, unlocked the door and turned on the light. Two strange suitcases sat on the floor and a corpulent black man was asleep in the second bed. Apparently they were sharing the room.

He gathered up his things and went downstairs. No one was at the front desk so he put his key on the hook and went out to the street. It was good to be in the night air. He would sleep near the boat. Hopefully the rain would hold off until boarding time.

He disappeared around the corner just as the black Renault rolled up in front of the hotel.

Four burly men, two carrying pieces of metal pipe the size of baseball bats, got out. Dressed in casual Western clothes and adorned with bulky gold jewelry, they resembled a troop of rap star bodyguards. They liberated the key to No. 21 from its hook and moved quietly up the stairs. One of the men silently worked the key in the lock and opened the door. They gathered in the dark around the figure snoring on the bed. The man with the key grunted, and the pipes came down hard on the lump beneath the covers. When the sounds from the bed stopped, they bundled up the blankets and dragged their package down the hall to the stairwell. The tire salesman from Dakar groaned each time his battered body hit a step on the way down.

44

The *Tombouctou*'s railings were already jammed with passengers when Jake arrived at the wharf, and the electricity of a departure was in the air. He joined the line on the gangplank and handed his ticket to the man at the top. A young boy led him to a paint-scabbed metal door on the upper deck, let him in, and turned on the air conditioner, disappearing into the hubbub before Jake could organize a tip.

Two lumpy beds draped with mosquito netting sat on the grimy floor. A lopsided cane chair, a dresser, and a too-quiet refrigerator completed the ensemble. The bathroom had a shower, toilet and sink, all discolored by rusty water, the fittings badly corroded. An assortment of insect carcasses covered the window ledge and a foot-tall can of bug spray sat atop an ancient short-wave radio. It was best not to examine the surroundings too closely: he would pretend he was camping. He emptied half the bug spray into the room and exited quickly to avoid asphyxiation.

The railing just outside the stateroom provided a good view of the commotion below. A parade of women with improbably large baskets perched on their heads – mangoes, squash, cabbage and peppers, miniature red potatoes, perfectly round watermelons, pale orange yams – marched up the gangplank and headed toward the galley like a file of ants. Men wrestled piles of plump fish and thick slabs of beef onto the stern with lines and pulleys and a hand-made wooden crane.

Sheep and cattle protested loudly as they were herded into pens, stored fresh for some future menu, no refrigeration required. A section of the lower deck was turned into a hideous abattoir: outraged chickens slaughtered on the fantail, intestines from a dismembered cow strung across the deck like mooring lines, the smell of blood in the air.

Jake disembarked to acquire some emergency vegetarian provisions. The shoreside vendors descended on him with boiled eggs, roasted peanuts, homemade cheese in foil wrappers, baguettes. He returned to find a crush of passengers jostling for precious deck space, staking their claims with tied-up bundles and reed mats. He side-stepped an unattended man on a branch stretcher. There didn't seem to be enough room for everyone to sit down, let alone sleep.

He stashed everything inside the lifeless refrigerator and returned to his spot at the rail. Without warning, the *Tombouctou* began to separate from the wharf. The bow swung into the river and slowly turned until it was pointed downstream. Jake waved to the onshore crowd like everyone else, disliking the feeling of being alone. The engines spooled up and he could feel the strong vibration through the soles of his feet. A group of barefoot children raced the boat along the shore.

Once Ségou disappeared astern, he moved forward to get upwind of the diesel smoke and exotic smells that rose from the lower decks. A large black man at the railing stared hard at him when he passed, and didn't avert his eyes when Jake stared back. Despite the orange boubou and pointed clogs, Jake marked him as an American.

He found a plastic chair near the bow and nested there until the sun was gone, the buzz-saw whine of mosquitoes finally driving him inside. The dining room door was locked so he went to his cabin and ate peanuts until he was thirsty, then went to bed, the air conditioner eventually catching up with the day's dissipating heat.

Hours later he was awakened by a jolt, followed by the clamor of raised voices and stampeding feet. The boat was stopped. He went on deck. The *Tombouctou* was beached on a sandy bank that sloped down to the river from a small village. Despite the hour, everyone seemed to be there, even the children, who scampered beneath bare bulbs strung on overhead poles, past market tables and smoking barbecues.

Merchants battled up the narrow gangplank against a stream of disembarking passengers and circulated through the decks like ballpark vendors, hawking straw hats and cheap watches. Jake bought a ballpoint pen from China. The market was being run on fast-forward, negotiations completed at top speed, nobody sure exactly when the boat would push off again. When the bell signaled the *Tombouctou's* imminent departure, the bargaining reached frantic levels.

The process was repeated more than once during the night and he dragged himself out of bed each time, not wanting to miss the show. When he woke for good in mid-morning it was to the sound of laughter and splashing and the ominous silence of the boat's engines.

People swam in the coolness of the boat's shaded side while crewmembers and passengers with long poles tried to push the *Tombouctou* off a sandbar. Mothers bathed their naked tots on the fantail with buckets of river water. A continuous loop of laughing boys jumped into the water from the upper deck and were helped back on board to do it again. It could have been Daniel, Jake and Finis at the same age, the sun beating down as they played in the warm, shallow waters of Utsalady Bay – except for the guinea worms and medieval life expectancies.

As they grew older, Daniel started to miss out on a lot of the fun, the fishing and crabbing, sailing and swimming, the campfires on the beach and touch football games in the orchards. He spent his summers working with One-Man-One-

Day, taking on more and more of the chores as arthritis stole his father's hands. Daniel didn't have access to a car like most of their friends, but tried to make it up to the cabin on weekends, sometimes hitchhiking or taking the train to Mount Vernon where Jake would pick him up.

On Saturday nights Daniel would negotiate beer-buying joint ventures with down-and-outers; then the three of them would cruise in Jake's blue panel truck, always on the lookout for the antipodal girls they knew were out there somewhere, in their own car, looking for a bunch of boys to have sex with.

Daniel never had any money to spend, everything going toward college, and he begged off from any venture that required cash. When they took the camping trip down the coast he bought a sleeping bag at Sears and returned it a few days down the road, then bought another and did the same, all the way there and back. He was always teased about it, being such a cheapskate, until the day Jake took a look in Daniel's refrigerator – bare except for two stuffed meatballs and half a yellow onion – and finally got it. After that they found things to do that didn't cost money and stopped talking about new cars and family trips to Hawaii.

Things hadn't changed much. When it was Daniel's turn to pay Jake still slipped cash on the table when they were done, knowing there would be no tip added to the charge slip.

He was a good friend though, in the old days.

Jake snacked in the cabin on cheese and a stale baguette while he checked the GPS against the map. The faded red hula-dancer curtains filtered the harsh sunlight, bathing the room in a rosy glow. He was on a slow boat to nothingness, but the GPS confirmed he was going there on purpose. He moved outside to the bow and watched the water slide by as the river bent around imperceptible rises in the flat land. Starting out only 150 miles from the ocean, the Niger headed in the opposite direction, into the Sahara, traveling over 2,500 miles through some of the most desolate land on earth before staggering into the Gulf of Guinea, abused and filthy. Nothing was easy around here.

It was already very hot, the breeze no longer pleasant. A group of pirogues loitered in the middle of the river, out of sight of land. The *Tombouctou* slowed and drifted through them, the boats gathering at her stern before she came to a full stop. Heavy-set women in garish pagnes opened chests of tea and flour and balloons, and pushed soap and rough cubes of sugar on passengers on the afterdeck, while their muscled paddlers looked on impassively. Minutes later the *Tombouctou* was on the move again, the pirogues trailing in her wake, trying to prolong business hours.

Shortly after noon Jake happily answered the lunch bell. He was seated with a mousy French couple bound for Timbuktu, drawn there by the exotic name and already disappointed, just like with San Diego. Waiters hurried through the room with plates of bony fish and corn-on-the-cob. Jake's teeth stripped off the sweet kernels with machine-like efficiency. The woman muttered in French that corn was fit only for chickens and Americans. He finished his rice pudding and a good cup of coffee without any attempt at conversation, and returned to his spot at the bow.

The river's southern bank appeared in the distance, low and flat. A thin line of green separated the muddy brown water from the baked brown earth. He could see little in the way of agriculture. Here at the edge of the desert, where the people had nothing, even the valuable water flowed right by them without leaving anything, or evaporated into the white hot skies to rain down later on the heads of more fortunate people in more blessed places.

The *Tombouctou* meandered across the water as though a child were at the helm, no obvious reason for the route, the water glassy smooth and featureless, more like a lake than a river, spreading to the horizon in every direction. The breeze came from dead astern, exactly matching the speed of the boat, enveloping them in a fog of diesel fumes. The metal deck was like a hot-plate.

The day rolled on: herons seemed to stand on the surface of the river; fishermen patiently eyed the water for the same fish; European backpackers lounged on the deck playing cards but put them away, mystified, when a passenger in Islamic green politely asked them to stop; a low village appeared along the shore, looking deserted, and Jake realized it was half submerged, its softly-contoured mud buildings looking like sand castles eroded by an incoming tide.

When the sun began to close on the horizon and the day cooled, the tall black man who stared at Jake the day before walked to the bow and took up a position a few yards down the railing. He wore a faded pinstripe suit with frayed cuffs and a shine, but still managed to look elegant, moving with the grace of a natural athlete, his enormous ass sticking out behind him like a shelf.

"Imbeciles," he said after a moment, pointing to a pinasse floating at the edge of a green mat of vegetation that stretched for dozens of acres along the shore.

Jake ignored the man, who moved a few steps closer.

"See that there?" He pointed to two men who were reaching down and pulling plants from the water and piling them in the narrow boat. "It's water hyacinth. Chokes the life out of every lake and river in Africa, except the Shire, and it'll get there soon enough. Cancer. You know what they're doing, those two men?"

"It looks like they're picking it," Jake said, breaking his long-standing rule to never make conversation with a travel-mate unless on final approach.

"Hah! They're weeding the river!"

It would take months to clear the patch and they had passed hundreds just like it.

"It's growing faster than they're cutting it," the man said softly to himself, as though Jake were no longer there.

Two men on the deck below began trading punches, cheered on by a gathering crowd, and Jake turned to watch the commotion. When the dinner bell finally rang, the smaller combatant, with a bloodied nose, was being swung around like a tetherball. The Deluxe and First Class passengers scrambled for the dining room. Jake's new friend extended his hand, exuding refinement. "Horace J. Washington. Perhaps you would join me for supper?"

"Sure," Jake said, shaking his hand, "Ronny Knoll."

They made their way to the dining room. The maître d' greeted them at the door. "Monsieur will be your guest for dinner this evening?" he asked, nodding at Horace who stood slightly behind Jake.

"Yes, we're together," Jake said.

They were seated at a nice table near the mirrored disco ball. Horace took a packet from the cracker basket, fumbled the wrapper off and devoured the contents. "I came here a little over three years ago. I was with WHEEP." He spewed feathery crumbs across the table, dispelling, a bit, the aura of sophistication. "That's *Water Hyacinth Education and Eradication Project*. It's UN."

The waiter brought them bowls of plain onion soup. Jake was still examining his for impurities visible to the naked eye, when Horace finished and set down his spoon, then picked up the bowl and drained the last of it.

He's hungry, Jake thought.

"I don't do anything for them anymore. WHEEP. Got out of it over a year ago. I used to traipse up and down the river buttonholing any village leader I could sneak up on. About helping with the hyacinth. It's wrecking the river, and the river is everything down here. They bathe in it, wash their animals and clothes in it. It's their drinking water and sewer."

Jake set down his spoon and pushed the bowl away.

"The fish are already disappearing. When the hyacinth sops up the rest of the oxygen and the river dies, it's going to destroy everything. It will be a bigger disaster here than AIDS, much bigger, and nobody has a clue yet. I might as well have been peddling lampshades."

Jake already felt pretty low and didn't want to listen to someone else's troubles right then. "So what are you doing in Mali now?"

Horace just sat there, head bowed and eyes closed, a painful expression on his face, like he was suffering from indigestion, or saying a belated grace. He might not have heard the question. "Can you keep a secret?" he finally whispered, leaning across the table, his voice low and hoarse. Jake didn't have a chance to answer before Horace plowed ahead, looking like he might cry.

"I have a son. Skitch. He's 11."

Jake already regretted having lunch with the man, who could very well be a lunatic.

"I haven't seen him in over a year. When I went home for supplies."

The waiter arrived with paper plates of steak and onions. The meat had an iridescent sheen to it, like a pigeon's neck. Horace regained his composure and ordered two large beers for each of them. The waiter left and Horace glanced around the room, then reached into his pocket and pulled something out, cupped in his hand. He gave Jake a peek. It was a twisty gold nugget the size of a walnut.

"One day I arrived at a little village for the usual bash-my-head-against-the-wall session with the tribal leaders. They ushered me into the chief's hut and brought me tea, three cups, each sweeter than the last. After a while a man showed up carrying a leather container, like a small shoebox. It was half-filled with gold dust. There had been a mistake. They thought I was there to buy gold, not talk about pulling weeds."

The *Tombouctou*'s captain sauntered up to the table, making the rounds in a boubou and ridiculous sailor's cap. "Have fun! Have fun!" he cheerfully admonished them.

"How long will it take to get to Kona?" Jake said.

The captain's smile disappeared. "A day or two."

Raising the question might have been another Jake Morrow cultural faux pas. "How are you able to find the channel?" he said, trying to recover. "Very impressive how you do that."

The captain shrugged. "God's will." He headed for the next table, the grin already pasted back on.

Horace picked up where he left off. "This country is filled with gold. It's everywhere. Tens of thousands of people collect it. More than that if a drought wipes out the crops."

Jake worked on a piece of meat that seemed to get bigger the longer he chewed it.

"I started to take an interest. I bought a sample and sent it up to Germany for assay and it came back 95% pure. Right out of the riverbed. Artisans can turn it into jewelry without any refining. He held up his closed fist with the nugget inside. "Six ounces. Picked up in a riverbed like a penny off the street."

"Wow," Jake said politely. The sound of an Asian martial arts movie blared from the wall-mounted television and made it difficult to hear.

"It's like a river system, a river of gold. Little kids walk the streambeds looking for nuggets. Adults pan for dust along the riverbanks, or work primitive mines. Dozens of families gather up what they've collected and bring it to an elder, who takes it to the chief, who takes it to a regional chief. It's hundreds of little streams of gold turning into bigger streams, then rivers, then bigger rivers. By the time the regional chiefs bring me the gold in Bamako, it's the Mississippi.

"I assay it right in my hotel room, buy it well below the London price, ship it to Germany. My markups are huge. I coordinate the buys with Air France's flights to Munich – out here you don't want to be sitting on a pile of the stuff for too long. My gold flights leave twice a week."

Jake concentrated hard on peeling his orange.

"Maybe you would like to get involved?"

"No thanks. Out of my league." He was unable to square two gold flights a week with the man's hungry look.

"Maybe you would like a little more information?" There was a hint of desperation in his voice.

"Do you know Kona? A little town past Mopti?"

"I know it well. I've been there many times." Horace was clearly disappointed by the change of subject.

"Is it possible to hire a car and driver there?"

Horace brightened. "Of course it is. I can take care of that for you."

"I might need to go into the bush."

"No problem. I can get a Land Rover. Let's meet up on the quay right after we disembark."

"You're getting off in Kona?"

"Yes. Why not? I have business there." He took a card out of his wallet, wrote something on the back and handed it to Jake. "My card."

Horace finished Jake's orange while Jake paid for the four beers and Horace's dinner. When no food of any kind remained on the table, Horace rose and excused himself. He didn't take the stairway that led up to the Deluxe cabins, but instead moved astern and down.

Jake nursed his second beer and examined the card: Horace J. Washington, Chairman, Mali Gold Consortium. Scrawled on the back was: "Ronny, I'm here to help any way I can."

Crew members began to transform the dining room into a discothèque. A trio of city women arrived and stood haughtily in a corner, looking out of place in flimsy camisoles and tight Capri pants. Hookers maybe. A group of army officers stared him down until he stopped looking at the women. The officers continued to eye him, speaking something other than French, and occasionally erupted in laughter that seemed to be at his expense. He waited until the next burst and joined in, guffawing loudly, and the men turned sullen.

He drained the last of his beer and left the dining room. One of the army officers deliberately bumped him in the narrow corridor and Jake apologized. He made his way to the outer deck and watched the beam from the oversized rooftop searchlight sweep the river, looking for the channel. The lights of the *Tombouctou* were the only ones visible, the riverbank dark and the moon and stars hidden behind clouds.

He strolled the decks, past charcoal grills and cauldrons of boiling oil. Cooks dispensed fried yams, rice and beans, flour beignets. Passengers gathered near the fires, sitting on millet stalk mats, and ate with their fingers from shared bowls. The cries of babies mixed with the squawks and bleats of the animals. A young mother in corn-rows stirred a pot and sipped a beer, a baby nursing quietly at her breast. Jake stood outside his cabin for a long time, until the only sounds left were the low hum of the diesel engine and the water slipping past the hull.

45

It was early morning, the sun just starting to crawl over the horizon. They were stopped at a village slightly larger than most, tied to a stone quay. Jake was at the upper-deck railing, killing time until breakfast. He didn't want to process any more food, but badly needed hydration after a night half-spent in the bathroom. The warning bell signaled their imminent departure, and then a panicked cry wafted over the murmur of the crowd.

"Ronny! Ronny! Over here!"

It took a moment to locate Horace in the swarm of people on shore, but finally there he was, standing next to a couple of full-sized steamer trunks and an untidy mound of boxes and bundles, hollering and waving his arms.

"This is Kona!"

Jake bolted for the cabin and threw his things together, barely making it down the gangplank before it was reeled in. He worked his way to Horace through the mob. The two men shook hands, then moved up the dirt street toward the center of town, transporting the baggage in relays, going back and forth like mountain climbers, until Jake had enough of it and paid the boys shadowing them to haul the stuff the rest of the way.

Horace turned down a sandy alley and led the procession to a cinderblock building with a smooth metal roof and no markings of any kind. Sweating profusely, he supervised the stacking of his belongings against an outside wall. "It's not good to leave the stuff unguarded, even for a few minutes," he said, nodding toward two of the young porters and rubbing his thumb across his fingers.

Jake paid the boys to watch the gear, and followed Horace inside. A bouncer in a chair by the door eyed him suspiciously, then turned back to scolding a grubby amputee. A handful of lonely liquor bottles languished on a single shelf behind a counter, all of them nearly empty. The gloomy room felt like a cave after the glare in the alley, and smelled like stale beer and surrender.

"Something to drink?" Horace asked.

"Sure." He was dehydrated from the diarrheal night, and seemed to recall that anything carbonated was safe. "A beer. Something imported if they have it." He turned to examine the room. The tables looked sticky; the men sitting at them anesthetized. Except for two with their heads on their arms, they all stared at him with drooping faces.

He spotted the lavatory in the back and headed for it. There was no lock on the door, no light, no visible toilet paper. A sloping square with a hole in it was set flush to the ground, the porcelain completely obscured by badly aimed excreta. He decided to retreat to the bar and hang on, already nostalgic for the *Tombouctou*.

Horace was engaged in an animated conversation with the bartender. Jake sat down at one of the empty tables and unfolded his map. Black flies ambled out of the way on foot, not yet warmed or worried enough to consider getting airborne.

Horace brought over a couple of Star beers in dark green 20-ounce bottles. "Green Death. Imported from Nigeria. Hope you're not allergic to formaldehyde." He set the bottles down on the outspread map and took a seat across from Jake. "The Land Rover isn't available right now, but I was able to get a Citroën. It's pricey, but it'll get us there."

Jake ignored the "us" and sipped the warm beer like it was bad-tasting medicine. He would be expected to show an interest in the cost of the car. "How much?"

"It depends on where we're going exactly."

"A number of possible places." He pointed to six sets of penciled-in crosshairs on the map. "These are the coordinates. I can steer us there with a GPS. I want to hit the ones closest to Kona first, then work my way out. If I find what I'm looking for, I don't need to bother with the rest."

"What exactly are you looking for, Ronny?"

"I'm not sure. I'll know it when I see it."

Horace stared at the map. "Let me have that for a second." He carried the map to the bar and laid it out. The bartender leaned over, the dark heads of the two men almost touching across the counter. Minutes later, he was back. He put the map on the table and pointed to a spot southwest of town. "We should try this one first. He says white people are out there. Thinks it might be dangerous though. We'll need a little extra for the driver. Better give me 25,000 CFA to get things started."

"We might have to go off-road," Jake said, pulling a fistful of currency from his pocket.

"No problem." Horace seemed hypnotized by the rhythmic peeling of the bills from the thick wad. "The driver will be here in an hour. I'll take my stuff to the hotel and be back before then."

Jake gagged down the rest of his beer. He felt a sinking spell coming on. This was mosquito, parasite, and liver-abscess land. He was closing in on something, but then what? Like the time the dog got into the bacon grease and threw up on the carpet, he had a nasty mess on his hands and wasn't quite sure he was up to the job.

His fellow patrons were still staring at him with thick-lidded eyes. What *was* that look exactly? He hadn't seen it before in Mali. Not malice exactly, or anger either. Revulsion maybe. And they were afraid. He scared them. Revulsion mixed with fear. And yes, there was some malice in there after all.

Probably no one would mind if he waited outside.

"WATCH OUT FOR pickpockets," came the cheery voice behind him. Horace was dressed in leather sandals, an Aloha shirt, and baggy green mental-patient pants with an elastic waistband. He looked ready for a day of sightseeing.

An ancient Deux Cheveux rattled down the alleyway toward them. The snail-shaped four-door was painted white, the brush strokes clearly visible. It had one hand-hammered green fender and three purple ones, all looking like they were fabricated in someone's backyard. Indecipherable words were painted on the rounded rear hump of the little car, and the whole thing listed seriously to port. Horace settled into the passenger seat and Jake climbed in back.

The driver started off in second gear, the car bucking and jerking, then jammed into fourth, gears grinding. They stopped for gas at a thatch-covered shed at the edge of the village. Horace fronted the cost of the fuel out of the day's fare. The driver filled the tank from a collection of pots, bottles and jars sitting on a table in front of the shack.

They headed out of town on a dirt road. After bumping along for nearly 20 minutes Jake checked the GPS. They weren't getting any closer to the first set of coordinates.

"No straight lines out here," Horace said.

The driver bought firewood from a lonely vendor who had set up shop in the middle of the road. Horace helped the man lash the branches to the roof.

A little later Horace pointed to a track that cut away from the road at an angle. After a protracted argument in the front seat, the driver turned the car, muttering under his breath.

Horace twisted around to face Jake. "I want to show you something. It's almost on the way."

THEY STOOD ON top of a small rise and watched a woman in a puddle at the river's edge. She stooped and added water to a black bowl filled with sand, then swirled it, trance-like, swaying gracefully to music only she could hear, doing it as naturally as breathing.

Jake watched transfixed. She continued her dance, adding more water, using smaller and smaller bowls. When nothing was left in the black bottom of the littlest bowl but a few tiny flecks of gold, gleaming like stars in a pitch dark sky, she used a feather to gently transfer them to a leather pouch tied to her wrist.

Horace broke the silence. "She's a good panner. She'll go through a quarter ton of sand today. If that's a decent spot she's in, she'll add enough gold to her pouch every few hours to dust a fingernail." He held up his pinkie. "A few shakes of a salt shaker. She might get a quarter gram for the day, maybe an ounce for the whole season. Every couple of years she'll find a nugget, nothing like the one I showed you on the boat, but a nugget nevertheless. Those are worth a lot more than just their weight in gold." His eyes suddenly gleamed. "But can you im- agine what she could do with a shovel and a sluice?"

All along the edge of the river other women were doing the same dance, a hallucinatory flock of herons: bending, dip- ping, swaying, pouring, bending, dipping, swaying. Children were scattered among them, walking the dry washes looking for nuggets, sifting dirt, carrying drinking water to the panners. A girl about five years old skipped up to the woman below them and delivered a calabash full of rice and fish and stayed for a long time, clasping her mother's leg.

"Where are the men?" Jake asked.

"Back in the village mostly. They take turns giving each other shaves in the afternoon. It's the women who keep it together here, same as the rest of Africa."

"Don't the kids go to school?"

"They have it easy here. The nasty work's further west. They dig shafts with hoes there. Forty or fifty feet deep and barely wide enough for a kid's shoulders. A child gets lowered down and stands in waist-deep mud and water at the bottom all day, scraping dirt into a bucket."

"I can't believe they're allowed to do that, even here."

"It's illegal, working the kids, but nobody would ever stop it. It beats the alternative."

"What's worse than the bottom of a 50-foot mud hole?"

"Starving to death. They're panning for their lives. A tiny bit of gold can be the difference." He pointed to a depression in the ground where water had collected. "Before that dries out they'll plant it, hoping to get a little millet before the sun bakes the ground so hard a jackhammer wouldn't dent it. But even in a good year they can't stay alive on that, and there aren't any good years anymore."

"What if the gold runs out?"

"Won't happen. It's a renewable resource. You know how Iowa's perfect for growing corn? Well Mali's perfect for collecting gold. The rains uncover a new batch each year and then the water goes away so they can get it. They've been doing it forever. The buckets are plastic now and the bowls are ceramic instead of wood, but otherwise it's the same as always."

They headed for the car, past a group of men sitting at a table under a tree. One ladled water into a cup from a large earthenware pot filled from the river, enough liquid sweating through its porous sides and evaporating into the hot air to keep the rest of the water cool all day. Another man raised a flat brass pan with narrowing edges to his mouth and gently puffed into the shallow open end, sending everything lighter than gold into the slight breeze, leaving just the heavy gold dust in the back, then used a miniature spoon to move it to a smooth leather box.

"Man's work," Horace said, as they passed the shady retreat.

The driver was slumped in his seat looking seriously demoralized. The car was quiet as they bounced back down the track to the road.

HORACE COULDN'T STOP thinking about the little girl hugging her mother's leg, just a baby really. The plan was to get the kids out of the shafts, keep them safe, put them in day-care and real schools, let them just be children, even if it were only for a little while.

It was a wonder he could get himself out of bed in the morning anymore.

It seemed so simple, so foolproof. He would provide grubstakes: shovels; picks; wheelbarrows; lumber; clothing; rice and sugar and cooking oil – everything on credit with reasonable markups, to be reimbursed later in gold. He would give them little gas pumps to suck the water out of the shafts, and hoses, spare parts and fuel. They would go through the old tailings with simple jigs, and get the other half of the gold the calabashes missed.

There would be motorbikes for taking supplies into the field and bringing back the gold. Radios would keep everyone in instant touch. Clinics for the sick and injured. Safe drinking water. Everyone would be better fed, stronger, healthier. Poverty and illiteracy would be vanquished, and with every improvement, production would go up. He would get a Land Rover for himself.

There would be a fair price for the gold too, much more than the Djati paid. That cabal had been manipulating prices for way too long, cheating the gold gatherers, getting rich on their backs. He would tie the price right to the London market, stay in constant touch with a satellite phone.

The tools and higher prices would lure people into the gold fields, double, maybe triple the size of the workforce. Even the men might get off their skinny asses and help.

Every year he would take out tons of pure unadulterated gold, enough to make a good-sized mining company envious. It would be grassroots, no government interference – no applications or permits, taxes or fees, red tape or bribery. And it would be dirt-cheap too: no dredgers, excavators, screeners, loaders, crushers or conveyors to buy. No bulldozers or dump-trucks to maintain. And no cyanide to leach the metal from the earth; no mercury and arsenic to dump into the river.

He could do it all with little more than a crate of tools from Home Depot and his organizational skills, well-honed after years of toiling in the bureaucracies.

The profits would be enormous.

He preached his message to the elders: he would help them get more gold, lots more, and pay better for it. All he asked in return was the exclusive right to their output. They listened and gave him their word. They shook his hand on it.

And why not? What businessman wouldn't want to increase production and get a higher price, and with no capital outlay whatsoever? Everyone was going to be a winner. Except the thieving Djati, of course.

It seemed like much longer than 18 months had passed since he headed to Brooklyn to raise a million dollars. A different person made that trip.

He tried his stockbroker first, and then the venture capitalists, which was a joke, and then the Yellow Pages and finally the lenders offering money in the newspaper.

The schools and clinics would have to come later, after the thing started to pay for itself. When even the loan sharks wouldn't lend him money, he cut out the potable water and day care.

In the end, it was his mother, brothers and sisters, aunts and uncles and cousins, friends from high school, people from the church and the neighborhood, who ponied up. It was an easy sell, he was always the shining star, the smart one, the guy who escaped and went to college and made it big. Everyone gave eagerly, but they barely had anything to give, and the total gathered from the whole group amounted to less than $35,000.

He emptied his bank account, cashed in the 401k (he could deal with the IRS after the gold money was rolling in), sold his five-year old car, and took out a whopping second mortgage on the house, the one he was born in, where Skitch grew up. With the divorce final, and being in Mali and all, he didn't need it anyway.

When everything was liquidated, the pot had grown to $185,000. Plus Jim Johnson agreed to get him a practically new Land Rover, valued at over 70 grand, and ship it to Africa.

He spent $80,000 for picks; shovels; lumber and tools; a portable gold assay kit; hoses; jigs; medical supplies; wheelbarrows; a dozen gas pumps that could draw over 300 gallons a minute; a satellite phone; dozens of VHF radios; and rice, sugar and oil for the company store. He wanted 20 motorbikes, but settled for five mountain bikes instead. Everything fit into a single container, which was shipped off to Africa with great fanfare, the entire neighborhood turning up at the dock to watch the crane drop it onto the boat.

He set aside $25,000 for living expenses. He could stretch that for three months, maybe more. Another $50,000 was earmarked to purchase the first batch of gold. The rest would be set aside for the emergencies and unexpected expenses that his year in Mali taught him were sure to arise.

The Land Rover never materialized. Only half the tools and none of the mountain bikes made it through Malian customs, and he paid more than a third of his remaining cash to get the rest of the gear out. Practically all the food supplies were spoiled, wet from their extended stay outside the customs shed. His passport went missing soon after he turned it in, as required, at the hotel desk, and he didn't leave his room for over a month, sick as a dog, guessing he might have contracted malaria.

And then things started to go downhill.

46

"Bear left about ten degrees; we're maybe two miles away," Jake said, surfacing from the GPS where he was viewing the display through cupped hands, trying to make out the faint numbers in the bright sunlight. He leaned over the seat and pointed: "About there."

Horace relayed the message to the driver, who so far was doing what he was told. The muttering got louder every mile though, and the man's mood had noticeably soured since they'd lost the tail pipe. The Deux Cheveux left the minimal dirt road and banged down a barely discernible track. The driver suddenly brought them to a jolting halt and mumbled something to Horace.

Horace looked back at Jake. "He won't go any further."

"We're almost there."

"Nevertheless."

"Why not?"

The driver had a rigid grasp of the wheel and was staring straight ahead.

"He's uncomfortable going any further."

"So you said. Why is that?"

"Says there's evil ahead."

There was nothing but low, barren earth around them. "We're only a few thousand yards away."

Horace shrugged.

Jake opened the door and got out, leaving his suitcase on the back seat. "I'll walk. If this is the right place I may be all day, otherwise I should be back in less than an hour and we can try the next spot. Can you tell him to wait right here?"

After a brief conversation, Horace reported back: "He wants more money. If you want him to wait."

"I thought we had him for the day."

"Well he wants more money. He won't stay unless you pay."

"*Combien?*" Jake said to the driver.

"40,000 CFA," Horace said.

"That's more than the rental."

Horace seemed to be out of things to say. Jake counted out the bills and started to pass them through the window to the driver when Horace leaned across the steering wheel and intercepted the money. "I'll handle this guy. Not to worry."

Jake locked their position into the GPS. "Don't move from this exact spot, okay? I'm programmed to get back to right here."

Horace was counting the CFA. "No problem. We'll be standing by."

Only a handful of bedraggled acacias interrupted the monotonous sandy scrubland that extended in all directions. The river must be close though, spreading like spilled milk, lapping up the flatlands to the north of him. Jake left the faint car track and set out across the brown earth, following the heading displayed on the GPS.

He got barely a hundred yards before the Deux Cheveux began to slowly back down the track. By the time he stopped concentrating on the emptiness in front of him and turned to get his bearings, the car was on the horizon, hull-down in a smudge of dust.

47

Jake stopped at the edge of the shimmering water. It wasn't a mirage after all. He double-checked the GPS then squinted across the river and downstream to where the coordinates lay. He would need to get wet.

He moved along the shore, looking for an easy place to cross. Black flying beetles tormented him, their numbers steadily increasing as he trudged along. They homed in on his eyes and nose, looking for moisture, setting at him like picadors, making him crazy. He flailed away with his arms, to no effect: might as well try to swat away the wind. It was better finally to not fight at all, to let them have their way. He imagined them as allies, friends gathering to urge him along in his quest, provide moral support, keep him company, show the way.

He was close enough – within a half mile – that he should be able to see something by now. The other side of the river offered nothing but flooded shrubs and bare brown hummocks, rising slightly to better take their beating from the sun. He was losing confidence in this set of coordinates anyway. Except for the green carpet of a rizière near the horizon, there was nothing in sight to indicate humans had ever set foot here, and Horace's suggestion in the bar that this was likely the place now seemed tainted by self-interest. If he didn't spot something in the next five minutes, ten max, he would head back and try the next set of numbers. And heaven help Horace if the car wasn't there.

The thought of the disappearing Deux Cheveux got him swatting at the beetles again.

THE BAREFOOT GRANDFATHER sat on his haunches beneath a scarred acacia, motionless, mulling over his troubles, not an ounce of fat under the dark-grained skin. He moved instinctively to stay in a tiny patch of shade that shifted beneath the tree with the morning sun. The demands, the pleas, it was all too much for a simple ferryman, way too much, finally, on his shoulders. He was being pounded like millet.

The six sons he sacrificed for were now all gone: one a teacher in Abidjan, two to Bamako, three dead. They hardly came back anymore, and brought less and less each time; they could barely take care of their own families, they said.

It was hard to know what to do. His wife wanted cloth and sheets to sell in the market and something nice to wear for Ramadan. A daughter wanted a flatiron and washtubs so she could set herself up in business cleaning clothes for taxi drivers. A brother wanted a donkey and a plow and another needed money for a call on the village phone. The hospital had medicine for his auntie but she needed her own needle. The cow needed medicine too, and a son-in-law had to have a battery for his flatbed truck. He himself could use a new mosquito net and mother coughed all night and wanted plastic chairs and his cousins and four men from their village were sleeping on the porch, expecting to be fed.

His face was serene, the eyes half closed, but inside he was churning. His nephew with the government job visited for only two days and left suddenly without passing on anything. It had never been this bad. He was so tired. Everyone looked to him, but who could he look to?

JAKE CAME STRAIGHT over the top of the slight rise, wanting the extra few feet of elevation. He checked the numbers again. He was directly perpendicular to the coordinates. More walking downstream would just take him further away. He raised his head from the GPS and there they were, right at his feet: three tapered pirogues, pulled up at the water's edge.

He walked down and stood in the middle of a car track, probably the one they had been on. He would have been here an hour ago if the driver didn't chicken out. No one was around except a little black man squatting under a tree.

Tire tracks led into the water and out the other side, about a hundred yards away. It appeared to be an island, the water stretching out and enveloping both ends. A decrepit, bowed chain-link fence was barely visible along the opposite shore: it followed the contour of the land, sometimes partially submerged, sometimes completely out of the water, like an undulating sea snake. There was a gate in the fence, and slightly higher ground and trees beyond. The water wasn't usually here: it would have come with the floods.

The man under the scrawny tree slowly uncoiled and got to his feet, conserving energy and precious calories, using his long pole as a staff. The heat rose off the ground in waves between the two men.

"Hello," Jake said as the old fellow walked toward him.

The man passed by without any acknowledgement and headed for the largest of the three pirogues.

Jake tried again: *"Bon jour."* No response. *"Parlez francais?"* He was talking to the man's back. He tried to dredge up some French: *"Quesce que se la?* Over there? *La. Savez vous quel est* over there, *la,* past *la fenétre...*no...*la clôture?"*

The old man set his long pole on the ground beside the pirogue and reached into the boat. He was getting ready to leave.

Jake pointed to the gate on the other side of the river and affected a comical French accent, hoping it might aid the comprehension: "*Connaisez vous qui est la?*"

The man picked up a bleach bottle, its bottom cut away. He scooped water out of the low point of the boat. His bony back was to Jake, the arm muscles well-developed and out of proportion with the rest of the lean body. He looked like a purple-black Popeye.

"*Portez-vous moi*...across?" Jake said, about ready to give up on the French, wishing he had paid more attention in class the day they covered asking a man for a canoe ride, thinking maybe this fellow spoke Bombara or something else anyway.

The man finished emptying the pirogue and stood beside it, knee-deep in the river, holding the side, ready to go. Jake moved toward him, arms out, palms up: "*S'il vous plait.*"

The man looked at Jake and shifted from one foot to the other in the murky water, made eye contact for the first time, then looked down at the boat.

Ah, he wants me to get in.

He was barely seated when the old man pushed the pirogue into the water and turned it around, letting the current help, until the bow pointed like an arrow at the coordinates, then lithely pulled himself over the gunwales and into the stern. He stood up and poled them into deeper water, accelerating smoothly.

Jake balanced on his narrow seat. The boatman didn't seem surprised when he wandered in from nowhere. It almost seemed the old guy was expecting him.

48

The boatman's pole was worn smooth where he gripped it, polished over time by his now-rough hands. He angled the boat slightly upstream, compensating for the drift, and aimed for a spot where the sandy shore sloped gently into the water. He beached them 75 yards downriver from the gate, close enough for Jake to see two men squatting in the meager shade of the fence, their weapons leaning against it, their heads slumped over, possibly asleep.

Jake got out of the pirogue and looked in the other direction. Fifty yards down the fenceline the rusting barbed-wire along its top sagged, marking a spot where the river had washed the earth from beneath a fence post.

The boatman was standing next to him, silent and motionless, like a bellhop waiting for a tip. Jake pulled out his CFA and separated a third of the bills from the wad and passed them over, knowing he was seriously overpaying but wanting to get out of there quickly before the two moribund guards noticed him. "*Merci beaucoup,*" Jake said in a whisper, crouching to make himself smaller. "*Pouvez vous…returnez?*…pick me up, *moi, ici?*…later today…*aujourd'hui?*…in a few hours?"

The boatman was silent, staring hard at the bills, better than a year's pay sitting in his palm.

Jake was positive he paid way more than enough, but the man was just standing there, his hand still outstretched with the money in it, looking stricken, not saying a word, so he passed over the rest of the wad, having plenty of U.S. dollars in reserve in his belt and more in the suitcase (wherever that might be).

He hurried down the fenceline and pulled himself underneath it like a dog escaping a kennel, then scrambled into waist-high grass and over a berm. When he was out of sight of the guards he knelt and checked the GPS: 100 yards from the spot. Might as well follow it all the way home.

He continued through the grass toward a clearing. The angles on the readout became more pronounced as the distance shortened, and finally the GPS showed he was at Daniel's coordinates.

It was a concrete pad. A large helicopter sat in the dirt nearby. Blocky and decrepit, its markings crudely painted over, it looked ex-government issue, like a mail truck bought at auction, probably a Soviet castoff from a long time back.

A thick red circle was painted around the periphery of the pad. He stood right in the middle, where the bull's-eye would go.

49

Horace peeled off more CFA and handed them to the driver. It was like feeding a payphone. The driver took the bills and stuffed them in his pocket without taking his eyes off the road. He had brightened a bit once Jake left the car, but still stopped three more times, and refused to carry on, before the two men settled into a cadence of passed-over bills that kept his foot on the gas.

Horace twisted to the backseat and rummaged through Jake's suitcase. He came up with a too-small blazer and put it on with some difficulty, smacking the driver in the process and causing them to momentarily swerve off the track.

You have to show a little flash when dealing with these people. Nobody wants to do business with a loser.

When they finally rattled down the track to the village it was clear where to go. Two SUVs, black under thick coatings of dust, were parked in the shade of the largest hut. Their oval plates ended with "RG", marking them as Guinean. A pair of brawny men flanked the entrance to the hut, looking out of place in the austere village. Horace passed over more bills and opened the car door.

The men patted him down before allowing him inside. Less than 30 minutes later he was back in the sunlight, lugging a leather bowl the size of a basketball, its curved lid sealed with red wax. He was sweating heavily, although it had been cool in the hut. He climbed into the backseat and clutched the heavy bowl on his lap.

The driver turned the car around. They bumped back down the track toward the main road. One of the SUVs followed in the distance, a sheepdog providing loose cover for a lamb.

50

To the east of the helipad, the island tapered into the water behind a high fence crowned with barbed wire. To the
west, a wide sandy path led through the undergrowth. What
appeared from the pirogue to be low brush was in fact the
thatched roofs of mud-brick buildings tucked in behind the
berm.

Jake stepped softly down the alleyway, keeping to the
edge. He paused at a hut with a missing door. Mounds of elec-
tronic gear covered the floor and antennae sprouted from the
rooftop like metallic weeds.

Further down was an elaborate play area for children, a
miniature village with dozens of huts and a schoolhouse, even
a square with a tiny pump in the center. Part of a day-care facil-
ity maybe, but no children anywhere.

The track opened out and a large Quonset hut appeared, a
string of silent air conditioners jutting from its side wall. There
were several more huts, long and low, then a half-dozen tradi-
tionally styled mud buildings, with patched metal roofs and
earth-stain creeping up their whitewashed sides like reddish
mold. A cluster of tents with wooden porches sat apart on a
slight rise. The whole place looked more like a deserted POW
camp than someplace people lived.

The door to the nearest building suddenly opened and a
white man in his early twenties emerged. Jake backed into the
scrub. The man blinked in the equatorial light, and headed for

the tents, a backpack tugging at his shoulders. He could have been dropped unnoticed onto any college campus in America.

Jake approached the door and stood beside it, listening. He pressed with two fingers and it opened. Inside, a dozen people were scattered at desks and drafting tables, or talking in small groups. It looked like a grade school science fair with handmade posters on the walls and cardboard cutouts of animals lined up on metal shelves. A tattered banner sagged across the back wall admonishing everyone to MAKE THE WORLD A BIGGER PLACE. A man at a card table near the door dipped a strip of newspaper into a floury paste and laid it on the wing of an airplane taking shape in front of him.

If I wanted this, I could have gone to kindergarten.

The man with the airplane looked up at Jake. He nudged the woman next to him. The process rippled through the room, the noise steadily decreasing, as though someone were slowly turning down the volume. Finally they were all staring at him, silent as stone, and he remembered he was caked with mud from his crawl under the fence.

They were young and evenly split between men and women. Was this some sort of Peace Corps center? If these people were dangerous, they were dangerous nerds.

"Good afternoon, sir," came the eager voice of a plain-faced woman from the far side of the room. She strode toward him, an angry rash gripping her neck. Her frizzy black hair bounced up and down her forehead, giving her a poodlelike air. "Francie Pagano, head of Social Section." When Jake didn't reciprocate, she soldiered on: "Would you like a briefing, sir?"

He scrutinized the beaming faces. They were like children with clean rooms, waiting for a parental inspection. "I don't see why not."

They scurried into a semicircle around the largest whiteboard. Two young men competed to bring Jake the best chair. "Will the Deputy Director be joining us?" Francie asked.

"Well, I'm not sure. Not this minute, no. Maybe in a while. Why don't you just give me the once-over and we can do something more elaborate with the Deputy Director later."

"Do you want me to start at the beginning?"

"Assume I've just stumbled in from the bush and don't know a thing." He was anxious to get on with it before something bad happened.

The room was quiet. Eyes flitted between Jake and the woman: nobody wanted to miss anything. Francie motioned to the back of the room and the lights went out. A man bent over a laptop computer. Seconds later a line-drawing of a naked man with indistinct genitalia appeared on the whiteboard. Francie took a sip of water from her plastic bottle.

"When isolated on small islands, without predators, large mammals tend to evolve toward smaller sizes. They don't have to fight off attackers, so why not? That way they can get by with fewer resources. Witness the Stegadon." A picture of an elephant the size of a cow flashed onto the wall next to the naked man. "This type of island reduction has also been seen in deer and hippos." Miniature versions of those animals joined the line-up.

"Earth is an island. We are large mammals. We have no predators."

Great. The Discovery Channel. Jake's foot started tapping on its own.

"We should be getting smaller. But we're not. We're breaking the Island Rule. Humans have been getting bigger instead, and doing it at an astonishing rate."

The stunted animals disappeared and were replaced by two humans, one wearing bell bottoms and a tie-dyed shirt; the other taller and more rotund, in jeans and a Boden vest.

"Since 1968, the height of the average American male increased two inches, to 5'11". During that same period his average weight ballooned over 25 pounds to 191. And the rate of increase is accelerating."

The next slide showed two women. "Similar increases have occurred in women: more than an inch and over 25 pounds, to 164." She turned slightly sidewise so Jake could see she was, at least in this area, way below average.

"The typical ten-year old is 11 pounds heavier now than in 1968. That's just a little kid, a fourth-grader. My great-grandfather was a six-footer and considered a very tall man. Now he would be pretty average. What will the norm be in a hundred years? Eight-foot, 500-pound men? Petite women looking like today's NFL tackles?" There was a smattering of polite laughter. Everyone looked at Jake for his reaction: they all had heard the line before.

"And where will our food come from as we get bigger? Until now technology and fertilizer have kept up in the United States, but we've reached the point of diminishing returns. Arable land is disappearing." She quickly clicked through a montage of depressing photos: wastelands, failed cornfields, salt pans. "Despite the tons of pesticides that are heaped on our best farmland, resistant forms of insects and disease are getting harder to beat back. Every day the water situation becomes more tenuous too: pollution; aquifers being sucked dry; dams silting up – before long they'll just be big waterfalls. And most of the rest of the world? Forget it. They're already going under."

"What is it you actually do here?" Jake said.

"Okay. Well then. The charter for Social Section is two-fold: plan for the future, of course, but also deal with the here-and-now. Identify the problems, devise solutions, get the data to Political Section and the Press Secretary." She looked at Jake, appearing to need some sort of reassurance, so he nodded.

"There are obviously some concerns. Getting subjects to cooperate for the beta testing has proven much more difficult than expected, despite, I understand, assurances from the highest levels of government, ours and theirs." She flashed Jake a quick look of gratitude. "But promises haven't been kept. The local people think we're doing something ungodly out here. There has been a bit of hysteria. I don't think that's overstating it. Rumblings about slavery too. And some sabotage. We don't go into town anymore."

So far the only thing on the island that seemed to have even a remote connection to Daniel was the papier-maché airplane on the card-table by the door.

Francie motioned for the next slide. The door in the back opened, momentarily washing out the picture of a big potato next to a much smaller one. Jake turned around. It was dark in the back but no mistaking the familiar voice.

"Jake! About time!"

"Hey Finis, how's it going?" Jake said, as if he had bumped into his old friend at a Seattle restaurant.

"Daniel said you were coming. I didn't hear a chopper. How did you get here?"

"I walked."

Finis had a laugh that made you think he was choking on a piece of meat. "Did he tell you I'm the lead bio-geneticist now? Since July?"

"I thought you were a nuclear physicist."

"I'm working on a unified theory."

"Where *is* Daniel?"

"He gets in today. That's why everything's so spiffed up."

Jake glanced around the room. It looked like someone was moving out and had given up on the deposit.

"The satellite phones are down – we're kind of incommunicado – so I can't say exactly what time. The flooding won't slow him down though; he comes by helicopter, even when the weather's good. What are you doing in Social Section?"

"Getting a briefing."

"Great. I'm glad I poked my head in. I've got a quick meeting at the cafeteria. It'll take ten minutes tops. If you want to tag along I can give you the grand tour when I'm done."

"Sure." Jake looked back at the assemblage. "Thank you, everyone. Ms. Pagano." They were crestfallen. "I'll be back." A few mustered weak smiles. "Keep up the good work."

"BOTTOM LINE, WHAT'S going on here?" Jake said as they walked across a dusty square populated with pecking chickens.

"Come on!"

"Is this about feeding the planet?"

"Hardly. We're fixing everything."

"Like what?"

"Name a problem."

"I'm really thirsty."

"Here's the cafeteria. See? Problem fixed."

They were at the mess tent, a large canvas structure with one side rolled up for ventilation and draped with mosquito netting. Dozens of metal folding tables filled the space inside and a cookshack was visible behind piles of branches out back. Women sat in the courtyard in ones and twos, stripping and cleaning leaves, tending to pots, hammering corn with club-shaped pestles. An oversized barbecue belched smoke through a stone chimney.

Finis pointed to a table in the corner. "There's the Deputy Director. He got in last night." A slump-shouldered man in full safari regalia sat silhouetted against the bright netting, his neck spilling over the top of his buttoned collar like a soufflé.

Snap Pease turned when he heard Finis. His booming voice reverberated through the tent: "Well pour me out and call me buttermilk! Don't just stand there holding your pecker, Jake. Pull up a chair and join your old cousin for some of this Kad-fen-oo. Looks like shit but tastes like shit 'n' peppers!"

51

"Good afternoon, Mr. Deputy Director," Jake said. "I trust you had a pleasant flight?"

"The flippin' helicopter looked like a tractor. One that'd been left out a lot. Emergency instructions all in Russian. Couldn't make out the letters let alone the words, and I really wanted to. Hey, how do you like our little place?"

"Well sir, it certainly beats those sticky summers in Langley."

Despite the grin pasted on his sweaty face, Snap looked a bit ambivalent about Jake's arrival, like his father had shown up to bail him out of the drunk tank. "By golly, Jake, we thought we'd lost you. Supposed to be on that plane and you're a pretty reliable guy. Dodged a bullet. Need to dedicate your life to God now. When did Daniel finally get you on board?"

"On board what?"

Finis excused himself and headed for a nearby table packed with young men and women in lab coats. Snap leaned forward in his seat. "Well just between you and me, pardner, Daniel's got his tit in a wringer on this one. You know anything about that?"

"I know nothing."

"Serious? You still in the dark?"

"Can't see a thing."

"I never understood why he wouldn't get you involved. Argued with him about it enough times, the small-minded little shithead." Snap took a single piece of long-grain rice off his plate and balanced it on the tip of his finger. "See what I got here?"

"A piece of rice?"

"Life. Nourishment. Civilization. One-twentieth of a calorie of carbohydrate, a little bit of protein, even a dab of fat."

Jake remembered the green rizière he spotted on his walk down the river. "So this is a rice project? You're developing some new kind of rice?"

"Hell no. Look, you weigh about 200, right? You're burning 15 calories a day to support each of those pounds." He held up his finger again and wagged it. "That's 55,000 of these little buggers."

"A day?"

"Each and every. One a second, if you don't count sleeping."

"I should just take them by IV."

"It's two uncooked pounds a day. A ten-pound sack every five. A ton of rice a year to maintain you and your wife and a couple of kids. If you had kids."

"A little teriyaki with that would be nice."

"Course it would, but you know, if you run it through an animal first you need almost ten times more to get the same calories. That meat's a real extravagance."

Jake once watched Snap put away an eight-pound sirloin, blood-rare, at the Steak Place, free to anyone who could get it all down and the baked potato and side dishes too.

"Imagine the human race is one big animal, Jake, each of us just a tiny part of it, like seven billion cells or whatever. Can you picture that?"

"I see an enormous beast."

"It's a Pandemos.

"Ah."

"About 500 million tons of biomass. It needs 16 *trillion* calories every day to stay alive. Hunt 'em, fish 'em, scrape 'em out of the ground. That's getting to be too much for this tired old planet. Like trying to graze a two-ton bull on a quarter-acre pasture."

Snap glanced at the little grain of cooked rice that was still sticking precariously to the tip of his finger, like he was noticing it for the first time, then picked it up between his teeth as gently as a lioness lifting her cub, and it was gone.

"And that Pandemos is getting bigger every day. We're multiplying like cane toads, getting taller and fatter and living 40% longer. We're gonna need double the food in 30 years, and we got people starving as it is. But if that biomass was a lot smaller, we might stand a chance."

Snap scraped his chair around until he was square with Jake and very close, their knees alternating.

"Now Jake, if you were to lose say 50 pounds, it'd take a lot less calories to support what was left of you. So instead of 800 pounds of rice a year, you'd need 600. Do you know where that extra rice goes?"

"Where?"

"Here. To one of these skinny pickaninnies running around in the dust. That's right, pardner, all you got to do is lose 50 pounds to keep one of these kids fed. Everyone in America can stand to lose that much on average. We're talking 15 million extra sacks of rice *every day*."

"So you're working on a diet program? Fat Americans creating surplus food for Africans—"

"Hell, if everyone just got the small fries instead of the big, that's gotta be billions of potatoes, don't it?"

"But you need to get the food to the starving people. Hunger over here has always been a logistics problem, not a food problem."

"Exactly. So why not cut out the middleman? Have the *starving children* lose the 50 pounds. That way, you see, you've created your food surplus right where you need it."

Snap's face was thrust out, earnest, inches away. It might be best to humor him, like Jake did with his father toward the end, when the conversations devolved into long monologues about getting fly-fishing tapes into the hands of the Chinese. "What kind of diet are you working on?"

"I'm not talking about a diet. What if I told you we could make it so we were, say, half as tall or even less?"

"You've got a people-shrinking machine. Neat."

"No, no. Not us. Children to be born in the future."

"I'd say that would be quite a trick."

"You ain't just a woofin', woof dog. And a person that's half as tall is about one-fourth the weight. Only needs one-fourth the calories. Did you see the chickens outside? Make the people around here half as tall and presto, you've got four times as many chickens running around."

"Huge eggs."

"Exactly! Exactly!" Snap popped out of his seat and jabbed at Jake with his spoon. "And it's not just about the food. The bigger we are the bigger our houses and cars and airplanes got to be, the more oil we need to heat us, haul us around, push us through the air. Have you heard of Hubbert's Peak?"

"Colorado?"

"It's the point where we've pretty much used up more oil than we got left, including the stuff we haven't found yet. Do you know when we're gonna hit that point?"

"Soon?"

"It's already way in the rear-view mirror. And we're gulping the stuff down like iced tea on a hot day. In a few decades it'll all be gone. But if we start downsizing pretty quick, it's like we push Hubbert's Peak back out in front of us again, like we've discovered an unbelievable new oil field."

"You're going to downbreed us? Like you do with your little cows?"

"We're not fruit flies, Jake."

"Of course not."

"We can't wait that long. We need a quick fix. Plus we can't shrink cars and houses a tiny bit every year – we've gotta do it in one big bang."

"Is there money in this?" Jake said, looking for the tie-in with Daniel.

"Supposed to be, but hell, probably not." Snap sat down, his exuberance beginning to ebb. "It'd be nice to get back what we put in though."

Finis returned to the table and handed Jake a liter of cloudy water. Snap excused himself, saying he had to see a man about a horse, and headed for the back door, threading his way through a cluster of people waiting patiently to meet him.

"I want to show you something across the square," Finis said. "It'll just take a minute and we can talk on the way. Did the Deputy Director fill you in?"

"He said you're going to shrink people so they eat less and get great mileage."

Finis held the door open. "Well, we're not shrinking anyone, of course. We're tinkering with the DNA just enough so mothers can give birth to children more appropriately sized to our current predicament. We call them Veehees. Perfectly proportioned miniatures."

"How do these Veejays–"

"Veehees. Engineering Section's been working on two sizes: VHS and Beta. The Veehees are half our height; the Betas one fourth. The Veehees would reduce caloric requirements by about 75%; the Betas by 94%. We're looking for the right balance: enough of a downsizing to rescue the world, but without shocking the infrastructure any more than necessary. We've pretty much settled on VHS for the first go-round, even though the Betas are technically superior."

"You're going to resize the human race?"

"We've got a very narrow window. Until a century ago we needed more people not fewer; and brawn was critical to survival. Making smaller people wouldn't have done any good anyway – they'd just be pushing smaller plows through smaller fields and getting smaller harvests. But we have a mechanical advantage now. A very small weapon can provide protection against the biggest predator. A miniature man can drive an enormous tractor. With hydraulics and electronics, a one-inch pilot can fly a 747 if you give him the right interface."

"You'd have to sit him on a huge stack of tiny phone books so he could see out the window."

"The plane would hold tens of thousands of people on more decks than a cruise ship, but the amount of fuel burned would be the same as right now. The world can support an almost infinite number of people if we get small enough. We can become viruses if we have to."

"How exactly is that possible?"

"We've been doing similar stuff for centuries, grafting hybrid grains, things like that. Now we're ready for humans. We harvest women's fertilized eggs and inject them with reengineered DNA, coded for the smaller size. About one-percent of the time the new DNA replaces the old DNA in the nucleus and gives us the genome we want."

"So you do a thousand eggs to get ten good ones?"

"More like five or six good ones. We test to see which ones took, then grow those cells in the lab and implant them into normal embryos. The babies that are born have some of the new genes and some of the altered ones. We separate out the babies whose sex cells have the reengineered small-person gene, and let them mate with each other when they reach reproductive age. After that our job is done. They carry on naturally, and their offspring are pure Veehee. Over the course of a few generations the world is repopulated at a new, better gauge."

They were almost to a large earthen building on the far side of the square. Finis fumbled with a bulky set of keys.

"So you're cloning people?"

"No, we're just making an adjustment in the DNA sequencing, like correcting for a genetic disease, and then letting people evolve naturally. We're not changing the words, just the size of the font."

"This is an odd place to be doing it."

Finis let them into the building. "It's the perfect place. They're starving here. Disease is picking them off at a pretty good clip too. Their genes will be wiped out anyway, so there's nothing to lose. Plus they've been selling each other as slaves forever and the women have a long tradition of doing what they're told. Daniel's landmen had no problem cutting deals with the government and some of the local big dogs to get research subjects." Finis snapped on the light and led Jake past rows of ceiling-high metal shelves crammed with document boxes. At the back of the room a blue plastic tarp, large enough to cover a boat, lay draped over an outsized table. "Give me a hand with this, will you?"

They gently pulled the dusty tarp away. Under it was an architect's model of a campus-like complex: brick dorms and steel and glass buildings in a neatly landscaped circle. In the middle of the ring, shadowed and dwarfed by the imposing bulk and glitter of the modern buildings that surrounded it, was a city of thatched mud huts laid out on irregular dirt streets, everything a uniform beige, like something from another century.

"Looks like Detroit," Jake said.

"The outer ring is the medical center, administration, staff housing, athletic facilities, Cineplex, research labs, restaurants – a complete city for the support staff. Everything is world-class." He pointed to a five-story burnished-brick building. "This is the birthing center. The Veehees will get superb medical care, pre-natal to adult. Don't want to lose any." His finger moved to a row of long, low buildings connected by breezeways. "The newborns go from the birthing center to here. Yearlings here. Two-year-olds here, and so forth. The children are raised together, like in a kibbutz. When they're old enough to take care of themselves they move into the main village in the middle here."

"How long do you keep them?"

"The first few thousand are experimental. They'll spend their entire lives here, so we can study them as they age. But once we get a few years under our belt, we'll go high-volume and start stocking children in their home villages – mainstreaming them – when they're about ten days old and over the critical infant mortality hump. They'll live normal lives in their traditional homes and we'll be totally hands-off. Won't even try to track who's mating with who, because, you know, how can you ever tell anyway?" A flicker of sorrow crossed his face, and then was gone.

"Where is this place?"

"You're standing right in the middle of it." He pointed to the corner of the bowling alley. "We're here."

"So none of it exists," Jake said, remembering the Ségou Hilton's swimming pool.

"We break ground as soon as the big funding gets buttoned down. I'm pretty sure that's what Daniel's visit is all about. We don't have to wait until everything's built though. We'll make babies during the construction phase, in the facilities we've already got."

"Where do the mothers come from? Who wants a walnut-sized baby?"

"Are you kidding? Who wants a big cell phone? The problem won't be finding people to do it, it'll be making them wait their turn. For parents, their burden is quartered. For the Veehees, they'll have a huge edge, a ticket to the future, better than a free college education. The small kids will push out the big. Definitely. Gresham's Law. And they'll be more like mangoes than walnuts when they're born."

"So you're turning the third world into the one-third world."

"After the bugs are worked out over here, and the economic advantages become obvious, we'll start to convert the U.S."

"You can barely work with stem cells there."

"True, it's tough. But if not the U.S., then other developed countries."

"They're going to let you shrink their citizens?"

"Have to. Whoever goes the furthest and the fastest with this thing will have a huge advantage over the rest. Their natural resources will quadruple. It'll be like they have computers and everyone else is counting on their fingers. Countries that miss the boat will drop to second-rate status, or worse. Believe me, if we can get traction somewhere, anywhere, competition and Darwin will take care of the rest. And regardless of what governments do, the multinationals are going to have a real appetite for Veehees."

"They only have to give them tiny little paychecks."

"The financial rewards are automatic. A buck buys a Veehee four times more food, car, house. It's like there's a huge tax on being big."

"I picture the little guys with these enormous cigarettes."

"Everything new will be sized to the Veehees and everything old will be converted: two-lane highways become 20;

there'll be gracious homes the size of storage sheds. Little cars, clothes, cans of baked beans. After a while being big will be like being left-handed: it'll be hard to find good stuff. It's not all about consuming either, it's just that if we have four times more of everything we can say goodbye to scarcity. And that means goodbye to crime. And war."

"People never have enough. They'll just reset the bar. An autoworker lives better than the richest king did a few centuries ago, but he's still not happy, even with buckets of chicken and two-ply toilet paper."

"That stuff's for Psychology Section."

Finis locked up and they headed back across the square. The smell of garbage wafted over on the slight breeze. "No more overflowing landfills. You'll be able to get a campsite at a national park whenever you want. Room at the beach on a hot day. And don't worry about global warming – reduced consumption will stop it dead. Pollution disappears. Fish come back. Rain forests are saved. Airport noise? Prison overcrowding? Rush-hour traffic? Name me one problem this doesn't solve."

"Mental illness."

"Inversely proportional to the amount of living space you have. Fixed."

"Religious nuts."

"Besides that."

"Old guys buying Harleys."

"Okay. If you don't want to be serious. Like Daniel always says: better to light one candle than curse the darkness. Besides, what's the alternative? Right now we're on a short trip to living on a garbage heap with nothing to eat or keep us warm."

"I thought we were moving to other planets when we finished with this one."

"Come on, Jake. That's just science fiction."

"I was looking at the Toyota hybrid."

"That's a joke. Like trying to stop a supertanker by whistling over the rail."

"Snap says there's not much time—"

"There isn't, but it won't take long to improve things. Six-footers die off; three-footers take their place. Once we start, the rate of population growth gets tempered immediately. Once we hit a 75% conversion rate for newborns, the human biomass begins a permanent downward spiral.

"The Pandemos?"

"The what?"

"Never mind."

"Converting even one big city in Bangladesh will have a noticeable impact."

"I don't think the Bangladeshis are eating that much of the food."

"It'll take a few generations to get up to a 100% conversion rate, and then another century until the last big person dies off. By that time we'll be living in Eden again."

"Not you and me. At least all the cemeteries will be bigger though."

"I'm not giving up. Change one gene in a worm and it lives six times longer. We're close to beating death, but it'll all be a waste if there's no place to sit."

"This is going to play hell with sports records."

They passed a tattered tent squeezed between two large buildings. "This is Civil Rights Section," Finis said. "The Veehees will have exactly the same rights as big people, no more, no less."

"Will they be able to marry big people?"

"Of course not. That would be an abomination."

They were almost back to the mess tent when the sound of the helicopter reached them. Moments later the chopper passed directly overhead on its way to the landing pad.

"There's Daniel. You can joke about it, Jake, but he's saving the planet."

"Our hero."

52

Moments after Finis ran off to meet the helicopter, Snap returned from the latrine and plopped down at the table. "Just thinking about this place gives me the trots."

"Is this for real?"

"Rough as a cob, isn't it? I figured it would be all glass and stainless steel and panels of blinking lights. A thousand people in matching uniforms. Daniel's really been blowing smoke up my ass."

"The thing about those James Bond deals, how do they keep the unions out?"

"Yeah. Where do the eggs come from every morning?"

"What are you the Deputy Director of anyway?"

"Hell, Jake, I don't know. That's Daniel's idea. Said it would be good for the troops."

"So these people think they work for the government?"

"The kids? I don't think they've actually been told that. Not in so many words. Guess they think they're in some kind of scientific Peace Corps or something."

"Have you been here before?"

"Nope. First time. Been trying for over a year though. Finally insisted. I needed to see it with my own eyes."

"Daniel always says there's no substitute for a close personal inspection."

"True, except he wouldn't let me come until I ponied up another five million. Like asking a man to take his shit before lunch."

"But you gave him the money."

"I gave him the money. The project was history if I didn't."

"Do you know anything about the two million I was taking to Liberia?"

"Nope. Not in on that."

"You have other money in this? Besides the five million?"

Snap bent over and lightly tapped his head on the table, then sat up again. "I get the big tour from your old buddy Finis this morning. Starts off good. Nice lab. Lots of people in gowns and masks and such. Then he takes me to the Data Center. The server banks look great but the thing is, they're made of cardboard. Just mock-ups, Finis says, placeholders until the real stuff arrives. Then we go to the animal labs. He shows me empty cages. 'This used to be the monkeys' he says, 'this used to be the cats.' Everything's pretty much got away, I guess. Then right at the end we go to a locked room. The big finale I figure. It's filled with cages, a tiny little rabbit inside each one. 'Miniaturized?' I say. 'Baby bunnies' he says."

Snap pushed the food around his plate. He was starting to sag. "I'm not getting screwed again. Daniel fixes this one on his own, or I'll make him fix it."

"How do you plan on doing that?"

"Like getting a horse into a trailer. You make everywhere else a worse place to be."

"He's not an easy guy to push around."

"I've got a big old atomic bomb ready and I'm a hog's hair away from letting it go. He makes this right or it's scorched earth. I swear I'll dress him out and hang him on my den wall."

There was a swell of approaching voices, and the mess tent doors suddenly flew open. Daniel strode in, his entourage strung out behind him. He worked the cafeteria like a politician, taking a while to get to Jake's table. "Hi Snap," he said, when he finally arrived.

Snap looked like he was having a bad dream. "Daniel, Jake's skeptical about the financial viability of our project. Give him the figures."

Daniel looked at Jake for the first time, his eyes cold. "Jake's a cynic. It doesn't always have to be about the money. We're changing the world here."

"He's joking, Jake. Tell him about the money, Daniel."

Daniel turned to the group gathered around the table and held up both hands. "Folks? Can you give us a few minutes? We just need a few minutes here." Everyone but Finis shuffled away, leaving the four men alone.

"We're in the process of performing the greatest financial feat in history." Daniel spoke quickly, in a flat voice, like he was reciting his catechism. "We're creating a new industry, one that will dwarf all others, an enormous medical effort, decades of in vitro fertilizations, tens of billions of conceptions, country-by-country franchises and no competition. But the patents and royalties and conversions are just the tip of the iceberg."

Snap was beginning to perk up, like a recently watered plant.

"We're not just leading a bio-technological revolution, we're going to remake the whole physical world – dismantle, retool and rebuild a thousand years of infrastructure; convert it to accommodate a new human race. FDR built a few dams and lodges to restart the American economy. We're talking about transforming every road, bridge, building, vehicle and appliance in the world. The accumulation of wealth will be like nothing we've ever seen before. Snap will be Ford, Rockefeller, Gates and the Sultan of Brunei rolled into one. Okay, that's it," he said, slamming the book shut at the best part. "I need to talk to Jake. Finis, make sure Snap gets fed. Jake, you come with me."

Daniel marched to the door. Jake shrugged at Snap and Finis, then followed him out.

THREE MEN FELL in behind them like bodyguards. This would be the local muscle – Thug Section – no resemblance whatsoever to the benign student-scientists Jake first encountered. A thick gold lunette hung from the neck of the tallest of the three: he exuded hostility from every pore and was clearly the goon-in-charge.

Daniel led them down a beaten dirt track on the backside of the compound and came to a stop at a small earthen house with a corrugated metal roof. The windows were shuttered and secured from the outside with thick planks.

A half-dozen men and adolescent boys loitered nearby, casually displaying their automatic weapons. Two dirty vans sat in the shade across from the building. They must have been there since before the rains.

One of the men pulled open the hut door. Daniel said something to him in French, too fast and low to pick up, and motioned Jake inside. It felt like being taken behind the woodshed for a strapping.

A bare bulb hung from the ceiling by its cord and gave off a harsh light. The room contained a table, two chairs made of branches, a single bed with a rubber sleeping pad, and a wooden desk. The hearth was in the center of the floor, beneath a small hole in the roof for the smoke. A couple of pots hung on the wall like artwork. It was typical middle-class rural Mali – a teacher's house maybe – the tea service on the table and some books on the desk the only hints of indulgence.

The door was pushed shut from outside and Daniel wheeled on Jake, seething, standing too close. "I think you have something that belongs to me."

He wasn't sure if Daniel was talking about the $2 million he got from Maddie in New York, the $82 million he swept from the partnership accounts in Victoria, or the *Nadalia*, nestled under 170 fathoms of water at the bottom of Haro Strait.

"How could you steal from me?" Daniel went on, spittle flying, "after everything I've done for you, you fucking bastard."

It was extremely unusual for Daniel to use bad language. It was best to go on the offensive. "Why did you blow up my plane?"

"That was *my* plane, asshole. Why would I blow it up?"

"I asked first. Are you a member of the Liberian Revolutionary Front?"

"You're the romantic, Jake, not me."

"How about insurance fraud then? You have a $90 million hull policy and the plane isn't worth anywhere near that."

"Don't be stupid. What did I do? Build a bomb in my basement?"

"I have complete confidence in your ability to acquire anything you want."

"Where does all that superiority come from, Jake? At least I have a reason for mine. Even if I didn't come from a goddamn pioneer family."

"It wasn't just coincidence I happened to be on that plane, you *put* me on it. You begged me to go—"

"I don't beg for anything."

"I'm your friend—"

"You're pathetic. Everything handed to you on a platter your whole life. Zero gravel in your gut. Play on your goddamn computer all day and call it a job. You spoiled over-privileged little piece of shit."

He may have underestimated the extent their relationship had deteriorated. "Don't sugar-coat it, Daniel."

Daniel walked to the table and poured tea into one of the cups. Jake had seen it before: he was willing himself back into control, slowing his heartbeat, forcing the flush from his face, practicing the biofeedback methods he learned at Arroyo Ranch. There was no tremor in his hand when he picked up the cup. When he began again, it was in the dispassionate voice of a businessman. "What would you guess that airplane is worth today?"

"I'd have to say very little, since it's at the bottom of the ocean."

"But for the crash."

"With Liberian maintenance and West African corrosion? $50 million. Tops."

"I think that's a little optimistic, considering what's been happening to the market. But assuming you're right, a $50 million asset. So the plane is over-insured by $40 million. It's *always* been over-insured, from day one. You negotiated that, remember? So why all of a sudden do I blow it up?"

"Lloyds was downsizing your hull policy. You had less than 30 days to cash out."

"That makes no sense." Daniel was caught by surprise, but barely missed a beat. "The insurers would just raise my rates for the next couple of years to recoup their losses. That's how they work. It's really just self-insurance."

"Nothing beats cash in your pants," Jake said, parroting one of Daniel's favorite mantras. "And Liberia has to pay your premiums regardless of how high they go, so who cares?"

"If I wanted the insurance money, I could have destroyed the plane on the ground in Liberia. Nobody gets hurt and it's not splashed all over the news forever." He motioned toward the door. "It would be easy to get someone to total it. Take about two minutes and cost less than a good pair of skis."

Jake stared at him. He did seem to have a point.

"So what exactly do you think is going on, Jake?"

"You could have gotten a courier to carry that money to Liberia, but you insisted I take it." And then, like from someone else's mouth: "Did you want my wife?" He didn't mean to say it, but there it was.

Daniel choked on his tea, a bit of it slopping down his chin. "Sheila? Oh right."

For the first time ever Jake felt a flash of hatred for his best friend; and for the first time in a very long time, a wave of tenderness for the woman he loved in high-school.

"I want *your* wife so I put you on *my* airplane with $2 million of *my* money and blow it up? That's your theory?"

"You're always looking for opportunities; need to be an even bigger elephant I guess. A chance comes along to make a quick $40 million from the insurers. You didn't get where you are by leaving a nickel sitting on the sidewalk. I'm sent off with two million bucks because it'll divert suspicion if a buddy and some of your cash go down with the plane. But you have Maddie switch briefcases. Can't stand the thought of all those hundred-dollar bills fluttering down in an Atlantic breeze. You sucker Haruna into carrying a bomb on board in a locked spare parts case – he thinks it's an HSI – and have him place it right over my head. Then you sit back and wait for your payday."

Daniel always had a talent for sifting through large amounts of data and focusing on the critical piece. "What do you mean," he said, "Maddie switched briefcases?"

53

They talked quietly for 30 minutes. Daniel poured them each another cup of tea. It seemed so normal: the two of them sitting at a table, dissecting a problem.

"Stay objective, Jake. It's not complicated. She stole my money then blew up the plane to cover her tracks."

"She wasn't capable of that."

"The Internet is an amazing thing."

"I mean, she would never do something like that."

"Oh that's right. You two have a *personal* relationship. Look, two million is chump change to me – I pay that in taxes every week – but in her world, that's a lot of dough. About 40 years of paychecks. A $2,000,000 score and she's set for life. And even if I decided to blow hundreds of people out of the sky for a little insurance money, I'm going to partner-up with Maddie for a lousy two million?"

Daniel was ringing true again, except for the part about paying taxes, which he studiously avoided. Partners? He suffered them only if they forked over big bucks and stayed quiet. As for Maddie, he would never have her as an accomplice; she was beneath him. Daniel's cost-benefit analysis would have told him that $2,000,000 was way too much to pay to divert a little suspicion from a plane crash anyway. And despite his fondness for money, it was still a stretch to picture Daniel actually killing people for it.

"Okay, so you thought your money went down with the plane."

"Of course I did."

"Why did you send me to Liberia with it?"

"I told you, to get the 747 lease renewed."

"But that was already signed — more than a week before you asked me to go."

It was a well-landed left hook, coming out of nowhere. Daniel was caught by surprise again, and this time took a split-second longer to shake it off. "It was for this," he said, waving his arm. "To keep it going."

Jake made a show of examining the mud hut.

"We're getting close to a breakthrough, to actually producing a few of Snap's midgets. But we need to get over a hump."

"Why make up a story about a 747 lease?"

Daniel hesitated, as if trying to decide whether the truth might be an option. "Snap wanted to keep you in the dark. Everything was super-double top secret for him. Need-to-know only."

Strike three. Jake could remember being astounded when someone lied right to his face, but that was a long time ago. "The people here seem to think they're working for the government."

"They think what they think. I can't help that."

"Is this thing for real?"

"Honest?"

"Yes."

"No."

"It's not for real?"

"It may be technically sound, but it's still politically impractical."

"Why put all this together if you're not going to carry through?"

"Self-indulgence. Not mine, Snap's. It's his baby, he's obsessed. Wants to 'discover' fifty times more oil than there's ever been in Texas. Make his ancestors proud. I was happy to give it a try, see if anything came of it, but I don't have any illusions."

"Snap doesn't think there's much to show for his investment."

"Everyone's an expert. There's lots of hidden costs. A big burn rate."

"He was disappointed the computers were made of cardboard."

"I'm disappointed I don't have a foot-long dick. So what?"

"I think he wants his money back."

"Snap's going to have to take his lumps, just like always."

Daniel took a slow draw on his tea. Jake waited, knowing what was next.

"Some money is missing."

"The two million?"

"The 82 million."

"Is that chump change?"

"No it's not. It was transferred out of 22 of my limited partnerships by mistake. I need it back."

"Was it transferred by someone who's not on the signature card? Because that would make it the bank's problem, not yours."

"Don't mess with me, Jake. I need it back. Right away. Return it and all is forgiven. We start over. It never happened."

"And if you don't get it back? Are you in trouble with your partners?"

"Look, I don't give a damn about those partnerships or partners. It's all about Zakian Global now. That's where the big exposure is."

"What do the 22 partnerships have to do with the hedge fund?"

"I need to move some money in as quickly as possible. I'm being hammered by the redemption rate. It's out of control. A run on the bank."

"Tough break."

"Not at all. It's a good thing. A godsend, really."

Daniel didn't like to be bested by anything. If you told him he had terminal cancer he'd say he was beating dementia. "How exactly is a run on the bank a godsend?"

"If I can cover the redemptions until the panic recedes, I'll seem stronger than ever when I come out the other end."

"So you were going to loot the partnerships to keep the hedge fund afloat?"

"Borrow."

"And repay?"

"Sure. Of course."

"But if you don't get the 82 million the fund craters."

"That's why I need your help."

Daniel is one of those self-entitled people who thinks a chance to help him out is a powerful motivator for others. "Why was I on the signature cards?"

"I trust you. I need to delegate more. What difference does it make?"

"Ah. I see. The money in those partnerships doesn't belong to you. Your limited partners won't let you use it, they think they're building beachfront condos and making artificial assholes, not investing in your hedge fund."

Daniel blew across his now-cool tea and nodded.

"You can't just come right out and steal the money so you decide to have me do it for you. I'm given authority over the accounts but nobody tells me about it. You transfer the funds out, they disappear into the ether, then magically reappear in Zakian Global. Incriminating files are left in my office. Everyone thinks I took the money. The banks don't care, the paperwork's in order, my signature's on file. The only people bent out of shape are your limited partners. They're told a crooked lawyer made off with the money, the matter's been turned over to the authorities, don't hold your breath for a recovery."

Daniel sat there looking smug. He was proud of himself.

"You've been diverting Snap's money into the hedge fund too, but you've got to keep showing him progress down here or he'll stop pouring in the cash. Everything's on the verge of imploding."

Daniel stirred his tea, even though he hadn't put anything in it.

"The insurance payoff on the plane is just icing on the cake."

"Will you forget about the damn plane? You think I'd kill a lot of people for a few bucks? I'm not a tobacco executive. And you brought some of the troubles on yourself, by the way."

He didn't think so, except possibly in some general karmic way. And something didn't quite add up: a piece of the jigsaw puzzle was being forced into a place it didn't belong. Carly should be here. She would figure it out.

"I'm a big loose end aren't I? I could scream I've been framed and someone might listen. That's why the plane couldn't be destroyed on the ground. I needed to be on it."

Daniel was silent for a moment, then began slowly. "I see things a little differently. Your life was coming down around your ears. Wife troubles at home. Unreliable and unproductive at work. You were about to lose Daniel Zakian as a client, which would destroy your firm and wipe you out. You've been talking for years about chucking it all and running away to Barbados with Maddie."

It was Jake's turn to be surprised, and unlike Daniel, he didn't hide it well.

"Your gullible client entrusts you with $2,000,000 that needs to be delivered to Africa and all of a sudden you see a way out. You decide to keep the money for yourself. You pick it up and sign the receipt. Carry the cash on the plane and sneak off minutes before takeoff. You go into hiding and decide to transfer another 82 million to yourself out of accounts where you're a trusted fiduciary. The plane crashes. Perfect. Maybe you did it, maybe you didn't. Either way, you have 84 million dollars and the trail of retribution for your wrongdoing ends with the crash. No reason to chase a dead man."

"So you tell me at ten in the morning to go to New York and I pack my bag and whip up a bomb and head for the airport?"

"I told your special friend Maddie to get the money ready more than a week before you left for New York. You had plenty of time."

"Snap was in the office when you told me to go to New York."

"He was gone before we started talking about the trip, and who says he'll even make it out of here? Mali can be dangerous."

"Nobody needs to get hurt," Jake said, taken aback. "This is just money we're talking about."

"Jake, the important thing for you at this point is to keep your head down, stay hidden, and that works for me too. And the good news is I'm here to give you the money to do it."

"I don't need your money. I'm rich."

"That's not your money."

"It's not yours either."

"It's more mine than yours."

"We're operating a little outside the system here, don't you think?"

"Jake, I want you to have enough to live out the rest of your life in seedy splendor, safe from any legal entanglements.

We can be partners on this. Partners in setting up a private witness-protection program for you. Look, maybe you didn't volunteer for this and maybe some things broke the wrong way, but you're the guy who's going to take the fall one way or another. The only question is how hard you hit the ground. And I'm just coming in and saying, hey, I'm willing to help out. I'm willing to fund a new life for you. Someplace over here would be best; you can be a bwana on very little."

"It's like you stick up a gas station while I'm sitting in the car like a sap. You get all the money and want me to do your time too. I'm not your sidekick. My life is just as important as yours. I lettered in three sports."

"Like I said, we're partners. And friends. For a long time. And you have more to lose than I do."

"It would be cheaper for you, and safer really, if I were dead. Even Africa will be a sizable long-term expense. And there's always the chance I'll pop up someday."

"As long as you don't get stupid the money keeps coming. Every month. Like clockwork. I promise. Money is the key here. It can buy you a decent life. And if you pop up anyway? I guarantee that would be a huge mistake."

Daniel opened a leather envelope, carefully extracted a single sheet of paper, and laid it on the table in front of Jake.

"What's this?"

"A power-of-attorney. It gives John Moritz power over your bank accounts."

"Who's John Moritz?"

"Nobody. A lackey. You sign it, I get my money back. Everything else sorts itself out."

Jake stared at the paper but wasn't reading it. He was listening to Carly's voice in his head, telling him the piece that didn't fit. Daniel had no way of knowing he would miss his flight. And nothing marks time more dramatically than a plane crash. Daniel didn't try to transfer the money out of the partnership accounts until Monday morning, more than two days after the plane went down.

"You expected me to make it to Liberia in one piece."

"You're retarded, Jake. That's what I've been telling you for almost an hour."

"Bello was going to force me to transfer the money out of the accounts from Liberia. So when the plane crashed you were screwed."

"I was."

"You couldn't make the transfers with me dead."

"I could make them. I had the passwords and codes—"

"But it wouldn't look good. Even a half-assed investigation would have problems with a dead man initiating wire transfers. You must have been pretty upset when you thought I'd gone down with the plane."

"Devastated. I couldn't believe it. Then you surfaced in Seattle and did a beautiful thing. You *did* transfer the money. I couldn't have planned it better. It was perfect."

"Except you don't have the money."

"Not yet."

"I'm thinking I might keep it."

"Jake, I'm not negotiating. You're on your own in the middle of Africa. I've got unlimited resources here. You do what I tell you. You take what I give you. You just need to get the money back to me. Today. Sign the power-of-attorney and tell me what bank you deposited it in."

"If I don't sign?"

"And I need to know where my boat is."

"I'm thinking of not signing."

"You'll sign. Those aren't nice people standing around out there. Some of them like to cause suffering, even when it serves no purpose. You're not a strong man. There are worse things than dying and one of them is not signing."

It was best to stall. Snap's atomic bomb hadn't been dropped yet. That should scramble things up. "I don't know the account information. It's in my briefcase. In Kona."

"Don't need it. This is a blanket power. It'll work for any account you have. I just need your signature and the name of the bank."

"I have to think about it."

A vein on Daniel's forehead began to pulse. Jake counted the beats for a while, wondering if it were literally possible to pop a vessel.

Daniel stood up. "I have to see Snap about something. I'll be back in ten minutes. The power-of-attorney needs to be signed by then. If you don't care about yourself, think about your fat friend."

Daniel turned and rapped on the door. After it closed behind him and the plank slid into place, Jake reached for the teapot. His hand shook so hard the lid came off and rolled across the table and shattered on the floor.

54

The promised ten-minute wait stretched into hours, and darkness now showed through the cracks in the shutters. Only the soft murmur of the guards and their occasional laughter disturbed the quiet. A car may have started up but it was hard to figure where it could go. Jake poked around the room again: the mud walls were still a foot thick and hard as cement; the packed-dirt floor still impenetrable; the heavy shutters and door still well-anchored in their frames. Nothing in the sparsely furnished room held much promise as a tool. For all its primitiveness, the little hut made a pretty good jail cell.

No news was good news though. Daniel probably didn't expect an onslaught from Snap: bombs away and screw the fallout.

He read the power-of-attorney again, the words now so familiar he could recite them from memory. The one-pager gave Daniel's guy unlimited authority over any account in Jake's name. Once signed it was irrevocable. Banks saw these things every day; they could definitely be used to empty an account.

The plank scraped outside. Seconds later the door was wrenched open. Snap filled the frame. Jake felt a moment of elation, like a child waking to the smiling faces of his parents, before Snap came hurtling across the room, his body moving unnaturally, arms flailing, and landed on the dirt floor like a sack of feed. Three men stood in the doorway, each of them much smaller than Snap but all muscle. The door slammed shut and the plank scraped back into place.

Snap struggled to his feet. "Whoo! It's getting a little western out there." He looked scuffed up, like a baseball.

Jake helped pull him upright. "What happened to the atomic bomb?"

"I dropped it. Right on his little pinhead."

"And?"

"Pretty much bounced off. He laughed, actually."

"What kind of a bomb was it exactly?"

"I told him I was going to sue his ass. And I wasn't bluffing."

"That was the atomic bomb? Scorched earth? Hang him on your den wall? A *lawsuit*? Daniel gets sued twice a week. He likes it, I think. My whole firm lives quite comfortably off him getting sued."

Snap slumped into one of the hard chairs. "What did you think I was going to do, Jake? Garrote him behind the shitter with my guitar string? You've got to stop watching the TV."

DANIEL ARRIVED AT the hut a few minutes later and carefully closed the door behind him. He looked corpselike in the light from the bare bulb, thinner than usual, yellowed, his cheeks sunken and shadowed.

"Sorry for the rough stuff, Snap. I hate being extorted is all."

"No problem Daniel, I'm sure I had it coming."

"Why don't you go sit on the bed and shut up so I can finish things with Jake and we can all get out of here?" He turned to Jake. "I've been thinking this through. It's time for some plain talk and honesty, okay? I'll be honest. You be honest."

"Okay."

"I've always been a good friend. I basically built your firm for you. I paid you good money, more than I needed to. I gave you bonuses and took you on vacations. I was very generous."

"Sometimes I had to pinch myself to make sure I wasn't dreaming."

"There's been some poor decisions made, some by me, some by you. And some bad luck too. What do you say we both get smart and cut our losses?"

"Getting smart sounds great, Daniel."

"I don't know exactly how everything's going to play out. I'm sure there'll be surprises, but if we stick together we can work through this thing. Forget what I said about you living over here. We'll go back to Seattle together and fix this together, like we've always done."

"Being able to go home would be nice."

"We'll both come out good. More than good. We'll make sure things are a lot better for you than before." He handed Jake a pen.

"What about the investors in the 22 partnerships?"

"I'll deal with them. I'm not going to tell you I've got all the answers right now. But I do know the hedge fund has to weather this storm, and for that to happen I need the money back from the 22 partnerships, and to get the money back I need the power-of-attorney. If Zakian Global survives we'll have resources, options, a flood of cash. We can pay back the partnerships, if not immediately then at least soon. But if the fund craters we're both dead meat."

Jake looked at the pen, then into Daniel's eyes, sizing him up like a witness on the stand. They had known each other for a lifetime, been through some stuff together. "Doesn't it need to be notarized?"

"Ruth at the Administration Building can do that before we leave."

"So I'm going to come out okay on this?"

"You have my word."

"For sure?"

"If you get screwed, I get screwed. The Gulfstream's at the Bamako airport. We'll take the helicopter there and be in New York before the sun comes up."

"Snap too?"

"Snap too."

Jake leaned both hands on the table and stared hard at the power-of-attorney.

"I kind of need you on this one buddy," Daniel said.

Jake gave an audible sigh, bent over and signed his name.

"What's the bank?" Daniel said, picking up the sheet and licking his lips.

"Klöden. In Luxembourg. Off Boulevard Royal."

"Sure. We used them on the Varig engine deal." Real golfers remember every stroke, sailors every windshift. Daniel remembered the details of every transaction. "I'm going to run up to the office and get this notarized and faxed off to the bank. I'll grab you guys in about ten minutes, on my way to the chopper.

Jake stepped toward the door. "I'll come with you."

"Better stay put. It's pouring out there." Daniel quickly closed the door behind him. The plank scraped into place. Jake and Snap looked at each other.

"He really wants to make sure we don't get wet," Jake said.

"I thought all the communications were down," Snap replied.

THEY WERE BOTH pacing in the small room, trying not to run into each other. "I appreciate you trying to help me out," Snap said, "signing that paper and all."

"No big deal. How much have you put into this Mali thing anyway? If you don't mind me asking."

"A lot."

"Ten million?"

"A big lot."

"Fifty?"

Snap was silent.

"A hundred?"

"I wish."

"Well, I'm guessing he's siphoned most of it to his hedge fund." Jake's words were drowned out by the helicopter passing directly overhead, its rotors beating the rain down on the hut's metal roof. Daniel probably selected the flight path himself.

Snap eased into one of the wooden chairs. "He was out of here faster than green corn through the new French maid."

THEY WORKED ON the back window for almost an hour, trying to pry the shutter loose without making any noise. "If we wanted this thing to stay put it'd be popping right off," Snap said, leaning against the wall.

"If you want it to come loose, it sticks. If you want it to stick, it comes loose. Everyone knows that."

"I want these shutters solid as a cheesemaker's turd."

"You can't fool the gods, Snap."

"If you want to buy something, it's priceless. If you want to sell the same damn thing, it's worthless as tits on a boar."

"If you want rain, go on a picnic."

"If you want to get called on, get a boner."

The two men sat down side-by-side on the narrow bed.

"I can't believe he coyoted on us like that, Jake. I always figured you were his chum."

"Like bait?"

"Like a pal."

"That's what I figured too. I don't think he plans on us leaving."

"Shit."

Jake stared at the window. "If we could just get that damn shutter open we could slip across the river and go to Kona. I know a guy there with a car. If we got to it we could make it over the border to an airport."

"If we had ham we could have ham and eggs," said Snap. "If we had eggs."

55

Finis Foster had a dilemma.

He watched Daniel and Jake go down the path, and noticed that only Daniel returned. Later, crouched behind a refuse container, his eyes smarting from the smoking garbage pits, he saw three men frog-step the Deputy Director to the guarded hut and toss him inside, then slam the door and secure it with a plank.

He hurried to the Administration Building and barged into Daniel's office. Jake's working out details for the next round of funding, Daniel said, he's ironing out a few wrinkles with the Deputy Director.

He tried to tell Daniel that the Deputy Director was being treated roughly, but Daniel cut him off at the knees, told him to stay out of the financial side, reminded him that he had higher duties and allegiances, pointed to the government badge Finis fingered while they spoke.

When Finis persisted, Daniel asked how long he had worked on the project, not counting tomorrow.

In fact, he had been on the project for over three years now, the best years of his life. Daniel hired him when no one else would take the chance. He owed him for that. If he lost this job it would be a catastrophe, a double whammy after the fiasco at the Energy Labs.

He sat in the latrine stall under the rain-drummed roof and tried to think things through.

HIS FATHER HAD been bullheaded and persistent, dead-set from the start on having a dozen children, reveling in the fact the archbishop himself would come to baptize the twelfth. Finis was the eleventh and the baby of the family, named by his finally assertive mother.

She brought him home from the hospital to the new place on Stone Lake, her dream house, the one she waited a lifetime to have.

Things began to unravel on a quiet spring morning, his mother half-asleep on the garden chaise, Finis snuggled at her breast, the spicy-sweet smell of viburnum and quince in the air. A light easterly blew up the valley and brought with it the faintest murmur of the highway below. At first she didn't believe it, the sound of traffic intruding on her idyll. She couldn't stop the noise though, and each day it grew louder. Eventually she could hear it even when the highway was empty. She tried to fight it, conjuring up an imaginary brook beyond the border of their wooded lot, the sounds just the gurgle of water over mossy rocks, but it was no use. The depression set in hard.

She took her life in the middle of a normal day, the contour sheet she was trying to fold left crumpled on the floor, her baby asleep in the next room.

Finis always knew it was his fault.

He transferred to Jesuit High in the middle of his freshman year and met Jake the first day. They became instant friends, partners on the debate team before the end of the week, and then Daniel became his friend too. Shy and thin as a stick, Finis was always the smartest kid in the class. He barely had a life outside of school except for Jake and Daniel and their friends. In the summers at the cabin Jake taught him how to swim and sail and he showed Jake how to navigate, schooled him on astronomy and the stunning order of the heavens, the two of them sleeping outside on the cabin porch with alarm clocks in their sleeping bags so they wouldn't miss a meteor shower or the return of Jupiter.

When Jake showed up at their ten-year reunion wearing a tiny short-sleeved shirt with a pocket protector and pants pulled halfway to his chest, sporting two-tone horn rims held together with electrical tape and a 'Finis Foster' name tag, he laughed as hard as anyone.

He picked up his doctorate and went straight to the high-security job at the Federal Energy Labs in the desert outside Kennewick, where the Yakima and Columbia rivers meet, three hours to the east of Seattle by car. After an uneventful decade there he went on his first real date, lost his virginity, contracted genital warts and got married, all in the space of five days.

Fiona was gorgeous and worked as a filing clerk in Logistics. He barely knew her name but one day she walked into his office and asked him out. That night she bought him dinner at the Steak 'n' Suds and took him to a production of *The Fantasticks* at the Community Theater, then invited herself back to his place and insisted on having sex, laboring diligently over him for hours to make sure it worked out after a couple of initial misfires. Barely seven months later he was the proud father of an eight-pound premature baby boy.

He had been amazed and overwhelmed by Fiona, and staggered by the physical intimacy too. A lifetime of puppy love, infatuation, helpless passion and romance came to him all at once, in a burst, compressed, overpowering, suffocating, like a sack of cement sitting on his chest. And then the baby came and bowled him over a second time.

He spent months designing and crafting a pair of diamond earrings and presented them to Fiona in the hospital on the day the baby was born. She carped about the size of the stones from time-to-time, but never took them off, not even to sleep. Looking back, it was probably the only thing he ever did that truly pleased her.

Things between them went downhill almost from the start. Fiona's first-night craving for sex gave way to less than indifference, the handful of couplings over the next three years directly correlating to the offer on the new house in Brindle-Wood, a spa trip to the California desert, Fiona's solo cruise to Alaska, the new luxury car.

At work there was more than one conversation in the coffee room that ended abruptly when he walked in, certain he had heard Fiona's name. A co-worker once asked if she still had blisters on her knees. Six months of evening knitting classes produced not even a shoelace, and on the bus to work one morning he overheard a student from the community college talking about the married woman he bonked the night before in the backseat of her black Lexus LS, of which there were probably dozens in Kennewick, if not more.

One day he returned home early from a conference in San Mateo and found Fiona in the bedroom sandwiched between what appeared to be, by the clothes on the floor, a couple of golfers. He bumbled around, doing all the talking, the trio in bed blank-faced and mute (he later thought he might have apologized but couldn't be certain). He finally backed out of the room and walked to Denny's for a Lumberjack Slam, not knowing where else to go.

Fiona filed for divorce the next morning and forced him to move to the Fission Motel, claiming he was suffocating her. Once her initial anger subsided, she seemed to have a change-of-heart. There was no serious downside to being married to Finis: he let her do as she pleased; required minimal closet space; was the equivalent of a fair to middling annuity. She began to hint at reconciliation, the hints growing broader as the weeks went by, all of it seeming to go over the head of the smartest kid in the class.

Despite very specific ethical constraints, Fiona's lawyer partook in an active and intimate relationship with her that began in the middle of the initial client interview and continued until she was handed her final decree. Like a child with no boundaries, the lawyer pressed Finis with outrageous demands, amazing even himself with the extent of his overreaching. Finis also had a lawyer, but he seemed quite familiar with Fiona too, and offered only token resistance to her ultimatums; and so the divorce proceeded smoothly.

The one thing Finis refused to roll over on was visitation rights, the boy almost three years old and Finis fearful of losing him completely. Fiona refused to budge though, mean as a snake, and insisted on full custody with no visitation, intending to send the boy to his grandmother as soon as the support payments were settled.

Then Finis took another blow, learning in a late-night phone call that his elderly father had died in a tragic automobile accident, mistaking the Washington Street boat ramp for a surprisingly available parking spot.

After that he just seemed to give up.

The final property agreement (including a lifetime of spousal maintenance well in excess of his gross pay and no visitation rights whatsoever) was ready to be signed when Jake spoke to him at the funeral, learned the basics of the divorce proceedings and offered to help. Finis numbly insisted everything was under control.

Before Finis packed the U-Haul with his share of the lifetime accumulations of his parents, Jake had been to Kennewick and back on the chartered King Air. He met separately with the lawyers for both sides, left them spinning, then met with them again together, mediating a redraft of the settlement agreement to better reflect current practice, no need to bring the Bar Association into the matter after all.

Finis never told Jake he found out about the trip.

Finis took the probate documents to a consumer-loan franchise and borrowed $35,000 against his share of the inheritance. He brought the money straight to Wolfe Jewelers and purchased two exquisite loose diamonds, pear-cut, over two carats each.

Back in Kennewick, he asked Fiona's permission to dig through the attic for his jewelry-making tools, and when she refused he bought a new set, and some design books for inspiration, and threw himself wholeheartedly into his old hobby.

He made the settings himself, hunched over in his big suit and mask, looking like an alien in the little jewelry factory he assembled in the motel room. He poured his feelings into the earrings and they turned out beautifully, the settings elegant, simple, not distractive from the gems at all, the silvery finish of the alloy slightly roughened and unique, exuding an aura of mystery and risk, worthy of the two stunning diamonds he mounted in them. When the earrings were perfect he stared at them for a long time before carefully placing them in a custom metal box with red-satin backing.

On the day the final decree was entered he met Fiona on her way out of the courthouse, her attorney at her side. He gave the lawyer an unkind glance then offered Fiona the little box. "I know things haven't been good," he said. "These show what's in my heart."

She put the earrings on right there, thanked him like he was a waiter bringing the check, wanted to know the exact size, color and clarity of the stones. Before walking off with the smirking lawyer, she announced to Finis the little boy wasn't his, which of course the smartest kid in the class had known all along.

He also knew Fiona was really going to love those earrings and would wear them religiously and never take them off, just like the smaller ones they replaced. That made him happy, even though it was bad it did, and he was ashamed of his feelings.

Eight months later he was forced out of his job at the Energy Labs, partially because he was depressed – both his attendance and performance had gotten spotty – and partially because of the isotope audit, which somewhat implicated him in the disappearance of four ounces of pure enriched uranium, albeit only because he had access to the substance, and not due to any compelling direct evidence he actually took it. Highly radioactive, the malleable metal was of course dangerous to humans, especially in close proximity and over long periods of time, but the amount was too small to be of any real use to terrorists and the follow-up was less than comprehensive. The incident was soon forgotten, except in his personnel file.

He was going through a pretty bad patch, employed as a part-time hourly technical writer at a Seattle biotech company, when Daniel ran him down and offered salvation: a dream job on a government contract, his new employer a thinly-veiled arm of a covert service. His redemption was complete: from the outhouse to the penthouse in an instant. He spent eleven months of experimental design and logistics-planning stateside, then headed to Mali to oversee the grandest scientific project of all time.

Because of his problems at the Energy Labs he knew he would never be permitted to officially work for the federal government again, nor in academia for that matter, and a decent scientific job in the private sector would depend upon lax recruitment procedures and inadequate screening. But that would be nothing compared to being dropped from the team right now, right before the Superbowl, when it was in large part due to his efforts they made it this far.

THE CONSEQUENCES WERE dreadful and it didn't help to catalog them again. If he didn't stay clear of this thing with Jake he would lose his position, and everything would go downhill from there. He hadn't talked to Jake in over five years, hadn't seen him for longer than that, not since father's funeral. Why couldn't he have just stayed in Seattle at his fancy law firm and minded his own damn business?

Finis fingered the identification card that dangled around his neck. He had listened many times to Daniel's explanations about the trust placed in him, the sanctity of the program and the security of the United States. In the end, none of that really carried any weight at all, and even if he believed Daniel it would have made no difference.

Jake was his friend and Jake was in trouble, and the smartest kid in the class was going to do something about it.

56

They had dismembered the table in an effort to arm themselves. Jake was the first to hear the scraping sound. It came from the back of the room, soft but clearly distinct from the pelting rain. Someone was trying to open the shutter from the outside. Each man picked up a leg of the table. Jake went to the window and Snap guarded the door.

The noise at the window stopped. A moment later the shutters creaked open. It was Finis, caught in the glare of the room's bare bulb, drenched, his glasses beaded over with raindrops, threadlike hair plastered to his scalp, and Jake's first thought was how much he had aged.

"I have sandwiches," Finis said, holding a damp sack up to the window, "and money and a flashlight."

Jake positioned a chair beneath the window and struggled to push Snap through the slightly too-small opening. Finis pulled from the other side. The frame suddenly released Snap's hips and he popped loose like a champagne cork. His legs jackknifed behind him and toppled the chair. Jake followed him through the window with surprising agility, and landed on top of him.

THE YOUNGEST OF the guards pressed up against the front door, squeezing under the narrow eave, most of the water passing over him like a waterfall. The rest of the men were packed into the vans, smoking and staying dry, waiting for Bel-

lo to arrive and the fun to begin. He heard the racket and signaled to the others, then set down his rifle and lifted the heavy
plank from the door. Why are the prisoners warm and dry inside, he thought, while the soldiers are left to stand outside in
the rain?

JAKE WATCHED FINIS lurch down the track: he was
moving erratically, skirting the brush, silhouetted by a weak
glow from the center of the compound. The men from the
vans would be able to see him, but not too well, an oyster-
catcher with a broken wing, pulling the predators away from
the nest.

"Let's go." Jake led Snap through the scrub, staying off
the track and away from the buildings. By the time they
reached the helicopter pad Snap was gasping for air. They
stumbled over the berm and came to a stop at the fence. The
ground was very wet.

"This should be about where I landed."

"How can you possibly tell?" Snap said. The darkness
near the river was complete: they could have been blindfolded.

Jake switched on his flashlight and darted the beam along
the fenceline, looking for the gap he had crawled under. The
bottom of the fence was covered with water as far as the light
would carry. "We need to climb."

Snap struggled over the top and Jake followed right behind him, cutting his arm on the barbed wire. They ended up
in ankle-deep water and moved upstream to a dry spot, then
pressed their backs against the fence. Jake tried the flashlight
again.

At first he didn't recognize it – the gate where the two
lounging guards had leaned their weapons. The men were gone
now, and the gate was partially submerged. The river was coming up fast, like a sinister tide.

Jake snapped off the light. "This is pretty much the narrowest stretch we'll find."

A half-dozen flashlights appeared downriver, jerking through the raindrops and along the ground, moving up the fenceline toward them. A second group of lights, very close, came over a rise in the road and headed for the fence.

The distance to the other side was much farther now, but still swimmable, the current slight despite the increased volume of the river. Jake was thinking about crocodiles and parasites and whether he should take off his shoes when Snap broke the silence with an urgent whisper.

"How do we get across?"

"We swim."

"I can't."

"You have to."

"I don't know how."

"What?"

"I can't swim."

"You just need to float," Jake said sharply.

The flashlights closed in from both directions like pincers. Snap should bob like a cork, his fat riding him high in the water. If they both stayed calm he could pull the big man across.

"Look Jake, I just can't go into that water. I can't do it. You go ahead. I think I broke a rib. I might be having a heart attack. Just get going for chrissakes."

"It's easy. We wade part way and when it gets too deep you lie on your back and I pull you. We go slow, no problem. You don't want to be on this side, trust me." Daniel's claim of things way worse than death was nagging at him.

"No. Really. I can't."

They were only inches apart. Jake couldn't see him in the dark, but felt the hot bursts of Snap's breath on his face. "Come on."

"No."

A powerful flashlight beam caught them and moved away, then quickly returned and stayed. The pursuers began to shout. A dozen lights played wildly off the two men.

Suddenly the old ferryman was tugging at Jake's arm. "I am here for you," he said, in French or Bombara or some other language, and Jake understood him perfectly.

57

Wind swept down the river, muffling the shouts of the men on shore. By the time the pirogue slid onto the sandy bank, grinding along the bottom, Snap was stiff and couldn't swing his legs over the side. The boatman helped Jake roll him out, then refused to take any money for the ride.

"Kona?" Jake said.

The man pointed into the dark.

"*Merci.*"

Jake and Snap stumbled off, holding hands like improbable lovers. Waiting until dawn wasn't an option: they needed to put distance between themselves and the compound, extend the search radius. It was best to keep the river close on the right. If the sky cleared they could angle off and intersect the road, using the stars to keep them in a straight line. If it didn't clear, at least they wouldn't end up walking in circles. He wished he had the GPS.

They staggered along like drunks for almost an hour. The mosquitoes feasted on them: there would be no making friends with these bloodsuckers. Snap was having a hard time breathing.

"Let's rest a minute, then we'll take it a little slower," Jake said. "You're doing good."

"Hell I am."

A light flickered across the ground, startling them both, their senses deprived in the quiet blackness. They turned.

Headlights were approaching, still a ways off, but on their side of the river and closing fast.

"What now?" Snap said.

"They could miss us." Seconds later the lights caught them square on. The vehicle changed course slightly and accelerated.

"What's Plan B?"

Jake sized up the lights. "I don't think it's my guy from Kona." They shouldn't have left their table legs at the riverbank.

"We could split up. Make it harder for them."

"No."

"Shit, Jake, just get out of here. I'm dead meat anyway. Go get us some help." He yanked his arm away and started toward the lights, then looked back over his shoulder: "Please."

Unless he tackled him, Snap was gone.

Jake loped away toward the river, perpendicular to their old path, hoping for a slight rise in the ground to get behind. He glanced back. It definitely wasn't the Deux Cheveux. The lights were too high and far apart. Whatever it was, Snap was hailing it like a taxi.

Snap disappeared from the cone of light. There was the sound of a door opening and slamming shut again. The transmission whined and the vehicle lurched forward. It turned 90 degrees and picked up speed. Jake flattened himself in the dirt. The ground vibrated and the headlights caught him.

Then it was Snap bellowing into the night: "All is well. All is well."

58

It was an old flatbed truck with branches for side-rails. The ferryman's son-in-law wore a tattered shirt and khaki shorts, and couldn't have weighed more than a hundred pounds. His head barely protruded above the steering wheel. Jake squeezed in beside Snap, who was radiating heat like a potbelly stove.

"Kona," the driver said, eyes fully forward, as he turned the truck to the south.

"*Bon*," said Jake, warm relief flooding through his body.

They rode in silence to the boat landing in Kona. The truck jerked to a halt and the engine died, the vehicle without a serviceable clutch. The elfin driver refused Jake's money with a shake of his head.

They walked toward the center of town, avoiding the pools of light thrown off by kerosene lamps in the huts. The driver was still at the landing, trying to restart his truck, the battery completely gone, the sad clicking of the solenoid audible from a hundred yards away.

They retraced the route to Horace's bar, then continued down a narrow lane. Rats scurried behind a conical bread oven that squatted in the middle of the alleyway like a smoke-blackened termite hill. They stopped in front of a two-story building, the only place so far with electricity. Snap pressed into the shadows while Jake crossed the street for a closer look.

The haunting sound of an acoustic guitar floated into the night from the lobby bar. The raspy-voiced guitarist, singing in an unfamiliar language, put out a mesmerizing beat, lilting, with sensual riffs, then a blazing run, raw as dirt. It was John Lee Hooker and delta blues, but different, and transcended all of the day's ugliness and filth. Maybe it was the ascetic environment, life here reduced to its simplest terms and tempered in the blistering sun, or maybe it was just food for a starving man, but as he stood in the forlorn alley and listened, it seemed the finest music he ever heard.

Snap coughed pointedly, breaking the spell. Jake scanned the small bar. Bare bulbs hung from the ceiling and threw a garish light over the people scattered at a half-dozen wooden tables. Three old men in traditional garb sat in a corner, heads bent slightly forward, looking like a photo negative with their ebony faces and pure white hair. Across the table from them, bulging out of Jake's new blazer, his features softened by the room's blue haze of cigarette smoke, sat Horace J. Washington, holding court.

Jake crossed back to the shadows. Children were pestering Snap for *cadeaux*, their uncanny sonar at work on the starless night. Jake took the oldest boy aside and led him to the lobby window. He handed him a thousand-CFA note and the business card Horace gave him on the boat. "*Prenez a l'Americain*," he said, pointing to the table in the corner, the money already tucked away in the boy's ragged shorts.

HORACE EMERGED FROM the building and looked up and down the street. He called out softly, a slight waver in his voice: "Ronny?"

Snap looked at Jake, who shrugged and stepped into the light. "Over here."

"Sorry about the mix-up with the car."

"Is there someplace we can talk?"

Horace noticed Snap and recoiled.

"A friend," Jake said.

Horace pulled a bare skeleton key out of his pocket. "We can use my room." He pointed to a passageway that ran along the side of the hotel. "Take the back stairs. It's number six. I just have to finish something. I'll be up in a minute."

THEY MOVED TOWARD the hum of a generator, Snap angling his shoulders to fit in the narrow walkway. A rickety staircase climbed the back of the building. They took it gingerly, and Jake let them into the room. It looked like a storage locker, the furniture lost beneath the clutter. A shovel and two picks were propped against the wall and brown bottles of chemicals lined the bathroom windowsill like toxic shampoo and conditioner. Snap moved a water pump and hose and sat down on the narrow bed.

Jake's suitcarrier hung in an alcove. His passport and wallet were still inside the zippered pocket, and appeared to be unmolested. He dug deeper and held up two miniature bottles of gin and a packet of dates from the Air Maroc flight. "Cocktail party."

"HE COULD BE turning us in right now." Snap said, nursing his drink.

"We need help. There's only one real airport here, one main road, no trains east of Bamako. It won't be hard to block us in. Or find us. We stick out."

"Like pink boots at the Cattleman's Club."

The sound of footsteps, a lot of them, came down the hallway and stopped in front of the door. Someone knocked, then knocked again harder. Jake slid the door open a crack. It was Horace, with the three men from downstairs.

"What's this?" Jake said.

"They'll just be a minute."

The new arrivals crammed into the room. The old men eyed Snap and fidgeted. One finally produced a leather box and opened it on the table. Inside were dozens of small cloth packets secured with thread. Jake had seen them before in the markets: filled with an exact quantity of gold dust, they were used like currency.

Another man brought out a small two-pan scale, turned his palm upwards and balanced it from a string looped over the ball of his thumb. The third man opened a packet and poured gold dust onto one side of the scale, then placed a small weight on the other.

When everyone was satisfied with the result, Horace carefully counted out CFA and passed them over. The man with the box scooped the gold back into its little cloth jacket and handed it to Horace, who re-poured it onto a metal plate in the center of the table and began pounding it with a hammer. He had the jagged look of someone on amphetamines, and the room's bare bulb gave him a demonic glow.

"If I had a spectrometer, I could just put a little of this in, push a button and zappo, an instant print-out of what I had, the gold and whatever else, and the exact amounts. Or I could use that," he said, pointing to a muzzle furnace about the size of a shoe-box that sat unplugged in the corner. "It turns everything liquid. I've blown dozens of hotel fuses with it. Never could quite get the hang of it. Always afraid I'd evaporate the dust in a cloud of gold chloride. But it doesn't matter anyway. They have their own idea of what they have here. Printouts and graphs and assays won't change that a bit."

He continued to hammer the already-pulverized gold dust with a vengeance, then took a large bottle of Lugol's Iodine down from the windowsill. "After I gave up on the furnace, my brother Dwayne went to Church Drugs and bought up every bottle of this they had, 40 of them. Eight made it through customs. Whatever they have planned for the other 32, I hope it's not internal."

Snap eyed a big box of cornmeal on the shelf.

"It's for stripping oxygen from the lead oxide," Horace said.

Snap leaned back on the bed. Moments later his soft snoring filled the room. The faces of the gold sellers relaxed.

Horace poured his little pile of gold dust into an empty baby food jar; the blond infant on the half-peeled label looking alien in the roomful of dark men. He added two scoops of coffee and covered it with the iodine solution, then screwed on the top and began to shake the jar fiercely.

The three local men watched with half-lidded eyes, like horses asleep on their feet.

When the liquid in the jar turned from maroon to a clear urine-yellow, Horace funneled it through a coffee filter into a second jar, then added a drop of mercury and shook it again. He let the contents settle, then poured off the liquid and added nitric acid and more water and shook it again. "I can use bleach to recover the mercury and use it again and again," he said, as he poured it down the sink, then held the jar of brown sludge up to the light: "Gold."

It looked much less like gold than what he started with.

"I have no idea how much is here, but you've got to put on a show. I'll offer them 10% less than they're asking so they won't think I'm a total idiot, not that it matters."

Snap shifted on the bed and released some gas into the atmosphere.

One of the old men lined up the packets on the table. Horace counted out more CFA, probably from the Deux Cheveux money.

After the gold sellers shuffled out of the room, Horace and Jake sat at the table.

"I'm sorry I missed you. I went to run a quick errand and the driver refused to go back. I was going to head out there as soon as it got light."

"I need to get out of Mali. Quickly and quietly. I can pay if you can help."

"Where do you want to go?"

"Anywhere with an international airport."

"No problem. I know a way. Who are we trying to avoid?"

"It doesn't really matter."

"Doesn't matter. When do you want to go?"

"Now."

"We can go in the morning."

"You're coming?"

"Just to Mopti. I'll leave you there. And you don't have to pay. Just the expenses. But I could use a favor. I need some gold dropped off in Europe."

"Am I smuggling?"

"No. Yes. Not really. Anyway, that's not a problem here, trust me."

"Why don't you just put it on one of your gold flights?"

Horace sagged. "Yes. One of the gold flights. That would be easiest, wouldn't it?"

The room was quiet except for Snap's rhythmic snoring. "I'm fine with taking the gold out," Jake said after a few moments, wanting to get Horace back on track.

Horace slowly revived. "I was going to change everything. Help them get even with the land. Rip the gold right out of it. Make a fortune while I was at it. After I lost most of my gear in customs, I made some adjustments. Figured I'd just be a middleman for a while, like the Djati, do it long enough to get the pump primed. The equipment and sluices, radios and Land Rovers, that could all wait a bit."

"The Djati?"

"The 'men-with-weighing-scales.' Gold brokers. The competition. They work the villages, control the gold trade."

Horace shuffled the hammer and metal plate around the table.

"After the malaria passed, I sat in Bamako for weeks, burning through my money. I got proposals from every tout in town, they flocked to me like kids to tourists. Everyone was ready to drop tons of gold in my lap. At half the London price. I just needed to say the word."

"Why so cheap?"

"Nobody's got a subscription to the *Financial Times*, I guess. They operate in their own world down here. Finally I meet this fellow I like a lot, he's enthusiastic, ambitious. I test him out, send him to a village with a thousand dollars. He's back in my room the next day with the gold. Worth twice what I'd paid for it, after all the expenses. I try it a few more times. It works the same. 'The villages are just waiting for you', he says, 'waiting with baskets of gold'. I need a success. I give him most of my stake, in one big chunk. Over $90,000. He was supposed to be back in two days with twice that much in gold."

Horace seemed to be having another sinking spell, gravity tugging at his features.

"I saw him six weeks later, but only because he didn't see me first. At least it got me off my ass. I went out to the villages myself, hit more than a hundred in three months. I didn't have the money to buy any gold but I set up the framework, met with chiefs and elders and Imams and mayors and anyone else with a finger in the pie. I went to birth ceremonies, burials, prayer meetings, ate some challenging food. It was worse than being a real estate agent. I played the African-American card too, but to them I couldn't have been any more foreign – it was like I'd stepped off the moon.

"I explained how the Djati were robbing them, fixing the price at half what it should be, moving it up and down every day, 20, 30 percent, just to keep everyone off balance. The scales and weights are all rigged too. And if someone new shows up to compete with them, the Djati pay a little more for a while, pick up a few school fees and doctor bills, whatever, just long enough for the new guy to disappear, then the villagers start getting shafted again."

"Big airline behavior."

"In the end though, seven village leaders solemnly promised to sell me their gold, and damn the Djati, so I won. I just needed cash. So I headed back to Brooklyn to scrape up another stake."

Horace walked over to the bed and pulled a covered leather bowl, sealed with red wax, from beneath it. "This is gold. I've gathered it up, grain by grain, over the last six months. I've walked the soles off my shoes doing it, showered with buckets from hotel wells, spent three days in jail in Foutaka. I need to get it to my refiner in Germany right away."

"Why don't you just take it there?"

"The Djati. They don't like me in their pumpkin patch. They pulled strings, got my passport confiscated. They'd be happy to see me go though, as long as this stays behind." He shielded the leather bowl with his hands as if Jake might try to snatch it. "But if I go anywhere near an airport or a border this gold is gone, and maybe me with it."

"I'll get it to Germany for you."

"No, it's not dangerous, not at all," Horace said, and Jake didn't recall asking.

59

It was getting light. Horace carefully slit the red-wax seal and removed the lid. He emptied each of the cloth packets into the leather bowl and replaced the top, secured it with duct tape, and placed it in a green vinyl bowling-ball bag. He stood up.

"Time to go."

Jake and Snap followed him down the back stairs. They tramped through a maze of narrow passageways and emerged 100 yards from the hotel. The Deux Cheveux was in a dusty lane barely wide enough to open the doors. A half-hour later they hit the outskirts of Mopti and Horace broke the silence, arguing with the driver, then turned to Jake in the backseat. "Give him ten thousand CFA."

Jake counted the money and passed it over. "What's up?"

"Visitors are supposed to register at the police station. He was taking us there. I told him to go straight to the bus stop and keep the change."

A few minutes later the taxi dropped them at the transportation square. They were early, and Snap lobbied hard for breakfast. Horace led them down a side street to an almost-deserted restaurant and took the table closest to the back door.

"When I went to Brooklyn to raise money the second time," he said as they waited for their food, "everyone was tapped out. But my brother Dwayne found someone who knew a guy who could maybe help get me what I needed. On a short term basis. I ended up borrowing $130,000."

"Loan shark?" Snap asked.

"Interest is accruing."

The waiter returned with three glasses of warm hibiscus juice and food that bore little resemblance to what they ordered.

"I missed a deadline, then a few more. Things got bad. They threatened Dwayne. He was their collateral. I collected every ounce of gold I could. Sold the equipment – gave it away really – to come up with money for a little more." He tapped the bowling bag. "It's all in here now. But I'm out of time. They're going to hurt Dwayne if I don't get the money to them by Wednesday. Then they'll start on his family. There are two little girls."

"Hurt?" said Jake.

"They say they'll kill him."

"You're in even worse shape than me," Snap said through a mouthful of porridge.

Horace turned to Jake and measured out each word: "The Djati, they skinned me alive. But I have the gold now and once you get it to Germany everything will be okay. They are five and six. My nieces." His eyes were watering up.

Something seemed called for, so Jake patted his arm.

"I don't care about myself," Horace said. "I don't care if I get out of here alive, as long as you tell me those two little girls won't get hurt, or their daddy either."

"I'll take care of it, Horace."

"You absolutely cannot let me down."

"I won't."

"You go to Munich," he said, passing over a half sheet of soiled paper. "Here's the address for Rodenburg and my account number. Take the gold to them. Get a receipt. They'll assay and weigh the gold and post its value to the account."

Jake nodded toward the green bag clutched on Horace's lap. "How much is in there?"

"Should be right around $250,000, with what I added this morning."

"So it's more than enough."

"I hope it's enough, with the interest." He held out the big gold nugget he first showed Jake on the boat. "Add this to it when you get to Munich."

Jake slipped the nugget into his pocket.

"We better go," Horace said. "The bus could be here any time."

They walked to an empty stretch of curb and sat on frayed lawn chairs under a leafless flame tree. "The bus to Bobo-Dioulasso goes from here. Bobo's across the border, so it should be safer. You change buses there for Ouagadougou and can grab a flight straight to Europe if your timing's right."

A worn bus with no markings pulled up at the curb. Snap struggled to his feet.

"No, no. Not this one."

"No?"

"You're taking the express."

Snap sat down. They were in the open, exposed, in a park-like setting. Jake caught people staring at them. A few looked slightly familiar. From breakfast, maybe?

The bowling bag sat on Horace's lap. He caressed it with one hand, like a near-term pregnant woman. A plastic grocery bag was in his other hand. He reached in and pulled out two cloth-swaddled bundles the size of demi-baguettes, no weight to them at all, and handed them to Jake. "Can you take these too? They're little dolls for the girls. Made locally. I've been promising forever." He handed Jake a scrap of paper torn from his assay book. "Here's the address for my nieces. Wait until you're inside the U.S. then Fed Ex them. You don't have to declare them at Customs, they're not worth anything." Horace flinched as Jake stuffed the little packages into his suitcase. "They *are* fragile, though."

Another bus rolled in and Snap looked expectantly at Horace, who ignored him. The bus loaded up and pulled out while the meager shade beneath the tree continued to shrink.

Horace was on his feet before the third bus came to a complete stop. "Wait here."

He muscled his way to the front of the crowd and got on the bus, then talked to the driver for a long time. When they were finished, he stood on the step and waved for Jake and Snap.

He led them down the aisle. "This whole last row is yours. I paid for all five seats. Don't let anyone take them from you." After Jake and Snap were settled, Horace hesitated, then thrust the gold at Jake. "This is my lifeblood."

"Don't worry." Jake stowed the bowling bag under his seat.

Horace grabbed Jake's hand and shook it, holding on for a while. "God bless you, Ronny." He abruptly let go and walked to the front of the bus, stepped off and waded into the crowd.

The driver called out names. People jostled to the door and boarded, until all the seats were filled except the three extras in the back row. The driver called another name and a large woman got on and came bumping toward them fully loaded. Jake and Snap scooted to one side to make room, but she turned and folded down a middle seat, blocking the aisle, and sat down.

More names were called and each newcomer folded down the seat in the preceding row until the aisle was erased. It was tight, even without the children, who didn't seem to have seats of their own and squirmed on laps and snuggled into crevices. The strong smell of the crowd competed with unusual odors from the baskets and small animals that were stuffed everywhere. The air conditioner had little effect beyond steaming up the windows, making it impossible to see out.

"If I wanted this," Jake said, "I could have taken Delta Airlines."

"Even *slightly* smaller people would be nice," Snap said, having a hard time getting comfortable in the last row, there being plenty of length to it but no width at all.

They pulled out and headed south. The shadow from the mountain of luggage on the roof ran alongside them. Hopefully there would be no overpasses.

Snap eyed the food, water, mats and blankets that people had carried on with them. "How long did Horace say this would take?"

"20 hours."

"My personal opinion, Jake, my personal opinion is that we're really in for it now."

Children sneaked occasional looks to the back, unable to resist the sight of the white man and his 340-pound alabaster sidekick, sweating through their shirts.

The unpaved road was almost free of traffic. Useless telephone poles marked the route to the horizon, the wire gone, stolen for its copper. Jake savored every flat, brown mile they put between themselves and Mopti. They stopped for gas, the engine running while the driver smoked and filled the tank, passengers puffing alongside him on the shady side of the bus. Jake and Snap scattered into the brush to relieve themselves.

Hours later, the bus stopped with nothing in sight but a lone woman selling cooking oil and ginger candies. Two passengers got off and walked away. The bus sat for a long time. A dusty car appeared and dropped off a man in flowing robes. He climbed aboard and took the freshly vacated front row.

"He's a local chief," Jake said. "He waits in his village until word comes that the bus has arrived, then leaves to catch it.

He's a leader, so he can't sit behind anyone. It's hell getting these guys into a taxi."

They drove for hours down the wrong side of the road, their half badly pot-holed, oncoming vehicles visible miles ahead as plumes of dust. The driver played chicken, swerving back to his lane at the last moment.

It turned dark and the bus rolled on. Much later it came to a stop in the middle of the road, and passengers in the aisle folded down their seats and filed off. The driver motioned for Jake and Snap to follow them.

"What do we do?" Snap asked.

"Stay put."

The other passengers weighed in, raising a chorus of unintelligible words and pointing to the door.

"They really want us to get off," Snap said.

Jake looked out at the emptiness. "Why in hell?"

He gathered up his suitcase and the gold and headed down the aisle, followed by Snap. Passengers grabbed at the bags as he went by. After he hit the ground the others began to reboard, leaving three rough-looking men behind, conversing softly in the shadows. When Jake tried to get back on the bus the driver closed the door in his face.

SNAP AND JAKE stood in the middle of the road watching the bus get smaller. The other three men looked them over.

"If the loan sharks don't kill Horace," Jake said, "I will."

The three men walked 20 yards into the brush, stopped and looked back, like dogs waiting for their owner to catch up.

"Maybe this is where we change buses," Jake said.

"Maybe this is where they keep the grain, said the steer at the slaughterhouse gate."

The three men seemed to lose patience and set off into the dark.

Jake picked up his bags. "The devil you know is better than the devil you don't know, Daniel always says." He headed after the trio, Snap close behind.

THEY WERE ON a footpath of sorts, lit by the stars. They marched hard for over twenty minutes, trying to keep the three men in sight. Snap tripped on a rock and crashed to the ground, cutting both palms as he broke the fall.

"I'm so fat," he puffed, struggling to his feet. "It's like I'm hauling a 200-pound sack of fat on my back."

"I'm the one with the damn gold."

"But you don't have to feed it. I've got to pump oxygen to the fat."

They came out of a slight depression and caught sight of the three men again, now nearly two hundred yards ahead and almost to a bus that was idling in the road with its headlights on.

"We *are* changing buses," Jake said. He sped up, leaving Snap behind, wanting to make sure the bus didn't take off without them.

A dozen passengers loitered near the door. Some looked familiar. It was the same driver. They lugged the bags down the aisle and settled into their old seats.

"Why did we do that?" Snap said.

"We were avoiding something. A military checkpoint maybe. Or the border."

"Who were the other three guys?"

"Fellow delinquents."

Snap picked the gravel out of his palms. "Well I'm glad that's over."

The second time, they left everything on the bus except the gold.

IT WAS WELL past midnight when they stopped for the third time. Jake and Snap gathered themselves up to go, but this time everyone followed the driver off the bus with their mats and blankets and scattered along the roadside. Snap stretched across the back row and began to snore. Jake lay in the aisle, wide awake.

Did he envy Daniel's life? Money, power, golf tournaments, charity galas, box seats, sycophants, enough lovers to fill three sheets of college-ruled paper? Like a tandem bicycle, it probably looked like a lot more fun than it really was. If Daniel's life was shallow and meaningless though, he certainly didn't seem to realize it.

Jake tried to get comfortable on the uneven metal floor. *He,* on the other hand, was smart enough to know how unhappy he should be. He had no children. His only human contact for years was the brush of the barista's fingers when she handed him his morning latté. He was getting older – old enough to remember when you raked leaves and parked downtown for free; when blow jobs were higher up the ladder than regular sex and really meant something.

The thing is though, wouldn't the richest man in the world, on say his 80th birthday, give every last penny to switch lives with the most pathetic teenager in town, straight across? So even his own ridiculous life, at 40, should be worth quite a lot, billions maybe, if you looked at it that way, a little less if you needed to live it out in Africa.

He didn't really care about Seattle, but he did want to be with Carly. Was it love? Infinite nuances got dumbed down to that one word. He needed a better one, a bigger word for how he felt. But yes. She was wonderful, flawless, perfect.

Except she probably liked to dance, and would be good at it too, and would want to go all the time.

60

The sleepy-eyed passengers straggled back to the bus at dawn and took their regular seats. The monotonous brown earth offered no clue to what country they were in.

The black sedan appeared behind them an hour after they set out. It barreled up the road, flashing its headlights, and pulled alongside. The bus driver didn't seem to notice. A man brandished an automatic pistol from the car's side window, and the bus came to a sudden stop.

The front door of the car opened and a man in a black silk shirt stepped out, a moon-shaped pendant around his neck.

"Uh oh," said Jake.

"What?"

"That's one of Daniel's guys. From the compound."

Three other men emerged, smoothed their clothes and stretched like insolent black cats, then stood with their backs to the car, making certain their weapons were clearly visible. The road was empty in both directions all the way to the horizon.

Daniel's man tapped on the bus door with his ring. The driver opened it with a shrug, resigned to being violated. The man boarded and examined the rows of motionless passengers. Everyone but the children stared straight ahead, as though something worth seeing might suddenly appear in the windshield.

The man's eyes stopped at the back row. Snap's face was the color of a pomegranate. Jake tried to make himself smaller. The people in the aisle scrambled off the bus.

Jake reached in his pocket and palmed Horace's gold nugget.

The intruder came down the aisle, taking his time, and stood over Jake. "Get off."

"Is this Ouagadougou? I'm for Ouagadougou."

The man bent down and grabbed Jake's neck with one hand and stretched him upward. The hand was hot, like it had been wrapped around a cup of coffee. The gold pendant banged into Jake's face. "Get off. You are come to me."

"Hey now, pardner," Snap said. "Hey now."

Jake held up the nugget and gasped for air. "I want to stay on the bus."

The man eased his grip and took the nugget with his free hand. He gave it a cursory glance and slipped it into his pocket. "*Merci beaucoup.* Thank you very much." A gold tooth flashed at the front of his mouth. "Get off autobus."

Jake met his gaze. This guy wasn't a petty thug on the lookout for a small bribe. He was an executive; he probably took a lot of pride in his work. "Would you like to be a rich man?" Jake said, carefully enunciating each word.

The enormous hand around Jake's neck didn't loosen, but there was a change in the eyes. "How rich?"

"Big gold. *Beaucoup* gold."

"Aw shit," said Snap.

"You need to get off this bus and tell your boys I wasn't on it–"

"I do not need to tell anything," snarled the man, tightening his grip, snapping the spell.

"Very rich," Jake said, backtracking to where things were better.

The man took his hand from Jake's neck and straightened up. "How much gold?"

Jake held both hands in front of him, cradling an imaginary pile of gold the size of a mushmelon.

The man frowned, trying to squeeze out an idea.

He's thinking he'll get me *and* the gold. Tear the bus apart if he has to. "The gold is not for your bosses," Jake said, the slight quaver gone from his voice. He nodded toward the three men standing by the car. "Or for them. The gold is only for you. *Seulement pour toi...vous.* If your boys know you have the gold, they will want to share it, or they will tell the bosses. If the bosses know you have the gold, they will not let you keep it. All the gold is for you. Take the gold and go."

It seemed like a lot of time went by. "Show."

Jake bent down, pulled the green bag from under the seat, and opened it. He lifted out the leather bowl, peeled off the tape and removed the lid. The man stared at the bare gold for a moment before pulling his eyes away. Jake replaced the cover and put the bowl back into the bag and zipped it.

"*D'accord.*" The man reached down and grabbed the bag off Jake's lap. He turned and went down the aisle, holding Horace's lifeblood over the heads of the seated passengers as though it were feathers, then stepped off the bus and was gone.

61

They pulled into Bobo-Dioulasso and the driver walked them over to another bus: a proper one this time, with nice seats and air-conditioning and nothing lashed on top. They had time to spare so found a small café and ordered fresh orange juice and *croque-monsieurs*.

When the food was gone, Snap settled back in his chair. "I'm a little worried about the Horace stuff, the two little girls."

"The thing about Horace, it's never the way he says it is."

"But still…"

Jake held up both hands and that was that.

IT WAS LATE afternoon when the bus deposited them in the heart of Ouagadougou. Jake told the taxi driver to take them to the grandest hotel in town. He secured two rooms without difficulty, both in Ronny Knoll's name, and paid from his diminishing store of ready cash.

He napped in his clothes on top of the bedcovers. When he woke, it was nighttime and the power was off. He took a shower by candlelight, getting out when the water turned cold, and changed into cleaner clothes. He walked around the sprawling city for hours, dodging motorbikes, happy to be in the bustle, then headed back to the hotel for Snap, knowing he would want to eat.

They ducked into a small restaurant for a late dinner and asked about the curries and perch kebobs, the mutton ragout and lamb in peanut sauce. Jake settled on the *steak au poivre*. Snap put in a surprise order for the *steak tartare du cheval*. (Jake knew what *cheval* meant, and *tartare* too, and that the two words didn't belong together, especially on a menu, but decided to leave Snap in peace.) Each dish they inquired about ended up at their table, six entrees, the platters overlapped so all would fit.

"I was in Greece once," Snap said, halfway through his *cheval*. "I was starving. Went into a restaurant but couldn't understand what they had, different alphabet and all. So I just pointed to things on the menu. Ended up with two glasses of booze that tasted like Good & Plentys and a bunch of little octopuses. Delicious though."

"When I first went to France I always ordered *boeuf*," Jake said. "It was a safe word on the menu, I knew what it meant. Turns out that *boeufs* have kidneys and glands, tongues and brains."

On the way back to the hotel they stopped at a bar for a beer and stayed for a few more. A good band was playing. Free-lance drummers wandered in and joined the group on stage – there were at least a dozen up there with the band, pounding out a hypnotic beat, when Jake and Snap left.

Jake couldn't sleep. He should have stayed longer at the bar. He dozed off as the sun came up, but the alarm woke him again. He opened his suitcarrier and lifted out the two small packages from Horace. He carefully unwrapped one: it was a ceramic figurine, about eight inches tall, with one arm missing. Old and crudely done, it looked like it was made by a child. The other package contained a clay figure of a woman seated on the ground with her arms crossed over her chest. He examined it for signs of secreted drugs or explosives, but it was light and delicate and seemed to have no hidden purpose. It was difficult, though, to picture the little sculptures lasting long in the hands of a five year-old girl.

He rewrapped the figurines and carried them downstairs in a paper laundry bag. Snap was sitting at a table on the pool terrace, pretending his boxer shorts were swimwear.

"I'm plugged up tighter'n a three-pint oil well. Should of appreciated the trots while I had 'em."

"I'm on my way to get plane tickets. Where do you want to go?"

"I need to go to New York, I guess. Lucille is there. What about you?"

Well that was easy. He wanted to go to Utsalady Bay. To the familiar beach and mountains, the sunsets and sailing waters. To Carly. She was smart, confident. It was the best sex ever. She could be his partner and lover, the mother of his children. It would be worth taking a few risks for that.

But then again, serious people were after him, police and a former best friend. A small town, close to home, was no place to hide. It made more sense to take cover someplace he could be anonymous, maybe a huge apartment complex in a big city: go unnoticed, fade away. No job and no co-workers, no kids bringing friends home, no neighbors over the back fence, nobody with any interest in him at all. It might be better than prison.

He left Snap and found a café with a balcony that looked down on the market. His father would have loved all this. When he was nine they were at the Albuquerque airport together, waiting for a connecting flight. His dad insisted on a whirlwind taxi tour of the city while the other passengers sat in the boarding area and stared at ads on the ceiling-mounted monitors. A huge eight-bedroom house could barely contain the man's life: the skis and telescopes and camping gear; cameras and kayaks and bikes and fly rods; easels in the attic and piles of wood for toy cars and boats in the basement; books spilling out everywhere; orchids, gardening tools, the king-sized bed. As he got older the things he loved were gradually taken from him; he needed less space every year. The tiny room at Sylvan Glen was barely big enough to squeeze in a three-drawer dresser, narrow bed, and the soundless television with its pixilated transmissions to keep him company.

Jake finished his omelette and picked up the bag with the dolls. He would not live in a box.

He asked the waiter for directions to the Air Faso office and the man hung up his apron and took him there. The airline had three flights a week to Paris, its only destination outside West Africa. A gentle lady at the ticket office regretted to inform him that the afternoon flight was sold out. The next one didn't leave for three days. He booked two seats to Abidjan instead, not wanting to stay in one place too long, confident they could get out of Africa from there.

The woman handed him his tickets. He asked for directions to the Fed Ex office, and made it there on foot in less than ten minutes. He carefully packed the two figurines into a medium box and cushioned them with waste paper from the bin under the counter. He grabbed a blank airbill and selected Priority Overnight Delivery (whatever that meant over here) and printed the name and address in large block letters: *CU-RATOR, NATIONAL MUSEUM, BAMAKO, MALI.* He slipped the airbill into its plastic pouch and handed the box to the agent.

On the way back to the hotel he picked up mangoes and lemons from a street vendor and asked the waiter at the hotel restaurant to prepare the fruit and deliver it to Snap on the terrace.

Later that night the two men walked in their shirtsleeves to L'Eau Vive and ate in a bougainvillea-packed courtyard.

"I'm afraid Daniel has really done me in," Snap said, a terrible sadness in his voice.

"You're still breathing," Jake said.

"I don't know what to tell Lucille." Nuns began to sere nade the diners with the *Ave Maria*. "I'd kill myself except I've got shirts at the cleaners."

THEY MET IN the deserted hotel lobby at five the next morning, anxious to be on their way, not sure of Daniel's reach. Jake commandeered a taxi driver who came in looking for another guest. The sun was up by the time they reached the airport. They were quickly processed through the terminal and joined the queue on the tarmac, next to an ancient Dutch jet, waiting for the plane door to be opened.

There was a fuel shortage at the airport and flights were canceled. Disappointed passengers, some camping out for days, massed behind a chain-link fence and stared at the plane like kids at a candy store window. Three men scrambled over the fence and joined the tidy line of passengers on the ramp. Seeing their success, a few more followed, then the crowd be-gan to pour over the top. The orderly queue crumbled from the rear, the people at the back realizing they would be the ones left without seats. Jake and Snap joined the forward press. Passengers climbed the outside of the airstairs; flight attendants stepped on their fingers to make them drop off. The whole thing looked like the fall of Saigon.

There were at least a hundred people on the 65-seater when the door finally closed. The extras stood in the aisle all the way to Abidjan.

Jake and Snap deplaned and went to the transit lounge. The Departures board showed a flight to New York in 90 minutes. Jake bought Snap a ticket and scanned the board for other options: Rio, Johannesburg, Moscow, Bahrain.

They called Snap's flight. He looked diminished, a foot shorter than he was in Daniel's office, and the moisture sucked out of him. Jake got a big bear-hug at the gate. After Snap was safely on board, Jake sat down on a hard chair, his suitcase on his lap.

He really had nowhere to go.

ONE YEAR LATER

62

The former Mrs. Jake Morrow walked out of the aroma-therapy shop laden with candles and oils and tried to remember where she parked the car. She was Sheila Smith again – her childhood name still sounding strange after twenty years in storage. Tonight was the one-year anniversary of this new life of hers, this wonderful thing. God bless Daniel. God bless that darling man.

She couldn't wait to get back to the vintage Laurelhurst home she bought with the divorce money, to her leaded-glass windows and claw-footed tub. She would have a chance to organize her samples before dinner. As one of only a handful of raw food coaches in Seattle she was not as busy as you might expect, but things were bound to get better over time, and money wasn't an issue anyway, there was plenty of that.

She hadn't heard Jake's voice in over a year. The last time was the voicemail, telling her he was going to Liberia for five days; it couldn't be helped he said. Her old life was about to end and he was playing his role, disappearing like molted skin.

The next evening Daniel called and announced she was going to the Poulsbo Spa for the Labor Day weekend, all expenses paid, the driver already on his way to pick her up. She had been pretty much a zombie forever, and Daniel must have seen it. He insisted she go, wouldn't take no for an answer, went on about enzyme peels and organic facials, lip smoothies and amazing meals with no calories or fat, until she gave in. He certainly was a persuasive man, and thank god for that.

He even came by the house to see her off. Said he would feed the cats and lock up – he needed to drop some files in the den anyway.

She felt a dark cloud beginning to lurk around the edges of her happiness, and dispelled it immediately with thoughts of Cam and the wonderful celebration they would have tonight.

On that first evening at the spa Cam gave her a massage and it was so intimate, so sensual, so much better than sex with Jake had ever been, she thought she might have her first orgasm in a decade right there on the Shiatsu table. Cam was young and single, strong, chiseled, swaggering, and had a great tan, the exact opposite of Jake in every way. By the end of the massage she was smitten and, she learned later, Cam felt it too.

Cam was her soulmate for sure, and loved the three cats as much as she did. (Jake never could disguise his dislike for them, wouldn't even say their names, just called them all the Kennedys – they were beautiful and pampered without deserving to be, he said – and was more embarrassed to be sent to the store for cat food than tampons.)

And the baby! She was finally going to be a mother. It didn't happen with Jake, but now with Cam her dream was coming true. She felt like a Bohemian, having a child and not even being married, but with things progressing the way they were, that could very well change.

They were going to Dromo's to mark the anniversary, her treat. Cam would be dead-set against any alcohol because of the pregnancy. But it was a big night: just a smidgeon of champagne would surely be in order.

She stepped off the curb and into the crosswalk, not bothering to check for traffic, and didn't notice the oversized van barreling down the street until it was almost on top of her.

THE DRIVER SLAMMED on the brakes and braced for a collision. The truck stopped inches short of the woman. "Jesus Christ," he said. He turned to look at the pile of laundry bags that had thumped up against the steel-mesh bulkhead behind his head.

"Bitch," muttered the man in the passenger seat, instinctively flipping the woman off, forgetting there were no fingers on his hand. He looked down at the coffee splashed over his white pants, then turned his attention to the buck-toothed driver: "This is my last clean uniform, numbnuts."

SHEILA STOOD IN a cloud of burning rubber and glared at the men in the truck. One of them raised his fist at her. The nerve! She pointed to the white stripes painted on the street. "Crosswalk, baby," she sneered, then continued across.

She just loved being with Cam, loved hanging out with her, it was like having that very best friend in high school she missed out on. They weren't lesbians (she couldn't stop giggling when the drunken woman on the cruise ship asked) though she could see how someone might make the mistake. No, they were just two people who liked to read the Sunday paper together in their jammies, who could stay up all night chatting about anything, who felt incomplete when they were apart.

And the sex, well, that was just being naughty.

63

Snap Pease glanced at his watch to see if he was early or the boat late, and noticed the date. It was a year since he stepped onto the plane in Abidjan, not knowing what was worse: Daniel's thugs behind him on that incomprehensible continent, or Lucille ahead of him in New York, needing to be told the truth.

HE HAD MADE it through the sea of smiling hotel staffers in New York, all of them happy to see him again and hopeful he would enjoy his stay, nobody appearing to notice his disheveled state. He looked for Lucille in both suites (the extra secured for storing packages) before settling on the immense bed to await her return from the shops.

She was thrilled to see him, didn't know he was coming, wanted to show him everything she bought so far. He let her go through the shopping bags and boxes one-by-one, glad to put off for just a little longer the hardest thing he would ever have to do.

Lucille set down the last bag, happy and excited, a thin layer of perspiration showing on her upper lip. She said they should go to Gasperetti's straightaway, that he looked a little peckish. He talked her into room service, wanting the privacy and worried about the credit card.

Halfway through dinner he was still trying to figure out how to bring it all up, and then she asked how the trip went, and he said not so good and pushed ahead. The first moments were painful, like plunging into the lake in December, then everything just poured out.

She listened sympathetically, nodded her head and muttered "oh my" at all the right places, and when he was done she told him she was sure it would all work out and he told her it wouldn't.

She said they would cut back and he told her they were ruined, he had personally guaranteed everything, they had a negative net worth and it was a big one; the banks would take it all and there was no way to ever get it back.

She set down her silver knife and fork with a stunned look. He thought for a moment she was having a stroke.

"Well, we'll just change some things, Pumpkin, readjust," she finally said.

"Yes." He gritted his teeth.

"I'll take all of these things back tomorrow." She waved her hand at the roomful of packages.

"That would be good," he said, head bent.

"The kids will be fine, they're really good kids. They are." She said it as though he might have missed that fact while they were growing up, and he knew she was right.

"We don't need all those houses, all those bathrooms to clean, you've said that lots of times. Why have a bunch of stuff anyway? Machines that break, things that gather dust? I've got my mother's jewelry, I think that's something no one can take away from me. We can sell it for a stake. I can get a job."

"What kind of a job could you get?" he asked, not meaning to be unkind, really just curious; she hadn't worked a day in her life.

"Maybe a restaurant job. I could be a waitress. I've eaten two-thirds of my meals out since I was three years old."

She came over to him then and put her arms around his slumped shoulders and told him not to worry, they were in this thing together. It was time she took over some of the worries, she said. The kids are extremely well-educated, certainly old enough to fend for themselves. They could rent, maybe get a place of their own later on. She just wanted it to be someplace warm is all, and she'd prefer if it weren't Texas; if it had to be Texas that would be okay, but all-in-all she'd rather start fresh and not be running into people they knew if she didn't have to.

When she told him they could go on picnics, that she would make the chicken, and potato salad, and the Jell-O with carrots and celery in it that he liked, and they could go to the park and watch the people play softball, it would be fun and free too, he just broke down and sobbed, his whole body heaving. It was the last thing in the world he wanted to do but he was tired from the trip and couldn't help himself.

THE PROW OF the big ship finally appeared from behind the point. He was so grateful for the past year; it was the best one ever. Lucille was like a new person, volunteering down at the school with the younger children, the ones with the extra problems, taking classes so she could do more. He had never seen her happier; it was what she should have been doing all along.

He loved his job too, if you could call it that. He met some people who came ashore on a day trip. They told their friends who came on later ships, and then those people told their friends too. The chain kept growing until it seemed he was always showing someone around to his favorite bars and restaurants and all the rest, and then the cruise ship company called and asked if he wanted to make it official.

It was only two weeks since the girls left but they'd be back for Thanksgiving. He was already figuring the days. It wouldn't be long before grandchildren would be coming too, little boys and girls, lots of them, sagging diapers and laughing faces, creases of fat on their tiny wrists, coming to visit grandpa, climbing up and sliding off.

He wanted to spend a lot of years with them, Lucille and his baby girls and the grandbabies.

He made his way down to the wharf, excited to meet some new friends. Maybe it was time to take another stab at a diet.

64

It was warm in Boise and the smog much worse than usual. The former cab driver fiddled with the Bertolucci while he drove, waiting for the woman at the escrow company to come back on the line. He rolled the watch across his fingers like worry beads, loving its heft, and read the inscription again: "To My Dearest Husband." Well, that was never going to happen. The girls down at the Riverside were easier on the eyes and a lot cheaper in the long run.

The woman came back on the line and told him nothing had changed in the last two hours: his deal still wasn't going to close until Thursday.

"You oughta, you know, get your shit together," he said, then muttered "bitch," just loud enough to be heard but still deniable, as he slapped down the cover of the cell phone.

He adjusted his papakha and took the next exit. He loved being a real estate agent, and loved Boise too – it was paradise-on-earth compared to New York, even with all the yokels.

Things were so different now.

65

Horace Washington stopped pacing in the small room and checked his watch again. It seemed to be running slow. He gazed through the barred window to the street below and absently rolled a thick coin along the sill. A raggedy man maneuvered a grocery cart full of empty bottles across a vacant corner lot, his three-legged dog working hard to keep up.

It was impossible to relax. He paced some more then edged back up to the window. The anxiety was palpable, a throbbing behind his eyes. He had waited a year. It was time to put an end to the story. It was painful, but he dredged it all up.

HE HAD MADE it out of Mali, but just barely. Stripped naked in the airport guardroom before a bunch of grinning thugs, poked and penetrated, he got to the plane with nothing but his passport and a few CFA for the airport tax in Dakar, lucky to still have that.

The Djati didn't want to just run him off. They wanted to make a statement.

At least it made it easier to stiff the Guinea gold smugglers. They followed him to the airport and were watching when the police dragged him out of the line. They must have known right then their gold was gone for good, and their mule too. They were big boys, though. *Caveat emptor.*

The connecting flight to New York was already gone by the time he touched down in Dakar, so he rebooked for the following day and slept at the boarding gate, the chair punishing his body like a pair of cheap shoes. He watched his slim cushion of time bleed away on the terminal clock and started to have chest pains. When they announced the delay he thought he might pass out. When they finally called the flight he was a quivering puddle and barely made it on the plane.

The loan shark was expecting just under $255,000. The Guinea dust was going to come up a little short, but there was the bit of gold he'd extracted from the villages himself and the one big nugget. The price of gold was up almost six dollars the past week, so that would help some too. But what if he had the interest wrong? He didn't think they compounded it, but maybe they did.

And if Ronny let him down? If the money never showed up at all? Well, he just wasn't going to let his thoughts travel in that direction.

He cleared customs in New York and went straight to an ΛTM and withdrew twenty dollars from his Chase account. The receipt showed he had $31.15 left, so he took out another twenty.

He made it to the front of the taxi line, then let a few people skip ahead. He wanted to sync up with a brother: it would be easier in case money issues cropped up at the other end. The taxi dropped him at a coffee place with bars on the windows and Internet access. He pushed the last of his money across the counter to buy a little computer time.

He had checked from a café in Bamako almost 48 hours earlier. The gold should have been at Rodenburg by then, but the account showed a zero balance. Things never go as planned on the Ouagadougou route though, and maybe Ronny had trouble getting a seat up to Germany. Or maybe the Rodenburg computers were down. There were a thousand possible explanations.

Yes, two days ago the delay was still on the cusp of reasonableness, no cause for panic. But now the money needed to be there. He logged onto the Rodenburg website and looked for his current balance, praying it would be close to $255,000.

And there it was, like a slap across the face: *Account Balance 0.00 (United States Dollars).*

He waited as long as he could, about three minutes, then checked the balance again. No change. Rodenburg was closed for the day but the assaying labs operated around the clock: the money would be posted as soon as the gold was evaluated, day or night.

He lined up at the counter and asked the woman ahead of him if she could buy him a caffé Mocha and she said yes, and then he asked about an eight-grain roll and she said all right, and then he asked if she could spare some money for computer time and she said no. The coffee was expensive, the paltry change from the woman's ten-dollar bill going into the tip jar, and he thought maybe that was where the money was: selling people something really addictive that was mostly water.

He promised to check the account only every fifteen minutes, but couldn't keep to it. The place got busier. Frowning patrons hovered near his computer, glanced at their watches, rolled their eyes, but he was oblivious: his universe the screen in front of him and a ticking clock. As time went by he became more agitated and the customers moved off to stand behind other users. Twice more he had to cadge donations to keep the computer going.

Finally, like a gambler realizing that the printed score on the sports page was never going to change, he knew the money wasn't coming.

He called the apartment and spoke to Dwayne's wife. She was excited to hear from him, not a hint of worry in her voice: Dwayne must be keeping things from her. She knew about the meeting though; gave him the address of the private club. He could hear the little girls chirping in the background, unaware of the calamity looming over them like a breaking wave. He hung up without saying goodbye.

He was going to be late, a bad way to start. He needed to convince these people they would get their money. He could rob a bank. He might get lucky in the lottery. He could buy life insurance and make them the beneficiary and then kill himself, once the exclusion-period elapsed. He still had a lot of options.

A woman approached the empty seat beside him, then turned and scurried off. He was starting to smell from the fear and the long trip, and his eyes, in an otherwise slack and ex-pressionless face, were screaming.

He looked at the clock again. The Chase branch would close in a few minutes. If he couldn't transfer the money from Rodenburg by then, that would be the end of it. He raised his hands to the keyboard one last time. His leaden fingers entered the account number with no conscious help from him. He thought about the two little girls, and what he had done, and began to softly wail, not realizing he was doing it, and the people within hearing distance cleared out like he had Semtex strapped to his chest.

The webpage appeared and this time something was dif-ferent. It showed *1,000,000.00 (United States Dollars)*.

Money, lots of it, had arrived.

It was doubly peculiar: so much in the account and in such a round number, no odd dollars and cents to reflect the untidy grains of gold dust in the leather bowl. He thought it might be a dream, the whole Mali debacle just a nightmare, but he didn't want to wake himself up and risk losing the money.

Rodenburg must have made a mistake, gotten the deposit wrong. And the thing was, if he could transfer some of the money out right away, before they corrected the error, just enough to cover the debt, he and Dwayne would be in the clear. He would owe Rodenburg, sure, but that was infinitely better than owing Dwayne's people, no doubt about that whatsoever.

He selected "Transfer Funds" and filled in the routing information for his Chase account. When the screen prompted him to enter an amount, he typed in $255,000 and looked at it for a moment, then changed it to $275,000 (in case he had miscalculated the interest), then changed it again to $300,000 (two months rent up front, damage deposit, some kind of transportation until he could get back on his feet – he would need a few suits too, and some walking-around money).

He clicked on "Send" and the screen flashed "Transaction Completed" – too quickly, he thought, for anything to have actually happened. He attributed the wave of giddiness to dehydration, or his recent lack of food, or maybe getting up from the table too quickly, and he knocked over a display of coffee grinders as he ran out to the sidewalk and headed for the bank.

He arrived at the private club – nothing more than a seedy restaurant – with the cash in a couple of pastry bags. Dwayne was with a group of people in the back. He handed the money to a surly man with no eyebrows and waited for a receipt, but apparently that wasn't the way they did things. On their way out he told Dwayne he hoped he hadn't been too worried, and Dwayne didn't know what he was talking about, and that was the amazing thing: Dwayne never doubted for a single moment he would show up with the money.

That was when he made the solemn vow, right there on the sidewalk outside the restaurant, to never ever put himself in that position again, where people had any faith in him.

He didn't have to be the big man in the neighborhood anymore, the star at every family gathering. He would get a job in Brooklyn, wait tables, drive a cab if that's what it came to, get settled in a cheap apartment. Lord knows, he was beyond embarrassment. A warm room in the winter, three good meals a day, precious time with Skitch, that's all he needed. Forget the floorside seats to the Knicks, it would be good enough to watch them on TV once in a while with his little guy.

At the top of the subway stairs Dwayne told him how proud everyone was of him and his accomplishments in Africa and he told Dwayne he needed to wrap up a few loose ends, then left and checked into the Marriott and slept for two days.

When he woke up he ordered room service (two cartfuls) and logged onto the Rodenburg website from the Business Center. His account showed a balance of $700,000 so he transferred another $100,000 to New York.

Might as well be shot for a sheep as a goat.

He used the money to pay back his investors, with interest, and apologized for not hitting the jackpot. On the night of his homecoming party he promised himself, on Skitch's life, to leave the other $600,000 in the account for one year from the moment it first appeared: if Rodenburg didn't take it back by then, well, they would have had their chance, end of story.

HE LEFT THE window and went to his desk and sat down. He gained back the 50 pounds, plus another ten, but looked healthy, not bad at all, and the new double-breasted suit was really sharp. He put the Kruggerand back in his pocket: he always kept it on him, a reminder of the gold fever, like a recovering alcoholic with an unopened bottle in the cupboard.

His assistant brought in the phone messages. She smiled at him and he smiled back, the sight of the attractive woman reminding him that Tania would be over tonight to cook dinner and celebrate his last night at the apartment. He knew it from the moment they met on the lobbying trip to Albany: she would be the icing on his new cake.

It felt comfortable being a bureaucrat again – the security, the structure, the nine-to-five. He was asked to join the Black History Month Committee, but that would be the last outside commitment. He would reserve the rest of his free time for

Skitch. There were hints he might be able to have him a little more than the custody decree allowed, and if his ex-wife didn't change her mind he was definitely going to take her up on it, once things settled down a bit.

The muted television in the corner was tuned to C-SPAN. He watched the pantomime for a moment, a man moving his lips behind a flag-flanked podium, then turned back to the papers on his desk.

THE MEMBERS OF the press didn't even pretend to take any of it down as the spokesman lauded the outstanding cooperation of the CIA, the FBI and the Pentagon, with special thanks to the U.S. Navy and a cursory nod to Woods Hole. The congratulations continued unabated for an unconscionably long time, like a nightmare Oscar-acceptance speech, dwarfing the NTSB report itself when they finally got around to it.

The report was brief and to the point. Terrorists were not involved in the crash of Liberia 53 after all, despite the fervid claims of the Amoudi Jihad, a fractious group of suburban lightweights who could no more down an airplane than put out the sun.

The depth of the water at the crash site made it impossible to recover anything heavier than 150 pounds, but the Navy's little submersible was able to retrieve both black boxes and a critical piece of the forward cargo door. The door fragment contained a counterfeit spare part, an ersatz latch whose substandard metallurgy and lack of tempering were not discernible to the naked eye. It was only a matter of time before the latch bent like cooked spaghetti and failed at high-altitude. When the door blew out it was like a balloon being pricked with a pin: the explosive force from the pressure differential ripped a hole in the fuselage and hurled debris at the engines and control surfaces.

HORACE USED THE remote to turn off the television and began to pack his briefcase. He paused to read the escrow documents for the fifth time since noon, loving the words – *hereditaments, tenements, appurtenances* – all of it coming back to him tomorrow.

He had gone to the new owners a month ago and offered to buy back the house. The price was inflated, nearly double what they stole it for at the foreclosure sale, but it would be worth it. When Skitch came on weekends he would have his own room back and could see his old friends. Things would be just like before.

He checked his watch. His self-imposed moratorium was over. He logged onto the Rodenburg site just like he did every day for the past year, and just like every other day the $600,000 was sitting there (accruing no interest, which was a shame).

He must have been the worst assayer in the world. Things were crazy though, it was a wonder he could even dress himself back then. It was still a mystery why exactly $1,000,000 was deposited. Maybe Ronny took everything over that as a commission. Well, God bless him if he did and he was welcome to it, wherever he might be. It was upsetting the two figurines never showed up though, and not a single word of explanation. A simple apology would have been nice.

He hit the "Send" button and the money was on its way.

He had promised to take Skitch to Disney World after they closed on the house, just the two of them. Skitch was ecstatic and hadn't talked about anything else for weeks: he devoured the maps and brochures, made lists of things to do each day. He already knew enough about the place to work there as a tour guide.

The other possibility, though – it just popped up the day before – might be Bermuda. That could be an even better bet. Some ex-University of Miami football players rented a house there and his new friend from the Jets invited him to go and meet them, so maybe he could kill two birds with one stone. It was a lifelong fraternity with those guys, being black and coming through the program and making it in the pros. If you hooked up with any of them, if they liked and trusted you, you were hooked up with them all, and all those to come. The Hurricane Mafia. Good guys looking to make some serious money.

He had been giving some thought to that old incinerator building: how it could be turned into a hotel with real character. Big, big upside. The 'Canes would be the perfect investors. Maybe Bermuda was the better choice. Skitch would like the beach and they could go fishing in the ocean. He could write the whole thing off. Skitch wouldn't mind hanging out in the room for an hour or two while he went to meet the guys and tried to click with them. It would be much better for Skitch in the long run, for his future, than an empty trip to Disney World, even if it meant a little disappointment in the here and now.

The excitement began to percolate. He got up and paced some more. If he went to Bermuda he would have to show a little flash – nobody wanted to waste time or money on a loser. He would probably need to put a little of his own cash into the deal too, to show he believed in it, and maybe guarantee some debt. It might be worth it to set aside part of the $600,000, not too much, to pursue the thing a little further.

66

Jake's car came around the freeway bend and suddenly Seattle was right there in front of him, the downtown towers sticking up like prairie silos. It was cool and drizzly, a low marine overcast pressing down hard, the often-perfect September weather nowhere to be seen. The drive into town was quicker than expected. He had plenty of time to find the place before heading for the cemetery.

He took the exit and dropped down to Lake Union, skirting its eastern shore. The unmarked shop materialized on the third pass, tucked behind a tavern, its entrance off the alley. It wasn't easy to score one of these things, you just had to show up in person and hope you got lucky.

He handed over $2,000 and the ex-aerospace machinist pushed a small box across the counter at him. The man, wild-eyed and unkempt, wouldn't let go and Jake had to gently tug it away.

He walked to a one-bench park at the end of the street and opened the box. The reel was aircraft-quality titanium, cut from bar stock like a marble sculpture, a work-of-art. He pictured Carly concentrating hard and biting her tongue, her face wet, working a salmon on a saltwater fly, the sun coming up through the gaps in the mountains. He was almost certain she would love it more than a piece of jewelry.

It was a year since Victoria. That last morning was his best ever, something to be celebrated. Amazing how those feelings spiked up at his age, and right in the middle of all the trouble. He had known her for such a short time. They were definitely on fast-forward though.

He liked looking out over the houseboats, thinking about her, but it was time to leave. He got up from the bench and she was gone, evaporating like a turned-off song.

It was almost five o'clock when he pulled into Lake View Cemetery. He sat in the car with the wipers going and watched the small clusters of people wend their way down the slope to the graveside. Even from a distance he could tell Gracie was crying. She was such a sweet, sensitive girl. Life was going to be hard on his little niece. He should be there for her.

Had he played it wrong?

HE WAS ABLE to use his PACER account to follow Daniel's downward trip through the bankruptcy courts. The pleadings and affidavits told the story: it was a rough slide.

The hedge fund cratered a few weeks after Daniel left Mali, then the partnerships started going down like dominoes. Money was missing from some accounts. Investors were screaming. The bankruptcy trustee was trying to prove fraud and found an old computer in a little room near Daniel's office. He thought he had his smoking gun, but the hard drive was missing.

There were references to Jake in the pleadings, but not by name. Some incriminating files were found at his house. He might still be radioactive.

Nothing criminal turned up on Daniel, but that stuff can take a while. There were a lot of heavy hitters invested with him, so maybe the fix was in. Usually when the money dries up though, so do the connections.

Daniel was gone. There were allegations he was in Costa Rica, Switzerland, Abu Dhabi. Some people thought the two of them were on the *Nadalia* somewhere, anchored in a tropical lagoon, drinking kamikazes and laughing their heads off.

To the public it looked like Daniel lost everything. Those best acquainted with him knew his fallbacks always had fallbacks. It was hard to believe Mr. Plan B didn't have a lifeboat parked someplace.

And what about Maddie? It took a while to figure it out. She steals the money, skips town, and is sitting in some airport bar waiting for her next flight. The Liberian crash is on the television. What to do? Any chance of her theft being discovered has just disappeared with the plane. Why not come back to New York like nothing's happened, $2,000,000 richer, cover your back and save the beaches for a little later?

FAMILY AND FRIENDS were gathered close around the striped canopy that sheltered the coffin from the rain. Jake climbed out of the car and caught his reflection in the side window. He had dropped 30 pounds. The outlines of his cheekbones were visible, and despite the new wrinkles at the corners of his eyes, he looked a decade younger.

He found a decent vantage point under the shelter of an old madrona tree, the nearby gravestones tilted by its roots. He wasn't dressed for the raw weather. Down the hill the old folks huddled in black coats, leaning on one another.

The coffin was lowered slowly into the earth. His baby nephew, barely four, walked up and stared into the hole. What thoughts were going through his little head, the curly blond hair whipped by the wind? Was he wondering what it was like for grandma to be in a box like that? She had started to disappear before he was even born.

It was best to leave while everyone was still occupied. He settled into the nondescript rental car and took a moment to figure out the headlights and wipers again. The sun was working its way to the horizon from somewhere behind the clouds,

Seattle on a dimmer-switch. He followed the side streets toward the freeway.

This was his hometown. He didn't actually descend from one of Seattle's pioneer families like Daniel said, but he could go back to the cemetery and visit the graves of great great-grandparents. He was born just over the hill at old Providence Hospital, gone to school, been married, lived his whole life here. So many streets, so many buildings held some shred of his life, some memory. All of his siblings and nieces and nephews lived here, and so did most of his uncles and aunts, friends from high school and college, people from work and the neighborhood.

He merged onto the freeway. The radio said a big storm was on the way. It was best to spend the night. He would need to find a hotel room.

67

Daniel Zakian stood by the pool and looked down the long side-garden to the orchard. Two of everything – apple, apricot, grapefruit, orange. Not efficient farming for sure, but fun to have them all.

He hoped she wouldn't be much longer.

He took a slow lap around the gardens on the brick path, trying not to step on the carefully cultivated moss in the cracks. The roses should have been pruned in the spring, they were getting leggy, but of course he was still in Seattle back then.

No question about it, the Montecito estate was even more spectacular than his place in Seattle, and that was saying something. Lots more upkeep though. It just comes with being so old.

It would be raining and cold up there, but still he missed it. You couldn't fault the weather here, it was certainly nice, but he never pictured himself ending up in Southern California. In Seattle he was right smack in the middle of everything; here he was on the outside, a stranger.

It definitely had been time for a change of scenery, though.

He arrived back at the pear-shaped pool and plopped down in a cushioned chair. It felt good to get off his feet. He breathed in the aroma of the freshly-mowed lawn that swept away before him. It would be great for touch-football, if it weren't for the slope. You needed someone to play with though.

The immaculate grass made him think of the dog. He had agreed to buy it only after the boys solemnly swore to handle the clean-up: any turd he found better still be steaming, he told them. It was a mistake to get rid of the mutt though, they were so little then, he should have just let it slide. He was always too hard on them, he could see that now. They sided with their mother, of course, but still he missed them more than he expected.

The evening sun sparkled on the gently-rippled surface of the pool. A swim would be nice. The pool in Seattle was used so little. He had to amortize it over less than 50 nice days a year. Here, you could swim almost every day.

He had unconsciously rolled the half-sheet of paper into a tube during his stroll. He smoothed it out on the table and put a small rock on it. It made him think of Jake, when they first met, the two of them scampering up and down the ravines on summer days as warm and sunny as this one.

It was crazy, of course, trying to kill Jake for money. That was wrong on a lot of levels. A serious loss of perspective on his part. He ignored other paths, much better ones. Ah, Monday-morning quarterbacking – he always hated that. Things were what they were. He made decisions every day. Lots of them. And lots of them were wrong. You just needed to keep making them; get as many right as possible.

Things certainly could have turned out a lot worse.

Hopefully Jake was okay. He was a smart guy and pretty tough with his back to the wall. A sap though, but maybe not so much anymore.

Jake had somehow screwed him with that power-of-attorney. He could tell from the Luxembourg banker's smirk he was at the right place, that Jake had been there, even if the toad wouldn't come right out and say it. And that was definitely Jake's signature on the power-of-attorney: he'd seen it ten thousand times. But for some reason it wouldn't unlock the door to the vault.

Never underestimate your adversary. He told Jake that a hundred times. Should have listened to his own damn advice. He wouldn't make the same mistake again.

He was a prick to send that list to his wife though. Ex-wife. Not at all like Jake, really, to be so mean-spirited, and not fair to the other women either. That and stealing the *Nadalia*. Not that he could have kept the boat anyway. A 50-foot asset wasn't going to escape anyone's attention, and it was in his own name. Galling though, that Jake somehow ended up with it. He always thought the *Nadalia* belonged to him, even though he was just an unpaid deckhand.

He caught the movement out of the corner of his eye as she descended the last few steps to the pool terrace. The magnificent body, the way she carried herself, you don't get that at a gym or dance school, you have to be born with it. She was truly a daughter of the gods.

It was four months now since they first met, right after his hasty retreat from Seattle, his life in total disarray. He was a little low then, his confidence dwindling, and understandably so. He knew right away she was perfect for him, tall and tan, dripping with class, with breasts that were not too big, not too small. She was someone he would be proud to show off. And rich too. That never hurt.

For a 40-year-old woman to be so attractive, so sexy, so much better than the younger ones he used to want, that was a surprise. Would she still look as good to him when she was 50? Or would some new 40-year-old be the perfect one then?

He rose quickly from his seat and drank her in as she approached, then caught himself. He didn't want to act like a pervert. He lowered his eyes.

"Sorry I took so long," she said, smiling like she was never so happy to see anyone in her life. "I got stuck on the phone."

"No problem." He smiled back, hoping it wasn't a foolish grin.

"How did everything go?"

"Great. Couldn't be better. Everything's ready for next week."

"Oh wonderful. You never let me down. As long as it's done before the Harvest Gala."

"That's not going to be a problem."

"Wonderful," she repeated, her mind already somewhere else, handing him the check.

"Thank you," he said, not wanting her to leave, snapping the half-sheet of paper out from under the small rock and holding it out.

She glanced quickly at the smudged invoice: "One-Man, One-Day."

"Do you want it for your records?" he said.

"Oh no. I don't need that." She turned and headed for the stairs, her smile disappearing like a rabbit down a hole, and then over her shoulder: "If you end up with any extra time, it's not too early to prune the roses."

68

Evelyn Schwab stared straight ahead, still not speaking to the driver, as the unmarked police car rolled across the bridge and onto Camano Island. Hook-shaped and hilled, the island scarcely deserved the descriptor anymore, the once-substantial waterway that separated it from the mainland now reduced to a narrow slough barely visible except at high water. The tide-lands were long ago stripped from the Indians, diked and filled by ambitious clans of flat-faced Scandinavian immigrants, their efforts fueled by cheese, whole cream and top-grade butterfat.

The road climbed steeply up a bluff that stared back across the cornfields and pumpkin patches to the mainland and the mountains to the east. A little further along, the car turned off the state highway and cruised down a narrow blacktop through dairy farms and pastureland, the beautiful setting suddenly at odds with a nauseating stench.

You're disgusting, Schwab thought, glancing at the driver.

"They're spreading liquefied cow manure," the young man said.

She wondered for a moment if she had spoken out loud, not trusting her mind anymore.

"The dairy farmers save it up for a year then lay it out with a traveling gun." He pointed to an insect-like mobile sprinkler that crawled across a pasture in the distance. "It's real good for the grass." They were the first words out of his mouth since she rebuffed his previous attempt at conversation more than an hour earlier.

THE SHERIFF, NO doubt taking valuable time away from the screenplay he was writing, personally summoned him into the office and told him to get down to Seattle and pick the woman up, pretty adamant she be kept happy. The job would require two round-trips and eat up the whole day, even if he beat the Everett traffic on the way back the second time, which he knew he wouldn't.

The briefing was cursory, less said than unsaid, and the fact the dildo skipped over the chain-of-command probably meant this was private business. He made a mental note to add it to his whistleblower file.

He glanced over at the dumpy woman in the passenger seat. She was uglier than a can of cheap tuna: thick brows, coarse skin, a double string of moles marking the path to her grainy nose like landing lights. It's hard to picture anyone banging this broad, he thought, but she sure seems juiced in with someone.

THE CAR SETTLED back into silence. Schwab slouched in her heavy brown overcoat and watched the barns and homesteads go by, the garages bigger than the houses, the names on the mailboxes the same as those on the cross streets.

They drove past a bare-bones airfield where faded farmers' planes, some without engines, sat tied down in islands of long grass the mower couldn't reach. An undulating runway, narrower than a good-sized driveway, ran downhill like a black ribbon between the trees and out of sight in the direction of the water. Cars and pickups sat in front of some of the aircraft, blocking them to the south, and Schwab remembered a big storm passed through the day before.

The car emerged from the woods and passed more open fields. Glacier-draped Rainier and Baker bracketed them like bookends, the mountains awesome even at a distance, but Schwab was lost in her thoughts and the driver had his eyes on the highway. At the end of a long forested hill the road crested and a sparkling bay appeared below them.

"Pull over there, by that gate," Schwab said, pointing to a gravel delta at the end of a farmhouse drive.

They looked down at the sweeping shoreline, packed shoulder-to-shoulder with small beach shacks and cabins, woodsmoke curling from random chimneys. Here and there a rich Seattleite's outsized house stuck out like a peacock in with the chickens.

"Utsalady Bay?" she asked.

"Yes." The driver hesitated. "Is he here?"

"Maybe."

"He can't be all that bright."

"No," she said, knowing it wasn't true.

IT WAS THE nastiest year ever. First Jake Morrow disappears like smoke, taking her career with him, the hunt totally botched, through no fault of her own. Then finally putting an end to it all with Gerald, their union always an unconventional one, she with the moustache, he the breasts, nothing at all between them anymore, but still a surprising empty spot, 24 years of anything bound to leave its mark.

Worst of all was the accident of course, waking up in the hospital with no memory of her evening walk. Witnesses reported a speeding car and a suddenly-opened passenger door, maybe a random act of maliciousness, maybe not. She made a lot of enemies over the years.

Her head just wasn't the same. Despite her efforts to hide the struggles, they pushed her out on a Medical. It wasn't exactly revenge she was after, but it would certainly be sweet to put a dent in Mr. Morrow.

Finding the EPIRB was the big break. One of her old subordinates at the Department called to say a boater, searching for guns and golf clubs stolen from his summer cabin, spotted it in a Stanwood pawnshop, and recognized the name of the now famously-missing *Nadalia*.

She could tell the jerk enjoyed it, tossing a crumb into her cubicle at Property Recovery Services. There was no mistaking the condescension in his voice: she might as well have been a school crossing guard.

A quick call to the FCC confirmed the EPIRB was indeed registered to Daniel Zakian's missing boat. The Stanwood police interviewed the pawnshop owner and recovered the ID ticket of the man who brought it in. The owner remembered him: Caucasian (but who wasn't up here?), about six-foot, brown hair – he'd seen him around town a few times.

The ticket listed an address on Utsalady Bay, and a call to the county auditor's office established the property was owned by Carly Spring, a woman with no prior record and no obvious connection to Daniel Zakian or Jake Morrow.

Schwab motioned for the driver to get moving again. They pulled back onto the road. The man was a dolt, but it was nice to have some muscle along.

A few minutes later they were in the driveway of a two-story beach house, old and weathered but meticulously kept. A thick rope fence enclosed the manicured lawn. She got out with her small duffel bag and looked into the carport, noted the catamaran on its trailer and the pair of mountain bikes hanging from a wall, but missed that the camping gear was in alphabetical order, and the paint cans sorted first by hue, then size. She walked past a kayak and a beat-up canoe, bottoms-up on the protected eastern side of the house, and headed for the small front porch.

The door opened before she could ring a third time. A young woman stood there, looking flushed and tucking in the last corner of her blouse.

"Carly Spring?"

"That's me."

"My name is Evelyn Schwab. I work for a company that locates missing property. I have a few questions."

"This really isn't a good time."

"It will only take a minute."

Carly pointed to the man in the car. "Would you mind asking him to move? My boyfriend has a thing about oil stains."

Schwab turned and motioned to the driver, garnered only a cocked head and quizzical look in return, then acted out increasingly emphatic charades until the light finally went on and the man backed down the driveway.

"What kind of questions?" Carly said, as the car pulled onto the shoulder next to the mailboxes.

"Do you know a Jake Morrow?"

"Who's asking?" said a good-looking man, coming up behind Carly. He was thin and well-muscled, his pressed white shirt, untucked and unbuttoned, revealing six-pack abs.

Schwab carefully scanned the man's face, then unabashedly looked him up and down, trying to determine if he could possibly be the pale and pudgy 40-year-old from the photos. "Do you mind if I come in?" she said, starting over.

The barefoot man glanced at a dozen pairs of new work gloves that sat on top of a cabinet by the door, then quickly looked back to Schwab. "Do you have a warrant?"

Dickhead. "I'm not a cop. I'm an investigator for a company that recovers assets."

The man slid in between her and Carly, cementing his position as spokesperson for the household. "Who's he then?" He nodded toward the driver, standing next to his unmarked sedan, which couldn't have looked any more like a police car if the lights and siren were going.

"He's my driver. I'm trying to find a missing boat." It was best to get right to it before the door slammed in her face.

"We don't know anything about a boat," the man said.

"Do you mind if I come in for a minute?"

"All right," Carly said. "I'll make some coffee."

They sat down at a worn kitchen table with a nice view of the beach. Schwab noticed the small box at the far end, resting on torn wrapping paper, a gleaming piece of titanium peeking out.

"That's a very nice reel."

"Thank you," Carly said. "I haven't tried it yet. Just came today."

"May I?" said Schwab, nodding at the box.

"Sure." Carly slid it down the table.

Schwab turned the reel over in her hand. "This is beautiful." She had never seen anything like it: dramatically ported and so light. It made her remember cold autumn days on the Skagit with the earthy firefighter from Bellingham.

"We really can't help you," the man said, the reel seeming to irritate him.

He was bathed in sunlight streaming through the window. Schwab examined him closely. This wasn't Jake Morrow. Too short, too slight, wrong colored eyes. Way too young: 25 at most. The best plastic surgeon in the world and a year's worth of nips and tucks and tanning beds couldn't have turned that flaccid, pasty-skinned lawyer into this little punk in pressed jeans and long hair.

Schwab stared out the window past the well-used crab-boiler, to a heron standing on a partially uncovered rock, then gently set the reel on the table and pulled the EPIRB from her duffel bag. "This was pawned," she said, holding it up for everyone to see.

Carly looked sharply at the man.

"Yeah, so what?" he said to Schwab, "I pawned it."

"Where did you get it?"

"I found it at the art shrine." He pointed through the side window to a miniature gazebo set up on the lawn near the road, a sign on its roof encouraging people to take some art or leave some. "People are always putting junk there like it was a Goodwill drop-off."

"You just found it there?"

"Yep. Just sitting there."

"Did you know what it was?"

"I knew it wasn't art."

A bald eagle sailed above the beach, pestered by three motley seagulls, cawing pissants to the majestic bird. Why doesn't it just snap their little necks thought Schwab, not yet at peace with the Department.

Carly set a mug of steaming coffee in front of her.

"Are you familiar with the *Nadalia*?" Schwab asked, looking at Carly and pointing to the handwritten black letters on the side of the bright orange EPIRB.

"Don't know her," the man said.

"It's a sailboat. Owned by a Daniel Zakian."

"We don't know anything about a boat like that," the man said.

Schwab continued to look at Carly until she shook her head and looked down. "Never heard of Jake Morrow or Daniel Zakian," Schwab said. "Never heard of the *Nadalia*. Found this thing on the art shrine." She didn't know where to go next. In the past she would have asked shrewd questions, led them down hidden paths and trapped them into the truth, intimidated them until they begged to tell her what they knew, but now she was just dry.

CARLY STOOD ON the porch and watched the stout woman limp back to her car, then turned to the man, trying not to smile. She loved the way he tried to protect her from the woman, was excited somehow by the facile lying, liked being with him, this gentle obsessive man, so much younger than she was, like a child really, a weekend artist with taps on his shoes. She wished he would stop coming home from Boeing with stuff in his lunchbox though.

"You jerk. You're pawning my things now?"

"It was junk. It was cluttering up the electronics shelf. I thought we could get a few bucks."

"Well ask next time."

"What am I?" he said, "your lapdog?" and this time she couldn't hold back the smile as he took her hand and led her back into the house.

She hoped Jake had landed on his feet.

69

Jake pressed his face against the window as the plane made its final approach. Bermuda was such an incongruous little speck, sitting there all by itself in the middle of the ocean. Three of them would fit into Snap's old ranch with room to spare.

He could see the dump sprawled out beneath him – rusted cars and appliances, steel drums and construction debris – a hundred fresh truckloads of plastic bags and paint cans every day. The garbage climbed over itself and crept into Castle Harbour. If everyone here were a Veehee, it would be only 25 truckloads a day.

There was a slight snap to his step as he walked across the ramp and through the terminal, the sea air lifting him up. Nothing beats coming home.

"Good morning Mr. Knoll!" chirped the driver, stepping forward and trying unsuccessfully to snatch his bag away.

They drove by the Captain's House and up the hill, past the estates hidden behind hibiscus hedges, the houses with names instead of numbers: Fore & Aft, Peace & Plenty, Bonnybrook. The driver allowed the car to slow at a steep curve; the long driveway coming up fast on the other side. They turned in just past the small *Utsalady Bay* sign staked in the grass, its gold-leaf letters glinting in the sun, then wound their way up the oleander-lined drive. The limestone roof appeared first, eye-hurting white, patiently waiting for some rain to route to the basement cistern, the water needed for the gardens and swimming pool. Then there was the pink house itself. He loved it from the first moment he saw it.

The pest-control man's tiny unmarked car was parked in the circle. He didn't seem to own any equipment. The guy probably went after the giant roaches one-at-a-time, with his bare hands. There was a carton of toads in the open trunk, the big ones with dark blotches on their backs. Someone must have seen a centipede.

Jake opened the unlocked front door. He set his bag in the foyer and sifted through the overflowing mail basket. Despite successfully hiding from Daniel and god knows who else, the solicitations for *Gay Travel Magazine* and the Rainbow Card had found their way to him.

His skipper's license was there too. They could officially take tourists out fishing on the new boat. Now *that* was going to be a lot of fun.

The house was cool and dark, its shutters closed against the early afternoon sun. He stopped on his way through the living room. The purple-and-white urn was gone from the mantle. Excellent. In its place was a framed photo of two kids in cowboy hats and boots, nine or ten, leaning against a dusty rodeo fence. They would be Maddie's boys.

He hurried through the library to the empty kitchen. Cook was probably at market; Maddie would be by the pool or down in the gardens. He stepped into the bright sun on the upper terrace. His sunglasses were back in the foyer, but he didn't want to take the time to retrieve them. He shaded his eyes with his hand. A cruise ship glided along in the distance, heading for Hamilton.

There she was in the farthest garden, half hidden by the banana and loquat trees that ringed the lower lawn. He watched for a while as she cut the flowers and put them in her basket. So graceful. Like a dancer who moves through space with no friction at all. He knew the prettiest flower would be in her hair when she came up to the house.

She must have felt him watching, and turned. She left the basket and clippers on the ground and headed for the steps. They met halfway to the middle lawn and gently held each other's forearms, like they were getting ready to learn how to dance.

The anxiety half-evaporated. She was glad now she waited to tell him. It was time to stop second-guessing herself.

"I saw the picture of the boys on the mantle."

"Yes."

"It's a nice spot for it."

"He's going to let me visit."

"That's good."

They started back up the stone steps to the house. "Finis called," she said. "He's getting in from Korea tomorrow."

The day was getting better and better. "Why early?"

"He's finished with the peer comments on his paper."

"That's great. He's been buried in that Mali data for a year."

"He sent you another dead mouse."

"Wonderful."

"I put it in the freezer with the others."

"At least he's moving on. We'll be famous if he comes up with the world's oldest mouse. Really famous if he wipes out death."

"I'd rather get my ice cream in peace. Are you going to the orchard?"

"Not today." He liked it best in the mornings, when it was cool and the dew was still on the leaves. And right now he wanted to be with her.

"Maybe Finis can help you with the hybrids."

He didn't know anything about fruit trees when he bought the small orchard. But he liked being outdoors. The physical work was good. Much better than fighting other people's battles from a high-rise box filled with paper. Daniel always said if you did something religiously, for a good part of each day, you'd be an expert in a year, and it seemed to be working out pretty well. If he got over a few hurdles he might have a mango that would actually thrive in Bermuda.

"Is Snap around?"

Maddie pointed to the matching pink cottage perched on the green lip of the hillside. An enormous man, closing in on 400 pounds, was manning a barbecue, smoke from a split 55-gallon drum rising slowly in the warm air. Snap spotted them just as Jake looked up.

"Welcome home, pardner!" he boomed, holding up a rack of bloody ribs in each hand like a demented butcher. "Biscuit, Jake's home!"

Lucille hurried out of the house and waved down to them.

Jake waved back. It would be a barbecue at Snap's tonight, the sauce imported from Amarillo, the corn grown right here in the garden, basted in cayenne butter and lime. After dinner they would play Scrabble: Maddie focused, competitive; Lucille delighted if someone had the good fortune to hit a triple-word square; Snap insistent that poontang was a word.

He was glad he'd followed Snap onto that plane in Abidjan; happy they bought the gatehouse with some of the money he gave them. It looked like the middle girl, Janie, would be married here in the spring.

They continued up the path to the house, holding hands like eighth-graders. He was already picturing himself in the room, the ceiling fan gently moving the frangipani-scented air, lying on his back, listening to the cheery redbirds and watching the shadows play against the wall, her sleeping tight against him on her side, breathing softly on his neck, her leg crooked over his thigh.

"Did you see her?" Maddie said, interrupting his reverie.

They were standing on the bedroom terrace. He didn't remember taking the last flight of stairs. "Her?" he said, knowing who she meant.

"Her. The love of your life."

"No."

The pressure in her head dissipated, just like when he massaged her shoulders.

"How come?" she said after a moment.

"Because *you're* the love of my life."

"Hah," she laughed, even her involuntary snort sounding attractive. "I'm not the love of your life."

"Then what am I doing with this tattoo?"

"Too many gin and tonics. You were impaired. Seriously impaired. You did something crazy for once…twice…in your life."

"I knew what I was doing."

"I'm sure you did. You got one where my name could easily be turned into an anchor and some line."

He impulsively scooped her up and cradled her in his arms, regretting it immediately, not noticing the slight swelling of her belly. "Cynic."

She rested her head on his shoulder and put her arms around his neck, easing his burden. "And I know why you're *really* with me."

"I've got two million good reasons."

"That's nothing to you. Guess again."

"Because I love you so much."

"No. Yes. But that's not why you're with me instead of her."

"Who says I could be with her?"

"You know you could."

"She needs Utsalady Bay."

"Utsalady Bay can be anywhere. She would have figured that out soon enough if she's as smart as you say. Come on, why aren't you with the perfect woman, your soulmate?"

He stopped a moment to readjust his load. "Because," he finally said, telling her at the same time he was first telling himself, "eventually I would have disappointed her."

Bingo, she thought, as he carried her through the terrace door and laid her on the bed, gently, like he was putting a baby in its crib. And she would have disappointed you too.

www.ingramcontent.com/pod-product-compliance
Lightning Source LLC
Chambersburg PA
CBHW020329180626
46812CB00001B/109